Inter SECTIONS

Intersections

Fiction and Poetry from The Banff Centre for the Arts

Edited by Edna Alford and Rhea Tregebov

The Banff Centre Press

CANADIAN CATALOGUING IN PUBLICATION DATA

Main entry under title:

Intersections
ISBN 0-920159-73-7

1. Canadian literature (English)—20th century.* 2. American literature—20th century.
3. English literature—20th century. I. Alford, Edna, 1947– II. Tregebov, Rhea, 1953– III. Banff Centre for the Arts.
PN6014.I57 2000 820.8'00914 C00-910377-5

Cover and book design by Alan Brownoff
Cover photos
(top left): Dorothy Livesay in the Hemingway Studio
(bottom right): Yolanda Van Dyck in the Henriquez Studio
Photographer credits
Front Cover (clockwise from top left): Kim Chan, Don Lee, Monte Greenshields, Kim Chan, Don Lee
Back Cover: Don Lee
Pages vii, x, xvi: Kim Chan
Pages xi, xii, xiii, xv, xix: Don Lee
Pages xiv, xvii: Monte Greenshields
All photos are property of The Banff Centre
Printed and bound in Canada by Houghton Boston Printers

The Banff Centre Press gratefully acknowledges the support of the Canada Council for the Arts for its support of our publishing program.

BANFF CENTRE PRESS
The Banff Centre for the Arts
Box 1020–17
Banff, Alberta Canada T0L 0C0
http://www.banffcentre.ab.ca/Writing/Press

Contents

The Leighton Studios

AT THE BANFF CENTRE

In 1972, The Banff Centre began to consider founding an artists' colony along the lines of MacDowell in New Hampshire and Yaddo in New York. A gift from the Kahanoff Foundation of Calgary and matching funds from the Government of Alberta

made the idea a reality. In 1983, plans for the Leighton Artist Colony were set in place and in 1984 the studios accepted their first artists. The colony was named after David Leighton, president of The Banff Centre from 1970 to 1982, and his wife, Peggy. The colony was renamed the Leighton Studios in 1992.

The excerpts as follows are from a 1983 document setting forth The Banff Centre's plan for an artists' colony. Documents were provided by the Paul D. Fleck Library and Archives, The Banff Centre.

The Leighton Artist Colony

An Introduction—Function and Purpose

AN ARTISTS' COLONY, simply stated, is an attempt to meet the need which artists throughout the ages have felt for functional and inspiring work space and uninterrupted solitude. In addition to providing the time and space to work, a colony functions as something of a sanctuary for the artist, an environment where there is respect for an artist's gifts and will—where needs (even eccentric ones) are anticipated—where the creative compulsion is sympathetically understood. An important factor in this regard is the encouraging fellowship of other artists working in a variety of disciplines.

A high level of support services has proven to be crucial to the success of artists' colonies. Living and working routines are sensitively tended by others in order to free the full extent of the artists' energy and thought for creative work. The supporting context is sufficiently flexible to accommodate the varied daily schedules which differing individuals may regard as essential to the process of unfolding their creative ideas.

There are a number of successful colonies currently in operation in the United States. The best established of these are the MacDowell and

Yaddo colonies, both of which have served as the creative haven for thousands of artists since being founded in the early part of this century. Many of America's most distinguished writers, composers, and visual artists have created their finest works at MacDowell or Yaddo, including dozens of Pulitzer Prize winning books and compositions. Both colonies have developed over the years a successful way of nurturing the work of artists at the highest level essentially by guaranteeing three things: privacy of working hours; limited but stimulating fellowship with other colonists; and individual studios that carry with them a rich and unique history of significant artistic accomplishment.

The Leighton Artist Colony consists of eight studios: two 600-square-foot studios to be used by visual artists, three 300-square-foot studios designed to be used by composers, and three 300-square-foot studios primarily designed for the use of writers.

Each private studio building is designed by a different architect. The resulting architectural variation will allow the artists to select studio environments closely suited to their working habits and temperaments. Each design focuses on the relationship between ambience or character of the working environment and the ability to carry out creative work within it. The multi-architect concept states in concrete terms a commitment to and respect for individual creativity and human needs.

Design Statement (excerpt)

THE EIGHT STUDIOS will be designed to be compatible with the natural environment, based on a set of user requirements and a specified range of materials ... The individual studios will be designed to maximize creative production and minimize stress during long, uninterrupted hours of daily work. Simplicity, even aesthetic austerity, may be required in the interior space, to allow the working context to give way to the presence of artist and the creative work in process.

The Site for the Colony

THE COLONY WILL BE LOCATED in a wooded area immediately southwest of The Banff Centre Campus. The Colony site has been approved by Parks Canada.

Criteria for the selection of the studio sites included existing clearances, stands of dead trees, the location of trees that could not be cut, the view, and the necessity to protect the isolation of the working artists.

The Colony will be constructed with a minimal environmental impact and will have no access by road. A footpath leading from the Colony site to the main Campus will be the only access for both artists and service personnel. Materials cannot be trucked to the site.

Visual Arts Studio

Architect: GUY GERIN-LAJOIE, *Montreal*

"To emphasize the building's relationship with nature, the roof concept is designed in metal over each of the five feet modules, associating its sloping shape and apex in line with the Rundle mountain ridge in the background. The steps created in the roofline are made to harmonize and blend with the rock formation of the surrounding mountains."

GUY GERIN-LAJOIE

Composer's Studio

Architect: DOUGLAS CARDINAL, *Edmonton*

"The design takes the form of a spiralling shell that seems to grow out of the ground and wrap itself around the composer, like a sea shell around a sea urchin, turning its back to the road and pathway, and terminating in a large window."

DOUGLAS CARDINAL

~~Visual Arts Studio~~

Architect: RON THOM, *Toronto*

"The studio space was kept as open and simple in its configuration as possible. This allows the artist the greatest degree of flexibility in arranging the working components within the studio to best suit his or her particular needs."

RON THOM

Composer's Studio

Architect: IAN DAVIDSON, *Vancouver*

"The beautiful site for this studio is on a north-south axis. To the south is a tree-filtered view of the mountains . . . Our response to the site and the program is a multi-faceted structure with a pyramid roof. The north facing entry side is without windows for privacy and energy conservation. The south facing view side has large windows and a private outdoor deck thrust into the wonderful view."

IAN DAVIDSON

Composer's Studio

Architect: FRED VALENTINE, Calgary

"The concept illustrated relies on a primary 'cathedral' space to enhance the sound of instruments and to dignify and enlarge the activity of writing music. The servant spaces are scaled down as seemed appropriate."

FRED VALENTINE

~~Writer's Studio~~

Architect: RICHARD HENRIQUEZ, *Vancouver*

"The treatment of the boat in the wooded site is similar to that which would be done by a curator finding 'Noah's Ark' at Banff."

RICHARD HENRIQUEZ

Writer's Studio

Architect: PETER HEMINGWAY, *Edmonton*

"This studio is conceived as an enclosure for a ceramic sculpture located in the woods which just happens to be at the same time a fireplace. I want to develop the feeling that this sculpture grew from the Banff soil, just like a morel or a Douglas fir." *

PETER HEMINGWAY

* *Although this ceramic fireplace sculpture was built by art students in The Banff Centre Ceramics Department, under the direction of department head Leslie Manning, it could not be installed because of building regulations for the site set forth by Parks Canada.*

Writer's Studio

Architect: MICHAEL EVAMY, *Calgary*

"The studio sits in a small clearing of spruce and pine forest and faces a gently sloping ridge only a few metres to the south. The ridge forms the wall of a small ravine moving downward to the southeast and upward to the southwest, offering direct views along the forest floor. A tall, narrow gash running east and west opens the forest canopy. One can see a thin band of blue sky directly above and follow it all the way to the east horizon where Rundle Mountain sits in the perfectly framed juncture. The studio itself is split into two halves along the same opening of the forest canopy."

MICHAEL EVAMY

A Gift of Intersections

THE LEIGHTON STUDIOS

1 We arrive here thinking of all the time we will have in which to create: tune in on the imagination,

turn up the intellect, strain the brain. But wait. We quickly discover that skin too is an organ of knowing. We touch and are touched by place.

To write is at once to enter into isolation from community and to enter community. This double experience is acted out quite literally by the writers who become guests of the Leighton Studios. The writer becomes a member of a community of artists who work and live in close proximity in The Banff Centre for the Arts. Yet each writer, sitting down to work, is in a studio unique in design, located in a stand of lodgepole pines on the south slope of Tunnel Mountain.

I am a guest in the Davidson, designed by the architect Ian Davidson to, in his own words, "include maximum visual and acoustical privacy." To get to the Davidson on these September mornings just as the sun snags on the peak of Mount Rundle, I follow a forest trail that takes me from my room in Lloyd Hall, a six-storey residence, into a green solitude that comes close to being scary. I step around fresh elk droppings, the richly dark brown turds shaped exactly as if the elk themselves were tempted by a forest aesthetic of abundance and economy. The path is pleasantly uncertain, as if I must each morning once again discover my way. The fear of rutting elk and black bears in a feeding frenzy as winter approaches reminds me that to write is always to risk one's life, even at the edge of paradise.

I enter my study with just the slightest sense of relief; I made it. I am once again safe in this writerly cocoon, this gift of isolation in which I can contemplate the varieties of community of which each of us is a member. The baby grand piano to the left of the door is permanently immune to my ability to play "Chopsticks." I have stowed the VCR out of reach behind the piano. Through all four large windows, I see the palisade of lodgepole pines, each lean tree trunk scaled as if it had once been a fish. A chipmunk, as if mocking my own delayed efforts, busily gathers whatever it is that chipmunks gather. I resist turning on the radio and instead turn on my computer.

It is my special privilege to be here writing about being here. Instead of sitting down I go to the bookcase, shuffle through sheets of music that I cannot read. I notice an oddly shaped book with a red cover. Casually, I flip through what turns out to be a guest book. I look, then look again. The abundance of ghosts comes as a surprise.

2 The Leighton Studios were only an idea back in 1979; six years later the group of eight studios was opened by Prince Philip.

The idea of an artists' retreat drew on the Yaddo Artists' Colony in upstate New York and the MacDowell Colony in New Hampshire, with the unique difference that the Leighton Studios were situated next to a busy arts centre that included work in theatre, ballet, the visual arts, and writing.

The Leighton Studios, each designed by a distinguished architect, were intended at first for the use of visual artists, writers, and composers. Today they are used as well by choreographers, media artists, songwriters, architects, and collaborative theatre groups.

Surely one of the communities we occupy is that of fellow artists, known or unknown, who are physically absent yet present as models or inspiration or simply as support. Alone in the Davidson, I am not alone. The guest book reminds me that the Alberta novelist Joan Crate worked in this studio while an elk calved outside. Karen Mulhallen, the busy editor of *Descant,* found time in this studio to complete a long poem. Another writer thanks "the ghost writer" who opens the studio door for her each morning. A composer waxes poetic: "The first draft of the opera *The Book of Jonah* was written at this window. The pine trees, all differently swaying, became for me the masts of many ships to ride out of *blank* into inspiration!" Another composer can't stand all the good news: "Glad everybody's so damn HAPPY!! I yelled, screamed, drank, threw things, wrestled with the fiddle/flute/bagpipes/lute, tried to write some musical notes that didn't want to be writ, fell asleep on the floor, started again, it's done, I'm outta here!" An Australian writer whose first name is Cassandra simply cautions, "Watch out for the coyote!"

This is indeed one of Coyote's places, a place watched over by the transformer, the trickster, the creator.

This is a place to make a copy editor squirm at the frequent use of exclamation marks.

3 To arrive at the Leighton retreat is to enter into a set of narratives, which is only appropriate for someone who has come here to write.

One of those narratives is the history of the Leighton retreat itself, the continuum of people who lug working materials down the trail for the first time, then look for a numbered studio, then gently open a door, close it from the inside, then confront what the composer so accurately called the *blank*. You have a whole crowd of collaborators cheering for you. And the bad news is, you're on your own. Page one, word one. Now what the hell am I doing here? Is the Sally Borden bar open at this hour? Should I get a good night's rest before beginning?

And yet, a week later, a month later, three months later, a plumper writer (the food in the dining hall is a wicked temptation) walks up the path and over a short wooden bridge and back to the world of publishers and readers—with a manuscript tucked into a folder. Okay, I'm outta here. But I don't really want to go.

Every writer here writes within the narrative of the Leighton Studios, just as she or he writes in larger narratives of Canadian or Japanese traditions, or the literatures written in English or French or Portuguese or Spanish. Even as I write this, I am in the company of a young Mexican poet in a neighbouring studio writing a sequence of poems on the migration of the grey whales, an Argentinian novelist and mathematician hurrying to complete his second novel before classes begin in Buenos Aires, a novelist from Calgary finishing the story of a woman's loss of a child in a prairie city.

Those are stories in progress. You, dear reader, now hold in your hands a collection of completed stories and poems. To write out of the past is also to write into the future. It is also to write the future. The finger touching a keyboard touches the elusive nexus where past and future meet. No wonder then that writers whine, cry, shout into culverts, sleep on floors, make unreasonable demands and improbable claims to success, sponge drinks from friends, hate reviewers, and love one another (sometimes). And then start over on page one, word one.

Our stories and poems guide our communities back into memory and forward into possibility. Every book, in a way (and I like the word "way") is a guidebook. The journey back is often a journey to the underworld, whether into the psyche or history or some other version of recovery. The journey forward is a seeking for the buried treasure, the promised land, the perfect mate, the happy isle. A writing studio is somewhere in between. As is the writer. For he or she is inextricably a portrayer and portrait of the community and its Janus face.

I'm not going to tell you a single thing about particular stories or poems in this collection; they speak eloquently for themselves. At this moment I ally myself with the readers; I become reader. And the reader, like the writer, enters into the risks and pleasures of transformation. The reader too lives in a tangle of narratives—of home, of work, of travel, of sexual fantasies, of altering memories, of impossible aspirations—and the reader too must create a unique and authentic story within the web of narrative we call a life or a culture.

Writing comes out of community. Community is configured in writing. We are caught in the old chicken or egg predicament. Paradoxically, there can be no first. A community is dependent on its artists. Artists are dependent on their community.

How would you go about reading a novel if you had never read a novel? We have all heard the anthropologist's story of showing a film to people who had never seen a film. After the showing they asked, Where did the chickens go when they ran off the edge of the screen?

No one has ever told me what the anthropologist answered.

4 As a reader now, I dare ask: Dear writers, What difference did it make to you that you wrote your poems and stories in the Leighton retreat?

On second thought, I take back the question. D. H. Lawrence told us trust the tale, not the teller. I don't quite believe that either. I delight in hearing writers talk, even when I have a suspicion they are lying, not to us, but to themselves.

To be honest (and always watch a writer who starts out by saying "to be honest"), I have met nearly half the writers represented in this book. So I may at times be speaking from a friendly bias. Writers have always come to know one another as friends, whether they were the Renaissance playwrights or the poets of the Romantic period or the writers of the Bloomsbury Group or the North American expatriates in Europe after

World War I or the Beat Generation in San Francisco or the Black Mountaineers or the Tish Poets in Vancouver.

In any case, I have met many of these writers, many of them here in Banff. Which sort of undoes my picture of all of us working in solitude. But to be honest and up front, I invite you to watch for the sly humour of Birk Sproxton, the gentle yet devastating insights of Rachel Wyatt. Put a hand to the warm granite of a Jan Zwicky poem. Tune in on the wry erotics of a story by Ven Begamudré or Gloria Sawai, the stressed erotics of a story by Linda Svendsen or Darlene Barry Quaife. Read a Jay Ruzesky poem as if you are lost in the rain forest. Read Barbara Sapergia as if you went homesteading on a glacier. Follow Geoffrey Ursell through the intricacies of Conradian desolation. Regret that Rhea Tregebov didn't give us one of her memory songs. Lament that Edna Alford didn't include one of her own wayward and enchanting fictions.

5 The more we know about writing, the more the mystery grows: Where *does* that next sentence come from?

The idea of the mind as a blank page (tabula rasa) is pretty much a spent notion. It turns out we are born with our minds scribbled over, so to speak, and our nursery bottles, our parents' reading us to sleep, our varieties of what we call education and experience, amount to further scribbling on a grand scale. Where *does* that focused and structured and articulated story come from?

The idea of writing as an isolated act, of the writer as an isolated figure, is by and large a romantic view. Writers, instead of avoiding messiness, get their hands stuck in the molasses when all they intended to do was steal a cookie.

Going to a writers' retreat is not a retirement to an ivory tower. Yes, the silence and comfort are gifts; the free time is more than a gift—it is a miracle. But the writer hauls into the studio the whole ball of wax or, more exactly, the whole tangle of string. I remember one time, here in Banff, a group of international writers watching an Inuit children's writer from Rankin Inlet turning a mere length of string into a fox catching a ptarmigan, a woman scraping a caribou hide, a hunter spearing a seal. We sat, all of us, as wide-eyed as children. But we were envious as well. Yes, that was all we wanted to do, really. Take that piece of string and fill the audience with wonder.

6 But I was asking: What difference does it make that these pieces of writing were written here in these studios?

This afternoon, going for a walk down to Bow Falls, I stepped over desiccated deer droppings, those engorged jelly beans (but all the same colour) returning to dust. I am seldom a metaphysician. For me, writing is in a way, a discharge from the body. And it is a discharge as important as sweat or saliva or tears, or any of the other two dozen or so excretions that leave our bodies. And our communality is just that, whether we are prime ministers or welfare recipients, astronomers or gang leaders. Or writers. Come off your high horse, dear artist. Belly up to the kitchen table.

To write is, in its simplest sense, to write. A matter of touch. It is the body working, much as a gardener works when he or she plants onions or tries to dig out dandelions. To write is to work with the body at a very particular task in a very particular place.

Again we come to the gift of a studio in a forest right smack alongside a community of other artists, and readers, and even those people who refuse to read. They are part of the narrative, too, those non-readers, and we as writers wish to convert them to the pleasurable smell of book, the caress of paper as one turns a page, the sheer astonishing pleasure of the eyes resolving alphabet into a reality as real as the whisky-jack on my balcony that is apparently curious as to why I don't share my tuna sandwich.

Okay, I will.

7 Later.

Somehow it is very Canadian to have the retreat so close to a centre where some people create computer art while others hold conferences on e-mail marketing. A place where mountain climbing and ballet are equally arts of resistance to gravity.

I was, three times during the 1960s and '70s, a guest at the Yaddo Artists' Colony in Saratoga Springs, New York. Granted, there were occasional evenings when one could hear the noise of the crowd at the famous race-track, but mostly the colony was removed from society—a wealthy couple's mansion and the house (also a mansion) built for the governess, turned into enough rooms and studios for numerous artists. For exercise, one strolled in the rose garden or walked in a garden-like forest. I hasten to say it is a truly wonderful location. I mention it now in an attempt to answer my own question: What is the effect of a writing place?

I remember a writer who lasted at Yaddo for three days, then fled back to New York City, leaving on his desk a simple note: "I can't stand the quiet." I would expect something similar has happened here in the Leighton Studios as well—silence is not always the stuff of story.

But silence is a space that invites story. I am not suggesting that Banff invites stories about Banff. Rather, Banff invites the tellers to swap tales; it returns the writer to the condition of scop or skald (and the word "skald" is related to "scold"). It says to the writer, Tell us a story of this or a distant place, of your own life and other lives, of imagined worlds. It puts us into complicity with whoever Homer was; blind bard, he told his listeners stories that recalled and foretold their own lives and dreams and past and future, all the while keeping his listeners immediately aware of the immediate moment.

I was telling you about Yaddo. One September afternoon a stout, near-sighted composer from Atlanta was out for a walk and bent down to pick up what he thought was a stick on the manicured path. The stick proved to be a migrating garter snake that had found itself chilled in the afternoon shade and had stopped moving. How far the composer, in his exclamation, threw the snake, we never determined. But all of us assured him that garter snakes are harmless. And all of us took to treading carefully on garden paths.

The composers' studios at Yaddo are far out in the woods. One fall when I arrived there to try to complete the last pages of a novel, I was assigned the farthest studio—and not because I was a composer. There had been reports of hooligans prowling through the grounds. The severe lady who assigned studios and maintained quiet (she made famous painters tiptoe to the lounge for their gin bottles and loudmouthed novelists whisper and skulk in the ping-pong room) explained to me that since I was a big fellow I wouldn't be afraid out there alone in the dark oak forest.

Like an ancient hero who has listened to praise poems from his bards, I was left with little choice but to go. Every time an acorn fell on the roof of the studio I jumped roughly a metre into the air. That was back in the days of manual typewriters. Fortunately, those typewriters made a lot of noise. I completed the ending of the novel in four days.

8 One enters into a dialogue with the place in which one is writing.

Consider how carefully writers arrange the sharpened pencils they will never use, how deliberately they position their desks in relation to morning light and the tilt of the planet. Have you ever watched a writer trying to lower or raise a blind to the appropriate height? Venetian blinds may well have caused madness on occasion.

What does one do with the Rocky Mountains?

Let me go back just a bit. We dialogue variously. Even to hesitate about what to wear to the studio, where one will not be seen, is to enter into dialogue. What if it's a sunny day and I decide to go downtown to shop for on-sale sneakers in one of the numerous sportswear shops near the Mount Royal Hotel? Should I check for my books in the Banff Book and Art Den? Should I go for a dip in the Upper Hot Springs? Should I finally enter the Sally Borden gym?

Writing is enormously just that: our numerous selves scrabbling to see who will get to hit which buttons, which keys. That, and not sloth, explains why writers miss deadlines.

We are alone, yet we expect very shortly to be seen (to be read, that is). Describe Mount Rundle's looming presence, keeping in mind Cézanne and his repeatedly painting Mont Sainte-Victoire, and the artist's compulsion to return to a landscape as to the scene of a crime. No, tell how you climbed Rundle one time and then, oxygen-starved, felt you could leap from the peak and float gently into the Bow Valley. No, simply record how it felt to hike down that long slope of loose rock, every step jarring your twisted left knee.

The composer and administrator Don Stein stopped by my studio to say hello. He once worked in this studio for three weeks. I asked him about the silence of the grand piano and its daring me to tackle a sonata in verbal form.

Don told me he didn't use the piano for his compositions; he made audios of sound walks through landscapes such as the Calgary Stampede. He then placed six one-watt radio transmitters (range one kilometre each) throughout Banff and (illegally?) broadcast alien landscapes into this idyllic setting.

To compose is to arrange according to proportion, relationship, contiguity, continuity. It also becomes a kind of testing, of venturing or exploring. But just what is proportion? Consider Johnston Canyon. What is continuity? Consider the Kicking Horse Pass.

Compose yourself, we whisper, experiencing the sublime that is associated with the mountains. But to compose ourselves is sometimes to fall into line, to behave in a more acceptable fashion. At that point we as writers entertain the idea of decomposition. I look at the elk droppings that remain there on the path to my studio and I decide they look like a heap of sun-dried figs in an open market in Sicily, and I turn off my judgmental self (which writers must learn to do at times, if they are going to explore). (Okay, so I'm wrong about the colour.)

9 Being present in a place like the Leighton Studios is a gift in that our being here nominates us into voice.

We are here; ergo, we must be writers. The gatekeepers in the field of writing are so vaguely defined (who decides who is what?) that even the most published writer surely has moments when he or she whispers in secret dialogue, Just who the hell am I fooling? I'm a fraud, I'm a fake, I haven't written three consecutive words in the past two months.

An artists' community, willingly and generously, gives us permission.

Stop thinking about it—do it.

Hey, buster. You just watch me write this three-hour play, this iambic pentameter epic, this four-volume novel.

10 This morning I turned up the radio and danced by myself for a while.

11 But I happened to mention madness. The tensions of self and community experienced in a retreat may be one of the reasons for creativity's being described as both the work of a divine muse and the work of one who is stark-raving mad. Bats. Bananas. Loony. Dodo. Out of it.

The divine part is easy. No end of agnostic artists have told me that The Banff Centre for the Arts is a sacred place. It inspires. The Native poet Louise Halfe assures us that the spirits walk here every night between 2 and 4 A.M. Two of the studios are circular. One is in fact a boat, hauled high into the mountains from Vancouver. Architecture itself is tempted by the iconic.

The madness part hits a little closer to home. It may have something to do with a loss of a sense of community. That happens in various ways. It may stem from an artist's sense of neglect, which further translates into a sense of being shunned, of being exiled. Sometimes it is a consequence of those very insights offered by the spirit of place—painters or dancers or writers see in ways that irritate or confuse the very audience for whom they paint or dance or write. Madness becomes a loss of language. The audience may feel the artist has lost any sense of the language that is necessary for communication. But is it possible that the audience has lost (the vitality of) its language to convention or repression and counts on the "shock" of the "mad" artist to do the renewing?

Banff is an atmosphere, a landscape, a community that encourages risk taking. Consider the violence and the hope in the expression "to break new ground."

12 Empty. Totally blank. My mind, not a scratch on it. So much for genetics and all that stuff about inherited deep grammar and a will to words. Tabula rasa in spades. Blankety-blank. The scourge and

from The Banff Centre for the Arts

blight of this place: to have this rare and precious time, an ideal work space—and not a goddamned word in the hollow of my skull. I thought for a blind wild instant the phone was ringing; it turned out to be a horny squirrel chasing a horny squirrel. Nature too is a text, and we read it variously. I head to my room. There is a large group staying in Lloyd Hall today, Japanese school kids from Tokyo; they crowd together, hold one another, laugh, talk and talk, have fun, talk, laugh. I listen to their quick, intimate language—I cannot understand a single syllable. I ask two laughing students where they are going today. They fall silent. Obviously, I haven't communicated. Then the younger girl tries a word. "Mountain," she says. She waits. She sees that I understand and squeezes her partner's arm and off they run, laughing. I turn away, come back to this cell to put my computer to sleep. I'm off to Lake Louse for a hike to Victoria glacier.

13 That guy Zeno, hanging around the Parthenon, which was its own kind of retreat.

Zeno, refusing to experience either joy or sorrow, pleasure or pain.

Sooner or later we must consider writing as an aspect of sexual excess. So much for Stoicism. Rather: the pleasure of writing; the taking of pleasure; the giving of pleasure.

I first came to Banff in 1947. Back then it was The Banff Summer School of the Arts and I was a kid who wanted to write. I thought I wanted to write short stories, and one sad day discovered I needed a wider street in which to turn my wagon.

Late on a Friday afternoon, a beautiful ballet dancer from Florida suggested that she and I hitchhike to Jasper the next morning and spend the day looking at the mountains and waterfalls and canyons and hot springs.

"But," I said, "we won't be able to do all that and get back here by tomorrow night."

She gave me a smile that I've never forgotten. "That's right," she said.

She was an older woman. Maybe twenty-eight. I was at most twenty and fresh from a rural corner of Alberta and kind of a gangly kid and she wasn't just beautiful, she was the most beautiful woman in the whole world and she was from Florida and beaches and sun and had delicate freckles.

It was then that I spoke the words I've regretted to this day.

"I have to write a novel this weekend," I said.

You see, writing is both a joining and a rupturing.

I was speaking of sexual excess. What I mean to suggest is that the fear I experienced when invited to love is somehow basic to the writing act. The loss we experience (in whatever way: the departure of a lover, the death of a mother or father or a child, the catastrophes of nature like flood and hurricane) is so great and so terrifying that we write and write, and still we cannot write enough to fill the hole, bridge the chasm, restart the stopped heart. We sit down to write a thank you note, a note of consolation, a farewell note even, but that isn't enough, so we write a book of poems and three novels, but that isn't enough.

Sexual. Conjoining (Webster's: to join together for a common purpose). I mean touching, whispering, hoping, kissing, sucking, dreaming, licking, wishing—doing it, as we used to say, in the school basement. A novel is a pathetic out-of-control love note. A poem is an eloquent and usually failed proposition—had we but world enough and time.

I lock myself in a cage to tell you I love you. You fall asleep in your bed, trying to guess what my book is saying.

So maybe writers are, in their awkward ways, adherents of Zeno's Stoicism.

14 Slight hangover.

Went downtown last night with Spanish-language writers to have one beer. Weak on details today. Mexican ceramist said she came here to make pots, is now writing poems. Offered to look at some. Forgot I can't read Spanish. Steep solitary climb up from graveyard.

15 I got lost there.

This is getting heavy. A love note from hell. You may, reader, want to skip to the next section. Later on I tell you a bear story.

About the excess. What I'm trying to say is that writing is a version of desire. An insatiable desire. Insatiable because it cannot ever completely name what it seeks. The paradox again: any community is larger than the story that describes it. A good story is greater than the community it describes.

The writer's desire cannot quite name its own object, its own intention. The writer's desire is libidinal and by definition indefinable, even unknowable, and so the need to write is as endless and compelling and blunt and crude and delicate and as irresistible as that mystery we call sex.

"What's love got to do with it?"

Or again: Is writing a forsaking rather than a seeking after?

Listen, don't ask me. It cannot be written; therefore we must write it.

You see, writing is a kind of going beyond. Beyond so-called common sense. Beyond so-called reason. Beyond the boundaries set by ethics and aesthetics and the cops and the intellectual bouncers and the code enforcers and worried parents and the city mayor and the ever-changing list of rules for safe sex. To write is to write up a storm.

This is where we return to the idea of sublime. While the Stoic remains unaffected, the writer of the sublime insists on emotion. The mountain poet Fred Wah speaks on affect. We desire a response. That first and most sublime of poets, Sappho herself, gave us a whole mountainous island to dream.

Wet September snow falling this evening. Snow turning evergreen branches into flowers of winter. Snow creasing Cascade Mountain. We do not look for meaning. We let our skin shiver its ambiguous delight.

So maybe all writers are, in their evasive ways, writers of the sublime.

16 Culture is transmission.

Writers, like Saskatchewan farmers, sometimes feel badly done by; we are at the bottom of the food chain and the first to be devoured. Writers and farmers like to point out that, but for them, no one would eat (or read). It is also obvious that if no one is eating (or reading), there won't be many farmers or writers. Hello, community.

There is always more than one system operating. Writers, like filmmakers and photographers and opera singers and painters, need the moon and the magpie. They need the library and the bodybuilding machines, the toddler reading a board book, and the old codger reading large type.

17 One time, a writer was at work late at night in Studio 6. He heard a mild commotion on the balcony of the studio, but ignored it. After a while the abnormal silence was more disturbing than the commotion. The writer turned out the solitary light on his desk and went to the windows facing onto the balcony and the night.

A bear was sitting in a plastic chair on the balcony.

Some accounts have it that the bear was reading an abandoned manuscript the writer had left on the chair, and appeared to be half amused. Another version has the bear munching on the manuscript—the writer was having his first experience of the Leighton Studios and had thought he might get started by imagining a visit from a friendly black bear. A kind of a ghost bear, you might say.

The bear scrambled over the balcony wall and disappeared, making a racket, banging into a couple of trees, there in the dark.

The writer turned on his studio lights and retrieved his manuscript—since most writers will risk their lives to retrieve an abandoned manuscript. Or even the scraps and crumbs.

Further, the writer had made four copies of his abandoned manuscript and had one of them in the small refrigerator in his studio. He was doubting his own five senses. Yet at the same time, he felt downright inspired. He wrote madly through the remainder of the night, and by sun-up the story was revised and completed.

The exhausted writer was reluctant to go to breakfast in Donald Cameron Hall and tell the other writers about the bear; he knew they'd laugh and call him a tenderfoot and a greenhorn, and a damned poor liar to boot. So instead of going for breakfast he made himself still another cup of instant coffee and went out onto the balcony to catch a breath of the brisk morning air and to light a cigarette.

He sat down in the white plastic chair where the bear had sat and he took a deep drag and sipped his coffee. He was getting the shakes, he noticed, from too much caffeine and nicotine. He listened to a distant raven and guessed that his own throat was in about the same shape.

And then he saw it. Not the bear. It was long gone.

He saw the first claw mark—on the tree right there beside the balcony.

The tree is an oldish poplar. The writer noticed more claw marks. Higher up. Then more. Bear claw marks. Or gouges may be a better word. Fresh, deep gouges, through the green bark and right down to white wood. Bear claw marks. From near the base of the trunk to five metres up, each mark three or four or even five claws wide and ripped down to raw wood and dripping fresh sap.

If you don't believe me, you can go have a look.

Ask permission first: writers hate to be disturbed; they can get growly. You can see the scars on the tree, like hieroglyphics. No, not that. Just plain gigantic claw marks that will give you the willies.

That's the good thing about being a writer and writing in the Leighton Studios. You're alone, but you're always alone in a community. You're with skeptical friends and a considerate, generous support staff and a whole crowd of potential readers. And the occasional large black bear, just to record and authenticate the truth of the tale.

ROBERT KROETSCH
Leighton Studios
September 1999

Icarus

DON MCKAY

Icarus
isn't sorry. We do not find him
doing penance, writing out the golden mean for all
eternity, or touring its high schools to tell student bodies
not to do what he done
done. Over and over he rehearses flight
and fall, tuning his moves, entering
with fresh rush into the mingling of the air
with spirit. This is his practice
and his prayer: to be translated into air, as air
with each breath enters lungs,
then blood. He feels resistance gather in his stiff
strange wings, angles his arms to shuck the sweet lift
from the drag, runs the full length
of a nameless corridor, his feet striking the paving stones
less and less heavily, then
they're bicycling above the ground,
a few shallow beats and he's up,
he's out of the story and into the song.

At the melting point of wax, which now he knows
the way Doug Harvey knows the blue line,
he will back-beat to create a pause, hover for maybe fifty
hummingbird heartbeats and then
lose it, tumbling into freefall, shedding feathers
like a lover shedding clothes. He may glide
in the long arc of a Tundra swan or pull up sharp
to Kingfisher into the sea which bears his name. Then,
giving it the full Ophelia, drown.

On the shore
the farmer plows his field, the dull ship
sails away, the poets moralize about our
unsignificance. But Icarus is thinking tremolo and
backflip, is thinking
next time with a half-twist
and a tuck and isn't
sorry.

Repertoire, technique. The beautiful contraptions bred from ingenuity and practice, and the names by which he claims them, into which—lift-off, loop-the-loop—they seem to bloom. Icarus could write a book. Instead he will stand for hours in that musing half-abstracted space, watching. During fall migrations he will often climb to the edge of a north-south running ridge where the soaring hawks find thermals like naturally occurring laughter, drawing his eyebeam up an unseen winding stair until they nearly vanish in the depth of sky. Lower down, Merlins slice the air with wings that say crisp crisp, precise as sushi chefs, while Sharp-shins alternately glide and flap, hunting as they go, each line break poised, ready to pivot like a point guard or Robert Creeley. Icarus notices how the Red-tails and Broadwings separate their primaries to spill a little air, giving up just enough lift to break their drag down into smaller trailing vortices. What does this remind him of? He thinks of the kind of gentle teasing that can dissipate a dark mood so it slips off as a bunch of skirmishes and quirks. Maybe that. Some little gift to acknowledge the many claims of drag and keep its big imperative at bay. Icarus knows all about that one.

In the spring he heads for a slough and makes himself a blind out of wolf willow and aspen, then climbs inside to let the marsh-mind claim his thinking. The soft splashdown of Scaup and Bufflehead, the dives which are simple shrugs and vanishings; the loon's wing, thin and sharp for flying in the underwater world, and the broad wing of the Mallard, powerful enough to break the water's grip with one sweep, a guffaw which lifts it straight up into the air. Icarus has already made the mistake of trying this at home, standing on a balustrade in the labyrinth and fanning like a manic punkah, the effort throwing him backwards off his perch and into a mock urn which the Minotaur had, more than once, used as a pisspot. Another gift of failure. Now his watching is humbler, less appropriative, a thoughtless thinking amid fly drone and dragonfly dart. Icarus will stay in the blind until his legs cramp up so badly that he has to move. He is really too large to be a fetus for more than an hour. He unbends creakily, stretches, and walks home, feeling gravity's pull upon him as a kind of wealth.

Sometimes Icarus dreams back into his early days with Daedalus in the labyrinth. Then he reflects upon the Minotaur, how seldom they saw him—did they ever?—while they shifted constantly from no-place to no-place, setting up false campsites and leaving decoy models of themselves. Sometimes they would come upon these replicas in strange postures, holding their heads in their laps or pointing to their private parts. Once they discovered two sticks stuck like horns in a decoy's head, which Daedalus took to be the worst of omens. Icarus was not so sure.

For today's replay he imagines himself sitting in a corridor reflecting on life as a Minotaur (*the* Minotaur) while waiting for his alter ego to come bumbling by. They were, he realizes, both children of technology—one its *enfant terrible,* the other the rash adolescent who, they will always say, should never have been given a pilot's licence in the first place. What will happen when they finally meet? Icarus imagines dodging like a Barn swallow, throwing out enough quick banter to deflect his rival's famous rage and pique his interest. How many minotaurs does it take to screw in a light bulb? What did the queen say to the machine? Should he wear two sticks on his head, or save that for later? He leaps ahead to scenes out of the Hardy Boys and Tom Sawyer. They will chaff and boast and punch each other on the arm. They will ridicule the weird obsessions of their parents. As they ramble, cul-de-sacs turn into secret hideouts and the institutional corridors take on the names of birds and athletes. They discover some imperfections in the rock face, nicks and juts which Daedalus neglected to chisel off, and which they will use to climb, boosting and balancing each other until they fall off. Together they will scheme and imagine. Somehow they will find a way to put their brute heads in the clouds.

Bread and Stone

CAROLINE ADDERSON

IF NAN TOOK ANOTHER MAN he could not be like her husband, Patrick. She did not want to delude herself into loving for mere resemblance. Also she had Lucifer Bill to consider. He claimed to remember his father, though she, sceptic, thought it was from the photographs, the stories she told. She was glad, though, that he hadn't turned out to despise Patrick for his absence, his untimely blameless death. Honour thy father and thy mother. That is what they had been doing the past four years. She had lost her own mother in the same accident and Joni, her only daughter.

The first time she went out with Stephen, she knew he was enough unlike Patrick. But she had met a lot of people who were repelled by tragedy and wasn't sure if Stephen would be, too. So she told it all. "We usually spent Christmas with Patrick's people. That year, though, Bill had to have a few tests at the hospital. Nothing serious, he was just, even at age two, how can I put it?" She made a gesture with her hands—pure energy.

"Frisky?"

"You're kind. Manic I was going to say. Anyway, Patrick and Joni and my mother drove up together. Bill and I stayed back, so we weren't in the car when it happened. End of story."

He didn't press her, but when he took her home, he asked to see Bill. Nan agreed enthusiastically; meeting an unconscious Bill was his best introduction. They crept up the stairs. As soon as she opened the door and looked at the room through someone else's eyes, she regretted it. Chaos and upheaval. Her son was a vandal.

He was in a pyjama top, crosswise on the bed, bare bottom glowing in the yellow light of his night lamp. A heat-maker, he warmed himself by his own inner fire and even in winter could not tolerate too much blanket.

"Cute little fellow."

"Little? He's a monster for his age."

"Where'd he get the red?"

"His father's beard. Joni was even brighter."

Downstairs, a wedding picture hung in the hallway. "Your husband was a bear," he said.

And this man Stephen, Nan decided, was a stag. Fine and sleek. She liked the way he kissed her cheek, not her lips, and even then, on the porch. Not in front of a photograph of Patrick.

Then she worried that since she had told Stephen the severed story of her life, he would be too familiar; even now she didn't want to hear Joni's name spoken as someone might name an object or a person gone out of the room. Or, worse, he might feign an ingratiating comprehension. So when they next met for a walk in the ravine, to prevent his disappointing her, she brought the subject up again.

"I told him they all joined hands and went to heaven."

"And he believed?"

"Of course. But he resents not having visiting rights."

When he asked what she believed in, she answered: doubt. "But I was raised Quaker. Silently." Little maxims always rang in her ear. Joy cometh in the morning. Where your treasure is, there will your heart be. What man, if his son asks bread, will give him a stone?

After a colourless winter, each unfolding leaf seemed intensely green. The ravine was ringing with the sound of running water. Below, chunks of old snow slid down the thawing bank into the river.

DINNER at Stephen's. She showed Bill how to carry the cake box by the string so the icing would not touch the cardboard. Stephen answered the door, squeezed her hand, squatted to Bill's level.

"How do you do?"

"Monkey poo," said Bill, deadpan.

"That's a game we play." She was exhausted from being sly all day long with Bill. Napping and fawning had put him in his behavioural prime, but he was already wandering toward the living room, the tranced steps of a child bent on exploration. A minute in the kitchen doorway with an eye on each man, then she slipped over to the stove.

"Smells wonderful."

Stephen put a glass of wine in her hands, lifted his own glass, dipped a finger. "Something special for Bill."

"What?"

"None of your business."

She laughed and at the same moment that she kissed him, his finger set the rim of the wineglass singing.

"Nan!" Bill cried from the doorway. "What are you doing?"

"Stephen's playing music on his glass, that's all."

They sat down to dinner. Bill gazed at her wistfully, pulling on his lip. Her playful, under-the-table kick offended him. Stephen brought a little pizza.

"Look, Bill," said Nan. "Red tomato cheeks. His nose is made of broccoli. Thank you, Stephen."

"I admit I'm trying to impress you, Bill."

"*I'm* impressed," she said.

They ate well, finished a bottle of wine. Bill even used his napkin. While Stephen made coffee, she asked Bill to bring the cake to the table. He sat on her lap, solemnly untying and opening the box. "William Lucifer," she whispered, kissing his red head, thinking: this is my beloved son in whom I am well pleased. She was not used to wine.

"The cake is just for you and me, right, Nanny?"

"It's for Stephen, too."

"Stephen didn't share with me."

"He made you something special. You wouldn't have liked the spicy food we ate."

"Nanny?" Earnest, innocent voice. "Stephen stinks, doesn't he?"

She put her hand over her face and thought, Oh God, but when she looked up, Stephen was laughing.

"BOUNCING around in the back seat like Wolf-Boy being driven to the vet. 'Sit down, Romulus,' I cry." Stephen re-enacting the scene in her living room.

"Oh, God. I'm sorry."

"We get there, Bill slavering—"

She had to laugh.

"Popcorn! Popcorn! I buy him a monster bag. We take our seats. The movie hasn't been rolling five minutes when I look at your boy beside me and see he's stuffing it up his nose!"

"Oh, God!"

"Bill, I say. I only want to direct him to the correct orifice, but he accidentally inhales. Cawing! Caterwauling! We spend half the film in the john blowing blood and snot and popcorn out of his nose."

"Why don't you sit down? I'll rub your back."

"Back in our seats, I'm concentrating on the film, trying to fill the thirty-minute gap in the plot. Suddenly I realize —"

She gasped. "He wasn't there!"

"Slippery little beggar. Gave me the old chase routine. To get him back to the car, I had to sling him screaming blue over my shoulder, everybody staring like I'm some child abuser."

"Last week he bit a girl at kindergarten."

Stephen slumped on the couch, groaning. "Is something wrong with Bill? It would help if I knew. A changeling maybe? The Future Ruler of the World?"

"Bill was wild even in the womb. When I was pregnant with him, I turned from vegetarian to raging carnivore. Then, after he was born . . ." She could laugh about it now. "We took him to psychiatrists and allergists, exorcists. The conclusion is character. He'll grow out of it. Patrick's mother isn't fazed. She says Patrick was worse."

"I don't know how you do it."

"He's tamed me."

"I'm still game on a package deal, Nan. The two of you, I mean. Even after today—would you believe it?"

That night was the first she let someone lie where Patrick had slept. She didn't feel she had dishonoured him in her mind or body, and there was no confusion over whom she touched and moved with or why. But she told Stephen she didn't want him there in the morning. He slipped away, honourable lover, saying he understood.

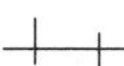

BILL telling her, "Patrick could do everything. He built houses and played guitar and made bowls."

"Wooden bowls on the lathe. You've seen Patrick's guitar, but you don't remember his playing."

"Nanny, I do! *Dear Abby dear Abby I never thought me and my girlfriend'd ever get caught.* He could get a fish with an arrow!"

"Mexico. Patrick speared fish in the Sea of Cortez. You were hardly two."

She wondered how far back she could go. Certainly not to her own father, dead of cancer before she could know him. Her mother had always been her friend, even in adolescence. No dogfights or power struggles. Other kids said: Nan's mom's not from this planet. How far back? She closed her eyes that night and tried, unwound her memory until it stopped at Nan on the sidewalk, aged four, finally able to skip rope, but backwards. Her mother, far away on the steps, is clapping. Stopped next at Nan in her bed. On the ceiling, pieces of glinting tin foil map the constellations. She grips her mother's soft arms, agony, curiosity—please, mommy, please, how was I born? But the room is too dark to see her face. No memorial then for a woman who salved so well the sting of growing.

She never asked why her mother didn't marry again. Now she needed the secret reasoning. Not that her mother would have given it if she were alive. The first time Nan made a pie on her own she used a cup of salt. I shouldn't rush, she said, spitting up on her plate. I should be more careful. Her mother said, not have-you-learned-your lesson-then, but, I rush too much myself. Later Nan remembered that her mother had watched her working and must have seen the motions of her mistake. Seen, but knew: patience leads to experience, and experience, to hope.

+ +

THE yard was lit by stars and the red spiral glow of mosquito coils. They were waiting for the aurora borealis.

"How long is Patrick going to mind? What's the difference—my going to bed with you, my staying the night?"

"Not Patrick. Bill sometimes comes in during the night. He collects me in the morning . . . There!"

It had begun, the vault and shiver, luminous unpleating of the night sky. Without speaking, they watched. Then she confessed, "I cleared you out a drawer ages ago."

The next morning she woke to Lucifer Bill standing at the side of the bed, naked, knocking on her shoulder. He was tip-toe, craning over her, staring at the occupied space. "Who's that?"

"Who do you think it is?"

"It's not Stephen!" He made a face.

"Do you want to come in?"

"Yuk!" He shook loose his wrist and ran out of the room. A moment later, a symphonic crash of pots and pans. She got up, put on her housecoat, and went downstairs to the kitchen.

"What are you doing, jaybird?"

He wouldn't answer.

"Are you jealous?"

"What's jealous?"

"Do you want all the good things for yourself?" Then she was sorry she said it. She knew, if he could, he would answer he wanted good for her, too. "Put on an apron. Bring me an egg."

When Stephen came down, she left the pancake batter settling and brought them each a cup of coffee to drink on the couch. "Good morning?"

"I'm happy," he said.

Bill flew across the room, loose apron like a cape wild behind him, dropped between them, half on her lap, the coffee sloshing out of their cups.

"Bill the Pill!"

Then he leaped up and charged again. Nan put out her bare foot to stop him. Gripping her heel, he closed his lips around her big toe and suckled noisily.

"That's silly. Go turn on the stove."

Nude, strutting, he pulled her along with him. At the kitchen door, she glanced over her shoulder at Stephen.

"Why don't you put him on a treadmill and power your house?" he called. "Or sell tickets? Kindergarten Burlesque."

Gingerly, she lifted the little brown cakes with the spatula. Bill carried the plate to Stephen, waiting now at the table, then stood a moment, head bowed, diligently working something in his mouth. A shiny worm of saliva. Clear and viscous, it trailed across the pancakes, still clinging to and stretching off his lip as he set the plate down.

Stephen, unflinching, opened the syrup bottle.

They had a hard day after that, Nan and Bill. Bill put his hand over the page she was reading, said, "Tell me about when I was a baby."

"You're not a baby. Soon you'll be in grade one."

The rest of the afternoon he was all anxiety, plaguing her with questions about school, twisting her answers, finally crying and purposely breaking a dish. She put him to bed before Stephen came, left him breathing heavily in dreams, as if his own badness were sitting on his chest.

Already Stephen was talking marriage.

"I don't know yet. Why force me?"

He didn't mean to, he said. If she knew the answer was no, she should say immediately, not keep him on cruelly. She said she hoped he thought more of her than that.

"I can't say the right thing tonight!"

So they vowed silence the rest of the evening, communicated through fingers, mouthed words. She laughed like a girl as he carried her, awkward, colliding with the walls of the stairwell. A picture slipped from its hook and crashed to the floor, this seeming so wildly funny they could barely stagger into the bedroom. He heaved her into the air and she fell giggling onto the bed, right onto Bill, who shrieked with the whole force of his savage throat.

Stephen found the light switch.

"I'm broken!" Bill wailed.

She was furious. "One, two, three, into your own room."

Stephen took each ankle and dragged Bill off the bed, held him a moment upside down while he thrashed like a landed fish.

Crawling between sheets, Nan tried to ignore the deadened thudding of her child hurling himself against the adjoining wall. Relentless shrieking, hysterical waves of fury, and now and then a lull, so she thought, thank God, but it was only his coming up for air. Finally she sat up.

Stephen held her back.

"Are you going to tell me not to go to him?"

"No. I just want to say I'm sorry for your trouble."

Now Lucifer Bill was bucking on the floor. When she touched him, he gave up struggling and clung to her nightgown. "What?" she asked, lifting his stained face. In the depths of his rage he had forgotten and began to cry again from confusion. She hushed him and brought him to his bed.

"Stephen's mean."

"He's not mean. He gets frustrated with you and no wonder. You have to get used to Stephen."

He put his mouth to her and breathed the word: mean.

This she promised him, promised herself: if she saw any sign of spite, however small, she would say goodbye to Stephen. She promised easily, half because she did not believe in a child's perception, half because she knew unkindness now would only grow through the years to animosity between two men. Any house divided against itself will not stand.

It was a long time before she left William Lucifer, breath exhausted and clotted, and went back to bed where Stephen, too, had fallen asleep. For her purposes then, she was alone. She lay back, lifted her arms over her head, inhaled, exhaled. The secret addiction of remembering her daughter. She was best indulged seeing Joni as she had been just before the accident, about Bill's age now, when they all realized she was growing into something almost perfect. Patrick had even said, I can't touch her anymore, she's too good for me. Hair red and eyes like the whole sky condensed. She had the most elegant carriage of any child and a way of being silent, not shyness—musing—then tipping off some extraordinary thought.

Even now Nan couldn't help thinking Joni was a mistake, that the accident was a way of retrieving something lost from that elsewhere place. As therapy she would imagine the car on that northern highway, afternoon sinking into early dusk. Patrick and Joni in front, her mother in the back with the Christmas cache. They are singing carols and, as in movies, their voices are audible all across the frozen fields, through the wind-breaks of naked trees. Then the truck appears speeding toward them in their own lane. Nothing can be done. In the next image, Joni is plucking glass out of the windshield, delicately, though glass could never cut her. She crawls out on the hood of the car, jumps down on a highway brightly littered with coloured parcels. She opens the driver's door and tugs her father's beard, as she always did to tease him, though now it is bloodied. In her green elfin parka, her buckle-up snow boots, Joni is unscathed, but Patrick is unrecognizable. He rises nonetheless. Joni wakes her broken grandmother with a kiss. Picking through the sideways wreckage of the moving van, they find the culpable driver who, even dead, sways from drunkenness. All together they set off cross-country, gore-red trail in the snow, going in the direction of a light behind the trees.

Then Stephen rolled over and she lost her vision. Looking at the fine line of his darkened face, she thought: if Joni were here instead of Bill, it would be a different life altogether. A decision would have been taken as spontaneously as a gift. Ease in her day life, night the struggle with the memory of her wayward prodigal son coming back to her as bad as ever, a celebration of his contrariness. And for a time she saw the car, her mother in the back seat, Patrick in the front with William Lucifer, not a toddler but almost six, pulling pieces of foam out of a hole in the seat, putting them in his mouth and spitting them at his grandmother. Patrick is telling him to cut it out when the truck comes barrelling down in their lane.

She sat up with a jerk, put her fist in her mouth to stop her own cry. *She had been thinking of life without Bill. She had been wishing away her only child.* Out of the tangle of covers she kicked, stumbled in the dark. She felt her way to the bathroom, then down the coolness of the toilet tank, urgent, fell forward. She had committed something in her heart, as bad as pushing him down the stairs or locking him out in winter. Her own finger she forced down her throat, stabbed, and heaved. When Stephen turned on the light, she was kneeling on the floor, hands clasped.

FROM a lawn chair she watched Stephen helping Bill around the big rocks, into the clear flow of the current. With arms extended, the boy looked like a bony marionette. Over the river noise, Stephen's voice: "Trust me. Yeah. Trust me."

Suddenly Bill was back on the shore, running to her.

"What? Don't cling to me! You're wet!"

"Stephen let the water go over my face!"

"It was an accident, I'm sure."

"Nanny, he pinched my arm!"

She looked at Stephen slogging out of the water. He shook his head and shrugged. "Put on a T-shirt, Bill. You'll catch cold."

She returned to her book. She hadn't turned a page yet, but instead was concentrating indulgently on her own bad humour. Perverse, her guilt pushing Bill away instead of bringing him closer. She was conscious of blaming him for the wrong she had done him, and this made her all the more irritable. When she looked up again, he was peeing in the river.

Stephen moved quietly about the picnic site. He set a glass of iced tea next to her without a word to disturb. Later, he took Bill off by the ear to light the coals. She could hear her boy's pugnacious voice shrill across the picnic site and was glad she did not have to be patient with him. Hers was a dire need for silence, silence to fill her life, like the calm she had grown up in. In another minute, Bill was wailing, coming toward her, fist in eye. "Stephen made the smoke—"

"Bill!" Stephen shouted. "Leave Nanny alone! She doesn't feel well, can't you see?"

Bill gaped at her, Stephen's scolding red on his face. Nan made a shooing motion with her hand. He hopped up and down on one foot, then scurried off down the riverbank.

The ruined myth: each generation betters the preceding. Her mother's grace and wisdom had been lost on her. How she blundered on. What hope was there then for William Lucifer, now filling his swimming trunks with river stones?

Her mother would have gotten up and done something, never brooded, sulked. This, and a wasp circling her head, goaded her out of the chair. She took the cloth from the hamper, shook it out over the picnic table, then began to unload the food. Bill came when she was slicing thick slabs of bread. He emptied his swimming trunks, laid fist-sized stones on the table among the picnic dishes.

Bill's job: transporting the chicken from fire to picnic table. He did this well and took a seat beside her. Stephen loaded the plates with salad.

"Bread please," said Bill.

"How are you?" Stephen asked her.

"All right. Don't worry."

"I said bread!"

She thought Stephen was going to shush Bill, but he reached past the basket of bread and picked up a stone. Held it a moment, palm up, as if to learn its weight or significance. Then he put it into Bill's waiting hand, not roughly or even with exasperation, just firmly, communicating. It shocked her more than if he had struck the boy.

Who would set a whole future on the whim of someone else's gesture?

A yellow wasp hovered over the table. She was not afraid. She gave her son a piece of bread.

Buffalo

TOM POW

The massed aspens rise from the earth
in a seam of black smoke contained
by the gentlest blue; though amongst them

on a path of all the leaves that have fallen
in a week they, and the white spruce too,
are silvered sunlight. I make up breath songs

dance along the track, take in the lake with
first man eyes, the wigeon and teal swimming
in and out among the cat-tails. "Stop

a moment. Listen." The last few aspen leaves
on the top branches, withered dry in the sun,
rattle like tokens, wishes in the breeze

"as if a spirit touches only them."
All else is silence and through the silence,
through the safety of the tall, quivering aspens

we approach a small herd of wood buffalo,
twenty, no more, moving across a clearing
in the forest. A straggling group

of refugees, they push great shoulders,
the weight of shaggy heads through sunlight
as if it were deepest snow. A calf trots

to keep up with its mother, a bull turns
the bevelled anvil of his nose, his black eyes
briefly acknowledge our presence. For the rest

there is only pulling their palettes, leaving
this moment behind. So few! So tame!
Picnicking later in the Indian summer

whose heat stokes up throughout the day, I feel
dampness gather round my collar, my forehead
beads with sweat. So when the rolls of thunder

finally come in the middle of the night
they shouldn't surprise me; yet I sit up
shaken and need to hear you calmly say the word.

That makes two of us who've smelled my fear—
of massed hooves thundering over dry earth
brushing all cover aside. Three, if you count

the lone buffalo who'd stood head on to us
as we parted from the trail. His mussel-
blue tongue, thick as my wrist, plays round his face

before, on legs slim as aspens, he swims
back into the forest's maze, leaving me
threadless, the last leaves trilling above my head.

Hazards

TOM POW

Cradling a bottle of bittersweet
McNally's, feet up, skimming a noir thriller,
a sharp-edged seductress on its cover;

with half an eye I take in game two
of the World Series, the Toronto Blue Jays
(one down) versus the Atlanta Braves.

I've given the aerials a good workout,
yet only in the slo-mo of a curving
pitch or in the real time of a sky-kissed

catch is it clear to me what's going on.
A blurred white trail at the foot of the screen
comes between me and my spicy dialogue.

Freezing rain's made road travel hazardous.
Police warn drivers to keep off the roads.
A moment later, the message repeats.

My wife sits where I'd encouraged her to go,
in the warm embrace of a dark theatre
staring toward the bright lights: her head's tipped

back to secure her glasses, her mind's alive,
generous, but framing questions, possibly
for a coffee house later—a caffe latte

of theatre talk. And all the time
the treacherous world grows more so. Rain welds
into ice where it falls, black roads glint

in moonlight. Cars helplessly collide.
In another room there's another pull.
Our son lies, his plump bottom up in the air,

the soles of his bare feet, two square-
nosed fish on a platter surrounded
by all the softness we want for his world.

I linger over him in the darkness,
edge him on his side and pull the blankets
over the drowsy question mark he makes:

this, the closest to prayer I get.
We're at the ninth inning when Ed Sprague
takes the ball mid-thigh and devours its heat.

The rest's History. The ball crashes
into an ocean of silenced Braves fans—
a two-run homer, 5 to 4, one game all

and all still to play for. "I could've crushed
their windpipes one by one and they couldn't
have done a thing to stop me," sings Easy

also on a roll. *CBC News at Ten*
warns conditions are extremely hazardous
for Croats, Serbs, Bosnians, Somalians,

Tajiks, emigrants, immigrants, and Jews.
I sit on the edge of my seat, my beer long
forgotten, waiting for your chopped, cold run

to the door. This is the symmetry of love:
the roots of sympathy growing wider,
deeper, watered by the freezing rains of dread.

Nesting

JULIA DARLING

GABRIELLE TOLD ME that she met Hilary in a beech wood behind the motorway.

She was alone, crumbling bread up in her pockets and dropping it, hoping no one would see her. It was a light, dry day, and she said the leaves crunched like cornflakes under her shoes. It was frosty.

Gabrielle always describes things this way, as if they were edible.

She said she heard a voice, calling her.

Gabrielle was thirteen, an unlucky age.

At the time I felt powerless, inadequate, and angry.

Our doctor, a great bulbous woman with greasy pores, would lecture me and Gabrielle as we sat before her, speechless.

She said that anorexia was like suicide, and that there would come a point from which Gabrielle could not return. I must make Gabrielle believe that she was worth saving, but the doctor didn't seem to know how. She had labradors, not children.

I even phoned up an expert in California who was reputed to have saved many girls. She said

"Honey, why can't you just put your arms around her and tell her that you love her, and that you'll never leave her," and I put the phone down, because I am a working mother, and the Californian's voice was sugary and over-rich, and I had the feeling she was blaming me, too.

I had Gabrielle when I was sixteen. I got pregnant with an amorous boy scout who was younger than me. I didn't realize boy scouts were capable of fatherhood. I don't think he did either. Neither of us was aware of the resilient seed that must have found its way through my regulation knickers to my ovaries, a hundred yards from a campfire, in a fumble of shorts and straps, while the rest of the troop sung "She'll Be Coming Round the Mountain."

My mother prayed for months, as I swelled. She is very devout. I got tired of being forgiven.

After two years of living at home in a state of perpetual shame, I moved into a council flat. Mother said I was moving in with Satan, but actually I was quite alone.

I trained as a beautician. She said that was wicked too. The house I grew up in was beige and ordinary, with chipped mugs on hooks in the kitchen and pale nylon covers from charity shops on the beds. I have always wanted beauty. My own daughter has dry, blotchy skin. That's another failure.

To goad my mother I sometimes dated a British Telecom engineer called Gary, but I only fancied him when he was up a ladder. I got a job on a skin counter in a department store, and I was due for promotion.

Then Gabrielle became anorexic, and Mother nodded and smirked as if Satan had been there all along, hiding in the fridge.

Perhaps he has.

Perhaps he is in me.

Sometimes I want to shake Gabrielle. Other times I am kind and make her small tasty meals that I try to feed her with a spoon.

I was at the end of my recipe book when Gabrielle met Hilary. That's why I went along with it. I would have believed anything.

She came home happy after her walk in the beech wood and told me that she had met a woman who lived up a tree.

"Really?" I said. "Eat a boiled egg."

But Gabrielle didn't answer. She sat down at the kitchen table and looked at me as if I was her jailer. She said

"I like being up in the air. Like a saint."

"Look," I said, "you'll have to go back into the hospital if you go on like that."

This is a conversation we have all the time.

It gets tedious.

Then she ate some boiled egg.

"I looked up and there she was."

"Who?"

"Hilary."

"Why is she living up a tree?"

"She says that living on the ground is too difficult."

+ +

THE next day I went to work. I had a woman come in with bags under her eyes and a shagreen complexion. I spent an hour smoothing it out with a small roller and filling in holes with putty. Eventually she looked ten years younger, although she couldn't shut her eyes. All the time I was worrying about Gabrielle and hoping that she was eating her lunch, not burying it in the garden, or feeding it to the neighbour's poodle.

When I got a break I went straight to the telephone, which staff are only supposed to use for emergencies, and rang home.

My mother answered.

"What the hell are you doing there?" I said, as the supervisor walked past.

"Forgive her, Lord," barked my mother. Then, nastily, "You shouldn't be working."

She always goes straight to the needle point in my stomach.

"Where's Gabrielle?" I shouted.

"Out."

The supervisor stood behind me twitching.

"I can't talk now," I snapped.

"I'd better find her for you, hadn't I?"

"She's probably gone to the shops, that's all."

"You know what I think."

"Yes." I slammed down the receiver.

I had to fill in on perfumes all afternoon because of that phone call. I stood there spraying the wrists of poor women who were as likely to buy a bottle of Desire as the Pope.

One woman said to me

"Smells like fly spray," and tripped off laughing. I sprayed the back of her coat with it, feeling like a tomcat with its hackles up, then met the supervisor's eyes across the shop floor.

Gabrielle and my mother were ruining my career.

Desire did smell like fly spray.

On the bus going home I kept thinking about Gabrielle.

I loved her when she was born. She had skin of satin and surprised eyes, and bore no resemblance to a boy scout. I hated it when they wouldn't let me hold her, when I could hear her crying upstairs in a shabby cot with a gloomy crucifix hanging above her tiny head while my breasts were leaking milk. When she was a little girl and we moved to the flat, we had treats all the time. We had chocolate for breakfast and bought clothes from catalogues.

She was quiet, and she was shy, but she had me. I would practise makeup skills on her tiny face. Once, she looked in the mirror and started to cry, because she thought I had made her look old, and I had to wipe it all off quickly with baby cream.

All the time my mother was coming round trying to save us and wanting to take Gabrielle back to the old house, but I put my foot down and wouldn't let her.

Gabrielle didn't understand and thought I was being cruel to her Nana. She liked the idea of angels. She liked nativity, and Noah, and even Moses, and the more I cursed these biblical ghosts the more she wanted them. She became pious and sanctimonious, until I felt persecuted by my mother and my daughter, and in the end I gave in and let Gabrielle go to church with my mother, even though it made me lonely. On Sundays I would go to bed and feel outcast, but then all my life I've felt lonely on Sundays.

The bus lurched into my estate, full of mothers with hairy legs who needed facials and who rushed away to their hothouse families, faces exposed to the wind. I walked carefully, determined to keep my poise.

At home Gabrielle was alone, sitting at the kitchen table. There was a lemon meringue pie cooking in the oven.

"Where's Nana?" I said.

Gabrielle didn't speak. She shrugged and said

"You look awful with all that lipstick on."

I rushed to the mirror. I looked miserable, but not awful.

"What's cooking?" I asked, trying to be cheerful.

"I'm making a pie, for Hilary."

"For Hilary?"

Dimly I recalled something the obese doctor had said—anorexics would do anything to avoid eating, even create fictional people who ate for them. I put my hand on Gabrielle's arm.

"Why don't we have some pie?" I said gently.

"I've already eaten," she said.

"Oh yes, what?"

"A sandwich."

I went to the bread bin. These days I count everything, even slices of bread, apples in the fruit bowl, eggs in the fridge. Some bread was gone.

"Did you really eat the sandwich?" I looked in the rubbish. It was empty.

"Of course I ate it. Hilary told me to."

"Is this your friend?"

"Yes. I already said. She lives in a tree."

I wondered if it was too late to phone the doctor and then decided I couldn't bear to listen to her voice again, with its pleated vowels and antiseptic morals. I would rather speak to one of her labradors.

"Will you eat something now?" I asked plaintively.

"No, I'm not hungry."

"Did you see Nana?"

"Oh, her." Gabrielle made a face. It cheered me up.

"What did she say?"

"She just went on."

"Oh yeah?"

"On and on. Hilary heard her. We were standing underneath the tree. Hilary dropped a fir cone on her head."

"Did she?" I was warming to Hilary. "Then what happened?"

"I came home with Nana, and I ate a sandwich."

GABRIELLE is not beautiful, but she is startling. She is a small yellow-haired girl with the frail bones of a sparrow. Her eyes are large and brown. It's an unusual combination. I don't know what to do about her. I have never really felt like a proper mother, like the women in supermarkets with children at their heels. She makes me feel clumsy and hard.

I weighed her. She looked so thin standing on the scales that I nearly cried. She had lost half a pound.

I tucked her up in bed that night and put a glass of milk on her bedside table.

She said, "I'm all right, you know. It's all right." I nodded, and stroked her bony head. A strand of hair came out in my hand.

Then she whispered, as if it was a guilty secret

"Hilary doesn't believe in God," before closing her eyes and turning her face away, so I couldn't answer.

The next morning I heard her getting out of bed at dawn. She went to the kitchen. I staggered in with my red silk dressing gown on. She was putting an old coat on over her pyjamas.

"What the hell are you doing?" I grunted.

"Going to see Hilary."

She stood there in the new light, holding the pie.

"You can come if you like."

I had not been out of the house with no lipstick on for some years, and I wasn't about to start. I went back to bed, but couldn't sleep. Birds were coughing in the trees.

I imagined Gabrielle walking through the drowsy estate, with tangled hair and half-closed eyes, carrying a lemon meringue pie. I suddenly thought how madness infects whole households, like a virus. It makes us do all kinds of things. It makes us be the opposite of what we are.

I felt powerless. I wanted to give up.

Gabrielle came back with an empty dish.

"Hilary liked the pie," she said. "I ate some too."

Her fictional friend was turning out to be extremely expensive.

I phoned work and said I was sick. In a manner of speaking I was.

Gabrielle watched television, the light flickering across her face in a room with the curtains drawn. I lay in the bath and smoked.

When my mother called, we both hid under the kitchen table.

We heard her marching off down the street huffing and puffing like an old gospel song.

I didn't tell Gabrielle to eat. I opened a tin of baked beans and gobbled them up myself with a spoon. It was a very peaceful, close day. In the evening Gabrielle baked a devil's food cake. I licked the bowl.

The next morning Gabrielle went again, carrying the weighty cake in a basket, like Little Red Riding Hood. I didn't stop her. I assumed she was burying it in the wood in some complicated ritual.

Later we had to go to the doctor's for a checkup. I knew that if we didn't go, someone would soon call, and that would be worse. I got dressed. I tidied Gabrielle's bedroom and found a shrivelled banana under the mattress.

When Gabrielle came back, the cake was gone.

"It was lovely," she said. "Hilary ate most of it. She likes food."

"What does Hilary look like?" I asked conversationally.

"Strange." Gabrielle didn't seem to want to expand.

"Do you climb the tree to see Hilary?" I asked foolishly.

"Yes. She's made a nest. It's very warm. We curl up."

"Nice," I said weakly.

Then she said

"Where are you going?"

"To the doctor's."

"But I'm all right!"

I made Gabrielle dress and wash. Her whole body was stiff and unhelpful. In another mood I might have slapped her, but I was tired of fighting.

"I'm worn out," said Gabrielle. Her face was pale. "I think I'm getting a cold."

I wound a scarf round her neck. It was as if she were a baby again. The phone rang loudly. We didn't answer it.

The doctor looked fatalistic. She sat with her broad knees spread before her and quoted medical journals at us for a while. Then she said she wanted to weigh Gabrielle. This is the part we hate. I wanted to say

"Why don't we weigh you for a change?" I bet her dogs are fat.

Gabrielle stood on the scales in a trance. She was staring up at the ceiling as if she wanted to fly away. The doctor said

"It looks to me as if we should have her in."

"I'm not working," I said quickly. "I'm off sick."

"And how is the reward system going?"

I struggled to remember the reward system. It was all about graphs and rules.

"Very well," I lied.

The doctor studied the scales.

"Oh," she said. She sounded disappointed.

"What?"

"The reward system must be working. She's put on two pounds. Well done."

I thought she was going to give me a dog biscuit.

On the way home Gabrielle said, "What's it like being fat?"

"Nice," I said.

"Hilary's fat."

"Fat and strange, eh?"

"Yes, that's right." Gabrielle was pale and serious.

At home my mother had left a note pinned to the door written on the back of a Christian postcard. It said

"Last night we prayed."

I tore it up, and Gabrielle said

"I don't want to go to church anymore. They shout too much."

I grinned.

AFTER a fortnight Gabrielle had put on half a stone. It was like watching a baby learn to walk. It even seemed as if our lives went from black and white to colour again. Gradually her face regained some of its features and colours; her arms looked less breakable, her legs plumped out, her eyes were brighter. When Mother came round, she was victorious. Her prayers were answered, she said. God had moved in mercifully before it was too late. I just nodded dumbly.

I didn't tell my mother about Hilary. Christians don't like imaginary people, apart from the Big One. I knew she would disapprove and say that Hilary was the henchwoman of the anti-Christ.

When she left, eyes raised to the heavens, stamping her way home, I felt bad. I hate it when Christians rejoice. It's worse than when they're miserable. I watched her going down the road in her badly fitting coat, one arm longer than the other from carrying her Bible. I wished that I was a more generous person.

All I cared about was Gabrielle returning to me, fatter and stronger.

I was proud of her.

WHEN Gabrielle was eight and a half stone, I applied for a job in a beauty parlour that specialized in anti-aging products and got the job. It was warm and intimate in the parlour, and I could use the telephone whenever I liked. I had a select and wealthy clientele who treated me with respect and gave tips in note form.

Gabrielle went back to school. She even began to menstruate. If she spoke of Hilary, I always humoured her. She still took food to the beech wood. I never complained about that either.

As far as I was concerned, Gabrielle had cured herself, with the help of her own imagination.

THEN one day I came in from work worn out from sanding down old ladies' wrinkles and plucking bristly old eyebrows and found Gabrielle in tears in her bedroom. She wouldn't speak. She just kept weeping. It was winter and outside, the earth was frosty and white. I thought she must have been bullied at school or jilted by some thoughtless lout. I kept on asking her what the matter was until she sat up and said

"It's Hilary. She's gone all stiff and cold."

I really didn't feel like going out, but I realized that she wouldn't be quiet until I did what she said. We got a torch and walked silently to the wood, which was damp and sinister. Gabrielle was holding my hand so tightly it hurt. I followed her down a brambly path into her private world. I was very nervous. I didn't know what to expect.

We came to a tree that was wide and gnarled. Gabrielle wouldn't let go. She climbed up first and I followed, catching my tights on the branches.

When I saw her I nearly screamed, but the sound stuck in my throat and so I just stared. She was lying in a curl in a nest of rags and bags. She was an old woman dressed in layers and layers of coats and dresses. Her eyes were wide open, and her silver hair coiled around her head in a halo. Her face was peaceful and she was smiling.

Gabrielle whimpered and lay down beside her like an animal seeking warmth. She reached into her pocket and brought out a chocolate bar, which she held to Hilary's stiff mouth. I reached out and pulled her hand away, and gently closed Hilary's eyes.

It was like turning off a light.

"Who is she?" I said, although I knew.

"She was my friend," sniffed Gabrielle.

There was a small paragraph about Hilary in the local newspaper. No one knew who she was or where she came from. I was afraid that her death would affect Gabrielle, but although she cried a lot she continued to eat.

In time the whole episode seemed dreamlike and insubstantial. My daughter was saved from death not by a doctor, or by her mother, or by God, but by a woman who lived in a tree.

I feel funny about it sometimes. I dream about Gabrielle curled up snug in the arms of a stranger. I have flashes of jealousy.

And sometimes, when I am patting cream onto the forehead of a client, or waxing a leg, or painting the contours of a cheekbone I think, It would be nice to stop this, to take off my overalls and walk into the quietest, greenest part of a forest and make a nest, away from everything.

A place just for me.

Going Places

HELEN FOGWILL PORTER

"HOW MANY DOORS do you have to open to get in 'ere?" The voice, a woman's, is half querulous, half resigned. I'm in a toilet cubicle in the washroom at the Corner Brook Holiday Inn. The washroom is reached through a kind of Russian-doll arrangement of doors. It reminds me, by some strange process of association, of the picture that used to be on the Pot of Gold chocolate box. Remember? It had a woman holding a box of chocolates, and on that box was a picture of the same woman holding a box of chocolates and on that box... When we were children, my sister Barbara and I used to wonder where, and if, the progression ended. It scared us in a pleasing way, similar to, but not as frightening as, our own mental investigations of eternity.

Somehow that voice makes me realize, more than anything else has done, that I'm back in Corner Brook. That mellow, h-dropping way of speaking was so familiar to me when I lived here. Not that it's a Corner Brook accent. I've never been able to define a Corner Brook accent, although my brothers claimed that Vicky sounded like a Corner Brooker when she first learned to talk. The men who moved here years ago to look for work in the paper mill talked in the accents of whichever bay they had come from. When their families followed, it was the same; there were pockets of people from Trinity Bay, Bonavista Bay, Notre Dame Bay, and White Bay. They identified themselves as being from Elliston or Greenspond, Herring Neck or Harbour Deep. It was their children and grandchildren who finally thought of themselves as Corner Brookers.

It's cold today, minus fifteen degrees Celsius. There's snow everywhere. I had to buy sunglasses earlier, to stop my eyes from watering. We don't see this much whiteness in St. John's except right after a fierce snowstorm. Here the snow looks as if it's settled in. The sidewalks are much higher than they are in summer; the snow has been packed down by hundreds of pedestrians and is hard as concrete to the foot. In the street itself the driving lanes don't have the salty blackness they do at home. With its many high hills where the slippery snow clings, it's a city I'd rather walk in than drive in.

When I turned the corner from the bed and breakfast this morning, I found myself on West Valley Road. I can't even remember the house number now; that's unusual for me. I've never forgotten 37 Avalon Terrace, 178 Topsail Road, 26 Monroe Street, 10 Penmore Drive, even 127 Southside Road East. In the fifties, we lived on West Valley Road in a two-room basement apartment, kitchen and bedroom, with a tiny washroom and no bathtub. The little boy who lived upstairs—Craig was his name—used to persecute Vicky. Every time he saw her, he'd hit her or try to push her downstairs. He was about three and a half; Vicky was twenty months, when we moved in. I was six months' pregnant with Alice.

Dad hated the apartment. "I can't stand to think about you living down here in this cellar," he said when he visited, his eyes filling with tears. For a moment I felt like crying, too, but then I began to get irritated. We were all right here, for the time being. Everything was fine, except for Craig. Tom wasn't home when Dad said that to me. I was glad. He hated it when my parents gave any indication that I might be worse off than before I was married.

Dad gave me twenty dollars when he was leaving. "Treat yourself the next time you go out," he said. "And for God's sake try to get another place before the baby comes. Mommy wouldn't want to see you in a place like this." When he kissed me goodbye I could feel the tears on his face. I wanted to cling to him, to beg him not to leave. At the same time, a part of me was glad he was going. I had grown used to the small world of Tom and me and Vicky.

The train was already moving; Dad had to jump aboard. He always did that, leaped on the train at the last minute. It drove Mom crazy when she was with him. He waved from the brakes and Vicky waved bye-bye from her stroller.

As I walked up the hill from the station, I remembered the twenty dollars and I felt oddly free. Now Vicky and I would be able to go to the drugstore on West Street. Perhaps I'd even buy a magazine. It wasn't often that Tom and I had any money left over after we paid the bills. Teachers' salaries were very low in those days and of course I "didn't work."

A twenty-dollar bill was a kind of symbol to me. I suppose it still is, in a way. These days I'm more often on the giving than on the receiving end.

The children are grown up now and have their own jobs. I sometimes still slip one or other of the boys a twenty, just before payday. But I'm more likely to give one to my sister Pam or to my brother's wife. They still have small children. I usually give Oscar and Rosalie a lesser amount, perhaps a five or a ten. Why do I have this need to pass out money? Perhaps it's in the genes.

The first time Aunt Winnie and Mrs. Long and Nonie and I went to the West Street drugstore I was twelve years old. That summer evening I noticed a girl and a boy in the booth opposite us. They were laughing and talking over Cokes, sucking the sweet liquid up through straws in the bottles. They looked about sixteen. The girl's hair was dark brown, shoulder-length, and shiny. The boy wore rolled-up dungarees and a white T-shirt. When they got up to leave, the girl pulled on a loose navy blue jacket with the words "Been Places, Going Places" on the back. Each white letter was stuck on separately. My heart ached at the sight.

"Betty, what are you dreaming about there now?" Aunt Winnie's voice was sharp. "Mrs. Long wants to know what kind of a soda you'd like. Nonie is having orange."

"My treat," whispered Mrs. Long, grinning at me. She almost always spoke in a whisper, glancing quickly over each shoulder. She was a distant cousin of Uncle Selby's. We were staying with her on Humber Road. Mrs. Long seemed to have lots of money, was always buying us ice cream and candy, comic books, and jacks with balls. She was a thin woman with a squint in one eye. Sometimes, when Nonie and I were alone in the bedroom we shared, we laughed at her and afterwards felt ashamed. She had a husband somewhere, but she never talked about him. Mom had hinted that he was in the asylum in St. John's. "But don't you dare utter a word about that," she warned me before I left home. "Poor man, he can't help it if he's off his head."

Why am I out here in Corner Brook right now, anyway? I'm supposed to be doing a piece on the fine arts college for the paper. I suggested to the editor a while ago that it might be a good idea. He wasn't too keen at first, but after I reminded him about the overpass syndrome he changed his mind. People from outside St. John's are always saying that townies think the world stops at Donovan's Overpass, and it *is* supposed to be a paper for the whole province. My boss is from the Great Northern Peninsula himself; although he's been living in St. John's for thirty years, he still calls himself a bayman.

What do I care about the fine arts college? Most people claim it was built in Corner Brook only because the Minister of Education is from there, that it should have been put in central Newfoundland. Or, of course, St. John's. The Holy City, as it's often called. But what do I really care about it, where it is, or anything else? Isn't all this just an excuse to get away?

Get away from what? My job at the paper, my family, my friends, the people who are always asking me to serve on committees? From my hangers-on? Yes, certainly, my hangers-on. Why don't my friends get involved with odd people the way I do? I've heard so much about codependency lately. You can't pick up a paper or a magazine or watch TV or listen to the radio without hearing about it. Do I actually need Oscar and Rosalie, and all the others? What would I do if I had no poor relations or friends, or at least none poorer than myself? Have I become an enabler? I'm so sick of all that jargon. I even came across a book of poetry about codependency the other day. Why does everything in the world have to fit neatly into a category?

Of course, I do it myself. I'm always trying to categorize people, even out here. Especially when I'm away from home. Now, as I cautiously continue my walk along West Street, I steal glances at the people I pass. That tight-lipped woman in the blue belted jacket and pants, the hood hiding all of her hair. Why does she look so angry? Is her husband an alcoholic? Did he leave her for another woman? Perhaps he's a child molester. Why do I automatically assume that husbands are responsible for most women's problems? Maybe this woman is annoyed because her feet are cold or maybe she hates her job.

My father used to slip me money whenever he had any to spare, and sometimes when he didn't. There's something about a twenty-dollar bill that makes me feel Dad's presence more than looking at his picture does, or hearing his voice on a tape recorder. I don't give Oscar or Rosalie twenty dollars very often, but when I do it makes me absolutely happy. People have always told me, especially now that I'm older, that I'm the image of my mother, but that's in appearance. A twenty-dollar bill, either to spend on something unnecessary or to graciously give away, is the same kind of talisman to me that it was to Dad. Sometimes when he was drunk, children would follow him along New Gower Street, their small dirty hands stretched out eagerly for the coins he couldn't help giving them. He would already have changed twenty dollars for just such a purpose.

Dad pitied those children as if they were his own. Most of them were poor, neglected, deprived, abused. He pitied me and my sisters and brothers too, to the point that he never forced us to go to school if we didn't feel like it. We probably would never have graduated if Mom hadn't kept after us. Yet we didn't always have fresh milk or juice to drink, things that most of our schoolmates took for granted. One day I heard Mom remind Dad that a quart of milk and a bottle of Jockey were exactly the same price.

The other night I went to a Toastmasters meeting with Rachel. She's Vicky's friend really, but I know her, too. As I listened to the speakers, I found myself falling into my old habit of pitying people. Especially the men. I empathize with the women, but I pity the men. Not as a group, of course. Just individually. Most of them seemed restive, ill at ease, anxious to please. So *unsure* of themselves. The women were more confident, more relaxed. Why is this? Perhaps the men are from more varied backgrounds, different roots. Maybe the women who come out for things like this are naturally the more assured ones. Is it that women's identities are not so bound up with success, or not yet, anyway? Not here? Margaret Atwood once said that what men fear most from women is being made a fool of. She also said that what women fear most from men is being killed.

Mrs. Long's husband tried to kill her. Aunt Winnie told me that, many years after our Corner Brook trip. "Poor Lucy, she's had a hard life." Aunt Winnie and my mother-in-law and I were sitting in a restaurant the night she told me, a new place on the outskirts of St. John's. I had recently gotten my driver's licence and had taken them for a drive to celebrate. Aunt Winnie had visited Mrs. Long that very afternoon at the Grace Hospital, where she was recovering from cancer surgery. "Joe—her husband—was nice enough when I first knew him. He stayed with us when he was working in St. John's; they were still living around the bay then. But when he was about fifty, he started to go right strange, always blaming poor Lucy for going out with other men. Can you imagine?" I couldn't. "Once he even thought she was carrying on with his own son; he was married before, you know. Anyhow, one night he went for her with the hatchet. She ran right out in the middle of the street in her nightgown and screamed. Her neighbours all rushed out, and two of the men grabbed Joe. They said he was some strong."

"Mental strength," said my mother-in-law. It was rare for Nan to speak up like that. She had been listening intently to what Aunt Winnie was saying.

"Anyway, they got the police," Aunt Winnie went on. "And the next day poor old Joe was brought in here to the asylum. They had him in a straitjacket on the train, never had the good drugs then, you know. Not like now."

"Poor mortal," said Nan, wiping her eyes with a tissue. Nan was never judgemental about that kind of thing, the way she was about people who enjoyed themselves on Sundays or played cards or drank. Perhaps she was thinking about her brother Jacob, a brilliant mathematician who had spent many months himself in the asylum, by that time called "the Mental."

In the restaurant that night I had trouble keeping myself from laughing. The corners of my mouth twitched as I pictured Mrs. Long's scrawny body in a long plain nightgown, standing and screaming in the middle of a quiet Corner Brook street. Was I ever really that cruel? I hope it was a kind of hysteria.

She's dead now, Mrs. Long. When I think of her these days it's never as a figure of fun. She was always good to Nonie and me, always wanted us to go downtown shopping with her when she came to St. John's. She walked so fast, with short, erratic steps, that it was hard to keep up with her. We mumbled to each other that she must be running away from something. Or someone. She laughed a lot herself then, putting her hand over her mouth when she caught people looking at her. Self-conscious, I suppose. Or hiding her slipping false teeth. She used to buy us sundaes at the Sweet Shoppe, ice cream piled high with strawberry, pineapple, or chocolate syrup, topped with nuts and swirly fake whipped cream. Sometimes she'd even order us banana splits. She'd get the same thing for herself, never content with the more sedate tea and pie Mom and Aunt Winnie usually settled for.

In those days almost every biggish store had large upright platform scales on which you could weigh yourself for one cent. We never called cents "pennies." Pennies were larger coins, left over from the past. They were worth two cents each. It was part of our routine to get weighed whenever we had a copper to spare. Nobody had bathroom scales back then. For that matter, most of us didn't have a bathroom, just a little toilet room squeezed into a small space. Mrs. Long and I were always trying to gain weight, Aunt Winnie and Nonie to lose it. Every time she stepped on the scales—the word was always plural to us—Mrs. Long would scan the indicator anxiously for her weight. If she was up even half a pound she'd be happy. Some of the scales offered fortunes on small square cards. Mrs. Long would read hers aloud to us. "Happy times await you," she'd say, sounding as if she believed the message absolutely. Or "Romance is just around the corner."

"Now see, I told you Neddy Barnes was looking at you in church last night," Aunt Winnie would remind her, and they'd giggle. There was no divorce in Newfoundland at that time.

"She's lonely, poor soul," Aunt Winnie would say when, as we got older, we complained about having to be with Mrs. Long so much. She never had any children of her own, and her stepson, married with a family, had little to do with her.

Mrs. Long loved my sister Barbara, who is six years younger than me. "Barbie Lou," she'd croon. "Barbie Lou went up in the flue / When she came down she thought of you." Barbie loved her, too, would cuddle into her skinny bosom and let herself be rocked to sleep. I wondered how she could stand being held tight against that bony body. Now, when I look back, I'm glad Barb liked her, and showed it. When I see Mrs. Long in my mind's eye, she reminds me of some of those men I met at the Toastmasters meeting—anxious to please, tentative, afraid of not being understood.

The night of the Toastmasters meeting, Rachel and I went out for coffee afterwards. She told me all about herself. I knew she was divorced but I didn't know the details. She left her husband, Dan, a nice man, steady, a good provider (how old-fashioned that sounds, like something Aunt Winnie would have said), because he bored her. Her two children lived alternately with her and with their father when they were growing up. She's had some real blow-ups with them, but they're friends now. She's a feminist; I'm a feminist. She's only about ten years younger than I am. We grew up in the same town, went to the same school, came from the same kind of family. What makes us so different?

Years ago, perhaps not so many, I might have yearned to be like Rachel. Now it doesn't matter. Tom bored me sometimes, but I would never have thought that just cause to leave him. Most other men would have bored me more. And surely I must have bored him, too? Since he died, I haven't really wanted another man. Oh sure, I still get sexual feelings, sometimes they're even associated with one particular man, but I know they'll go away, especially if I help them along.

When I was more active in the women's movement than I am now, a lesbian feminist asked me why I was still sleeping with the enemy. I never did think of individual men that way—Tom, my father, my sons, my sons-in-law. Yet there's no doubt that men as a whole have been incredibly cruel to women as a whole. (That sounds like a really sick pun.) And I don't want to sleep with women either, at least as far as I know. What is the answer? Is there an answer?

Aunt Winnie and Mrs. Long and their friends didn't spend much time with men. Even the ones like Mom and Aunt Winnie, who went places with their husbands occasionally, spent far more time with women. You'd see them going downtown in twos or threes on Saturday nights, arm in arm—"linked up," they called it—talking in low voices that never seemed to run out of things to say. They had their own card clubs, their own church groups, their own bowling leagues, their own lodge meetings. When they travelled, they stayed with friends or in boarding houses, often two to a bed. Sometimes they made suggestive remarks about the men left behind. They would have laughed at the idea of sexual love between women. There was warmth, though. They shared warmth.

When we lived in Corner Brook thirty years ago I didn't go out much. We had the children and I always seemed to be pregnant. If Tom and I went out at all at night, we went separately, he to band practice or a teachers meeting, while I stayed home; I to a movie or a baby shower, while he looked after the children. Was Mrs. Long still living here then? I can't remember. If she had been, Aunt Winnie would surely have ordered me to visit her. I wouldn't have wanted to go. Mrs. Long was too easy to please, too hungry for love. And, certainly at that time, I wouldn't have had any love left over to give her. Besides Tom there was Vicky, followed in rapid succession by Alice and Robert. Michael came later, after we moved back to St. John's. And then, of course, there were Mom and Dad, my sisters and brothers, my other close relatives, all my friends.

Mrs. Long probably would have made a good babysitter. But I wouldn't have wanted her in my house. To me she was a symbol of misfortune, bad luck, ill winds. A symbol of what women—what people—can become. I wouldn't have wanted to think of myself as an old, poor-looking (that's what we used to call unattractive people—poor-looking), unloved woman, living off the fragments of other people's lives. That last line sounds like it's straight out of *The Lonely Passion of Judith Hearne.* Perhaps it is.

And yet Mrs. Long's husband must once have thought of her as a creature of passion, an object of desire. Or was that a figment of his sick mind? Men's fears and beliefs about their women are remarkably standard; I know a number of men who've accused their wives of being cheats, whores, sluts. Most of these women never looked at another man. And yet none of those husbands would have been certified insane.

Tom never called me any such names. I don't think he ever even thought them. I often wondered what kinds of things he'd say if he ever got drunk. As he never had a drink in his life, I never found out.

My father was not physically violent, but he used to call my mother names. Only when he was drinking, of course. The first time I heard him call her fucker, bitch, cunt, I couldn't believe my ears. Not my soft-voiced, gentle father, with his clear blue eyes that filled with tears if one of his children was lonely or tired or sick or had a falling-out with a friend. "That was a lovely dinner, Mommy," he would say after every meal. Most men his age took good meals for granted, many of them more likely to complain than praise.

"It's the liquor talking," my mother would console me after one of Dad's drunken tirades. "He doesn't really mean what he says." But I couldn't forget those words. They rang in my head for years.

Dad never really got over Mom's death. In the eighteen years he lived without her, he never looked for a replacement, though several women would have gladly fitted into his life. He was wiry and active, looked much younger than his years. He often reminded us about how good he had been to Mom, how much he loved her, what a wonderful person she was. "She always had her own cheque book," he'd say. I didn't remind him about the cheques that bounced at the supermarket. I wondered if he ever felt guilty about his drinking, his verbal abuse. He never called my sisters or me those sickening names. He used them only when he lashed out at his own beloved wife. Where did those words come from? And why did he have to say them? At other times my parents appeared to be happy enough together.

Every morning of his adult life, my father worked out with dumbbells. Except when he'd had too much to drink the night before. Then he would lie in bed with the covers up to his eyes, looking white, and pathetic, and scared. Later he'd ask my mother to tell him what he'd said the night before, claiming he couldn't remember. He almost always called her Mommy; she called him Ted. "I'll never do it again, Mommy," he'd say after she told him.

"Honour bright, I won't." She would already have phoned the office to say that Dad was sick and wouldn't be in. Sometimes she sent me to Jean's Shop for Haig Ale, a near-beer that was the only kind allowed to be sold in grocery stores at that time. When I came home with it, Dad would drink thirstily, his hands shaking.

When we lived here in Corner Brook in the fifties, I was often jealous about Tom. He was a good-looking young man, shy but with his own kind of appeal that I'm sure was not lost on the female teachers, the women at the church. Even, perhaps, his students. I went wild with anger when he spent a Saturday afternoon playing badminton at the school gym with Stephen and Emily Sterns, a young English couple who had no children. "What was Emily wearing?" I screamed at him when he came home, happy and relaxed, after the game. He was astonished; I was usually accepting of his behaviour, which, of course, was almost always pretty acceptable. But I couldn't stop raging at him.

"You're up there jumping around like a teenager while I'm here with three crabby youngsters!" I yelled. I wanted to pound on his chest, to wipe that questioning smile off his face. Instead I ran into the bedroom, threw myself on the bed, and cried. He stayed in the living room with the children, making paper airplanes.

I miss Tom, sexually and in every other way. I think I miss him most of all for his unconditional comforting, his acceptance of my emotional highs and lows, his warm physical presence, his love. He died of a massive heart attack; we had slept in each other's arms the night before. Yet he irritated me often. His steadiness, his temperance, his reliability, the very qualities I'd married him for became annoyances later. His high expectations of behaviour for our children, his dependence on me for his social life, his unhidden impatience when my father and my brothers smoked in our house, all made me wish, more than once, that I was on my own. Yet I would never have left him, not if we had lived together for fifty years. And I'm as certain as I can be that he would never have left me.

Now I spend a great deal of my time avoiding people. When I see familiar faces on the street I turn my head away before I'm recognized. When I'm eating alone in a restaurant I pray that nobody I know will come in. Of course I still go to meetings, out to dinner with friends, to the occasional play or movie. Even, once in a blue moon, to a singles bar with my sister Pam. I'm with my family a lot, my sons and daughters, celebrating birthdays and holidays, babysitting my grandchildren. And then there's my work with the paper, the reason I'm out here to do this blessed article that I don't want to do. But I'm happiest when I'm alone. Really, happy is a word that doesn't apply to me anymore. It's a long, long time since I've been overtaken by joy, as C. S. Lewis puts it. But there's a kind of peace. And I suppose most women my age feel the same way.

And if I did decide to look for another man, as some of my friends recommend? What man would want a woman who has to wear Depends in bed? Disposable undergarments, as they euphemize so tactfully on the package. It's either that or pad myself with towels so I won't wet the sheets. Even if some stranger could overlook all that, how would I be able to stand it? Tom would have accepted it, and we would have laughed about it, as we laughed together about so many other things. I'm better off as I am, or is that just what I tell myself? Perhaps it's an excuse. Surely something could be done about my bladder problem if I really wanted it done.

The mill whistle is blowing. Must be lunchtime. I'm sitting in a booth with high walls at the Holiday Inn coffee shop, drinking my third cup of tea. How can it be noon already?

When I was small I used to have a recurring dream that my father would leave us. That's the way I always thought of it—*us*. For another woman. Never did I dream of my mother leaving my father, although that would have made more sense. Barbara thought Mom should leave Dad, and told her so. I never wanted that. Later, after I was married, the characters in the dream changed. Now Tom was leaving me (us?) for another woman, a beautiful young woman who spoke in a low voice and who was active, sympathetic, and well organized. Even now, years after his death, I still dream of him being with someone else. In the last dream it was a sixteen-year-old student. The core of the dream has changed, though. Now I'm always the one who's responsible for our separation. In the dreams, I question myself about why we stopped having sex, as if it was my fault. Tom's death was so sudden. There was no preparation at all.

My father lived with us for over a year after Mom died. I don't think Tom ever really wanted him there. We had never discussed the possibility of having Dad stay at our house. It just happened. I was working at the university then; it was good to have Dad to look after the children in my absence.

After several quiet months, Dad began drinking heavily again. One early morning, when he came home drunk, I told him to get out. He did, then and there. We did not become estranged. I visited him often at his various apartments, and he came to meals at our house sometimes. The Christmas after he left, he came for dinner with the rest of the family. He had been drinking; his face was chalky and his hands shook as he reached for his hat when he was getting ready to leave. "Where are you going, Dad?" I asked, thinking he might be planning to make some visits. "I'm going home," he said, and I wanted to weep, remembering the home we had all once shared and visualizing the tiny basement apartment he lived in now.

"Would you like some lunch?" The waitress is standing over me, holding out the menu. I study it intently, not taking in a word.

"It's nice and warm," I say. "I hope I haven't been sitting here too long."

"No problem. It's some cold out today, isn't it?" She rubs her hands together as if she's standing on the street. I can't identify her accent; she's probably a Corner Brook mixture.

As I wait for my soup and sandwich, I tune in to the voices from the booth behind. I used to do this a lot, when people interested me more. I do it today because there's no alternative—I have nothing to read, and I haven't got the energy or the inclination to write letters.

"I think I *am* going to leave him this time." The voice is a woman's, low, cautious. "I can't live like this much longer."

"He doesn't seem too bad to me," says the other voice, a woman's also. "I mean, he never hits you or anything. And he doesn't put you down in front of people. Does he do it when you're alone?"

"Oh no, Lloyd is not a bit like that. But he's just so—so cold, Marian. I feel like I don't know him at all. And now that the children are grown up and gone, we have nothing to say to each other. It's like living in a silent prison."

"Well, don't do anything hasty. There's a lot got it worse. And better the devil you know, after all."

"Don't worry, I'm not going to no other man. I've had enough of men to last me a lifetime." Her voice is bitter; I imagine the expression on her face. "Sometimes I think he's like his father. He died in the Mental, you know."

"Yes, but he was violent, wasn't he? Didn't you tell me he . . ."

"Shhh, here comes the waitress. What're we gonna have?"

The waitress brings my soup. It looks good, but I'm not hungry. Perhaps I can cancel the sandwich. I think of all the sad people I've ever heard of—this woman, her husband, his father, Mrs. Long, my father, those girls in Holyrood who were raped by their foster father, the little autistic boy Pam was telling me about, the woman on my street who has Alzheimer's and keeps running from house to house telling the same stories over and over again.

My mind turns sharply to a night in that summer of 1942 when we were staying with Mrs. Long in her big old house on Humber Road. Nonie and I were in bed when I remembered that I'd left my new Cherry Ames book downstairs. When I went down to get it, Mrs. Long and Aunt Winnie were still sitting at the kitchen table, their empty teacups in front of them.

"I don't know what I'm going to do when you goes back, Winnie, I just don't know." Mrs. Long was looking down at the white tablecloth, tracing patterns on it with the handle of her spoon. "It's so lonely here by myself."

"Life is lonely," said Aunt Winnie, reaching across the table to squeeze her friend's hand. I picked up my book and went upstairs without them even knowing I'd been there.

How long have I had this feeling of waiting, waiting, waiting? Waiting for what? Waiting for whom? Why am I so afraid of getting close to someone again? I get so mad at television shows like *The Golden Girls,* with their eternal emphasis on sex. And the movies. There are no movies these days without the obligatory steamy sex scene. This is all necessary, we're told. It's like life. Like whose life? Certainly not like my life. Not like the lives of most of the people I know.

Of course I do have those dreams. Dreams of lying naked in bed with Tom, feeling his hard penis against me. Dreams of sexual closeness with a stranger, or a man I know casually. Occasionally, dreams of physical intimacy with a woman.

Once, when I was thirteen or fourteen, I went to a movie by myself one afternoon. This was unusual; I almost always went with friends. It was as dark as midnight inside the theatre. Somehow—I don't know how it started—the young man in the next seat and I began kissing and touching. I seem to remember moving closer to him before we started. We kept it up all through the show. Afterwards, when the lights came on, I saw his face clearly for the first time. He was eighteen or nineteen, with greasy hair and pasty skin. He looked at me with a kind of contempt and said, "That was what you wanted, wasn't it?" Then he hurried past me into the crowd. Over the years I've nearly convinced myself that this never happened, that it was another dream. I've never told anyone about it, not even Tom. Perhaps especially not Tom.

The women in the next booth are talking about their children now—Nancy, who is getting married in June, and Lionel, living in Fort McMurray. I pick up my spoon and begin on the soup. I take a notebook and pen out of my purse, ready to list the names of the people I'll call this afternoon for interviews. It's time I got started.

Lombard Street

JAY RUZESKY

He says yes to the long drive knowing
there will be fights with the brother,
threats from the father,
the mother's silence and bad navigation
through complex American freeways.

Yes to Alcatraz, trolley cars,
someone he wishes he could be momentarily
skateboarding down a steep incline
toward the low and distant bay,
Chinatown, and Fisherman's Wharf.
Yes to dinner at the Hilton
with its palate-cleansing sorbets between courses.

Yes to Lombard Street, the most
twisted street in the world,
the family car climbing and
this small boy outlined in the rear window,
his balloon an empty word bubble in the frame;
some cartoon character who forgot
what he was about to say.

Yes to the evening drive out of town
across the Golden Gate Bridge,
the city closing its slow eye.
Yes to the next day and drive home again,
to the next year when his voice broke,
and to his first sexual experience.
Yes to the second one the next day,
then to the few women in his life
who taught him what he knows.
Yes to the birth of his child,
to the house and jewelled yard around it.
Yes to the dog.

And now he's well into it,
there's no turning back.
Around another hairpin climbing steadily
beyond the silence surrounding
the dog's inevitable end,
so yes even to the death of his parents and
yes to being there each time.
Yes to all the routes that sent him
corkscrewing forever up like an aria.
Yes to watching his daughter
back down the driveway
graduating high school. Then yes to
old age and to senior's discounts at Sears.
Yes to memory and forgetting,
the decline of his body,
to those who call on weekends,
and to the someone who pushes him
out to the park in a wheelchair.
Yes to light and dark and closing,
and Lombard Street's hedges and red bougainvillea.

Bruise

MARLENE COOKSHAW

Looking backward
we back into
life. Its finest particle
surprises. Through

the rear window of cars
in the years before seatbelts, or
standing on ship stern:
exquisite , unbearable arc

of each detail surging
away. Back
as shield, carapace
of bone and muscle, what splits

the world in two
—the right, the left—
and serves it up
in passing. What passes

for highway, landscape, ship's
wake, its populace of gulls.
I'm not certain I'm ready
to turn, or ever will be: someone

needs to note the extravagant
waste of our lives, its drop-dead
beauty. Like that splay
of prairie landfill I hand-fed

with remnants of
my mother's basement. Broken
televisions, calendars
across the heaps of glittering

trash—which bulldozers fold,
relentless, into earth, like laundry,
and in the distance sun picks out
the reds of lampshades, aprons.

The gulls lift off and land
with every turn of the machines.
This happens north of a town
whose only honoured road

runs east and west.
South is America, and north
the frontier. Always
I've packed and gone west,

over mountains, my back
to the town I grew up in,
to the wavering path my father traced
in this world, then abandoned.

Did he look backward
too? Back to back:
a strong position, good
defence, the last defence.

An embrace of a kind,
in its way.

First Steps First

ROYSTON TESTER

(an excerpt)

TO HELL WITH GOING BACK.

Nineteen and out of England for the first time, Enoch Jones had made up his mind to do a bunk. And the longer he mingled with this jinxed and disgruntled band of British holidaymakers, the opportunities for disappearance increased no end. What a doomed journey for these Mediterranean-seeking three hundred. Now stranded in Madrid.

Enoch leaned against a windowpane out of the sun, when a bearded Spaniard who smelled of lemons—Fabio, he said his name was—immediately set upon a conversation, in meticulous English, about staircases: Blenheim Palace, Chatsworth House. The man had stepped in the lot. Bodian, "the most fairy of English castles" as he put it, with its famous spiral.

With one ear attuned to the chatty man and the other to the announcements of delays and changes of itinerary that had long since got the better of the crowd's patience, Enoch attempted to plot an escape from the Conquerors Holidays "air-only." The stairs-I-have-known raconteur did go on a bit: Sissinghurst's tower steps,Winston Churchill's tricky Chartwell ones. He must be a Catholic in crisis, thought Enoch; the idea of pilgrimage—the up and down kind, on your knees preferably—appeals to that sort.

There was little enough for Enoch to plot, it seemed: he knew no one in Spain, knew nothing about his purported destination, and had money enough only for a night or two, the original courier arrangement being that he should return to England the following afternoon, once he had delivered the stack of documents.

It crossed Enoch's mind that he was being irresponsible, maybe even breaking down somehow. But he had nothing to lose; certainly he didn't feel loyalty to Chubbsy or to Riaz Mansour, who had sent him on this pipe dream of theirs, his suitcases laden with designs for a fish and chip shop built around a swimming pool. In fact the unlikelihood of any success after going missing—and dumping the cases—whetted his appetite all the more. If I don't do it now, he thought, I'll grow up gabbing to young men in jeans about staircases.

Not me, bro.

It was early August 1974 and the two travellers—or at least one of them—engaged in staircases were part of a jostling group of passengers—a very ugly mixture of the hot, much-tormented charter tourists recently arrived from London and a scattering of apprehensive locals—all on the tarmac at Madrid's Barajas airport, waiting to board an Iberia shuttle bus out to the plane.

"Franco! Look!" shouted a Spanish boy tugging at his mother's arm, "Generalísimo Franco!"

One or two people looked in the child's direction, but most of the English seemed more concerned about getting seats—or more correctly, a beer—on the flight ahead than paying heed to a youngster.

Already forming in the stifling air of high summer were the many versions of complaints to Conquerors Holidays, who had promised them a direct flight to the Mediterranean port of Alicante—not an unearthing in Spain's landlocked capital—followed by, in the words of the Conquerors' representative, whose breathing was resembling contractions, "quick *pop-over* to Barcelona," where a brand-new jet would be standing ready to "*taddle on* south."

"Ay, but will *this* bleeder make it?" said one tourist in neat, white soccer shorts.

Miss Conquerors Representative tried to laugh with the crowd.

"We didn't vote in Harold Wilson to be treated like this, young lady," said another, referring to Britain's new Labour prime minister and the glorious road ahead for the downtrodden.

"We want our money back!" shouted yet another.

The little Spanish boy was now jumping up and down, pointing excitedly at the airport's distant cargo area.

"We want! We want!" began a burly Scot trying to recreate the mood of the February ban on miners' overtime that had led to a national strike in the United Kingdom.

"*Guapo,* no," scolded the Spanish boy's mother—no, dear—looking around nervously at the rioting English and their embittered alien tongues. "El Caudillo's in hospital," she said. Spain's elderly leader, Francisco Franco, was recovering from a grave illness.

There was no stopping the boy. He had spotted Franco.

"Money back! Money back!" The chant hit a revolutionary stride.

Suddenly a fleet of six military vehicles emerged from behind a series of hangars and launched into a spritely escort across the main runway.

"Dios mío!" declared the boy's mother—my God!—clutching her son. "Get down from there, Pacito!"

Two or three Spaniards nudged one another and strained to see over the heads of the boisterous foreigners. "Franco," they were saying. *"El Pardo."* His palace. Recovery.

At the rear of the procession was a black Mercedes displaying on its roof the blood and sun stripes of the Spanish flag—unmistakably, judging by the awestruck faces in the crowd, this was the dictator's personal limousine.

"We want! Money back!" The Anglo-Saxon lament continued.

But the British protesters sensed attention falling away.

Tongues tied.

In the middle of the convoy was some kind of pyramid structure. A missile launcher perhaps. Or a glittering robot. Enoch couldn't quite make it out so far away in the brash sunlight.

The chanting petered out.

Groups of people appeared at the departure windows as the vehicles drew closer.

"Fuck you! Fuck you!" the burly Scot droned on gloriously, punching at the air, but now the sole voice. "Up yours! Fuck you!"

Clearly the armed escort was an event. And the spectators to this unannounced march-past by their ailing general fell into a deep, if not entirely respectful, hush.

"Lighten up, Eric!" One of the Scotsman's Cockney mates tapped him on the shoulder and indicated the runway. "Queen Mum's comin' wiv us. Look!"

Eric swayed to the perpendicular.

"Peasant butcher," whispered Fabio at Enoch's side, hastily replacing his sunglasses with spectacles.

"Who is then?" said Enoch.

"There's a saying about men like him from Galicia."

"General Franco?"

The man nodded warily. "If you meet a *gallego* on the stairs, you never know if he's going up or down."

Enoch shaded his eyes to get a better view of the approaching vehicles. "In the Black Country, where I'm from in England," he told the Spaniard, "it's seven years of bad luck if you meet *anyone* on the stairs."

Fabio chuckled. "In Spain's case that would be forty years, I'm afraid."

"He'll be dead soon, right? Franco? From what I've heard..."

The man looked to the heavens and held out his arms imploringly.

"Ah! And this is the Month of the Most Precious Blood!"

Then he crossed himself.

"Am I wrong?"

"Wrong?!" He fixed his eyes on Enoch. "Sometimes we get what we pray for, don't we?"

"Do we?"

"And then we *really* see."

"Oh, ah."

"That it's something else we wanted after all."

"Oh, that's a recipe for giving up," said Enoch.

"No," replied the man, adjusting his linen shirt, "it's a recipe for going further."

Enoch couldn't disagree.

"That's what's scary," Fabio continued.

Maybe there's more to a banister-clutcher than meets the eye, thought Enoch.

As the troop vehicles paraded in front of the main terminal building, people squinted and leaned forward to see who in fact was travelling at the rear of the party.

"It wouldn't be Juan Carlos in the limo, then?" asked Enoch.

"Our terrified king? Not a chance. Generals shrink his balls too much."

"Only a chauffeur in the car!" said a smartly dressed Catalan woman to her friend.

And she was right.

The back seat was bare.

It was now plain as day, however, that the dusty combat vehicles and the regal-looking Mercedes were in fact escorting a set of Iberia boarding steps.

Just steps. And there they were in the sweltering afternoon, heading out of the airport compound, the stairs hauled by chains attached to a personnel carrier.

A staircase, thought Enoch. And he turned to look at his new travelling companion.

Fabio was smirking.

"You saw them coming all along?" said Enoch.

"Of course."

"You don't miss much."

"Very quick. A little fuzzy around the edges."

Enoch scratched his head. He wasn't accustomed to being impressed by a man over thirty-five. "There are easier ways to move airline steps," he said.

"Of course."

"So?"

"Not where Franco's concerned."

"But he's not here," said Enoch.

"Dark Ages," whispered the man, "1974 and a flight of stairs brings Spain's major airport to a standstill. Not quite Heathrow, is it?"

"Pity," said Enoch, "I wanted a peek at the famous dictator."

"You did," he replied. "Those stairs are for him. To practise walking for the cameras."

Several British were ridiculing the military display, another absurdity cutting into their Conquerors "Magic Getaway."

"Did I see him?" asked Enoch.

The man shook his head impatiently and indicated the security guards, who were saluting even the boarding steps as they sailed out of the main gates to a waiting transporter. "You did indeed. All but the flesh," said Fabio glumly, putting his spectacles away again. "Quite enough for most."

Enoch watched as the stairs were raised onto a flatbed vehicle.

"Do you have a place in Barcelona?" enquired the Spaniard.

"Naturally," said Enoch, lying.

The man's fingers twirled at his beard. "I was going to offer you a room in my house."

"Does it have stairs?"

"Hundreds," he replied.

Enoch guessed the game. "I'll take you up on it," he said.

The Spaniard frowned. "All but the flesh," he said reassuringly.

"What are steps for anyway, Fabio?"

And they waited in silence for the Iberia bus.

Been in the Storm So Long *(an excerpt)*

TERRY JORDAN

PROLOGUE

HE ROSE A FINAL TIME in the slightest shadows of the coming dawn and reached to the night table for the portrait of his wife he kept there. He held it for a moment, searching her eyes for some answer of what was to come, some strength. He had talked to her most of the night, asking for a sign, some map he might follow to the place she would be beyond this world. Then he kissed her cold mouth, as he'd done each morning for the two years past. He was still dressed from the night before. It was the only photograph in the house he had not stored away.

In the earlier darkness the metronomic chiming of the family clock had become unbearable and he had wrapped it with a blanket wishing he could forestall midnight itself and not just its bells. Come morning he would judge the hour, as always, by the angle of the sun or the quality of cloud and light in the sky.

Like other watermen before him he believed that only a chosen few were blessed with the ability to hear the clouds, the rest of the world ignorant to the boomings, the scudding immensity of their movements. Anyone could see there had to be music there; only the touched, the gifted, could enter. The odd crack and rumble of thunder was mockery, a chance door opening to sound for the deaf.

He listened. Ducks went softly muttering in the autumn dark on the river marshland below. The thin ringing of bells from the milk cows in the hills behind. All as it should be, for all that it would be. Tomorrow.

He had started to shiver. It was a chill morning but he was not deceived. He held his hands out in front of him willing them peace. When they had quieted he thought, It's not your hands that'll fail you, you sorry old fool, and he paced the four steps from his bed to the washstand across the room. He was thirty-seven years old.

He took the lamp from its tin grotto on the wall, removed the glass, and struck a match to it. The flame faltered a bit then settled on the wick, and he replaced the glass. He poured water into a basin and splashed it on his face to clear the night away.

In the warped surface of the mirror, old even to him, he seemed thinner-faced than he actually was. His eyes, too, a tiny bit pinched, the width not proportionate to the height. He had seen that false image enough times that, by now, he might have described himself that way. He mouthed his names—first John, then Powell— as though each belonged to someone else.

He looked down into the basin water, and again in the mirror. Then he surprised himself, almost wondering if he was dreaming, when he heard himself whisper, "We come from the fishes." He had always been fascinated by the natural world. "And back to them we must go," he answered.

In the kitchen he stirred the night's ashes in the stove and added new wood so his children would awake to some warmth. A boy and a girl, both now old enough to fix their own food and go off to school. He considered looking in on them again but stopped himself. He had done so, many times, in the long hours before. He did not consider eating.

Some different sound made him turn to the window. He moved the curtains aside and saw the shapes of two men dimly silhouetted in the grey morning, faintly heard their voices. It was not odd that they had failed to knock. They were early.

"They can wait for a moment," he said to himself. "I've been too long waiting myself." One of the men was much taller than the other.

Over his shirt and trousers he donned wool, then oilskin ducking clothes, the same clothes he always wore those mornings hunting. Rubber gumboots he put aside, a cap on top of them for later.

He checked his coat for the shot shells he knew were there. He had studied them the previous day, had fogged and polished their brass, wiped down the shiny wax on their hulls, discarded the few that had even the slightest bulge at their crimps. He had chosen No. 2 shot and a heavy charge. He knew from experience there were over a hundred and thirty lead pellets in each of those shells. More than enough at close range. He finished dressing, tucked his double gun under an arm, and with one look back into his house, he walked outside into the morning.

He could just make out the faces of the two men now. A ground mist obscured their boots, their breath clouded above them. The tall man nodded. Aside from his stature, the shorter man was easily recognized by the rolled-brim hat worn constantly, it seemed—day, night, and all four seasons. He realized the man did not have it on.

It almost stopped him.

"Hey, men," he said quietly, instead.

At first, the short man misunderstood. He bowed his bare head. "Amen," he answered before he thought to stop himself.

THE hills there were long and tree-covered and regular, endless and repeated in the distance like wales in corduroy. The three men walked down the slope in silence, toward the slow, wide river, a bay and the sea to the north. They had been friends most of their lives. John had been born in the house where his own children now slept; the other two had arrived from the old country as boys.

The short man's father and grandfather, and on and beyond so that only the barest story remained with a name in the parish register, had worked the hard seas and lands of Ireland's Western Isles. Had cleared the land for centuries, piled stones into a warren of fences. Had rowed their leather curraghs from the coves. Hauled countless basketloads of seaweed from the shore and left it to rot into soil on their rocky land so that their children and ancestors might someday eat vegetables with their fish and fowl. Both of the short man's brothers had stayed home and gone into the priesthood. He had not seen either of them in the decades since. He had lost his accent almost as soon as he arrived. His father had been proud of this, said he was a true man of the New World.

The tall man's father had belonged to the constabulary in Belfast until the chanting inside him for the drink became too strong and he beat a young man, almost a boy it was said, while on duty one night. Moreover, he had allowed the next morning to find him lying senseless on a busy street near the station house, his pants having been pulled down for him, revealing the ignominy of his nakedness below the waist, was how it was put. He could not find another job after that, and the shame on his street was strong and bitter and unforgiving. Within a year the family had emigrated. The drinks the tall man had taken his entire life numbered less than his age.

"Did you manage any sleep, then, John?" the tall man said finally. Silence was his answer.

This thing that needed doing had been murmured about and fought over. The need, the reason for it, and finally, its cold inevitability. There was little left to say. There was no retreat.

"Jack Wilde's missus died yesterday." The tall man seemed to speak to himself. "Hydrophobia. Bitten by her own crazed dog."

"I know." He knew because everyone already knew. He wondered why the man had chosen that cruel subject to talk about.

"I saw her on the hills I think last week."

The short man seemed ready to interrupt. Instead, he offered the others a flask to drink from.

"Not this early morning, no," John said. When the short man again pressed him to drink, he pushed it away.

The short man shrugged. "Danny?" But the tall man, too, declined.

"None of your publican ways here," the tall man said. No one laughed.

The short man drank once, and then again. "Happens fast sometimes," he said, referring to the woman's death.

John said, "With any luck." And the others looked away.

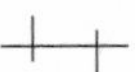

THE island was above the point in the river where, at high tide, the sea backed in and salt water met the sweet. They had hunted ducks, even as boys, and had constructed a permanent blind on the island's northeast marshy side. Until a hurricane had claimed it, there was a clubhouse, too, on the water—a shack on wood-and-barrel floats they could moor their boat under—secured with cables to thick trees on shore.

He shoved off in the punt that his father had paid a dollar and a half and a brace of ducks for. The two others followed in another.

They poled out rapidly into the dark river as they'd done thousands of times before. Three or four quick pushes and the boat would carry a lazy arc on the current to the northern tip of the island downstream, one of its oars used for a rudder.

Stowed neatly in both, in wooden racks under the seats and rails, were the decoys their fathers, and they after them, had carved and painted. Wrapped with anchor cord, dangling lead weights. Roughing out the blocks, hollowing the bodies had been a boy's job while his father fashioned heads from knot wood so they wouldn't crack, saw to it that the birds' curves and sleekness emerged, gave form and life. Painting with simple and muted colours, any detailing done with delicate brushwork, the salvaged wings of different ducks placed beside him on the table for reference.

Canvasback drakes and hens with their red, wary eyes. Blackducks dulled with charcoal and lampsoot. The demarcation of feathers like fish scales. He knew that birds had once been fishes, too. The road once taken and farther along. No turning back for ducks nor man.

He was the first to reach the shore of the island but he did not move, even after the others beached their boat. He had started to shake again.

"Has it really come to this?" he said.

The tall man nodded. He knew. The same and no different from what the other two knew.

His shotgun was wide-locked so the breech looked muscled, shaped like the head of an animal. The barrels and hammers were greyed and worn, the works of it loosened with age. Its walnut stock was dark and deep with layers of oil. He set it across his thighs.

"Could you do it for me, then?" he asked.

The tall man shook his head this time. "You know the plan, John. There's no secret to it now." He held the boat's bowline in his hand.

"Please, Dan. I thought I'd be all right," he said, part of him still not believing.

The short man moaned.

"I watched both your children grow. You'll not catch me walking that path," the tall man said. "Besides, they won't lack a thing. I'll see to it. I've said it before."

John's breathing was ragged. He wiped at his face with his coat sleeve. "I'll drift out to sea," he pleaded. "They'll never find me."

"There's two bends before the river mouth. You'll not get by them without snagging."

John began to stammer a prayer.

"Do it, man!" the tall man said loudly. "Stand up! You gave your word!"

The short man said, "Goodbye, John."

"Now!" the tall man ordered.

In the end his hands did fail him; palsied and paralyzed, he could not hope to settle his fingers on the triggers. He looked beseechingly to shore. The tall man shook his head a last time.

And then he wet himself. Strangely, that seemed to steady him. He set the hammers finally with one wrist and forced himself to stand for the second time that morning. Both hands gripped tightly high up on the barrel. He bent slightly at the waist. The tall man let the bowline go and the boat began to drift. When John banged the butt of his gunstock hard on the bottom of the boat, both barrels went off into his chest.

A raft of ducks from the marsh beside them rose thrashing from the water into the now-bright dawn. The roar echoed down the river channel, other birds rising in stages as it passed. "One. Two. Three. Four." The short man counted those startled flocks until the first bend in the river and he could see no farther. Later, he could hardly believe he had done this. But it had seemed to take minutes, so slow. He had not turned away from the killing as the tall man had, so fast. The short man would regret this the rest of his life.

After the explosion, the gun had hung for a moment by itself before it fell—barrel-first toward the shore—into the bow of the boat. The tall man had instinctively turned his body and thrown out a protective arm, then composed himself when no other shot came. The dead man had been knocked back into the stern. His body arched, his head and shoulders hanging over the transom. His cap was gone. The boat, by then, beginning to circle slowly as it rode the channel current away.

The short man was slumped over on shore, strings of saliva and whisky bile hanging from his mouth. The tall man plucking at the coat of the other, hauling him to his feet by the collar.

"Put your spine straight, lad." He passed him a handkerchief. "Clean yourself up, now."

The short man pressed the handkerchief to his forehead first and then wiped his mouth. "Please, God, have mercy on us for what we've done!" His voice was still throaty and clotted.

The tall man said, "Shut off your jabber, Matthew! It's not us that caused what happened here today. And petition God all you like, but John didn't believe in your God."

The short man pushed himself violently away from the other man. "Just once!" he said. He stood wild-eyed, glaring for such a time that the tall man looked away. "Just once I'd love to see you listen to someone besides yourself, have you notice someone else, you deaf and blind Black and Tan son of a bastard." He raised his fists. "And don't be talking about our John or our God that way or I'll ..." He closed his eyes for a second with the relief of having said it.

"God bless him," he said when he opened them. And there was only the short man's breathing in the moment that followed. "Say it, Danny."

The tall man stood silent, unmoving.

"Say it!" the short man shouted. He shouted again, "Now!"

"All right," the tall man said finally. "Yes. Fuck sake, God bless him, then." He shouldered the other aside and strode toward the punt. And both men, in nearly the same motion, looked up to gauge the growing light. As the tall man doubled back, kicking sand over the scuffle of footprints they had left on the beach, the short man caught him by the coat sleeve and shook his head as if to say it didn't matter. And after the moment the tall man took to pause, he shrugged. And then they set about quickly to make their way home.

Achill Ancestors and a Stranger

MAUREEN BRADY

FAR OUT ALONG THE HEADLANDS, Nuala picks up a stone and tries to scratch her name into the boggy ground but the mossy soil only indents for a second, then bounces back. Clouds streaming rapidly by quicken the beat of her heart and her skin tingles. A wild contentment vibrates in her, as if she's reached a destination she hadn't known she was heading for. She's on Achill Island—one of the farthest reaches of the west coast of Ireland. Soon the mist will come in to fade out the whole land. Soon, too—in one more day—she'll be on her way back home.

A dusky mauve enters the sky to turn the clouds pink. She tries to capture the wildness of the high cliffs in the distance with her camera.

Another half mile and she can see Bertie's, once the lighthouse property, now the perfect B & B, where she's staying. Whitewashed, squat and firm. Behind it there's a white picket fence, then the stone wall that takes the lick of the ocean when the tide comes in. Beyond the fence a man wearing a leather jacket now stands on the rocks, arms folded across his chest, his gaze upon the sea. She saved her last shot for Bertie's, but not sure she wants the man in her picture, she walks on a little closer.

She drove out that day from Sligo, taking several hours to achieve a hundred miles or so. Stopping often for sheep crossing the road, now and again cattle, sometimes simply a lazy dog. But she didn't mind being slowed, for at every peak she imagined she could almost see Mary McGowan and Michael McTigue—her great-grandmother and great-grandfather, whose papers are pressed flat back in Pennsylvania in her aunt's Bible. She's only recently woken up to the fact that they left here in 1846. That they were part of the potato famine. *That they left because they had to.*

Nuala's eyes are drawn once more to the drama of the cliffs and the graceful hamlet below her, silently holding the ages. The countryside is rugged, rural, fanciful. So is she. She has the seaworthy carriage of her father, who, indeed, went to sea, became a wanderer but not a searcher, didn't know what to look for.

She gazes down. The man's still there. He's become so much a part of the landscape that when he moves, it jars Nuala. Especially when he turns and looks up at her. She's not sure she wants to be seen while she has that fluttery stir in her chest. Not only that, he no longer has the peace she assigned him when he seemed so at one with the sea. Now that she's closer, she sees the ocean has swelled something up in him—a longing in his body that speaks of need. She's dead sure of it, even though she tells herself that she couldn't possibly know this about some total stranger.

As she approaches him, a broad "Hello" comes out of her, not the tentative greeting she might have uttered even the day before, when she'd been standing more aloof from the land of her ancestors.

He nods and greets her back. He has a German accent.

"A grand site, isn't it?" she states the obvious, gesturing to the ocean.

"Yes, yes," he agrees. "The wind blows everything out of your head."

"You stay here?" Her English becomes broken though his is not.

"Bertie's? Yes, yes." After a pause, he asks, "You too?"

"Yes."

"On holiday?"

"A short rest before I return home."

"You have been travelling a long time?"

"No, no," she tells him. "Working hard to finish a novel at an artist's colony over on the other side of the country."

"Ah, a writer," he says. "Successful."

She doesn't deny it, having achieved at least the momentary pleasure of coming to an ending and putting her book down to rest.

"And you?" she asks.

"I am a writer, too, only, a failed one."

His statement is blunt, hurtful to him and perhaps even to her by identification, for she had suffered so many years of bewilderment before this book came true for her, yet always stepped around a word like "failure." She wants to say, Surely you know a writer is just a writer no matter what happens to the work, but he seemed so firm about calling himself the failed one, she suspects this would deny him. So she falters, leaving a hole in the conversation.

He looks out at the sea again, then returns his gaze to her. "I'll soon be going to the restaurant up the road. There . . ." He gestures in the direction she just walked from.

"Is it a good one?"

"The only one."

"Oh."

"So I assume you may go there, too."

"Yes," she answers. She may be blushing. It's been years since a man asked her to join him.

"If you'd care to come along with me . . ."

"I need to go back to my room first."

"Very well." He stiffens a bit at her hesitation. "I'll be up there if you like . . ." He formally extends his hand, speaking his name, "Dieter."

"Nuala," she answers, offering him a firm handshake before turning up the footpath that leads to Bertie's.

In the interlude between his invitation and when she goes to meet him, a lusty desire, which has grown from mute to a nearly palpable buzz in her, raises the notion that she may conceivably sleep with him. Despite the fact that she doesn't sleep with men. Hasn't since she came out in her late twenties. *Now why is that?* she wonders as she stands perched on the same rock Dieter claimed for so long, casting to the sea for an answer.

She likes to believe her ideas are freely hers—not bound by the urgings of any collective voice—but now, as she rankles at her leaning toward Dieter, she wonders if she is, in fact, under the influence of the lesbian police. Because surely, if she wants to, she can sleep with a man, not as a serious straight thing but as part of her posture as outlaw. What could be more deviant?

The wind whips wildly about her head and the sea crashes in at her feet, leaving foam at the bottom of the rock. "Why not?" she calls out to no one. The moon is full. The clouds conceal it, then waft by, trailing it behind them. She doesn't think clouds move like this in America, or at least she never noticed them. Irish clouds make a wildness in the sky to match the landscape. She imagines the Celts worshipping the moon in those stone circles she saw just the day before on the great plateau of Carrowmore. She has been told all redheads are witches, which makes her wonder at her powers. Does that apply to women only? For Dieter is red-headed also and has a red moustache.

She spots him as soon as she walks in, his eyes cast down on his half-eaten dinner. When the maître d' approaches her with a menu, her feet don't know which way to go. Why does he not look up and help her out by beckoning? Perhaps she is too late to join him. But when the maître d' indicates a table on the other side of the room, Nuala points as if she's in a foreign country where she can't speak the language and guides him to Dieter's table. "Would you still like company?" she asks when she's beside him.

He half stands, bows. "Yes, yes, please. I'd be delighted."

His face brightens as she strips off her two jackets and unwinds the scarf from her neck and the sea air wafts off of her. Dieter seems washed by it.

She studies the menu; he studies her. She tells him to go ahead with his dinner, orders hers quickly. They talk of their homes: Berlin, Manhattan. He says Germany is not so good now. Difficult to get published unless you are very conventional. She wonders if he's unconventional. One couldn't tell by his looks, his slate grey wool sweater, corduroy trousers. "What do you write about?" she asks him.

"A man who goes on holiday and is waiting for something to happen to him."

His statement makes her tingle, as if she is standing back at the cliff's edge. She wonders if it's a proposition. It's been so long, she can't remember what men say if they want a woman to sleep with them.

Still, they talk easily together, despite or perhaps because of the excitement of having found a way to join each other. They avoid the sort of personal questions that would reveal a spouse or lover back home. Dieter announces he's celebrating his forty-fifth birthday with his holiday on Achill Island, and Nuala reveals they're the same age. Of course he tells her she doesn't look it, her Irish complexion may hold her youth forever. He wants to know if she's famous in America. Would he have read her books if he lived there? Not very likely, she tells him.

"Have they been translated into German?"

"Only one piece, in an anthology." She doesn't tell him it's a collection of stories by lesbians.

He sits forward. His face is lean and shapely. His hands are delicate. Thick brows frame his intelligent eyes with an arc of slight puzzlement, which attracts her. He's a university professor, teaches German literature. At the moment he's on sabbatical. Meant to write his own book this year but has no reason to believe he'll accomplish this, since for years he's been saying he'll do it but has not. But when she asks him why he can't do it now that he has the time, he grows foxy, and his eyes appear too wideset. Perhaps one is a wandering eye. He acts as if he can't talk about it—claims problems with his English, which is really quite adequate.

"Is this why you call yourself a failed writer?" she asks to draw him out.

He moves about uncomfortably in his seat, which makes her sorry she asked, afraid she's moved herself into a maternal role with him. Maybe she did that to blunt the question that makes her keep feeling like a bad girl: *Is she going to sleep with him?*

"I don't have enough to say," he says about the writing.

"Oh," she says and leaves it at that. Not *Of course you do, it's a question of daring to reveal it,* which may only reinforce the maternal.

Suddenly superimposed upon his man's face is his boy's face, full of yearning but also an almost flinching fear. It is this fear that draws her and makes him seem safe to go home with. But what does she really want from him? Does she think she's going to punish Anya, who turned into a tiresome baby as soon as she moved in with her? Or her lover before that, who whirled her high, then dropped her with a smashing blow by going back to her heavy-handed husband? Or will she sleep with him over nothing—no one, no reason?

But as soon as they come into the crispness of the open air, she remembers once again that it is not nothing propelling her, but Ireland, Achill Island, the full moon, her ancestors, her novel. It is finding home so far from home, sheep in her path, sea spray in her nostrils. And it is him too, with his wistfulness that stops short of a cry just at this moment when hers may be sated.

THEY are in Dieter's room because he had the presence of mind to invite her in for tea. He puts on the kettle while she's in the bathroom. There are no chairs—only single beds divided by a nightstand. "Please," he indicates stiffly, when she comes out. She takes the bed closest to the sea, which they can hear pounding Bertie's shore. She leans back awkwardly on her elbows. The overhead light is too bright, lighting up her consciousness of how very little she knows him.

Her voice comes out raspy with nerves, "Do you mind if I turn off the big light?"

"As you like," he says, so she turns on the small light and shuts off the overhead.

He brings the tea on a tray and sets it beside her, kicks off his shoes so they land, clunk, and rests back parallel to her. Asks if she knows Günter Grass, a writer who has influenced him.

"Yes," she replies, "*The Tin Drum* mesmerized me. I was a drummer as a child." The other girl drummer in her high school band pops into her mind—the one who slicked her hair back in a greasy DA. To keep from being associated with her, Nuala always stood at the opposite end from her, keeping the boys between them, but she secretly noted the girl's agile hands, which beat out such crisp drum rolls.

When the tea is steeped, she pours it the Irish way, which makes it more of a comfort drink. Milk first coating the bottom of the cup, then the tea, then the sugar. She holds the teacup daintily because it's the sort of fine china that commands gesture. Funny that she's been waiting for an Irish woman to invite her to her room for tea because she read in the lesbian and gay guidebook that this is code for "Will you come to my room and sleep with me?" Maybe it's the same for heterosexuals and Dieter knows that. Maybe once in the room, one is supposed to skip the tea. For certainly the tea service is now in the way and conversation is exhausted.

Finally Dieter relieves her of the cup and saucer, moves the service to the other bed, and returns to take her hands, study them, squeeze them. She squeezes back a little, realizing she is passing up the last possible moment to excuse herself and return to her silent communion with the sea as her solo lover.

She inclines slightly toward Dieter instead and he leans across to kiss her. Gently at first, quietly—almost as she remembers her first cousin kissing her once when they were children playing spin the bottle—his soft lips pressing hers, his tongue restrained but creating heat behind them. It's a tentative exploration, so unobtrusive Nuala relaxes and begins to encourage it to open out into desire. Unlike with her cousin, when her mind kept repeating to her, *Oh my God, you shouldn't.*

She lies back and Dieter comes up to hold the full length of her against him. He is warm and gentle. Still, she wishes he were a woman, for she wants to rub her cheek against another soft as hers. Her first time making love with a woman, this meant the most to her, this softness that told her to claim her vulnerability. Dieter rubs his clean-shaven face against hers. There's a prickle and his moustache tickles, but as he kisses her neck and her body begins to yield to him, she knows a vulnerability more profound than she has known in a while. Yet, when he crosses her breast, she catches his hand and keeps it pressed into her, and lets herself grow hungry.

He opens his eyes and rolls them in a signal of delirium.

When he lifts up, she strips off her shirt and her V-neck sweater in one stroke, overriding her shyness with a boldness she barely recognizes. She's never done this with a man. Always waited to be undressed, as if she were still a teenager and each item could be the last one permissible, the one that would raise objection.

She's braless and Dieter is apparently a bit shocked.

"You write about a man who goes on a holiday and is waiting for something to happen to him. What happens when something happens?" she teases him.

He smiles, licks his lips, narrows his wide-apart eyes, drops his own clothes beside the bed in a flash, and comes up to lie on top of her.

When he is in her and it feels good, she wonders why she has not thought to do this before. Her low belly draws toward a heavenly fullness, her chest tingles, and the sound of ocean pounding shore grows louder in the silence. They are two alone souls on a faraway night, why should they not come together?

She rides Dieter. She sees horses. She sees a great green valley like so many she saw as she drove westward. She is travelling along with Dieter, then suddenly she discovers that she has gone very far away from him, as if they veered off on different paths at a fork that divided.

She sees a small red-headed girl, her arms stretched wide to embrace a green field as if it can fill her up. But it cannot, for she is starving. The girl is Mary McGowan, her great-grandmother. She's ten years old. Others come in a blur before her eyes. Distended bellies, bumpy bones, hollows that haunt the bewilderment in their eyes. Her forebears? Some must have withered and died, just as the potatoes hollowed out beneath their skins.

She sees the fog that comes in so strong it leaves treetops standing ghost-like without the appearance of earthly communion. Faces form in the fog. Faces like hers. They flicker, then disappear, like the faces of the dead do.

These pictures arrive without invitation while Nuala is still in the middle of her business with Dieter, changing her valence so utterly that what is wet turns cold—the sweat on her belly, the glistening lube between her legs.

Dieter rises up on his arms, heat in his eyes, his mouth soft from kissing, and sees her eyes darting about. "What is it?" he asks, softening and shrinking a little inside her.

She catches a glimpse of his taut, red hair. There is a frizz to it that makes it clearly not Irish hair, and she is reassured by this distinction between them. "Distraction of the mind," she says. "I'm sorry."

He closes his eyes, opens them again, hesitates, like a man deciding what to write next. He starts to move in her again, but every little collision is felt like a ferry that comes bumping and bouncing into a dock. They are two, not one, their parts distinct and separate. She does not have to tell him to stop. He comes out of her and rolls onto his side, letting out a deep sigh.

"What is your real story?" he asks after a moment, his eyes narrowing as if to peg her.

"I'm a better lover to women," she says.

"Ah," he says. "Bisexual."

"No," she replies. "Lesbian."

He makes a face and curls into his midsection as if the word is a blunt axe that has struck him. She thinks of those labryses they sell in women's bookstores—harmless, miniature axes on silver chains. Can the word really be this lethal?

"Do you do this often?"

"Never."

"Why with me then?"

She shrugs. "I guess I was a woman on holiday waiting for something to happen. And besides that, I like you."

"What do you like about me?"

"That sadness you try so hard to hide."

"Oh," he says, keeping his face behind his arms.

"Come on," she says, touching the short, springy hair on the top of his head. "My being a lesbian is a choice or, even if I was born with it, we've already established I don't have eye teeth in my vagina or anything of that sort."

In the silence that follows, the air in the room takes on a greater charge than ever it held during their lovemaking.

"It's not you," he says, slowly unfolding from his fetal position. "It's Marlene."

"Who's Marlene?"

"She was my woman for the past twelve years. She went off with another woman three months ago."

Nuala sees the hurt come clean, Dieter's eyes no longer trying to look both ways at once. She tells him she's sorry, keeping hidden the little note of triumph she can't deny feeling for Marlene. It's nothing against Dieter, only an allegiance to her kind.

"Were you married?"

"No. She had one bad marriage and swore she'd never get married again. I would have married her. Now I think maybe it was partly because she knew she might fall in love with a woman."

"Um," Nuala agrees, lifting the blanket to cover them.

He looks squarely into her eyes. "And you," he says. "Do you have a broken heart, too?"

Does she? Now that he's put it this way, she feels her losses echo but not from up close, from far away. Her trials of the last decade often turning her inside out, nurturance more of an enticement than an actual experience.

Dieter is on his elbow awaiting her answer. The old way she's told her story suddenly no longer seems true. She can tell him anything; he is a stranger. But why should she hide from him or anyone?

Her eyes cast to the ceiling. "I had a major love," she tells him. "I left her a long time ago and have had some other lovers but never let myself all the way in since the first one."

"Why did you leave the first one?"

Her heart begins to pound again, as it did out there on the headlands. She's always told it the most obvious way: how her lover cheated on her, and, when she discovered the betrayal, couldn't bear it. But in this land of many angles of light, she sees an entirely different sight.

"I was always filled with longing," she says. "We kept each other busy, which held that feeling at bay, but whenever we would stop, I would find myself yearning with a hunger deep in my gut that made me want to blame her for anything she couldn't provide me. But then if she'd come at me, as if she could fill it up with her, I'd only want to step aside. I stepped aside enough that eventually she snuck off and had an affair with another woman, which blew us up."

"Was that your distraction?" Dieter asks, reminding Nuala of the moment she left him to ride off in a different direction.

She hears the waves crashing in, the undertow sucking the sand out. The sea's constancy steadies her. "No," she answers. "It was not. I was remembering my ancestors. Feeling their hunger and how it must have passed on to me." She closes her eyes, tries to tap the old yearning she knows so well, but it's not there. Dieter is. She looks past him, toward the sea. "Maybe *that hunger* gave me the longing. Because now that I'm here on their island, it's gone."

He nods his understanding, his now-calm eyes on hers. "Something is settled for you, no?" He cradles her face with the length of his hand. The gesture is not sexual.

"Yes."

"Now you are ready to go on."

She chuckles. "And you? Will you be able to finish your story?"

"Now we'll see if I have one." He says this lightly, then he adds, "Do you think I'm a man with a special attraction for lesbians?"

"Ah, yes, it would seem that you are. Perhaps you were a lesbian in an earlier life."

"Perhaps on Achill Island," he embellishes the fantasy. "My people are not here but I come here again and again because it's a place where I can hear myself. And when unusual things happen on Achill Island, I do not consider them so unusual."

Hosea's Children

GLORIA SAWAI

WHEN HOSEA DROVE UP FROM Medicine Hat to look for Gordon in Edmonton, she brought her two youngest children to her sister in Rocky Mountain House. The girl, Doloros, was seven and Bittern, her son, was ten. Her oldest child had already left home, and the last Hosea heard was living somewhere in British Columbia. She moved from place to place and didn't keep in touch with her mother. She'd left the Hat with a man named Joe, who worked the rigs, and had changed her name to Ann.

Hosea had thought about Edmonton on and off all spring. She still knew a couple of people in the city from the time she and Gordon lived there—she could stay with them for a while. She also thought that besides locating her husband, she might find work and move to the city permanently. So on April 11 she packed the children and an old suitcase of clothes and a few toys into her green Chev and headed north. It was the day the story came out about a seven-year-old girl, with her father and flight instructor, dying in an airplane crash in the United States. The girl had wanted to be the youngest pilot ever to fly across the country, but the plane, which had taken off in California, crashed somewhere in Wyoming.

Hosea listened to all this on the car radio as she drove north on Highway 2, then west on Number 11 into Rocky Mountain House. The girl, the *pilot,* was the same age as Doloros.

On the drive west, a snowy drizzle came down, wet and slushy against the windshield, and she had to lean close to the steering wheel and peer out past the clicking wipers in order to see the road ahead. She told Doloros, sitting beside her, to please be still, and Bittern, in the back seat, to stop asking questions. But the boy did not quit talking about the plane crash.

"Would you let Doloros drive an airplane in a snowstorm?" he asked. "If she wanted to?"

"Think, Bittern," Hosea said. "Just be quiet and think about it." She clutched more tightly at the steering wheel.

"I am thinking," Bittern said. "I'm thinking what if she wanted to do that."

"I do want to," Doloros said, snuggling into her small frayed blanket. "I want to drive an airplane in a snowstorm."

Right, Hosea thought. As if you won't have danger and treachery enough on the small path you'll walk here on Earth. Hosea could not understand people who seemed to find life easy, to feel comfortable with themselves and their situation, people who travelled light, her sister Judith, for instance.

Before they reached Rocky Mountain House, the snow stopped, and when they drove into town the sun was out and the western sky was a deep purplish blue. The mountain range on the far horizon shone silver.

Judith was waiting for them on her porch. She was sitting on a white plastic chair in a patch of sunlight, wearing her husband's curling sweater and drinking coffee from a yellow mug. The children saw her even before the car slowed down, and they waved and pounded the windows, and shouted, "Judith! Judith! There she is. Judith!"

When the car stopped at the curb, they scrambled out and ran into the yard and up the porch steps to their aunt. They threw themselves at her, the three of them a tangled bundle in the sunlight.

"Well, you," Judith said. "If it isn't you and you. Right here on my porch. Isn't that something. Isn't that just lovely."

"Me and her and you," Bittern said.

Hosea climbed the stairs, suitcase in hand. "Me too." And Judith reached out her arms to her sister.

"Do you know what Mom is going to let Doloros do?" Bittern asked. "Drive an airplane in a snowstorm. Even in a raging blizzard."

"So you heard about that."

"I'm a very good reader," said Doloros.

Bittern jumped down the steps. "I'm checking out the rabbits." He ran around the house to the backyard, his sister following.

Judith went into the house and returned with a fresh cup of coffee for Hosea and a refill for herself. The women sat down in the white chairs—Judith, her body softly round, brown hair curling about her face, Hosea, thin, almost gaunt, sandy hair tied at the back of her neck in a tight ponytail.

Judith had been thinking about Hosea and her children all morning. Particularly about Ann. She wondered if she should tell her sister what she knew, but Ann had asked that her mother not find out yet. So as Judith was making up the cot for Doloros in her daughter Carly's room and the sofa bed for Bittern in the small study across from it, she decided that today she would try to just listen to Hosea without offering opinions or advice. She'd *try*.

The last time the two sisters were together, Hosea had again lamented the disappearance of Gordon. And Judith's reply again was, "But he always leaves. You know that. He's a jerk. He thinks if you're a big-shot writer, which he isn't—how many books has he actually finished and published? *Zero*—but he thinks he is and therefore he's not required like ordinary human beings to be responsible. He can do anything he pleases. He can leave his own children . . ."

"Stop it, Judith, you don't know the whole story, so just stop talking." And she told Judith (again) in her strained voice that Gordon had signed a certificate with a gold seal on it, on July 8, 1980, in a church lit with white candles and decorated with pink carnations, and that he'd pledged his vows before God and Reverend Hunter ("You remember Norman") and before Thelma their mother, who died six months later, and all the other relatives and Gordon's folks as well. And she just wanted to remind Gordon of these facts.

The two women sat quiet in the sunlight, sipping their coffee.

"You've heard from Anxiety, haven't you," Hosea said finally.

Judith looked startled. She held her cup with both hands and waited a moment to answer. "Why do you keep calling her that?"

"It's her name," Hosea said.

"She wants to be called Ann. You of all people should know that. *Hosea.* Some old guy married to a *hooker.*"

"You've heard from her, haven't you."

Judith sighed. "She wrote to Carly, not me." Carly was the same age as Anxiety.

"It's funny," Hosea said. "It's her dad who left her, but it's me she can't stand. She has no respect for me."

"She's doing all right," Judith said. "Joe seems like a good person."

"Running off with a fifteen-year-old?"

"Sixteen now," Judith said. "You were only seventeen the first time you took up with Gordon. Remember?"

"Are they in B.C.?" Hosea asked.

"Revelstoke, but they're moving; she didn't say where." She stood up. "I've made sandwiches," she said. "Let's call the children."

Hosea drove out of town under a dark sky. On the road east it began to snow again, and when she turned north toward Edmonton the flakes were thick.

Leaving Rocky Mountain House, she had felt warm and safe. The children were with Judith, who enfolded them in her arms and cared for them with an easy confidence. But now the peace she'd felt began to unravel. Why was she doing this? Every book she'd read on the subject told her the same thing: drop him, he's a loser.

And then there was Anxiety. Where was the balm to heal the wound of a child gone?

Wet flakes splashed against the glass. Icy slush moved back and forth in small chunks on the windshield. She stared past them at the narrow road ahead.

Not that life with her daughter still at home had been happy or peaceful. Far from it. The girl was too angry for that, and closed.

Their last night together, Hosea had gotten up and gone into the kitchen for a glass of milk. She'd paced the living room, turned on the TV, watched the late-night ads. She'd checked Doloros and Bittern, safe and sleeping in their beds, and then gone back into her own bed and stared up at the darkness.

At 3 A.M. she heard the door opening and closing and footsteps creaking on the hall floor. What relief. Everyone was in and safe; she could go back to sleep. But instead she got out of bed and met her daughter in the hallway.

"Where were you?" she said and heard her voice, hard, accusing.

"Who needs to know?" Anxiety muttered.

"Don't talk to me like that."

"Like what?" Her voice was slurred.

"You've been drinking again."

Anxiety walked, straight and deliberate, past her mother toward her own room.

Hosea yelled, "Why are you so hateful?"

Anxiety swayed against the wall.

"Why not, Mama?"

Anxiety was thirteen.

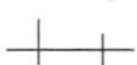

AT the Lacombe turnoff Hosea started to cry. Tears ran down her face and dripped off her chin onto her lap. Visibility was bad enough as it was, but she couldn't stop. She took her right hand off the steering wheel and wiped her eyes. She turned on the car radio. Heard only static.

The snow stopped before she reached the Leduc airport, and when she arrived at the southern outskirts of Edmonton a dry wind was blowing. She drove into a Husky station to use the washroom and make a phone call.

In the ladies room, a large woman with pale white skin and a black patch over one eye was trying to get her little girl to reach up to the sink to wash. Her small fingers could barely touch the stream of water pouring from the tap. The mother rubbed soap on the child's hands, lathering her palms, her wrists, and between each finger. Then she lifted her up closer to the tap so she could rinse.

"You never know, do you," the woman said to Hosea. "You just never know." Water splashed over the girl's skin and into the porcelain bowl. Hosea didn't answer. She examined her own splotchy face in the mirror above the sink.

"There's so much stuff out there," the woman continued. "It's all over ... you can't get away from it ... it gets on your skin and sticks there ... then your pores soak it up ... all that crud ... and what happens next? ... gets into the internal organs ... and then ... the blood ... have you ever thought about that?"

She turned to the girl, pretty, curly haired, her blue eyes bright and curious. "Are you finished, Junie? Are you nice and clean? Let's dry your hands now." She rubbed the girl's hands with a paper towel, threw the towel into the wastebasket, and headed for the exit. She bent forward, pushed the door open with her forehead, and the two disappeared.

Hosea stared after them. What is going on? Are mothers simply cracking up? She soaked a paper towel in cold water, washed her face, and decided that before she did anything else she needed a cup of coffee.

In the Husky café she chose a booth next to a window. She liked the sense of privacy a booth gave her, a pleasant sensation of being in her own yard but surrounded by neighbours who went about their business in a quiet yet friendly way. She looked out at the grey coldness. Melting snow and slushy mud had made ragged ditches in the parking lot, and the dry wind had hardened the edges into ridges of stiff dirt. She ordered coffee and a glazed doughnut, then unfolded a paper napkin. She dug in her purse for her ballpoint pen. "Things to Do," she printed at the top of the napkin. "Call the Letts, call Alfreda." Often she filled a whole page with her scribbling; today this was all she had to say.

A man with thick grey hair and wearing a yellow jacket got up as she was leaving. They bumped arms at the cash register.

"You're some looker, do you know that?" He was staring into her face. "Not a spring chicken, about forty I'd say, maybe forty-one on a bad day." She stepped aside and dug in her purse for money.

"Hey. No hard feelings."

"Back off, okay?" She laid the money on the counter and made her way to the phone booth.

"Well, a nice day to you, too," the man called after her.

First she dialed the Letts—they'd want her to stay with them a night or two—but she got their answering machine. Then she called Alfreda, who told her that her mother might be coming to town this week and her cat was shedding besides. Hosea hung up the receiver and slouched against the wall. Of course, she should have called them before she left. She realized that now. Sometimes her brain didn't click into the specifics of life. "You're *deep,*" Judith used to say, teasing. "You're a very *deep* person." She flipped through the Yellow Pages. There must be cheap lodging somewhere.

The YWCA was situated on the corner of 100th Avenue and 103rd Street. Across the street to the north was the Foster & McGarvey Funeral Chapel, and to the east, the Alano Club, a private club for ex-drunks, the Y receptionist told Hosea when she registered for the night, and a cheap place to eat when the Y dining room was closed, "which is right now," she added.

So it was at the Alano Club that Hosea found herself sitting alone at a Formica-covered table, eating a cheeseburger, drinking cold milk, and thinking of Gordon. She looked around, half expecting he would show up. You never knew. He could have decided he'd had enough and become an ex-drunk instead of a practising one. She decided years ago that if you came from Montana and called yourself a writer you were probably a drunk. Not that Gordon was *from* Montana. He'd only lived there a year. He was from Alberta actually. Cardston. Mormon country. But he wasn't a Mormon either. He was simply a drunk who thought he was a writer.

And where are you now? Gordon with the red beard, wide neck, broad back? Gordon with the smooth skin, the sweet words, the touch? You thought I was pretty and my hair was fine and soft, precious you said, and held the ends of it in your hand and breathed on it, and on my chin. Such a smooth little chip of a thing, you said, and my neck curved under your palm and my face was easy on your chest. You funny, funny bird, you said.

"Would you like company?" The woman standing in front of her was holding a coffee cup in one hand, a red purse in the other. "Or not?" she added. "It's up to you. I sometimes like to eat alone, but then again I get really starved for conversation."

"Please, sit down," Hosea said.

"Thirty days," the woman said. "Never thought I'd make it this far. But one day comes and then another, and before you know it you've got thirty days of sobriety. Unbelievable, isn't it?"

She set the red purse on the floor under the chair, her cup on the table, and sat across from Hosea. She was a thin woman with pale skin. The heavy makeup she wore did not conceal the tiny bumps covering her face. Even her eyelids bubbled. But her bright red lips were smooth and her black hair shiny.

"And totally unbelievable that I'm sitting here, with you," she continued. "I mean, two weeks ago I'd've been off by myself in some corner, hiding behind a newspaper, scared to death someone might talk to me and mad as hell if they didn't. Crazy, huh?"

"Do you come here often?" Hosea asked.

"Pretty well all the time, not having a job right now, which is a bummer. My name's Lily, by the way. And you are?"

"Hosea."

"Say that again?"

"Hosea."

"Some handle, eh? Whose idea was it?"

And Hosea told her the story of how her mother, when she was pregnant, was working in a hotel, cleaning rooms, and how one day she opened up a Gideon Bible to whatever page it opened to and there she saw it. Hosea. She never read far enough to know it was a man's name.

"So where are you from?" Hosea asked.

"Nowhere really. I wander around mostly. Here and there. Used to live in Ryley when I was young. Not far from here."

"Have a family?"

"Two kids. Social Services took them. That's why I'm here. I want them back. God, I do. But if I don't sober up . . ." She folded her hands and let out a long sigh. "How about you? Any kids?"

"Three. They're with my sister. Well, two of them are. One's off somewhere. She doesn't keep in touch."

"Sounds like me." She looked at the clock on the far wall. "Well, I have to go now or I won't make my meeting. Thirty days. They give you a red chip when you make thirty."

She leaned over and picked up her purse from under the chair. "So. Maybe I'll see you around."

"Sure," Hosea said. "Maybe."

The woman rose and walked away.

THEY'D had a pleasant supper together, the four of them sitting around the kitchen table eating spaghetti and soft Italian bread. It was summer, and the early evening was warm and rosy. Then purple-blue clouds piled up on the western horizon and the rain began. Silver-beaded chains slanted down from the sky, gentle at first, then harsher, until the kitchen window was streaming with water, and the yard outside—lilacs, fence, even the small garage—was hidden in the dark rain. But inside it was warm, the light glowed amber from the bamboo-shaded fixture above the table, and there was a softness about the family, a quiet gentleness.

"So what are we all doing tonight?" Hosea asked.

"Me? Nothing," Bittern said.

"Let's make popcorn and watch television and pretend it's Christmas," Doloros said.

Anxiety was quiet.

"And you?" Hosea asked.

"I don't know. I guess I'll do some laundry. I'm way behind."

"It looks like a good night to curl up with a mystery," Hosea said.

Bittern and Doloros made popcorn and snuggled in blankets in front of the TV. Hosea, in the big chair by the living room window, sipped hot tea and looked through magazines, and Anxiety did her wash. Hosea could hear the dryer thumping in the little laundry room at the end of the hall. When the wash was done, Anxiety joined her brother and sister on the floor. She watched television, drank cocoa, joked with Bittern, tousled Doloros's hair.

And the next morning she was gone. The clean laundry she'd piled at the foot of her bed was gone. Shoes from her closet, new jeans, diary, makeup, the pink-and-silver comb and mirror she'd gotten from Joe—all were gone. And Anxiety was gone.

HOSEA stood up and tugged at her coat, twisting her arms into the sleeves. On the television screen above the grill, a small crowd was gathered around the airplane that had crashed in Wyoming. The plane had landed in someone's front yard, on their driveway. Landed nose down and gouged out chunks of concrete. Hosea looked up at the screen and stood frozen for a moment, gazing at the image.

HER room at the Y was on the sixth floor. In it were four narrow beds, each with a thin metal rod as headboard, flush against the wall. The beds were five or six feet apart. At the foot of each was a small metal closet. The bathroom was down the hall.

When Hosea had registered, she'd paid the $6 fee for the dormitory room and chosen the bed farthest from the door. She'd shoved her case into the closet and laid a towel over the metal rod to reserve her space. She'd found the room empty and thought herself lucky to have the space to herself.

But now, returning from the Alano Club, she saw that the bed nearest the door had also been claimed. A canvas backpack was lying on the green blanket, and a pair of white panties hung over the metal rod. But her roommate was nowhere to be seen.

On the way to the bathroom, she passed the lounge. She saw in a glance the large television screen, the worn sofa, the small table strewn with pop cans and magazines, and three girls slouched in overstuffed chairs, watching TV. Only the television made any noise. She noticed that the girls were young and they all looked gloomy. One of the three was probably her roommate.

Back in her own room, the bed felt good. The mattress was thin but firm, the sheets clean, the blanket warm. She'd raised the shade on the small window between her bed and the one next to it, and a pale glow from a streetlight entered the room in a shaft of light that was comforting to her. Then she remembered. She hadn't called the children; she'd forgotten to call.

She saw them sitting together at the kitchen table in Rocky Mountain House—Bittern and Doloros side by side, Carly opposite them, Judith and Ralph each at an end. Ralph with his shaggy hair and thin lips, his funny nose and sharp chin, making comic faces and strange animal sounds. Bittern whooping with laughter, Doloros smiling, Carly feigning dismay.

She saw the woman with the bumpy skin sitting at the table in the Alano Club. Lily. *I want them back,* she'd said. *God, I do.* Where were these children now? Hosea wondered. And where was their father?

She saw the seven-year-old girl in California tugging at her mother's arm. "Please, Mama, please? I want to fly. Get me an airplane and let me fly." And her mother says, "How exciting. Yes, yes. We'll call your father." And the father says, "If that's what you want, why not? We'll set a world record." And Hosea saw them—the father, the flying instructor, the girl—in the snowy sky above Wyoming, excited and proud, speeding through morning. But suddenly the girl is shouting, "It's wrong, something's wrong!" And the instructor is pushing her out of the way, grabbing the controls. Only it's too late. The nose of the plane jerks downward. Down down through whirling snow. Mama Mama Mama ... oh please, Mama. And the father, what was he doing? Did he suddenly repent up there in the swirling madness? My God, save her ... I was wrong ... have mercy ... God ... And right then did the plane's nose smash into the concrete, hurling chunks of cement, bits of gravel, sharp flints of stone into the snowy air?

Hosea turned onto her side. She should try to get some sleep. In the morning she would start looking for Gordon.

A key turned in the lock, and the door opened and quietly closed. She heard light footsteps on the linoleum floor. She lay still, listened in silence to the movements. The tearing of the Velcro fastening on the backpack, crumpling plastic, the tugging and rustling of undressing and dressing. Then a deep sigh. And it was quiet.

Hosea waited several seconds before she opened her eyes. When she did she saw in the dim light a girl's form crouched on the floor beside the bed, her back to Hosea, her arms splayed out on the blanket. She was sighing, whispering very softly. Hosea strained to hear her. "Heavenly Father, Holy God, Almighty Lord." Her head was moving in small semicircles from side to side. She was *praying.* Kneeling by the bed and praying. Right there below the white panties hanging on the rod. Hosea closed her eyes. She was ashamed to be watching. But then she opened them again. And she saw the girl get up from the floor, saw her silhouette in the dim light, her thin body bending over the bed, then disappearing under the covers. She was slender, like Anxiety, but taller.

THE first time Gordon left was right after Anxiety was born. Hosea had just come home from the hospital with the new baby, her first. She was scared. The baby cried almost constantly. Hosea had tried to enjoy the infant, to sit on the sunny porch beside the morning glories and nurse her, to sing to her, to go for walks in the park pushing the baby in her small carriage. But she did these things without confidence, without energy. Her actions were awkward and rigid. The baby seemed to sense her mother's fear and became increasingly nervous and discontent, vomiting, bawling, her small face turning dark red from some deep and hopeless effort she was making right there in her mother's arms. Then Gordon left. When he returned two weeks later, he explained that he wasn't able to handle the confusion: meals disrupted, sleep disturbed, wife flustered, impatient, depressed.

One day while he was still gone, Hosea, with the baby in her arms, took the city bus downtown to the office of Vital Statistics. She stood in front of the clerk, a man with thick dark-rimmed glasses and bulbous eyes that peered out through the glass, who was in a hurry that day and did not want any arguments or fuss, and she announced without hesitation, loudly, with a confidence she had hitherto not experienced, "Her name is Anxiety."

SHE heard soft snoring from the other bed and pulled the blanket partway over her head. When she finally went to sleep, she dreamt of her father.

Beery they called him, although his name was Ben, actually Benjamin. "Hey, Beer, over here," they'd say. Hosea didn't think about him much. He was killed in a mining accident when she was ten. But tonight he was in her dream. She was swimming in the Atlantic Ocean, halfway between Europe and North America. It was dark, the water icy cold, and she was alone. She radioed to New York to tell someone that she couldn't make it; it was too far and she was tired. If she didn't get help soon she was going to sink. And her father came to her, red-faced and laughing. He grabbed her with his strong dusty arms and lifted her out of the murky water and carried her safely to shore.

When Hosea awoke, the girl was sitting cross-legged on her bed, digging into her backpack. Hosea could not see her face, but she saw the long straight hair, thin arms, grey-white T-shirt, loose on her skinny body. The white panties were gone from the rod. The girl must have sensed Hosea's awakening. She raised her head and looked at her, a sly look, Hosea thought, a bit of a sneaky look, the look of someone who had just played a trick on you or was about to. She was not as pretty as Anxiety.

"Well, good morning, sleepyhead!" the girl said in a voice loud and enthusiastic. "I'm just getting breakfast and you're welcome to have some." From her pack she lifted out a loaf of McGavin's bread, a jar of jam, and a sausage ring. She laughed. "I'm travelling third-class economy as you can see." She laughed again, louder. "Actually, I've been saving for a while for the Rose Benson weekend at the Westin Hotel. You've heard of Rose. She's a preacher on TV. From Texas. Everybody calls her the Yellow Rose of Texas. And she's *wonderful.* I myself came on the Greyhound. From Bawlf, ha ha."

Hosea stood. She took her towel from the iron rod, and picked up her bath kit.

"Would you care to join me?" the girl said. "Ten dollars a session, or twenty-five for three. You won't be sorry."

"Oh, no. I have business to look after. I'm kind of in a hurry. But thanks."

"No problem."

When Hosea returned from the shower, the girl was gone. But she'd left a note on Hosea's pillow: "Help yourself to the food on the table. I'll be back tonight for supper. (More bread and sausage. Ha!)"

Who was she anyway? Loud. Forward. Like an American, Hosea thought as she got dressed. Hosea didn't like Americans. She blamed the entire United States of America, especially Montana, for Gordon's behaviour; he hadn't been a runaround in Cardston. She checked her purse for keys, wallet, makeup.

In the lobby downstairs she stopped at the bulletin board and read the notices. Aerobics: Tuesday & Thursday. Makeup: Monday. Accessories: Wednesday. Self-esteem: Friday. Beside the announcements, someone had pinned a brochure announcing Sunday morning worship at the New Universal Church of Feminine Consciousness and Cosmic Awareness. "Get in touch with the Divine Feminine at the heart of the Universe. Connect with Her energy. Feel Her Power in your fingertips." In the lower corner of the board was a small poster of colour photographs of missing children: Tara, age 10, missing since November 10, 1987. Brent, age 4, missing since October 1992. Jonathan since 1988 . . .

Hosea looked at the pictures and wondered why she felt nothing. No sympathy. No sadness. Her mind remembered with exact detail the morning of Anxiety's disappearance. But her heart was blank.

In one glance from the bedroom doorway she had gotten the whole picture: the top of the dresser cleared of all its objects, the bed neatly made.

For several moments she didn't move. She stood in the doorway and felt the small grey hole at the centre of her stomach slowly expand, from below her navel up into her chest and throat, then quickly out to her arms and down her sides to her legs and ankles, until there was nothing inside of her to hold her up. She sat down on the bed.

Bittern came into the room. "Where's Annie?" He was the only one who called her that.

"Gone," Hosea said.

"Gone where?"

"With Joe."

"So where'd they go?"

"I don't know."

He moved to the closet and peered into its emptiness. Then he opened each dresser drawer, reached his hand to the far corners of one, and pulled out a pink sock. "One sock. Man. She *is* gone," he said.

THE Inn on Seventh Street was only four blocks from the YWCA. Hosea decided to walk the short distance and have breakfast there. The air was clear. The sun was shining. In front of the funeral chapel, bare branches of shrubs glistened in the light.

At the inn, she chose a booth by the window, ordered a carafe of coffee and a cinnamon bun, and got out her ballpoint pen. "What to Do," she wrote on the paper napkin. "Call Judith, go to the Cecil, the Strathcona, the Commercial." Someone would remember him. Someone would know where he was.

He liked to sit in taverns or coffee shops and write his ideas in little scrappy notebooks. He wrote mostly about gamblers and wild women, about ex-cons in dark and smoky bars. He wrote a poem about her once—in the Commercial Hotel on Whyte Avenue. About her body, naked in an amber light. Hosea filled her cup with hot coffee from the carafe and unrolled a long strip of cinnamon bun. His favourite colour: amber.

ON Anxiety's fourth birthday they had gone to Pancake Palace, just outside of Medicine Hat, for breakfast. Anxiety, Gordon, and Hosea. After the waiter had laid the plates of steaming hotcakes in front of them, Anxiety examined hers carefully, her nose close to the plate, and refused even to lift her fork to them.

"Eat up," Gordon said.

"I don't eat green pancakes," she said.

"They're not green," her mother said.

Anxiety pointed to a tiny speck in the centre of one pancake. "Do you see that?"

And since it was her birthday, she got a waffle instead, with whipped cream and strawberries.

IN the lobby, Hosea dialed her sister in Rocky Mountain House. No sooner had Judith answered the call than Hosea heard Bittern and Doloros arguing in the background.

"I want to! I want to!" Doloros was shouting.

"I said I was going to," Bittern said.

And Judith said, "Just a minute, I have to settle something here."

While she waited, Hosea unclasped her wallet and counted her money. Four 10's two 5's, some change. She'd need to fill the gas tank before she went back. She'd have to be careful with the spending.

Bittern came on the line. "Guess what?"

"What?"

"Guess."

"I can't guess."

"Guess who called."

"Who?"

"Guess."

Hosea's heart beat faster. Gordon. He must be trying to find her. "Your father," she said. "It was your dad."

"No. Annie."

"Anxiety?"

"Annie! That's what I said."

Judith picked up the phone. "She called last night. She wondered where you were, but I didn't know so I couldn't tell her anything."

"She wondered where *I* was? *Me?*" Hosea felt her heart speeding. "Where is she?"

"She didn't say. Where are you? She may call back."

"She called?"

"Yes," Judith said. "So where are you?"

"The Y. The YWCA."

THE policeman had asked dozens of questions. He'd sat at Hosea's kitchen table, pen in hand, yellow notepad on the blue placemat. Who is this guy? A guy. How old is he? Nineteen. Where does he work? The oilpatch. Is he abusive? I don't think so. Is she safe? The officer was a tall, lanky man. He spoke fast, got to the point. "We can find them, of course," he said. "But then what?" He stood up, stuffed the notepad and pen into his black case. "Do you have pictures?" he asked. "A recent snapshot?" Hosea gave him a school portrait of Anxiety when she was in grade eight. By the door he turned and looked at her.

"Anxiety," he said. "That's a hell of a name for a kid."

They'd found her the next day at the York Hotel in Calgary. With Joe. And when the police called Hosea, she heard her daughter yelling in the background. "I was not kidnapped. He didn't even know I was coming."

"Tell her to get home where she belongs!" Hosea shouted. "Right now!"

"Never!" Anxiety yelled back.

A policeman came on the line. "We can bring her home in handcuffs," he said. "Is that what you want? Or would you like to come to Calgary and talk to her?"

In the end, Hosea went to Calgary, Judith drove down from Rocky Mountain House, and Anxiety agreed to stay with Ralph and Judith until things calmed down. Then Hosea drove home. Anxiety stayed in Rocky Mountain House for five weeks, until her sixteenth birthday, when she called her mother. "I'm going now," she said calmly, without anger. "I'm going with Joe." And Hosea knew not to argue.

WHERE had her daughter gotten her formidable will? Gordon was not one to persist in anything. And Hosea herself had waffled her way through life. But Anxiety had some bottomless source of willpower that was there right from the beginning. How hard she had kicked against the walls of her mother's womb. Kick. Kick. Punch. Kick. And when she finally emerged—the tearing, the bruising, the incredible pain.

"Look at this head," the doctor had called to someone. "The size of it." And Hosea had thought in her drowsiness that she had delivered a monster. But no. The doctor raved on. "She'll be a stubborn one. A winner. A rare beauty." And she was a beauty. People would stop Hosea on the street to look at the new baby in her carriage and gush at her loveliness.

As the baby grew, she also became more affectionate. Even in her sleep she could sense her mother's presence hovering over the bed and would reach out her arms and pull Hosea down to her and hold her close.

Where had such love come from?

The waiter stopped at her table. "Would you like anything else?" he asked.

"No," Hosea said. "No thank you." She sipped the coffee and stared out the window at the traffic.

And where had it gone wrong?

Suddenly Hosea wanted to sleep. She wanted to undress and get into bed and sleep for a long time. She got up from the table, paid for the coffee, and walked back to the Y.

She asked the receptionist if there had been any calls for her.

"No," the girl said. "None."

"Oh," Hosea said. She remained standing by the front desk.

The receptionist looked up at her. "Was there something else?"

"No. Nothing."

"Oh."

"I'm going to my room now. I'll be in my room on the sixth floor."

"I see."

"My name's Hosea." She did not move from the spot.

"You're expecting a call?" the receptionist asked.

"Not really. But in case."

"I understand," the girl said. "The phone will ring in the hall up there, if there's a call for you."

Hosea took the elevator to her floor, checked the location of the phone, then unlocked the door of her room. She would have a long, quiet nap. She took off her shoes, sweater, and jeans and lay down under the blanket.

Anxiety had always hated naps. "Not all children take naps, you know," she announced when she was five. "Christine and Scott don't take naps. Tim Hanson doesn't. Jeff Merkel never does. He doesn't have to do anything he doesn't want to do."

"That's enough now," Hosea said.

"Do kangaroos take naps? Do fish? I know dolphins take naps, but only when they want to."

"Go to sleep," Hosea said. "You're not a fish."

WHEN Hosea woke up, it was mid-afternoon. She lay under the blanket and tried to remember her dream, something white and moving, but nothing more came to her. Instead, she remembered the day Anxiety stepped on a hornet's nest. Kicked into it. She was three years old and playing near a cement slab in their backyard. The hornets had built their nest under a ridge at the edge of the slab. Anxiety had seen it there, grey and papery, and kicked it. Hosea and Gordon were in the house. They didn't hear Anxiety's screams. They didn't see the insects swarming. They didn't realize what had happened until their neighbour came to the door, holding the child in his arms. She was panting for breath, her face deep red, beginning to blister.

"Baking soda," the neighbour said. "Mix it with water."

Gordon mixed the paste and the two men daubed Anxiety's face and arms with the white mixture. Hosea tried to hold Anxiety still, but the child was wild, yelling, arms flailing. They restrained her with a sheet and drove her to the hospital.

Why was she remembering this now? She got out of bed, dressed, and walked down the hall to the bathroom.

On her way back to the room, she saw a large woman in the lounge, lying on the sofa, watching *The Young and the Restless* on TV. A rerun. Hosea had seen the segment before. Victor Newman's blind wife, Hope, was feeding her son, Victor Junior, in the kitchen of her farm home in Kansas. Victor himself was in Genoa City; the couple was no longer together. Hosea sat on one of the overstuffed chairs and watched the show.

When it was over, she turned to the woman and said, "Isn't it something the way she can manage everything?"

No answer from the sofa.

"I mean being blind and still looking after the farm, the house, and the baby? She doesn't even have a hired girl."

The fat woman kept her eyes on the screen. Hosea rose from her chair. "Of course, it's all made up," she said and returned to her room.

She unlocked the door, stood in the doorway, and looked in. Her roommate was back. She was sitting on her bed, fumbling with a small tape recorder.

"Oh," Hosea said. "It's you."

The girl looked up and smiled broadly. She had a large mouth. "Right. Bread and sausage. Remember?" She pressed a button on the recorder. "Listen to this." The tape whirred backward. "It's Rose. Listen. Her voice. I mean you've never *heard* such a voice. She's all Texas. *Huge.* Her body just *rolls* when she's preaching. And that *voice.* Well you know Texas. *Big!*"

The rewinding stopped, and Hosea heard a soft, breathy woman's voice, low and seductive.

"Well, she *starts* soft," the girl said. "But wait. You'll see."

Hosea lay down on the bed.

"It's about the children," the girl explained, "what happened with the children, how they tried to keep the children away. Only he said no, let them come. It's all about those children . . ."

Hosea sat up. "Would you mind if we didn't listen to that right now? I'm kind of tired." She lay back on the bed.

"No problem," the girl said and stopped the tape. "Are you hungry? I'm starved. I'll make sandwiches."

Hosea stared at the ceiling. There'd been no phone call. And she hadn't even started looking for Gordon.

She turned on her side and watched the girl cutting slices of sausage onto a paper towel. She was using a pocket knife.

"You look a little like my daughter," Hosea said, kindly, her head still on the pillow.

"I do? Poor thing."

"I haven't seen her for several months or heard from her."

"Your daughter? Your own daughter?"

"She ran away with her boyfriend."

"Oh no." The girl stopped cutting, the knife poised in the air. "So you're here looking for her."

"No. I came to Edmonton to look for my husband."

"Your *husband's* gone, too? Your daughter *and* your husband?"

"Both of them," Hosea said.

"Took off together!" the girl said.

"No, Gordon left a couple of years ago."

"That's *awful,*" the girl said. "How can you *stand* it?"

"We didn't get along. Our house was chaos. Pure silence, or yelling and fighting."

"My God, he beat you."

"No. It was words mostly. But when I got mad at Gordon, I'd hit the kids."

"You didn't!"

"Yes I did. I hit them."

"But *why?* It wasn't their fault."

"I just did, that's all," Hosea said.

"So what did the kids do then?"

"Hide."

"*Hide!*"

"Once I found my oldest daughter hiding in the laundry room. She was five or six, I can't remember exactly. She'd piled all the sheets and towels and shirts and jeans and underwear—all of it—in a huge stack on the floor and she was lying under the clothes."

"*That is so terrible.*" The girl held up both hands, fingers splayed, as if she was about to catch a falling object. "Dirty clothes? Or clean."

"Both. She dumped them all in a pile on the floor, and she was lying under the pile. And when I found her she was red-faced from crying."

"My God!" the girl said again. She looked down at the small rings of sausage spread out on the paper towel. She began to carefully place the meat on the bread.

Hosea turned to face the wall. "Can I listen to your tape?" she asked.

"You wouldn't like this tape."

"Can I anyway?"

"You'd hate it."

"So?"

"All right, but I warned you. Here, have some bread." She went to Hosea's bed and handed her a sandwich, then returned to her own, and clicked on the recorder.

The voice was dark and husky.

What did he do what did he do what did he do? You know what he did? Lifted them up is what he did. Does that mean down? No. Does up mean down? Certainly not. And where did he lift them? In his arms, that's where. And then what? What did he do then? Says right here what he did. Laid his hands on them. On who? Who did he lay his hands on? The children. Who? Children! Say it louder. Children children children. That's right! You got that just right. And then what did he do? Did he beat them up with those hands? No! Slap them down? Nooo! Molest them in dirty ways? No! No! No! That is correct. So what was it he did? Says the answer right here. Right here it says. Blessed them. What? Blessed. Can't hear you. What did he do? Blessed them. Still can't hear. Blessed! Blessed! Blessed! That's exactly what he did. And what does that mean? Scoff at them? No. Ignore them? No! Call them names? Worthless? No-Good? Won't-Amount-to-Anything? Is that the meaning here? Of course not! He lifted them up entire and complete. His arms lifted them up, his hands lifted them, his words, his face, his thoughts, his spirit. They all did the lifting! He taught them. Lifted them up. Lifted them. Lifted. Oh blessed. Oh oh blessed.

The tape stopped rolling. The girl stuffed the recorder into her pack. Hosea sat on the bed, clutching the sandwich. Thank you, Yellow Rose of Texas. She bit into the bread, chewed on the crust.

"So, did you like it?" the girl asked.

"Just great," Hosea said.

When they finished eating, the girl packed up her stuff. "I won't be coming back here," she said. "I've got a ride home after the meeting."

She moved to Hosea and shook her hand, large pumping movements, up and down and again and again. And she was gone.

Hosea looked around at the sudden emptiness and thought she had to go outside, walk, breathe, get some air. She put on her jacket, picked up her purse, and left.

In the lobby she passed the receptionist's desk without speaking and opened the door.

Outside, the wind had risen. Bits of debris swirled down the street, twigs, dry leaves, scraps of paper. The air was cold, the sky darkening. Charcoal clouds were moving over the funeral chapel. Maybe she'd drive around for a while, go over to Whyte Avenue and check out a couple of spots. Tomorrow she'd call a few places, be more methodical in her search. Then she'd return to Rocky Mountain House.

She backed out of the Y parking lot, drove west to 109th, then south on the High Level Bridge to Whyte Avenue.

At the Renford Inn she parked on the ramp in the parkade, walked down the dusty concrete steps to the street below. She held her collar close to her neck, bent her head against the wind, and scrunched her way to the hotel entrance.

There were no customers in the restaurant. And no waiter. She'd hoped Jeanette would still be there, chattering, pouring coffee, bringing food, as she'd done in the past; but she saw no one. Then she heard a guitar and some drums, loud and pulsating, and she followed the sound down the hall to the tavern door. If Gordon was anywhere in Edmonton, this was the likely place. From the doorway she squinted into the dimness, moved slowly to the bar. The bartender was tall and wide-shouldered. Hosea hesitated, then spoke.

"Do you know a Gordon who comes here?" she asked.

"Gordon? Don't think so. Hey, Buck, you know a Gordon who hangs here?"

"You mean George?" The voice came from the other end of the bar.

The bartender leaned toward Hosea. "Are you thinking of George?"

"No," Hosea said. "Gordon."

"Gordon!" shouted the bartender.

"Don't know Gordon," the voice said. "But George, he's here every night—should be showing up any time."

"Sorry," the bartender said.

She saw four girls sitting at a table by the window. She walked past them, glanced at their faces. Strangers. She turned quickly and walked out.

In the café, she sat down at the far end, by the mirrors. A skinny man in a white shirt and black pants emerged through swinging doors from the kitchen. He brought a pot of coffee to her table and filled her cup.

"There used to be a Jeanette who worked here," Hosea said. "Curly hair? Friendly? Is she still around?"

"Works mornings," he said, "but she's off this week."

"Oh," she said.

She glanced at the *Journal* lying on the table next to her. On the front page was a picture of the fallen airplane in Cheyenne, Wyoming, covered with a tarp, a rough mound on the concrete. In the yard, grass was growing.

She lifted the cup, held it in both hands, and drank.

THAT night, she dreamt of dolphins. She was floating in blue water watching dozens of baby dolphins sleeping under the waves, lying on their backs and snoring. Their mother was scolding them, telling them to turn over. "Dolphins always lie on their stomachs," she said. "Why?" they asked in their high clicking voices. "So they won't snore," their mother said.

IN the morning it was raining. Hosea decided to stay at the Y for breakfast. It was ten o'clock. She'd slept later than she'd planned.

She chose a table by one of the tall windows at the far end of the coffee shop and sat down on the plastic chair beside it. She laid her arm on the tabletop, rested her hand beside a white vase holding a yellow daffodil. She watched thin streams of water run crookedly down the windowpane. Heard the traffic on the pavement outside. Saw the rain splash down on roofs of speeding cars, spray up in curves from under their black tires. Across the street the funeral home wavered, grey and distant in the slanting rain.

Hosea turned her head and saw the fat lady sitting by the far wall, alone, and at the table next to her, two old women, one in a white sweater, one in pink, sitting across from each other. She saw the clock on the wall above the urn and the muffins in a plastic case on the counter.

Then she saw a movement in the doorway.

A dark shape in the doorway.

Her heart began to pound.

Anxiety.

Filling the doorway.

Standing large and wet. Long hair dripping water. Grey coat soaked in rain.

Big-bellied. Huge.

Hosea sucked in her breath and stared. Anxiety didn't move, didn't speak. She just stood there. Unsmiling.

Hosea half rose from her chair, but her legs felt weak, and she sat down again. She lifted her hand, beckoned her daughter with a limp wave. And Anxiety moved, slowly and clumsily, toward her mother. And Hosea's breath was somewhere just below her lungs. And her heart was racing. And she saw her daughter moving. (That huge coat. That wetness. God.) And then she was standing by the table, solemn and dripping.

"Hi, Mom," she said.

"Oh," Hosea said. "Oh my, it's you."

"It's me all right." Anxiety gave a short laugh, nervous, more like a snort.

"It's really you," Hosea said.

"Are you surprised?"

"Well, yes," Hosea said. "Yes. Of course. I'm surprised."

Water dripped from the hem of her daughter's coat, forming small puddles on the floor by her feet. Her face was rosy pink from the cold. Her body seemed to spread, filling the aisle.

"Sit down," Hosea said. "Why don't you sit? You may as well sit down." She heard her own voice rising, getting shrill.

Anxiety sat crooked in the chair, her feet sprawled in the aisle.

Hosea tried not to look at the bulging stomach. But there it was. Bold and rude. Sticking out. Even so, she could not bring herself to acknowledge it. Instead she asked, "How did you know I was here?"

"Judith. I called her yesterday. Again."

"From Revelstoke?" Hosea wondered how Anxiety could have gotten to Edmonton in such short time.

"Oh no, I've been in town for a while. A week now." She seemed impatient that Hosea didn't know this.

"I'm pregnant," she said.

"Yes, I can see that," Hosea said.

"It shows, doesn't it," Anxiety said.

And then, because Hosea really didn't know what to say next, she said, "So when did all this happen?"

"I was pregnant when I left home, if that's what you're asking."

Hosea was silent. No, that is not what I'm asking. Where have you been? is what I'm asking. Why no word? I'm asking. Did you lose your memory? I ask. Forget the street you lived on? Forget your brother's name? Your sister's face? Did a dark wind from the end of the world carry all this away?

But out loud she said, "Is Joe with you?"

"Yes and no," Anxiety said. "Joe's in Kuwait." Her eyes were gazing on the rippling glass. She had unbuttoned her coat, and Hosea saw her neck, a mottled pink.

"Oh," Hosea said, "I didn't know that."

"He has a job in the oilfields. It's only for six months. He'll be sending me money. We're still together."

"I see," Hosea said, and her eyes glanced down at Anxiety's stomach pressed against the rim of the table. "You're staying with friends then? You have friends here?"

"Sort of. Don't you have a room here? My back's killing me. I either have to lie down or stand up against a wall."

"Yes," Hosea said. "Let's go on up." And they left the café and took the elevator to the sixth floor.

Inside the room, Anxiety struggled out of her coat, manoeuvring her arms and shoulders this way and that. She hung the damp garment over the iron bar at the head of the first bed, the one the girl from Bawlf had slept in. She stretched, yawned, rubbed her lower back with the knuckles of her fisted hand.

"Did your back get to you when you were pregnant?"

"Yes, the back's a real problem," Hosea said. She noticed Anxiety's outfit, a nubby pink top and leggings to match. It looked modern and expensive. She wore a gold chain around her neck.

Hosea sat down on her own bed at the end of the room. Anxiety waddled to the bed next to it and slowly lowered herself onto the green blanket. She sat upright, very straight, wiggled her feet out of her sneakers without unlacing them, using one foot to slide the shoe off the other.

"I hate being wet," she said.

"That's a pretty outfit," Hosea said.

"It's new. I got it here in Edmonton," Anxiety said.

"You look healthy," her mother said. "You look good. You must be taking care of yourself."

"Tell me about it," Anxiety said. "I had to watch all these videos in the clinic in Revelstoke. About food and exercise and smoking and drinking. Stuff like that. I saw these skinny babies and stunted babies and fetal alcohol babies with those weird eyes. You can screw up a kid even before it's born. Did you know that? Hey, would they kill me if I laid down on this bed?"

And without waiting for an answer, she stood up, lifted the green blanket, and lowered herself again, this time lying on her back, legs stretched out, head on the pillow. She pulled the blanket to her chin. "It's cold in here." She smoothed it over her belly, a green mound in the middle of the bed.

"So what are you doing here?" she asked her mother, who was still sitting on the edge of her bed.

"Looking for your father," Hosea said.

"Dad?"

"Well, yes."

"You're *still* looking for Dad?"

"He's still my husband," Hosea said.

Anxiety raised her head from the pillow. "*Mother,* pardon me for a minute here, but you two split up. Remember? I think it's time you got a new life."

Hosea sucked in her breath. Great, she thought. Just great. Miss Due-in-three-weeks-with-no-mate can now tell me how to live my life. She suddenly has the credentials for teaching me how to live.

"Go back to school or something," Anxiety said. "There's a college in Medicine Hat, isn't there?"

Hosea's anger rose. "Me?" she said. "*I* should go to school? You're telling me that I should go to college?" She meant for Anxiety to see her own predicament: quitting school and suffering all its worst consequences.

But instead Anxiety said, "Why not? You can read, can't you?"

Hosea felt the space between the two beds widen, the beds like small ships floating away in opposite directions on a murky and unmanageable sea. She was conscious as she drifted that she hadn't even touched her daughter—not a hug, a kiss, a handshake, not the slightest, tiniest tap of a hand on her daughter's arm or shoulder. She lay down, covered herself with the blanket. The room was chilly. The rain beat against the window.

And then, through the fog that surrounded her, through its thick haze, she heard the voice of Anxiety in the next bed. It cut through the greyness like thin steel.

"I've been with him."

"Who?" Hosea said.

"Dad. He lives here now. On the north side."

Hosea felt the fog pull close to her and contract and tighten and harden against her.

"He's changed," Anxiety said. "He's not the jerk he used to be. He's happier, I think."

Hosea's voice was hoarse. "You've kept in touch with your father?"

"On and off," Anxiety said. "When Joe left for Kuwait, Dad said I could stay with him."

"I see," Hosea said.

"Him and Bonnie."

"Bonnie." Hosea echoed the word from a distant mountain across the continent.

"Well, you know Dad."

Hosea was silent.

"But I think this one is permanent," Anxiety said. "A real relationship. And she's good for him—lots of life, makes him laugh."

Hosea's least favourite word: relationship.

"Fuck relationship," she said.

"Mother. Don't be crude."

"His make-him-laugh girlfriend doesn't say crude things?"

"Of course. But she's young."

Hosea felt herself at the top of a mountain, standing on a precipice, her feet on the very edge of it, her shoes slipping on loose rock. And she heard Anxiety's voice from across the chasm.

"She took me shopping last week. Bought me a bunch of baby stuff, a layette it's called, and a receiving blanket. I didn't even know there was such a thing. And this outfit. Well, Dad paid for it, I guess."

And Hosea's feet slipped on the rock and her body tumbled into space and her daughter's words faded, became distant, dissipated. Hosea floated, breathless. She knew one thing: don't land. If you land you'll break into pieces. You'll be a little pile of broken bits at the bottom of the chasm.

Then something caught her, held her. She sat up. Her neck was stiff, her back hard against the wall.

"Why are you here, Anxiety? Why have you come? Is this your big get-even-with-Mother thing? But you've already done that. No answers to letters. No phone calls. What happened? Was your memory turned off? Your imagination? You couldn't get the picture?"

Anxiety didn't answer. She lay with the green blanket over her belly, her head on the pillow, her damp hair swirling up and out, over the pillow's edge. The pink smock was crunched up over the edge of the blanket, and the gold chain had fallen in a loop away from her chest onto the pillow. Her neck was red and blotchy. And Hosea saw her there, a heap on the bed. God. She looked like a small whale. She must have gained fifty pounds. Even in that pink underwear outfit, she looked huge. Lord.

Hosea hadn't landed. She hadn't broken into pieces. She was stronger than she thought. Still in control. Let her daughter and Gordon both sail off into the sunset. Let the happy girl sail with them. And the new baby. She couldn't care less.

"So why *did* you come?" she asked again.

Anxiety turned her head slightly. Her face was flushed. Her hands lay on the blanket, fingers rigid.

"To ask you for something," she said.

Right, Hosea thought. Your father's out of cash. You need money.

"I was hoping you'd be with me when the baby comes," Anxiety said.

For a moment, Hosea stopped breathing. The room was still, the darkness hovered. She stared at her daughter, saw a small thin wetness seep out from the corners of her eyes.

"Me? You want me? Not..."

"I don't want them," Anxiety said. "But if you can't, well that's all right."

The blue darkness of the long rain seeped into the room.

Suddenly Anxiety jerked forward. "Oh my God," she said.

"What? What?" Hosea said. "Is it time?"

Anxiety fell back on the bed. "It's kicking. It's really kicking. Feel it. Put your hand here. Quick, or you'll miss it. Right here."

And before she realized it, Hosea was at her daughter's side, her hand pressed on her stomach, feeling the jabs and kicks.

"It moves," Anxiety said. "Did you know that? It actually moves. And it makes noise. The doctor said so." She grabbed her mother's shoulder and pulled her down. "Listen. See if you can hear it. Try to hear it."

Then Hosea's head was on Anxiety's stomach, her ear pressed close.

And Anxiety was crying and laughing. "It's wild. It's so crazy."

But Hosea was neither laughing nor crying. She was holding on tight to the mattress, her eyes closed. Oh, Hosea, what are you doing here bent over this girl, your head on the smooth mound of her belly? What are you doing with your eyelids shut and your lips pressed hard? Hold on, Hosea. Hold fast.

But what could she do? What was there to do when her cheek was pressed like this against her daughter? When her ear was receiving even now the bumps and thuds and general chaos of the life within?

And what else could she do when at this moment her daughter's arms came up and circled round her and held her there?

She could do only what she did. She let out a clumsy hiccup of a sob, and then another. And she opened her mouth and bawled.

And when Hosea's crying stopped, Anxiety lifted her mother's head with her own thin hands and raised her up and looked into her face and said, "Did you hear it?"

"Some thumps."

"That's all?"

"Some gurgling sounds."

"I want to hear it, too," Anxiety said, "but my ear can't reach that far." She crouched deeper under the blanket.

"My name is Ann," she murmured. She turned over on her side and yawned. "I thought of Beyond Repair for the baby's name."

"Annie!" Hosea said. "It could have been worse. I could have named you something a lot worse."

"I suppose," Annie said. "It's going to be a girl, you know. Amazing might be a good name. That has a nice sound to it. Or I could name her after you." She closed her eyes and breathed into her pillow.

Hosea sat on the edge of the bed and watched her daughter. Ann's mouth was partly open, a bead of spit bubbled on her lower lip, and she began to snore, a soft snore like purring. And Hosea noticed things about her she thought she had forgotten: the thin scar on the side of her chin from a fall on her tricycle when she was three, the birthmark below her left ear, the tiny beads of sweat that formed on the bridge of her nose when she was sleeping. Hosea did not move from the bed. She sat very still and looked at her daughter.

She thought of names for the baby. Karen, Marilyn, Sue, Kristi. And Naomi—that was a pretty name. So many to choose from. It was going to be a girl, she'd said.

When Ann awoke it was still raining. She yawned and stretched and looked up at her mother. "Have you decided?" she asked.

Hosea rose from the bed and stepped to the window. She loved weather, especially rain, but this downpour just came and came and came. It was too much.

"Yes," she said. "Yes. I'll call and let them know we're coming."

"My stuff's downstairs at the desk," Ann said.

IN Rocky Mountain House, the sun had dropped behind the ridge of mountains in the west. The air was cold, a blue-black air left behind by the sun. The earth was still hard with frost, but in wide patches the ground had crumbled and become soft.

On the porch the children waited in thick sweaters and mitts. They'd know the whirring and the small clicking sounds of the car's engine. They'd know the slanted beam of its headlights, and the crackling movement of the tires on the pavement. They'd know its curved shape looming out of the dark.

They sat on the steps and leaned toward the street and waited.

They breathed in the cold air and breathed it out and watched it form small clouds in front of their faces, then disappear into the darkness.

"It's about time she came home," Doloros said.

"I guess I'll have a thing or two to say to her," said Bittern.

The Garden of Edith Ashdown

BARBARA SAPERGIA

EDITH ASHDOWN STANDS IN THE DOORWAY listening to the man, not bothering to hide her impatience. He's younger than she is, about thirty-five, dressed for work in denim trousers and a blue chambray shirt with the sleeves rolled up. She has no time to talk. The children have gone to school, Arnold has drifted back to sleep, and it's time to do the housework. The April breeze is cold, cutting through her thin cotton housedress.

"No, thank you," she says. "I do all the gardening here." He stands his ground. "Those cottonwoods could use some pruning. Next big storm, you might find all those dead branches on your roof. That can do a lot of damage."

The garden is bare and bleached of colour, everything pale grey or soft mossy green. Only the grass has begun to take on spring colour, and the buds on the trees. She looks at the dead limbs on the cottonwood, the lilacs and roses she never found time to cut back in the fall, and is suddenly very tired. Her own muscles and bones have a dry, creaky feel, and she thinks that if she bends too quickly she might crack in two.

Edith Ashdown doesn't like people disagreeing with her. She thinks the man should have gone off when she said no, but he stands waiting. He wants her to say yes, but she's having trouble saying anything at all.

"And those lilacs are getting overgrown. I could prune them back for you."

"I do that," she says quickly.

"Lot of work keeping up a place like this," he says.

"Yes," she says, looking at the blue eyes in his tanned face, the light brown hair. It's ridiculous, but he reminds her of David, more a feel of David than an actual resemblance, because David's hair was golden blond and his eyes were brown. David was well educated, and this man is not. And this man has reached an age David never reached.

"All right," she says, surprising herself, "I'll hire you to do the pruning."

He nods and gets right to work. He's brought his own implements, his own ladder, in the back of his pickup truck. He seems to have nothing further to say to her, so she closes the door.

She watches from the kitchen window until she's satisfied he knows what he's doing. He works at a steady pace, not hurrying at all, but covering ground. Soon dead branches, large and small, are falling from the great cottonwoods onto the parched-looking lawn.

She goes back to her work, washing the breakfast dishes, tidying the kitchen and living room. She makes Arnold's midmorning tea and toast and climbs the stairs, suddenly aware of the stillness in the house. Halfway up she hears the old grandfather clock striking the hour. Ten o'clock. In their bedroom he lies with his head propped up by many pillows, his arms flung out at his sides. His mouth is wide open, his breathing deep and harsh. It disgusts her that he should be so lost in sleep, so far away from the daytime world in which she must move and work. She wants to shake him until he stops the ugly breathing. Instead she puts a gentle hand on his shoulder.

"Arnold," she says, "I've brought your tea and toast."

Amazingly, he comes awake straightaway. He looks with pleasure at the tray she's brought him, tea in a fine china pot, toast powdered with sugared cinnamon on a dainty pink porcelain plate. She puts the tray down as he struggles to raise himself in the bed, and helps lift him up, arranging the pillows to support him.

She sits on the bed and watches him eat. Without warning—as usual—Homer is there, sitting in the wing chair where Edith likes to sit.

"He was a milksop when you married him, and he's getting worse."

She ignores him, stirring sugar into Arnold's tea. She holds it out to Arnold, and he sips it happily; hot sweet tea is Arnold's favourite beverage now. Thank God he can eat and drink without help. She doesn't think she could stand doing that for him.

"Mind you, that's just the sort of thing you'd like, I should imagine. A man you can push around at will."

She doesn't speak aloud to Homer, not when other people are around. She sends him a message in her mind. *I bet you'd like to eat toast again yourself. But you'll never get any from me.*

For some reason this hits home. Homer looks rather deflated. He gets up from the chair and fades slowly from the room. She sees that Arnold is looking at her anxiously. She smiles at him and pours more tea. He smiles back at her, gratefully.

Through the window she sees the man gathering twigs and branches into a neat pile on the lawn. He has cut some of the larger boughs into shorter lengths for the fireplace. He bends and lifts and turns easily, does not look the least bit creaky.

Later, she is vacuuming the downstairs floors with the Electrolux when she hears the back doorbell. He has finished the work and come to be paid. She leaves him standing in the doorway while she goes into the living room to get her purse. When she comes back, he has stepped just inside the door. He looks at her thoughtfully, pleasantly. She is suddenly aware of her faded cotton dress as she hands him the money. She waits for him to thank her and go.

"I could come again later on and help put in your garden," he says.

"Oh no," she says, "I can do that. I always do."

She realizes that she expects him to offer counter-arguments as he did before. It's too much work, you need help with the lawn, or whatever. But he doesn't say anything, just looks at her.

"Mind you, I have a lot on my hands these days," she says, although he has no way of knowing what she has on her hands. He doesn't know her, doesn't know about Arnold. Unless somebody's told him. He waits.

"Why don't you come back in a couple of weeks, when the lawn's ready to cut? I could use some help with that."

"All right," he says. "I'll do that. I'll see you then."

He goes out the door, and she watches him through the various windows until he climbs into his truck and drives away. She realizes that she has seen him before. He helps Mr. Hayashi, who owns the greenhouse in the valley. Every spring she goes down to buy her bedding plants, and the man helps her find what she needs. In the fall she buys extra cucumbers and tomatoes from him. Perhaps that's why he seems so familiar. And yet he does also remind her of David in some way. She thinks about Arnold lying in bed and wonders what they're going to do. He has been sick for a long time, and even the doctor has given up trying to find out why. He doesn't get any worse, but he doesn't get better either. Arnold is only fifty-one, too young to give up on life and making a living, but at the same time too ill to work. They are living on the money his parents left, and that won't last forever. Edith has given up her cleaning lady to cut expenses, but she doesn't see what else she can do. Looking after the house and the children and Arnold is taking all her time.

H E has cut the grass and raked it into neat miniature haystacks all over the lawn. The yard smells sweetly of it, like a summer meadow, smells also of freshly turned earth where he has dug a plot for her vegetable garden. He has taken off his shirt in the warm sunshine. She enjoys looking at his bare chest, the contrast of pink nipples against the beginnings of a suntan, although she tries not to let him see her looking. She has always marvelled that men are allowed to go about this way. It seems so naked in a country where the winters are cold enough to kill.

She has come outside to show him the roses she wants pruned. She wears a smooth-fitting grey skirt that flares out slightly below her knees and a short-sleeved pink pullover that she knows brings out the auburn gloss in her hair.

The lawn has been invaded by robins, a dozen or more. She stops to watch a pair of them pulling rubbery-looking earthworms from the grass. She feels the warm sun on her head; a soft spring breeze tousles her hair. The blue sky is broken by patches of cloud that promise rain, as do the robins singing on the fencepost.

He sees her looking at the birds. "I like birds," he says. "You can learn a lot watching them."

She looks up at him, and he smiles, friendly, assuming nothing. She sees the fine dew of sweat on his forehead, the strong muscles in his forearms.

"I came to show you the roses," she says.

T H E new leaves and shoots take her by storm. Suddenly everything is green fire—new leaves so freshly green you could imagine eating them, spears of asparagus thrusting out of the soil almost as she watches, bark of her rose bushes turning green overnight. Nature is back in the business of growing and flowering.

S H E pauses at the back door; Homer is there, getting in her way.

"Where do you think you're going?" She ignores him. "You think I don't know what you're up to?"

"I don't care if you know," she says.

"Of course, it's no more than I'd expect from you," he says. "But I must admit I was surprised by the indecent haste. You used to be a bit more cautious."

"Maybe that was my problem," she says, sensing her own power. She is going out, and Homer never goes out. She doesn't think he can. She smiles at him, as nastily as she can, and enjoys the effect it has on him: he starts to fade, and she sees how he hates it. But she doesn't have time for him now. She slips out the back door and into the garden. The night is warm, perfumed by the flowering almond that always blooms in time for her birthday, late in May. She follows a stone path to the rose garden and the covered gazebo, which stands beside the fence overlooking the river. Before she sees his face, she feels his warmth coming toward her out of the shadows. Then she's in his arms, sinking softly to the floor, to the rough blanket he's spread there. She feels his kisses on her face, and his hands, warm and strong, as he unfastens her shirt and peels it away from her bare shoulders. He presses his face against her breasts and then begins to kiss them. If she didn't know better, she would say this was the finest, the best part.

Forty years she has lived, had a husband and two children, and only now is she beginning to have knowledge of her own body and of a man's body. People would say, if they knew, that she's wanton. And she is wanton, but it's more than that; she is filled with grace and fluency in everything she does, in every part of her body. She sees that a woman's body is perfect, right in every respect, and she has never known until this year, this spring. She loves her own breasts because it feels so good to hold his head against them. She loves her hands caressing him, her legs wrapped around his. She loves the place in her where he enters, a place that is warm and good and as limitless as her feeling for him.

She no longer feels dry and creaky. She feels moist as birch trees in spring rain. She feels like a sun that flows everywhere, warms everything it touches. Forty years have passed and meant nothing. She is a young woman again. She has a lover, a real lover, far different than her long-lost sweetheart. She thinks it has something to do with the garden. The years have been cold and dry, but all along she has kept her garden green and flourishing, kept herself alive in some small vital spot that is growing now until it warms and possesses her whole body. She has tended her garden well, and now it has given her a lover.

They are both naked on the blanket; she feels the soft breath of the night all over her skin, and his body against hers, giving off the warmth he has soaked up during the day. He will press that warmth against her and into her until it is very late, until it grows cold in the garden.

LATE in June she moves Arnold into the spare room, the one Homer had when he was ill. She tells him it will be easier to look after him there, that she won't disturb him when she gets up in the morning or comes to bed at night. The real reason is so he won't be able to look out into the garden when Tom is working there. Instead he will have a view of the river below, which she tells him will be a nice change.

Homer is very upset. He still thinks of it as his room. He sits in the chair and rails at her, in his white pyjamas and maroon dressing gown. She pays him very little mind. He has a nasty tongue, but she's always given as good as she's got, and lately she doesn't care that much what he says.

⊹

SHE tends her vegetable garden. She eats anything she can find, the moment it's ready. Nobody else gets asparagus, because she breaks the stalks off and eats them raw as soon as she sees anything there to eat. It gives her urine a peculiar odour, which she enjoys.

Homer is still with her in the house. He shows up at any time in any room. It's disgraceful, a person has no privacy. Even in the bathroom, he will suddenly appear, laughing at her flash of annoyance.

He accuses her of killing him. She says she did no such thing, much as she might have liked to. "Ah, that's the thing," he says. "Do you think wanting doesn't kill?"

Mostly she doesn't listen.

⊹

ARNOLD looks at Edith's face, hovering a few inches above his. Her lips are moving, and she's asking him something about breakfast cereal. Her face is not as he remembers it.

Edith Ashdown, as he still thinks of her, has always been a beautiful woman. That was why he wanted her in the first place. She'd had a cool queenly beauty, with just a touch of rosy colour in her cheeks, a flash of auburn glamour in her hair. She'd had something measured and controlled; she was his idea of a lady.

Now someone else is there in her place. Someone who gives off beauty like a scent, radiates power in waves that roll over him, making him feel faint and sick. He sees a sensuous lustre on her face, her throat, her limbs. It's the way her eyes look at him, full of knowledge; the way her lips move, languidly, as if exulting in their own warmth. She wears the same clothes as before, but there is nothing familiar about the way she looks in them, the way he senses her breasts and hips inside the clothes. He has some sense that her breasts are defiant now, boisterous, jubilant. He thinks this is a ridiculous thought to have. He remembers their moments of coupling, the pleasure he felt, the pride when he was able to create children in her, in the cool and beautiful Edith Ashdown.

Dimly he understands that a great change has come to his wife, as an earthquake or a massive avalanche changes all the old familiar territory, and that it has nothing to do with him. He has a peevish sense of injury—it's wrong for her to change when he feels so weak, so tired. The colours of her skin and hair deepen and glow as his own fade away. She is blooming, he is withering. Is she doing this to him, draining away his strength? But what a wild thought. This is only his wife, Edith Ashdown, asking him about breakfast cereal.

ONE night she is ready to step out the back door when she hears a noise on the stairs. Her daughter, Eleanor, has come down, stands at the foot of the stairs, looking like a small serious gnome.

Edith struggles to keep the irritation from showing on her face. Even now she has difficulty believing this is her child. But she was awake during the birth and there is no mistake. It's her son she loves, though, her son Lockwood, named for her mother's family, who favours Edith and is in turn favoured by her. He has her lovely hair, her grace and self-possession. Even at five years of age, he has the sense that he is someone to be taken into consideration. Eleanor has none of these things.

"I can't sleep," Eleanor says, eyes frightened, pleading.

"Of course you can," Edith says, as kindly as she is able. "Everything is all right."

"Don't go away," the child says. "I don't want you to go away."

Edith tries not to look at her with distaste. It's not the child's fault she's awkward and plain. "Of course not," she says. "Where did you get an idea like that?"

She takes Eleanor in her arms, trying to infuse into her eight-year-old daughter some of the tenderness she's learned. The child has a right to it. She lifts her and carries her up the stairs. Without her mind being quite aware of it, her arms promise the child that she will stay and look after her. She settles Eleanor in her bed, kisses her softly on the cheek.

She waits a quarter of an hour, listening, hoping the child is asleep. She has promised she won't leave, and perhaps the promise is stronger than one made to a loved child. It is sealed with a strong glue, the biting-sharp bond of guilt.

Quiet as a leaf, she turns the knob and slips out the back door and into the night.

+

DAY by day, Edith grows rounder and softer. Something coiled tight inside her has finally come loose, unravelled, melted away. She never understood it was there until it began to go away. Or perhaps she knew it was there, but mistook it for her own self and now knows this is false. It feels good to let it go.

+

ONE day Arnold understands that his wife, Edith Ashdown, is pregnant. There is no one definitive sign, but he feels sure she is, and it explains so much. Does she know about it? She must, if he can feel it, lying cold and still in a sickbed. He sees that she's pregnant and knows that it is none of his doing. He feels frightened, and tired to his very bones.

+

HIS name is Tom. He has a small house in the valley, left to him by his parents. He works for Hayashi, the greenhouse man, and does gardening for people on his own time. He saves most of his money, and in the winter he hardly works at all, except for clearing the snow from and flooding the outdoor rinks. It doesn't pay much, but it keeps him going, and he likes to go skating afterwards on the clean, swift ice.

Edith's first impression was that he reminded her of David, her fiancé who was lost in the war. Now she wonders how she could have thought this, because Tom is completely different. He is not particularly eloquent and seldom gives compliments. He's not particularly handsome, or maybe he's handsome in a plain and solid sort of way. She likes this solidity about him that says, I may not be much, but I'm all right. No one in Edith's family could ever think it was all right to do the work Tom does. But Tom is not part of the family and doesn't care what anyone in it thinks. He has a life that pleases him, a life that makes a pleasant shape, like a finely knit sweater. He is his own man and doesn't show himself to everybody, and in this, at least, he is like Edith. Edith has always prized the things that made her different from other people, raised her above them. Now she cuts these things out of her thoughts, focuses only on him and the thing they have together, which contains great pleasure and also goes beyond pleasure.

She feels they are caught in a river, and the river flows through them and in them. In fact she knows that she is the river, her soft inner places the headwaters of the river. And if that is so, he must be the rain and snow that feeds her. She only knows that the river is the best thing she has known. Her life before him seems almost comically unimportant in comparison. She doesn't know if she can hold on to this life, if she can always be a river, but she will stay with it as long as she can, because she loves its deep dark life, its flow and its swift shuddering currents.

She knows the dangers. Winter will come and their nest in the rose garden will fill up with snow. But even then, she knows the river will still be part of her, cold and slow under a layer of heavy ice, but ready to flow again in a season of warmth and rain.

SHE forces herself to remember David. She has kept his image alive since he was reported missing in the third year of the war. She has had difficulty lately seeing that image and has started to suspect why. She is afraid to compare him to Tom. He bore comparison with Arnold easily enough, but the notion of his perfection begins to fall apart when she thinks of Tom.

Without meaning to, she begins to understand many things that have never occurred to her before. She sees that David was only an untried boy when he went to war, and she was an untried girl. The years he spent in university while she waited for him in her father's house only delayed the time when he should have become a man. She sees that she has not yet forgiven him for going away, although it was never really his choice. His own parents expected it of him. It doesn't matter; she has blamed him for leaving her alone in the house with Homer, and for the long years of nursing Homer through his last illness.

Now she thinks she may be forgiving him at last. As she does so, his face and body fade out of her memory. She is forgetting the boy who was lost, forgetting the girl.

ARNOLD is afraid. They have not talked about the baby Edith is going to have. He's tired and sick, but he has to make himself think about it. How did she get a baby started? She almost never leaves the house. She has the groceries sent in. Hardly anyone visits them. Even the doctor has stopped coming, since he doesn't know what's wrong with Arnold and therefore also doesn't know what to do for him. If only Arnold could show some small sign of improvement, he could get the doctor interested again. If the doctor would come, he could consult him about Edith.

The thought of consulting anyone about Edith fills him with fear. Edith wouldn't like it, especially if they hadn't talked about it first. He wants to talk to her, but he doesn't know how. He knows women don't get pregnant by themselves, except perhaps in the case of the Virgin Mary, but at the same time, he can't think of a good explanation. He hasn't had sex with her for many months, that much he's sure of. Or did she come to him late one night, when he was too sleepy to fully realize or later remember it? Did she softly tease and stroke him until he was ready for her? Did she straddle him and take him inside her? Was that how it was done? He can't remember such a thing, but he finds the idea comforting and strangely exciting. Edith has never done anything like that, not that he can remember. But perhaps it happened, and that is why the thought of it pleases him like a memory.

She is getting rounder in front. Other people must be aware of it, the few that actually see her. That Ransome woman has come for tea, surely she'd notice a thing like that. Surely she'd wonder about it, with him sick in bed.

Each day he tells himself he must ask Edith about it, and each day he fails. She has such a confidence to her, such a boldness when she washes him or helps him turn in the bed. The warm strength in her fingers seems to give his own limbs a new vigour. She stands before him like a firm young tree, spreading, flourishing. How can he ask her how she comes to be pregnant? It seems too preposterous for words.

On Halloween she helps the children dress up and takes them out for treats. Lockwood she's dressed as Robin Hood, in a leather vest over a forest green shirt, with a little bow and a satin quiver full of tiny arrows. Eleanor she's done up as Little Red Riding Hood, with a charming scarlet cloak and dozens of tiny ringlets all over her head. Arnold thinks she looks almost pretty. Edith presents the results of her handiwork with a proud look, as if she's turned out to be better than she'd expected at the craft of mothering.

It snows that night, after they're all back safe inside, and in the morning Edith tells him there's ice on the river. When she comes into the room with his tea and toast, he looks at her in her yellow sweater that rounds gently over her belly and sets off her auburn hair, and finds that he can now speak.

"You're going to have a baby."

"Yes," she says matter-of-factly, as if satisfying an unimportant but perfectly natural curiosity.

"How?" he asks. "How did it happen?"

"In the usual way, I expect," she says, fluffing his pillows and helping him sit up. "Shall I fix your tea?"

He nods and watches as she adds milk and sugar, stirring them in with great thoroughness. He is fascinated by her grace and concentration, and then by her evident satisfaction when he drinks the tea. He decides he must come at the main question by indirection.

"When will it be due, do you think?"

"Oh, some time in March, probably, whenever it's ready. You know how babies are."

He doesn't know. He tries to concentrate on the meaning of what she's told him.

"So you've been pregnant since spring? Since May or June?"

"Something like that," she says. "It's so hard to know exactly. So hard to keep track."

She watches him expectantly, then when he seems puzzled, looks pointedly at the toast. He takes a bite and tastes the delicious flavour of sugar and cinnamon. He feels tears in his eyes, tears of gratitude that she's made it specially for him. She sees that he likes it and is pleased.

"But Edith," he hears himself say, "I don't see how that could be. I was so sick then. I mean, we didn't..." He stops, embarrassed.

"Didn't we?" she says, and looks right into his eyes. And it seems to him that he knows for a certainty two separate and quite opposite things. That Edith has gone with another man, and that Edith has come to his room late one night and crept under the covers beside him. It is quite extraordinary, but he can almost remember it.

"Did we not?" she says playfully and picks up a piece of toast and munches on it companionably. "Well, I certainly am going to have a baby. Even Maisie Ransome noticed. You know what I told her? I told her how pleased we are."

"You told her that?"

"Certainly I did. And I told her what we're going to name the baby."

"Did you now?" he asks. "And what are we going to name the baby?"

"We're going to call her Tira. It's such a wonderful sound."

"It's going to be a girl, is it, Edith?"

"Oh yes," she says.

Arnold feels something slipping away from him, something he can't quite put his finger on. At the same time he feels that Edith has spoken the truth. He is pleased. She looks so beautiful this way. And he likes babies. A little girl, Tira. That would be nice.

THE days are all right. She has so much energy now, flowing out of her. It starts around the place where the baby is growing and radiates through her and out her body by the same path the baby will take when she's born. With the first two pregnancies, she was tired beyond imagining, tired as a stone, but now she can do everything she has to do. She finds she is good at a remarkable number of things. She is even kind to Eleanor, and sees the child warming up a little, hesitant, but wanting to love this new Mother. This is the only guilt she feels: about Eleanor, not about Arnold. She's looking after him; he has no cause to complain. She is gentle with him, glad to be of help. She doesn't see how he could be dissatisfied with that. She even thinks he may be getting better. She's pleased about that, but it doesn't really affect her.

The nights are not all right. At night she is caught in the river that is really herself, feels it swirling around her. The river cannot flow, cannot find the channels to release its power. Sometimes she touches her body to find a release, to ease the relentless power of the river. But she never stops wanting him to come to her, as he did in the summer, although the feelings in her body are not the same now. Having made a baby with him, a part of her is sealed off from him. She has read that during pregnancy the opening of the cervix forms a mucus plug to prevent any more babies getting started, and this is the outward sign of her being sealed. But she still wants his touch, wants to take him inside her again and again, and even that would barely hold the river.

She has sent him away. She imagines him in his bachelor's house, lighting his cookstove, cooking his food, washing his clothes, and she thinks she will go mad. She thinks she is mad. One night he comes to the door, very late. He looks desperate, with dark smudges under his eyes as if he hasn't slept for a long time. She takes him in, and they make love on the thick living room rug all the night long. If either of the children comes down, there will be nothing she can do about it. She doesn't think Arnold can hear anything from his room, but she can't think how anyone could sleep in the presence of the appalling energy the two of them have loosed in the house.

In the morning he is gone and she is lying on the rug, and then Homer is there in the big plush armchair, his look of hatred and scorn corroding his face.

"Well, Edith, I always said you were a worthless slut. But last night's little performance confounds even me."

"Does it?" she says. And she feels a smile spreading over her lips, feels its delicious warmth. And as she smiles, he is fading, right there in front of her, a look of alarm in his eyes. She laughs out loud, gathers up her scattered clothes.

BY Christmas the doctor confirms two things. The baby is coming some time in March. And Arnold is getting better. The doctor actually examines Edith at home now, when he comes to see Arnold. If he has any questions about the baby's provenance, he keeps them to himself; and the amount of irony he allows into his eyes is not beyond what she can tolerate. Edith tells the doctor that anticipation of the new baby is helping Arnold recover, giving him something to focus on. On Christmas day, Arnold comes downstairs for the first time since his illness began, and Edith is pleased to have her family around her, her three children as it seems to her.

By the time the baby is due, Arnold is up and about, talking about getting back to work. His partner comes over to discuss the business of the law firm, and Edith sees how pleased he is that Arnold can once more offer the cogent arguments and subtle opinions that are his chief skill in life. One day she finds him in his room, polishing his dress shoes and then saddle-soaping his briefcase.

As the baby gathers her strength to be born, a great calm possesses Edith. She is tired at last, but still gets through her days, taking things more slowly. She sends Arnold's suits to the cleaners, takes his white shirts, which have grown yellowed and stale hanging in the closet, and washes, starches, and irons them afresh. She arranges for a hairdresser to come in and cut his hair. One morning, without anything being said, Arnold appears at the breakfast nook neatly dressed in suit and tie. He eats his breakfast, kisses her cheek, and leaves for work, walking the two blocks to the bus, as though he's never stopped doing it.

The baby comes on a fierce, windy day in March. She keeps the light labour at bay all morning, tidying the house and making a casserole for dinner. After lunch she runs down the block to arrange for Maisie Ransome to look after the children after school, and then she calls a taxi to take her to the hospital. She asks a nurse to call Arnold. Before he can come after work, she has delivered a baby girl, just as she'd predicted, a pretty red-haired baby she calls Tira.

After dinner Arnold visits her in her private room, all smiles in his clean suit and starched white shirt. A nurse brings in the baby and places her in his arms, and he is instantly enchanted. He talks of the new shawls and rattles and silver cups and knitted booties she will need. Edith is amused, but also pleased, to see him so transported. She herself is so well that the next day, before anyone can protest, she gets dressed and wraps the child in a receiving blanket, then calls a taxi and goes home.

Maisie Ransome, preparing a lunch of vegetable soup and cheese sandwiches is amazed to see her. When Edith gives her the baby to hold, she can see how impressed Maisie is, can see that she would like to have a baby like Tira, too. Edith cannot help but triumph. Soon her pleasure and her triumph drive Maisie Ransome home, because it is not pleasant to be around untempered triumph.

Homer waits till Maisie leaves before he appears. Either it is a rare display of tact, or there is something about the presence of outsiders that makes it hard for him to materialize. In any case he waits until Edith has cleared up the lunch things and sent the children back to school. Only then does she dive into the double bed that is all hers now, taking Tira with her. Homer stands over the bed. With a great effort, Edith subdues her triumph and simply holds the baby up for him to look at. She sees the bitterness drain from his face as he looks at her little girl. For the first time she can remember, he has no words; without effort or planning, she has finally vanquished him. She cannot help but triumph anew, but the triumph is less bitter than she would have expected. Forgiving or forgetting are not possible for them; but at the same time, unrelenting hatred is melting away. She has no room for it now, and he is utterly overthrown.

Homer comes to the head of the bed and looks down at her, tears in his eyes. He bends and presses a kiss on her cheek, soft like the touch of a moth's wing.

"Goodbye, Edith," he says. He walks to the door, stopping to turn and look at them one last time, and then he is gone. She knows she will never see him again.

WHEN the man who works for Hayashi comes to her door in the spring, she asks him in for tea. She shows him baby Tira and lets him hold her. The baby laughs when he picks her up, and he smiles a slow, amazed smile. He understands that she is his baby and is astounded that this has happened to him. He would like to have her live with him, but he has never looked after a child, and anyway he can see that Edith would never let her go. Edith is quite kind to him and doesn't treat him like a hired gardener at all. But now he sees her in a new way: as a wife and mother, as one of the well-off women he never expected to know. Last summer they were just man and woman. He had something she'd never known and suddenly found she wanted.

She chats on to him and clucks absently at the baby, supreme in her mother's role, and he can hardly believe there was a time when she needed him. She doesn't need him now. She still has the bloom on her of her triumphant motherhood, although he can see in the daylight how she has fine lines around her eyes and the first strands of grey in her auburn hair. He has come to the house wanting to go on as before, prepared to argue with her if need be, but argument now seems pointless. She no longer seems available to him, no longer open even to conversation. She could be any woman showing off a new baby to a family friend.

They have never really talked before, not for such a long time. His way of talking is simple but not stupid, but her way is a way of not talking. He has never met with it close up before, and never for more than a few moments. He is stunned by the perfection of her manner, like a wall with no opening anywhere, and a shiny hard surface.

And yet everything is acknowledged; they both know this is his child. Perhaps she will even let him visit again, see the child as she grows up. He does not feel anger toward her, although he understands that she will never love him again. He is glad of their time together, but he thinks that maybe she has taken something from him, something valuable. Before, his life seemed a pleasant and well-crafted thing, something he managed well. Now his life and thoughts are more complicated, and he has lost the thing that made such complexity seem worthwhile.

They finish the tea, and he sees that she would like him to go. He imagines coming to clean up the yard and put in the garden for her, then immediately sees it isn't possible.

+++

AS the child changes shape from a baby into a toddler with desires of her own and words to express them, Edith slowly eases back into something like her old self. The child, Tira, comes to seem a little more like an ordinary child, while her husband, Arnold, picks up a little more animation as he goes forward with his rediscovered career. Edith supports him in his career and continues to overindulge her son, Lockwood. She moves into middle age, outwardly the cool and controlled lady Arnold married. She hires a new cleaning woman and a gardener and buys a few pieces of new furniture for the house. Some years she forgets, but usually around the time of Tira's birthday, she invites the man who works for Hayashi over for afternoon tea, so that he's still there when the children come home from school. Over the years she watches as his hair turns from brown to grey, as a slightly puzzled expression creeps onto his face and then sets there.

Homer never comes back and she forgets about David, her sweetheart who was lost in the war. She imagines the neighbours sitting in their houses and occasionally speaking of her. They probably think nothing has changed. The riverbank is falling away, a little more each year, but she believes it will last until her children are grown and gone, until her husband is dead and gone, and as long as she has need of this strip of land to hold her house above the water.

Diamond Grill

FRED WAH

(excerpts)

IN THE DIAMOND, at the end of a long green vinyl aisle between booths of chrome, Naugahyde and Formica, are two large swinging wooden doors, each with a round hatch of face-sized window. Those kitchen doors can be kicked with such a slap they're heard all the way up to the soda fountain. On the other side of the doors, hardly audible to the customers, echoes a jargon of curses, jokes, and cryptic orders. Stack a hots! Half a dozen fry! Hot beef san! Fingers and tongues all over the place jibe and swear You mucka high!—Thloong you! And outside, running through and around the town, the creeks flow down to the lake with, maybe, a spring thaw. And the prairie sun over the mountains to the east, over my family's shoulders. The journal journey tilts tight-fisted through the gutter of the book, avoiding a place to start—or end. Maps don't have beginnings, just edges. Some frayed and hazy margin of possibility, absence, gap. Shouts in the kitchen. Fish an! Side a fries! Over easy! On brown! I pick up an order and turn, back through the doors, whap! My foot registers more than its own imprint, starts to read the stain of memory.

Thus: a kind of heterocellular recovery reverberates through the busy body, from the foot against that kitchen door on up the leg into the torso and hands, eyes thinking straight ahead, looking through doors and languages, skin recalling its own reconnaissance, cooked into the steamy food, replayed in the folds of elsewhere, always far away, tunnelling through the centre of the Earth, mouth saying can't forget, mouth saying what I want to know can feed me, what I don't can bleed me.

THOSE doors take quite a beating. Brass sheet nailed across the bottom. *Whap!* What a way to announce your presence. You kind of explode, going through one door onto the customers, through the other onto the cooks. It's so nifty when I discover how they work: you're supposed to go through only on the right-hand side and that's how you don't get hit not looking when someone steamrollers through the other door at full clip with a load of dirty dishes or food spread out along their hands and arms. *Boom!* You'd think the glass portholes'd fall out of the doors, but they're built to take it. Inch-and-a-half varnished fir plywood with big spring hinges. When I first start working in the cafe I love to wallop that brass as hard as I can. But my dad warns me early to not make such a noise because that disturbs the customers, so I come up with a way of placing my heel close to the bottom and then rocking the foot forward to squeeze the door open in a silent rush of air as I come through on the fly. But when we get real busy, like at lunchtime, all the waiters and waitresses, including my dad, will let loose in the shape and cacophony of busy-ness, the kicker of desire hidden in the isochronous torso, a necessary dance, a vital percussion, a critical persuasion, a playful permission fast and loud, *WhapBamBoom!*—feels so good.

FAMOUS Chinese Restaurant is the name of a small, strip-mall Chinese cafe a friend of mine eats at once in a while. We laugh at the innocent pretentiousness of the name, Famous.

But then I think of the pride with which my father names the Diamond Grill. For him, the name is neither innocent nor pretentious. The Diamond, he proudly regales the banquet at the grand opening, is the most modern, up-to-date restaurant in the interior of B.C. The angled design of the booths matches the angles of a diamond, and the diamond itself stands for good luck. We hope this new restaurant will bring good luck for all our families and for this town. Eat! Drink! Have a good time!

Almost everything in Chinese stands for good luck, it seems. You're not supposed to use words that might bring bad luck. Aunty Ethel is very upset when we choose a white casket for my father's funeral. She says That no good! White mean death, bad luck!

So I understand something of the dynamics of naming and desire when I think of the names of some Chinese cafes in my family's history. The big one, of course, is the Elite, which we, with no disrespect for the Queen's English, always pronounce the eee-light. In fact, everyone in town pronounces it that way. My dad works in an Elite in Swift Current and that's what he names his cafe in Trail when we move out to B.C. Elite is a fairly common

Chinese cafe name in the early fifties, but not anymore. I see one still on Edmonton Trail in Calgary and I know of one in Revelstoke. I like the resonant undertone in the word, *elite:* the privilege to choose. In the face of being denied the right to vote up until 1949, I smile a little at the recognition by the Chinese that choice is, indeed, a privilege.

Other names also play on the margins of fantasy and longing. Grampa Wah owns the Regal in Swift Current, and just around the corner are the Venice and the Paris. Just as Chiang escapes to Taiwan, my father gets into the New Star in Nelson.

During the fifties and sixties, coincidental with the rise of Canadian nationalism, we find small-town cafes with names like the Canadian, Canada Chinese Takeout, and, in respect of *Hockey Night in Canada,* the All Star. Along the border: American-Canadian Cafe and the Ambassador.

One could read more recent trends such as Bamboo Terrace, Heaven's Gate, Pearl Seafood Restaurant, and the Mandarin as indicative of both the recognized exoticization in Orientalism as well as, possibly, a slight turn, a deference, pride and longing for the homeland.

Perhaps we might regard more concretely what resonates for us when we walk into places like White Dove Cafe and Hotel in Mossbank, Saskatchewan, or the even-now famous Disappearing Moon Cafe, 50 East Pender Street, Vancouver, B.C.

ON the edge of Centre. Just off Main. Chinatown. The cafes, yes, but farther back, almost hidden, the ubiquitous Chinese store—an unmoving stratus of smoke, dusky and quiet, clock ticking. Dark brown wood panelling, some porcelain planters on the windowsill, maybe some goldfish. Goldfish for Gold Mountain men. Not so far, then, from the red carp of their childhood ponds. Brown skin stringy salt-and-pepper beard polished bent knuckles and at least one super-long fingernail for picking. Alone and on the edge of their world, far from the centre, no women, no family. This kind of edge in race we only half suspect as edge. A gap, really. Hollow.

I wander to it, tagging along with my father or with a cousin, sent there to get a jar of some strange herb or balm from an old man who forces salted candies on us or digs for a piece of licorice dirtied with grains of tobacco from his pocket, the background of old men's voices sure and argumentative within this grotto. Dominoes clacking. This store, part of a geography, mysterious to most, a migrant haven edge of outpost, of gossip, bavardage, foreign tenacity. But always in itself, on the edge of some great fold.

In a room at the back of the Chinese store, or above, like a room fifteen feet over the street din in Vancouver Chinatown, you can hear, amplified through the window, the click-clacking of mah-jong pieces being shuffled over the tabletops. The voices from up there or behind the curtain are hot-tempered, powerful, challenging, aggressive, bickering, accusatory, demeaning, bravado, superstitious, bluffing, gossipy, serious, goading, letting off steam, ticked off, fed up, hot under the collar, hungry for company, hungry for language, hungry for luck, edgy.

I hardly ever go into King's Family Restaurant because, when it comes to Chinese cafes and Chinatowns, I'd rather be transparent. Camouflaged enough so they know I'm there but can't see me, can't get to me. It's not safe. I need a clear coast for a getaway. Invisible. I don't know who I am in this territory and maybe don't want to. Yet I love to wander into Toronto's Chinatown and eat tofu and vegetables at my favourite barbecue joint and then meander indolently through the crowds, listening to the tones and watching the dark eyes, the black hair. Sometimes in a store, say, I'm picking up a pair of new kung-fu sandals and the guy checks my Mastercard as I sign and he says Wah! You Chinese? Heh heh heh! because he knows I'm not. Physically, I'm racially transpicuous and I've come to prefer that mode.

I want to be there but don't want to be seen being there. By the time I'm ten I'm only white. Until 1949 the few Chinese in my life are relatives and old men. Very few Chinese kids my age. After '49, when the Canadian government rescinds its Chinese Exclusion Act, a wave of young Chinese immigrate to Canada. Nelson's Chinese population visibly changes in the early fifties. In a few years there are enough teenage Chinese kids around to form not only an association, the Nelson Chinese Youth Association, but also a basketball team. And they're good, too. Fast, smart. I play on the junior high school team, and when the NCYA team comes to play us, I know a lot of the Chinese guys. But my buddies at school call them chinks and geeks and I feel a little embarrassed and don't talk much with the Chinese kids. I'm white enough to get away with it and that's what I do.

But downtown, working in the cafe, things are different. Some of the young guys start working at our cafe, and my dad's very involved with helping them all settle into their new circumstances. He acts as an interpreter for a lot of the legal negotiations. Everyone's trying to reunite with long-lost relatives. Anyway, I work alongside some of these new Chinese and become friends.

Shu brings his son over around 1953 and Lawrence is in the cafe business for the rest of his working life. Lawrence and I work together in the Diamond until I leave small-town Nelson for university at the coast. We're good friends. Even today, as aging men, we always exchange greetings whenever we meet on the street. But I hardly ever go into his cafe.

So now, standing across the street from King's Family Restaurant, I know I'd love to go in there and have a dish of beef and greens, but he would know me, he would have me clear in his sights, not Chinese but stained enough by genealogy to make a difference. When Lawrence and I work together, him just over from China, he's a boss's son and I'm a boss's son. His pure Chineseness and my impure Chineseness don't make any difference to us in the cafe. But I've assumed a dull and ambiguous edge of difference in myself; the hyphen always seems to demand negotiation.

I decide, finally, to cross the street. I push myself through the door, and his wife, Fay, catches me with the corner of her eye. She doesn't say anything and I wonder if she recognizes me. The white waitress takes my order and I ask if Lawrence is in the kitchen. He is, she says.

I go through Lawrence's kitchen door like I work there. I relish the little kick the door is built to take. He's happy to see me and stops slicing the chicken on the chopping block, wipes his hands on his apron, and shakes my hand. How's your mother? Whatchyou doing here? How's Ernie and Donnie? Family, that's what it is. The politics of the family.

He says something to the cook, a young guy. Then he turns to me and says Hey, Freddy, did you know this is your cousin? He's from the same area near Canton. His name is Quong. Then in Chinese, he gives a quick explanation to Quong; no doubt my entire Chinese family history. Lawrence smiles at me like he used to when we were kids: he knows something I don't. I suffer the negative capability of camouflage.

How many cousins do I have, I wonder. Thousands maybe. How could we recognize one another? Names.

The food, the names, the geography, the family history—the filiated dendrita of myself displayed before me. I can't escape, and don't want to, for a moment. Lawrence's kitchen seems one of the surest places I know. But then after we've exchanged our mutual family news and I've eaten a wonderful dish of tofu and vegetables, back outside, on the street, all my ambivalence gets covered over, camouflaged by a safety net of class and colourlessness—the racism within me that makes and consumes that neutral (white) version of myself, that allows me the sad privilege of being, in this white white world, not the target but the gun.

YOU never taught me how, but I remember your frown, particularly that, your frown, whenever you confronted something new in your world, like our basement, how to move around the furnace, or a gun, how to aim it, or logging, say, how Tak Mori's caulk boots sound on the running board of his deep green Fargo pickup, or, better still, your scowl of incredulity at how to

from The Banff Centre for the Arts

gulp quickly Granny Erickson's Christmas pickled herring while her beak-nosed challenge sat in the kitchen chair opposite your dark bird-eyed defiance (oof dah), or when Betty Goodman ordered stewed oysters for lunch and you got me to wait on her while you went to the can and puked, all those puzzled moments in the new world when your brown brow squinched up while you translated vectors or politesse or measurement or celebration or strange foods or weird Europeans or, through gold-rimmed reading glasses, the day's page 1 world wars, page 2 Baker Street, page 5 sports, *Nelson Daily News* spread out over the grey Formica tabletop in the back booth of the Diamond Grill, all these moments nothing but your river of truth, fiction, and history, nothing but the long nights of a Chinese winter waiting for the promised new/old world of mothers fathers brothers sisters, river of ocean, river of impossible passing, too large and formidable even later spinning your days out under Elephant Mountain, such encounters with possibility criss-crossed on your forehead, indeed, your whole body wired taut for daily brushes with what, the foreign, that jailed Juan de Fuca immigrant in your eyes as you looked, now look out to the sea this sentence makes, puzzled, cryptic, wild, bewildered, ex'd and perplexed thought so far away and other, but then your lower lip bites up under your teeth, hands, fingers, eyes, laughing, how, to ...

But then you by now, like everyone else in town, we've all, walked past the sign in the window of the Club Cafe—

SPECIAL CHRISTMAS DINNER

$1.50

ALL THE TRIMMINGS

—the same Christmas dinner Sammy Wong has cooked every year since he bought the Club in 1938 from his cousin, who went back to China to find a girl. Sammy didn't. Never bought or brought a wife. Only girls he knows are his waitresses, and Edna has been there the longest; she's a steamboat and makes sure Sammy keeps the place tip-top. She pretty much runs the front of the cafe. So, even the sign—she probably made that, a few sprigs of holly coloured with a green wax crayon and "All the Trimmings" in red—sits now getting stained from the condensation running down the window in the heated steamy and smoky cafe. The only thing Edna doesn't like about his Christmas dinner, and she tells him, too, is that special cranberry sauce he makes every year. You're not gonna make that again, it's too tart, the jellied canned stuff is nicer, sweeter, darker. Sammy just glares at her over the stove. He thinks, Tart? All the time I make this—what's a matter with you?

Just across the street, the New Grand Hotel has a sprayed-icing window stencilled with "Season's Greetings." Its dining room will be closed Christmas Day, but for New Year's Eve the hotel is holding a gala banquet and dance. For this, hotel magnate Dominic Rissuti, the cigar-smoking rotund president of the Columbo Lodge and local nickel Mafioso, has hired the Melodaires, who do mostly popular songs like "Mocking Bird Hill." (Their saxophonist, Lefty Black, regularly swoons a lot of the town's women with his lilting rendition of "Deep Purple.") For eight dollars a couple you get a sit-down dinner with a choice of ham, roast beef, or grilled salmon steak, a bar that opens at 6:30 (drinks three for a dollar), noisemakers, and a glass of special punch to welcome in the New Year. All this come-on appears on a big display ad that has bubbles rolling out of glasses on page 2 of the *Nelson Daily News*. The only problem Rissuti has run into is getting a liquor licence, because New Year's Eve falls on a Sunday this year. In Al's Barber Shop next door, he complains to some of the guys, That goddamned police chief says he won't sign the licence. What do I gotta do? Go to the mayor?

Eadie Petrella, the owner of the Shamrock Grill (gauze curtains, no jukebox), never could figure out how Lok Pon managed to get his turkey so moist (fifteen years cooking in logging camps), but what Lok remembers is that first Christmas he worked for Eadie she came into the kitchen and watched over him all morning garumphing around while he filled and trussed and basted, no smile, no talk, particularly the no talk, she usually talks non-stop, at least in the kitchen to the waitresses, always babbling something he can't understand anyway, so now, after six years of cooking at the Shamrock, he watches her cocked over his stove testing his gravy, smacking her lips, eyeing the three birds he's cooked racked over the warming oven, and her eyes pinch slightly with an *Mmmm* (he knows it's good) and she turns away with a haughty Better get those Brussels sprouts started! not to him but to his half-wit helper and dishwasher so he's left standing there by the steam table with lots to do yet and curses her under his breath—You mucka high!

Except, by the time the holidays are over, we've all, even at the Diamond Grill where the plum puddings with rum and maple sauce continue in high demand, we've had enough of turkey and ham and stuffing and mashed potatoes and know that the real gung hay fa choy Chinese New Year celebration sometime in January will bring on the Diamond's legendary Chinese banquet with local high muckamucks like the mayor, a few aldermen, the police chief and fire chief, steadies like the early-morning pensioners and CPR shift workers and cab drivers. Even the waitresses set places for their husbands or boyfriends in the booths disguised now with white tablecloths and dishes of quarters wrapped in red paper and lichee nuts, both chopsticks and cutlery, bottles of scotch and rye, this once-a-year feast tops the whole season as far as I'm concerned starting even with bird's nest soup and then the dishes come too fast, barbecue pork, chicken and almond chop suey (incredible washed down with Canada Dry ginger ale), beef and green pepper, snow peas, fried rice, steamed rice, deep-fried rock cod, abalone, jumbo shrimp and black beans finished off with ice cream or Jell-O and lots of leftover Christmas cake and a few speeches, even the mayor's toast to the shy Chinese cooks who stand just outside the swinging kitchen doors in their dirty aprons, faces glazed with sweat. Shu Ling Mar the chief cook looks to you and says something in Chinese and you translate He says please come back again you're all welcome, lots more in the kitchen! Then somehow, all that mess disappears and the floors washed by six the next morning when you open up.

Then what is that taste, mulled memory, kitchen sediment. Your hands and body fill, pour, stir. Dark brown eyes the Aleutian land bridge over the stove—and dancing. How do I make your tangy sauce for seafood cocktail so good my mouth waters in this sentence saying ketchup horseradish lemon Tabasco, maybe a dash of soy. Something gave pure zip. Your shoulders. I thought the sharp red bottle in the top cupboard. Reach. Was crabmeat. Even something creamy crunchy celery tomatoed and all that spooned into short glasses, fluted, what I thought were like sundae dishes first lined with a lettuce leaf, a few dozen made up in advance and kept on a shelf in the walk-in cooler. I'd sneak one. Or two. Boston cream pie on a slack and snowy Sunday afternoon. Where did that taste for such zip Charlie-chim-chong-say-wong-lung-chung come to your mouth in a shot shout as you clicked your tongue, eyes sparkled if it was too hot, too much kick, they'd water a bit and you'd cut the sauce with what, HP, or maybe that other dark brown steak sauce, A-1, under the counters by the cutlery trays. Not cayenne. No, that was never your spice. Chili powder. Some say you looked more Mexican than Chinese and right here on this page fiction wouldn't be awry making you out Philippino. So, of course, chili or Tabasco. But of yours, something with more smack than gut, not pepper, further forward on the palate to match the sea brine but with bang, Oooo-Eee, the boot to begin every banquet and Chinese New Year. That now then is winter lingulate imprint in December. Under the breath. Just outside. Massive dark hole swirl of Oriental nebulae, just outside. Or just next door, the mayor, the pool hall, anyone else, everyone else. And all time. What's a matter? You just smiled, laughed, and said Pretty good gung hey, eh, Freddy? Fa choy! That's how.

Wedding in Brighton Beach

EMIL A. DRAITSER

BRIGHTON BEACH WEDDINGS are such sumptuous extravaganzas, each could be the last on Earth: a wedding to end all weddings. Every time it seems like the Earth's energy has finally been depleted, and no one will ever again try to marry; how could anyone beat the celebration still winding down even as we speak? In the end, why live in this great big world, gentlemen—former comrades—if not to lavish such nuptials upon your children and grandchildren! So live it up with little Tanya and little Misha—you can relax later. Your last worldly concerns will have been satisfied ... And don't forget, the wedding you organize is also a notch in our memory of you. Make such a splash that afterwards, sighing and shaking their heads, everyone will remember Zuskind: What a man! What a wedding he threw his granddaughter! And such people have to die!

I was at such a wedding. Let me testify ...

1.

THEY say that nothing surprises America. Brighton Beach is an exception. Brighton, a.k.a. Little Odessa, is the fruit of an unprecedented transcontinental migration taking place right before our eyes, a huge city carrying itself here through the air, not a quantum of its soul lost. And what a city it is, still—more like a legend in the making! Set out now from Moscow for the south, for the Black Sea, and climb a steppe hill, to view the gulf from its northern shoreline. You'll see that the town no longer exists, the town where, once, a sixty-year-old arrival from Murmansk would feel a sudden lifting of his spirit and an unexpected desire to live another forty years. The facades of buildings designed by fugitive French architects on Deribasovskaya Street and Richelieu Boulevard and in the former Palais Royale still charm with their faded beauty, like aging Parisian women. Along splendid Pushkin Street autumn still unrolls carpeted pedestrian paths touched by ochre and vermilion, woven of chestnut, maple, and plane leaves. And the sea waves along the most delicate beaches still sneak up to your feet like playfully threatening puppies mistaking them for house slippers.

But the living city itself is no longer there. It's gone. It's clambered aboard TU-104 jets. Or onto trains that rushed across the former Soviet border and through clean little Viennese streets, Roman stations, and Tyrrhenian resort towns. Dragging suitcases and trunks stuffed with frying pans, pots, packages of porridge for infants (on the road anything can happen, including unplanned children), and little pillows needed to steady the unruly head of the traveller trying to fall asleep in foreign lands, this city gradually, grain by grain, settled in the southernmost protuberance of Brooklyn. Also near a huge water hulk—only not just another sea, but a rank higher—the ocean.

2.

WEDDINGS in Brighton take place in restaurants. Naturally, in the largest and most fashionable. The king of them all is the National (in honour of its unsurpassable Moscow namesake and by virtue of tradition, pronounced not just any way, but with a French intonation). Of course there are smaller restaurants and cafés in Brighton that seat a good hundred, let's say, even a hundred fifty. But a Brightonite would consider it indecent to make a wedding in any one of those. It would be like getting married in a snack bar.

Debts are heavy in Brighton. Everybody is everybody else's relative. Distant or close—among emigrants the distinction is meaningless. Someone may be only distantly related, but he lives nearby—so he's considered "close." Especially when it comes to weddings. And so sometimes you end up at two celebrations in a week. You ask your inviter, "Will there be a lot of people?" and expect the usual modest response: "Ah, what're you talking about? How many relatives have I got here! Only my own folks, a narrow circle." Which means, maybe, three hundred or so.

As a rule, nobody carries presents to the newlyweds. A bunch of flowers for the bride, yes, but no more than that. New times, new customs. With one arm a guest shakes the groom's hand, with the other he slips into his pocket unnoticed, as if into a mail slot, an envelope with a cheque. Everyone knows what the Russian restaurants charge per person. That's why, in the end, no one loses, despite the scale of the event—the more the merrier.

When you first peek into the restaurant hall, you see nothing but flowers. Posts of bouquets like frozen explosions, wafting a heart-stopping mixture of fragrances, hang over the guests and threaten to topple down. What smell so sweet are peonies, the favourite of Brightonites, surprisingly like Black Sea women in sumptuousness, spice, and beauty. Stalks of gladioli with little pink petal ears barely emerging from tight buds push upward timidly through the heaps of peonies—the way the arms of the Brightonites' daughters, the teenaged girls of an already new, American vintage, reach nervously for the shoulders of their young men for a first kiss.

You loiter awhile in the lobby and greet the person who invited you—some distant uncle on the girl's side. He might have arrived just two days before from Russia with bag and baggage, still somewhat befuddled and not sure himself he knows the bride. (He's last seen her as a pot-bellied infant with one tooth in her mouth in his grandniece's arms, during a short visit from Dushanbe in Tiraspol, where he'd come for the wedding of the son of his second cousin on his mother's side.) Then, inching sideways to your seat, you try your best to show that the food interests you only up to a point—more than anything, naturally, you're just overwhelmed with happiness that your relative is getting married.

At a Brighton wedding you expect not just to "proceed to reception," but to *live it up:* at a wedding you're to *eat, drink,* and *dance.* Now pay attention—that's eat, and not "dine" (if it's more toward evening). And certainly not—"have supper," which, back home, had meant a modest portion of blintzes with a glass of kefir or tea and a small sandwich the size of a beer mug coaster. None of this ascetic stupidity will be tolerated here. A true wedding—where the eating itself is essential to the ritual—is no place to "have a bite," snack, or, God forbid, "grab something on the run."

Once you cast your eyes over a Brighton wedding table, you understand: sitting down was easy, getting up will be harder. Say so long to your diet—as long as you're in Brighton, you won't see it again! If you're in the mood for a long walk, try searching the countless food shops for fat-free (or even low-fat) milk or cheese, or skinned chicken (evidently thus disfigured as punishment for some frightful misdeed). You won't find such "ersatz food" here, where they respect human, earthly pleasures. Tell someone you're "on a diet," and his or her eyes will moisten in sympathy. It's clear you haven't long to live.

3.

YOUR table is so crammed with platters and saucers, plates and little jam dishes and wineglasses and shot glasses and goblets, that you can't even see the tablecloth. Surveying the possibilities spread out before you, you realize your life is not yet over. The best is yet to come. Behold: a surge of earthly fruits, there for no other purpose than to offer you the endless energy of the sun, embodied in the best of its creations. In anticipation of this new landmark in your life, you secretly undo the shirt button near your belt. And one on your chest as well—there has to be room for your heart to expand, for at this moment it wants everything in the world, except to rest.

In ordinary American restaurants the food is arranged primitively, in horizontal order. Not so in the Russian restaurants of Brighton Beach. The plates making up this fantastic feast, like cars in Manhattan's municipal garages, tower in many-leveled pyramids. The upper tier is loaded with the starter food. The appetizer *pirozhki,* round little pastry-pies adorned with hills of red and black caviar, should be enough to reinvigorate your interest in life. Having sampled two or three of each kind, after a proper pause you're ready for a patty of normal dimensions—that is, the size of an Odessa longshoreman's palm. As you eat, slices of cold smoked Siberian salmon glimmer from the neighbouring dish with a languid moisture and now and then catch your eye, as if to say, "We're here, don't pass us by completely, you nice former comrade."

Representing the vegetable gardens are fresh cucumbers, sliced with such deft strokes that through the translucent flesh the seeds gleam, like tiny tooth roots through the gums of infants. Nearby, cheeks puffed out, New Jersey tomatoes watch you with a single squinting yellow-grey eye. Alas, despite their decent size and excellent flavour, they're only a dim reminder of those the Black Sea emigrants are used to from childhood—Fontanski tomatoes with an odour and taste (and this every Brightonite knows!) unequalled in this world or, it's suspected, in the next.

Other tomatoes, bashfully pink, under whose fine skin the juice languorously chases round a water-level bubble, are part of a salty-sour group. There's also white and red cabbage, lightly pickled, and homemade dill pickles. (Not trusting the restaurant's specialist, the bride's grandmother has pickled them herself—so they have a fresh-made crunch.) When that's almost gone, slices of pickled watermelon are at your disposal. And if you're up for marinade, you're welcome to the little field mushrooms.

At this point, the spreading fragrance of fresh coriander and tantalizingly acute scent of *khnel'* and *sunel'* (a cilantro-like aromatic grass) announce the favourite dish of the friendly Georgian people: *satsivi,* a complex conglomeration of chicken parts in a fancy sauce. Lovers of especially sharp sensations will appreciate the cheese paste, thoroughly seasoned with garlic and embellished with slices of pineapple, served in a delicate jam dish.

Dutch cheeses, among the upper-layer foods devoid of any special fantasy, will satisfy those who consider cheese an aristocratic delicacy. There are also the thinnest slices of Swiss—for the aesthetes, who think of it more as lace for supporting a line of ivory elephants on Grandmother's sideboard than as food. And if only for the sake of a full palette, the moistly sparkling Greek feta is an honest attempt to simulate the salty sheep's milk cheese of Privoz, the famous Odessa market of bygone times.

None of this, however, has the right to call itself appetizers, *zakuski.* It's only priming—a sprinkling of gunpowder in an ancient blunderbuss—to signal the approach of real food. It's a weak roulade from a Young Pioneer bugle of school days: "Get up, get up, put on your short pants!" To wake up your body for real business. So that you'll get the hint, extrapolate, set the imagination in motion, and prepare yourself physically and morally. Something much more essential, and even grandiose, is on its way.

4.

THE aroma from the tables reaches the nostrils of the invited. The torture becomes unbearable. Meanwhile the wedding ceremony hasn't even begun. It turns out there's no one to unite the betrothed—where's the rabbi? By now a woman scolds her round-eyed, sad-faced husband so loudly that those sitting nearby can hear, "Senya, why aren't you eating! Remember your ulcer, you're not allowed to stay away from food for so long!" She smears butter on some bread, spreads out little beads of red caviar like a set of Chinese checkers. She sighs deeply, weighed down by two thoughts: first, how primitive is human nature, that says "give me food, and to hell with the dignity of the moment," and second, how hard it is to live with a sick husband. What stoicism you need, and how rarely outsiders understand the special problems of human physiology. It's easy enough for them to accuse a sick person of gluttony!

But still no sign of the rabbi. Eventually it becomes clear he's not in Hawaii, or the Virgin Islands, or the Persian Gulf region—he's not that big a schmuck! He's here—in Brighton Beach. En route from another Russian wedding. He's already welded the newlyweds together with a valiant "Mazel Tov!," already drunk another toast to their happiness and unending health, already escaped from the teeming relatives' embraces into the fresh air. And it's done him in. The flood of emotions has overcome him. In his blue Toyota he's circling the block where the guests numbering three infantry regiments await him. He's searching for, but just can't find, a parking space. Finally someone from the bride's retinue has the good sense to lie down, waving his arms and legs, on the hood of the religious servant's car. As if to assure the rabbi it's okay to calm down and leave the wheel—they'll find a little space for the car, even if they have to move the vegetable store on the corner. The guests are utterly exhausted; the knees of the young bridegroom with the first fuzz on his chin are trembling from the advancing trial of manhood; the bride herself is by now unmistakably hot to trot. So how about it, rabbi, it's no time to drag your heels!

5.

WHILE the rabbi is caught and revived, the guests, ill at ease, avoid one another's look and make short work of the upper tier of food—that is, the priming. The layer beneath is the *zakuski* proper, there to open wide the bodily locks and conduct through them with a rumble, music, and applause an ocean liner filled with the principal food, splendid in quality and unsurpassed in quantity.

First are the cold hors d'oeuvres: Russian *Olivier* salad; fresh cucumber and tomato salad with huge gypsy earrings of onions, seasoned with oil as fragrant as Ukrainian black earth; and herring with split belly and eyes fixed wide in amazement—she obviously hadn't expected such a turn in her fate. (However, the Brightonites' love for her, undiminished with the years, must be of some comfort to her. Here they address her not without an anxious quivering of the stomach—"my dear little herring!") Also turning up at the Brighton table is an honoured guest and local foundling—señor avocado. And, naturally, pickled pepper. And stuffed pepper. And of course pâté made from eggplants, seasoned with garlic and grated tomatoes, known to the entire Russian culinary world by the Odessa name "little blue ones" *(sinen'kie)*. And right there in far-sighted wisdom—prune with a walnut's cerebral hemispheres adroitly hidden inside.

Now, when the guests are warmed up, they're ready for the hot hors d'oeuvres: baby potatoes with garlic and fresh dill, swimming in little puddles of butter as sweet-smelling as alpine meadows—they are cooed over in the most gentle and voluptuous terms—"my darling dear sweet little potato!" *kartoshechka;* duck, baked with apples; carp roasted by the slice; baked pudding with mushrooms and ground beef.

The only vodka served in Brighton, let's not forget, is Swedish, with self-promoting name Absolut (no need, so to speak, to look any further). The cognac, of course, is Hennessy—anything else would be an embarrassment. (Don't even mention Napoleon!) As a chaser, there's an extract of sour cherry and red grape juice.

6.

AFTER your dip into the hors d'oeuvres, before you get down to the serious consumption, you enter the dancing circle and shake it up for a while. Recovering your breath, you pretend that nothing has really been eaten yet, and it's time to return to the table and have a nosh . . .

First the young people dance. Then, the forty- and fifty-year-olds. And finally, during the first chords of "Freilechs" and "Hava Nagila," up from their chairs spring the elderly—those who ordinarily can't move without their relatives' help.

As a breather for the audience, the orchestra kindly switches to something measured, a popular tune brought from the old country:

On the steamship the music plays,
While alone I stand on the shore,
At the sounds of the song my heart stops,
I can do nothing more.

The hall listens with particular attention. For the emigrants, the song is all too real. Though in their case there hadn't been music. Not counting the upbeat singsong about Soviet space flight wailing from the station loudspeaker, with the refrain: "Fourteen minutes to start!" At that time, "to finish" seemed more to the point. After the turmoil of the last sleepless nights, the painstaking wrapping of grandmother's silver knives to save them from the customs thieves, the incoherent conversations with friends never, in all probability, to be seen again, in the head and heart there'd been nothing but fear and hollow melancholy:

On the steamship the music plays . . .

A steamship! How about a leaky dinghy? That was more likely. The sail would flare up with a shallow ripple, the mast, threatening to fall, would creak, the wind would get behind your collar, and time and again little Regina's doll carriage would get lost. Or maybe it was the doll and not the carriage that got lost . . .

While alone I stand on the shore . . .

The rapt, reliable audience sits around the tables. Expensive Italian leather, black, harshly figure hugging, glimmers with a dull shine; the striking forms of women predominate. The naturally Mediterranean faces of the guests look surprisingly like Kabuki masks. In the solemnity of the moment the muscles of the thickly powdered cheeks are motionless, the eyes are narrowed to a slot, the lips—done in fashionable carmine tints—are pursed primly.

Gradually gathering force from a tiny trickle, soon enough the table talk turns into a powerful turbulent flow and gets in full swing. As a rule, guests know one another only slightly: as a close friend of an aunt on the groom's side, as a co-worker of a cousin on the bride's side. The usual emigrant chit-chat: "Are you here long?" "Are you well settled?" "How's your English?" "Do you need it at work?" Those who've started a business here speak of it modestly, with a slight sigh. What else could they do? In America, without the language, their former occupation—warehouse clerk—had become pointless . . .

At the table is also a woman who'd come to America, with a small child, in complete despair—not only without a husband and without the language, but without any basic survival skills. But then, out of nowhere, after a short course in something as simple as giving facials to the natives, everything, little by little, had become possible—even a trip to the terrifying homeland to see dear girlfriends. Telling her simple story, the narrator can barely restrain her love for her own hands. It turns out they're such clever little ones! Up to now they'd pretended all they could do was write phony reports from the ghostly construction sites of communism, or newspaper articles, full of feigned enthusiasm, on the gala openings of public laundries: "A joyous surprise awaits the working mothers of the Primorsky region." In a surge of gratitude that her little hands could be such good providers, she kisses them . . .

Each person at the table considers it a duty to assure the neighbours that, except on family occasions, he or she rarely gets together with emigrants in restaurants. They more often see Americans. Generally, meetings with Americans, American friends, are a topic of pride—intended, no doubt, to invoke envy.

"I beg your pardon. Excuse me, I'm in a hurry," a middle-aged lady in a pink dress with sparkling gold epaulettes on the shoulders says with a reserved dignity as she gets up. "Sorry. Not to come would have been quite awkward. They just sent a limo from Manhattan. Madonna has to go to an opening. She sent a bodyguard for me."

"Madonna?" someone says. "Which Madonna?"

The wedding deserter's eyes roll upward. "Which? Which? The singer, of course! 'No one will do,' she says, 'but the Russian manicurist Rosa.'" In America the concept of "manicurist," it turns out, is old-fashioned. On Rosa's business card it reads "Nail Artist." Maybe Salvador Dali couldn't have unfolded his fantasies on such a tiny canvas, but the Russian Rosa manages just all right.

The conversations around the table are often such in name only. Unlike in American restaurants, which are as quiet as the admitting rooms of village hospitals, at Russian affairs the guests can't communicate other than by shouting in one another's ear. The orchestra so roars that you're sure the trumpets and saxophones are only rented. But the musicians have been paid in hard currency, so let them squeeze out as much music as possible, to the last note. Even if the instruments overheat to collapse, there's nothing to worry about: the insurance will cover it.

"Your first time here?" your neighbour on the left yells in your ear.

"First!" you bark.

"Thirst? So have another drink!" he screams.

"Good idea!" you chirp.

7.

IT'S either the importance of the occasion, or his hoarseness from the previous wedding, but in trying to conduct the ceremony over the thunder of the orchestra and din of voices, the rabbi slides his voice down to the lowest possible register. His tone is inappropriately tragic. The father and mother of the couples are called. Sisters and brothers. Uncles and aunts. Nephews and nieces. First cousins and second cousins.

"What about grandmother and grandfather?" it's grumbled around the tables.

In the confusion and heat, the rabbi has indeed gotten off track.

"Grandmother Lo-o-o-o-ba and Grandfather Ro-o-o-o-va!" he trumpets.

No one hears him. The wedding is already roaring louder than a Brighton subway train shooting up from the lower depths and rumbling between heaven and earth.

"*Pyzhalusta tykha!* Silence, please!" the American rabbi yells, employing his entire store of Russian, mastered specially for Brighton weddings.

A few natives always attend the parties—usually colleagues of the bride's and groom's parents whose ideas about Russians are gleaned from two-minute television reports on world events. Watching the Brighton merriment, the American guests shout "Wow!" and go nuts. Television Russians are gloomy; they glower into the camera. But this—it's no mere wedding of recent refugees, but a spectacle, the hands-down victor in razzle-dazzle over any Olympic Games opening ceremony...

Meanwhile, the waiters (mostly Russian "tourists" with expired visas who've cramped their cheek muscles from the effort of smiling) remove the hors d'oeuvre plates to make room for the main food of the party: roasted chicken with buckwheat kasha, side of lamb, shish kebab *(shashlyk po-karski),* chicken Kiev, and chicken *tabaka* (unfurled and spread out like monks before the altar).

"Your fork! Give me your fork!!!" my round-eyed neighbour (the fellow with the ulcer) cries out. For some time there hasn't been a trace of his usual melancholy. He's addressing an American, the only one at the table, who, his first time at a Russian wedding, is smiling a smile that could mean only one thing: he's completely stupefied. Round-Eyed is convinced that even if the natives have admittedly put together not too bad a country, they still have no idea how to live. And it's up to ex-Soviet citizens like him to teach them. Judging by how events are unfolding at the table, life, undoubtedly, has turned out well. He respectfully takes the fork from the American's hand and with great drama pierces a patty, glossy with butter, that's miraculously survived from the hors d'oeuvres. He gazes at it as a lover upon a daisy and returns it to the native guest. At the sight of the butter, the American strains to conceal his horror. The round-eyed Russian's face shows the pride of the tiller—he himself grew the grain, threshed it, and baked the patty. Get a load of us, Yankees!

The native guest is an American girl's dream—more than six feet tall, handsome, with a Clark Gable moustache. A fashionable suit, two elegant rings—one silver, from his university, and the other golden, antique, apparently inherited. He's an engineer, a specialist in metallic alloys. Learning of this, Round-Eyed declares that in America you have to be either a lawyer or a doctor, or, even better, a businessman. Everything else is child's play, not serious. Engineer-schmengineer ... But it's all right, the native comrade is still young—he looks no more than thirty-five. He still has time to come to his senses and go to law school. Round-Eyed struggles with his lack of words for imparting this good advice to the American.

"Well, well," he sighs. "I should be his age, with his health, and his language ... Oy, oy, oy!" He shakes his head; he can't even begin to list his missed prospects. Staring vacantly into the empty dishes, he mumbles a little and assembles a first sentence in English. Encouraged by this linguistic success, he turns to the American, having decided, apparently, that the first step is always the hardest. From there it will surely be downhill. But the orchestra once again bursts out, and the dancing catches fire.

Meanwhile, along the walls of the hall, they're laying the dessert tables. On them, watching above the heads of the guests, arms outstretched in amazement, tower huge dolls in hoop skirts of white, pink, and pale green marshmallow. Just above them rise multi-storeyed pagodas of wedding cakes. Among the mountains of sweets, of chiefly former-homeland make and nostalgic assortment—Little Bear Misha in the North, White Nights, Northern Palmyra—dessert king Strudel reigns, covered with marshmallow of all the colours of the rainbow and filled with five kinds of stuffing.

The pièce de résistance of the dessert repertoire, however, is the chocolate: in unexpected shapes and sizes, as well as three colours. There's white—shaped like a lifelike swan, a bare-breasted mermaid, and a hare thrice life-sized—and a large candy box containing dark chocolate. Most surprising is the pink chocolate in the form of a rather graceful, considering the material, life-sized woman's leg.

With his sturdy teeth, Round-Eyed breaks off his portion of the lady's ankle and returns to the table. His face shining with perspiration, he barks into the American's ear that still to come is the main wedding cake in a fountain of champagne.

8.

YOU wonder by what miracle, having stuffed themselves to the breaking point, Brightonites manage to dance?

There's no explanation. Just accept it—they dance!

Ah, how they dance in Brighton! Just watch them move—it's clear they love it and will never forget how. Even when still on the road, the future Brightonites couldn't let everyday pleasures pass them by. In Rome, for example, while they waited for their American visas, the travellers had to count and recount the few lire given out for subsistence. Every so often they'd visit the Round Market near the Termini Railroad Station and buy up the breastless chicken parts. The inexpensive fowl became popular with the emigrants and quickly took on a nickname—The Wings of the Soviets. The Odessans are true culinary masters, and even the gizzards and other entrails would turn out tasty.

They'd also fill the large basins, in which, by their southern habit, the arriving mothers would otherwise warm water in the sun and wash the children, with tiny fish from the same Round Market. Expertly pickled, the fish would make an excellent appetizer sprat.

Wine in Italy was inexpensive. Also sold was carbonated orangeade. (The emigrants would gulp it down and shout, "I can't believe it, it's completely natural! Got to have it! Nothing artificial!") From their suitcases they'd get the Stolichnaya, which practically everyone had carted out to sell in Europe. And in the jam-packed little rooms rented from the trusting Italians, who'd never have believed these refugees were capable of such carnival-like gaiety, there'd be such revelry that the local residents, though themselves by no means phlegmatic, could only marvel. How could a country as cold as Russia produce such human boilers, able to out-argue, out-yell, out-dance, and out-eat any Sicilian?

Ah, Odessa,

—it could be heard along the Roman streets from rented record players,

. . . the Pearl by the Sea.
Ah, Odessa, you've known so much sorrow.
Ah, Odessa, my beloved land.
May you bloom and flourish!

The trains rumble over Brighton; the wedding roars, deafening the neighbourhood with the hymn of life. The ritual banquet of the human clan—which no one has the power to destroy—thunders on.

Ah, Odessa, Pearl by the Sea! . . .

That's right, by the sea . . . Correction: by the ocean!

(Translated from Russian by Robert Glasser)

Remembering Mr. Fox

CHRISTOPHER WISEMAN

Dinner in the old hotel by the sea,
Out of season. And each of us assigned
To our own numbered tables. Pink cloths,
Pink curtains, pink walls, a pink satin flower
In a thin vase by the menu. Next to me
A man, by himself, facing the wrong way,
His back to the big windows, the sea, the room,
The other guests. Staring at the wall.

Thick with makeup, watching beadily,
Six women in a row talked to each other
Loudly, flashing rings, queens of this place.

Apprehensive, I introduced myself
To the old man and he half turned, shook
My hand, and said "My name is Fox and I'm
92. How nice of you to talk to me."
It was the waitress turned him round, he said,
Because his shaky hand sometimes spilled food
And other guests must never be embarrassed.
Furious, I asked him if he'd like
To face the room, but "No. I'd better not.

Less trouble staying where I am, I think."
He'd been there nearly two years, he told me.
"It's quite comfortable, really. Just a bit
noisy when the holidaymakers come."

Over the days I talked to him a lot.
He'd been to Cambridge, played high-class rugby,
Had successful children, near retirement now,
Always wore a suit, had read far more
Than I, loved opera, chamber music, art.
Knew Latin. Spoke French and German well.
At 7 P.M. he beamed when I sat down
And said "Good morning." Then frowned and asked me
To please forgive his forgetfulness. "Sometimes
Time confuses me."

On my last day
He shook hands, thanked me for taking time to talk,
And whispered fiercely "All the others here
are either stupid or potty and I won't talk
to them," and he stood as I got up, stood
And looked down and shook his head, and I saw,
Surprised, that he was crying silently.

If I went back there now, what would I see?
Big windows, the grey sea out of season,
Pink everywhere, enough to make you sick,
The parrot-widows clicking jewels and cackling,
And either an empty table with no number,
Or that dear man, alone with all his seasons,
Turned by time, staring through the wall.

Lenin's Mother

JANICE KULYK KEEFER

GENTLEMEN, you come to me with an offer framed to pierce a mother's heart; pierce and nail it down, in just the shape and size you want. Your hands are empty but I know all about that awkward, that embarrassing package you are planning to deliver. Because a midwife once tugged him from me like a turnip from the earth, you think I should split myself open now and pull him back, where no one would dare to look for him. Out there are lunatics, fanatics, true believers robbed of a short, squat body, a beard pointed like a garden trowel, an oily, alcoholic odour not even thousands of massed chrysanthemums can cut. You think they'd sniff him out anywhere, scrabble through dirt for shreds of the leather that was his skin, or whatever body parts can be stuck in reliquaries shaped like a nose or elbow or Adam's apple. And you've decided I'm the one inviolable tomb for this creature you've created: neither corpse nor ghost, but a prisoner, these fifty years, of a cage made from his own veins, pumped each month with fresh embalming fluid. Gentlemen, we must get a few things straight.

First of all, you must know that I am not merely a dead woman: I am a ghost. If you were to put your fingers over mine you would feel nothing; the shadow of your hands would fall to the slats of this bench on which we sit. If you were officials of another age, an altogether different breed of men, you might attempt to kiss my hand. I watched you walking like a pair of rivals through that long avenue of leafless trees; you walked toward a woman sitting on a wooden bench, her head bare, her hands gloved in ice. You thought you saw a woman, and you were mistaken.

Ghosts, like angels, have no gender, gentlemen: we do not speak of ghosts and ghostesses. Ghosts have neither breasts nor wombs, though they do have ears, transparent, like glass jars filled with coloured stones; the stones go nowhere and hear nothing. Ghosts have no social rank, and no familial role. We address one another by our given names alone; we wear the letters like jewelled chains around our throats. We cannot trust to appearances, you see—we don't always know one another from our former lives, and even if we do, we may have assumed the body, the face of a self so young or old that our friends or relatives will see us only as strangers. This was the case with my daughter Olga; I first met her ghost playing under the apple trees at our house in Simbirsk, the ghost of a six-year-old with a muddy face and a ripped pinafore. But I had forgotten what she looked like as a child, the huskiness of her voice, the fierce way she had of paying attention, whether to her dog's lame paw or to the sharps in a tricky piece of music. I had to read her name before I knew her. It was only then I could make out, haloing her small body, the outline of that twenty-year-old woman who died of typhus at the worst hospital in all of Petersbourg. The hospital to whose care my son committed her—the same son of whom we've just been speaking.

Typhus is one of the more disgusting diseases to die from. Eight to ten days after you're bitten, you suffer chills, and then acute pains in all your joints; this progresses to fever, prostration, and finally a livid rash, followed by pneumonia, if you are not cared for properly—pneumonia and death. May I remind you that I was the daughter of a physician, though I was not allowed to study medicine. If I had, I should never have married, and you would have been spared this most indelicate errand. I was a promising musician and had a marked gift for languages; unfortunately, my father's business affairs went into sharp decline just when I should have been sent abroad to study. Instead, I was tutored at home, by a deaf aunt. The small estate my father owned produced nothing but ice for skating in the winter and a pond for swimming in the dog days of July. I had only two dresses to wear, winter and summer: always calico, always with an open neck and elbow-length sleeves. Every winter, frost would make fine, white ladders of the hairs on my arms as I sat doing sums in the nursery; my father believed that stoves and fireplaces brought on degeneracy of the nervous system. Every day my sister and I would walk for miles across the fields, whether the snow was up to our knees or ankles. I became impervious to cold, a talent inherited by my second son. It proved to be of no small value during his imprisonment in Siberia and his exile in unheated rooms in Switzerland.

It is one of my favourite haunts, this park in Petersbourg. Especially in winter, when the trees hold out their arms like empty candelabras. Occasionally I am joined here by the ghost of the Tsarina Maria Alexandrovna. Alive, we shared two things: our given names and patronymics, and our being the mothers of infamous men. Dead, we are bound by the etiquette of ghosts. I never mention that her oldest son was responsible for the execution of mine; she never reminds me that my second son ordered the extermination of her grandson and his entire immediate family, plus assorted servants and retainers. Neither of us ever appears in mourning. She favours blue, the aqua of an early summer sky; I wear white, not out of nostalgia for my bridal days, but because only now can I walk through muddy fields, or rooms where dust lies thick as mould on ancient oranges, and never stain my dress.

I have a special attachment to Petersbourg, but not because I happen to be buried here. In fact, I am out of town as often as in; death hasn't changed that particular habit. Petersbourg, Moscow, Simbirsk, Kazan, Samara, Kiev. Once it was necessity, the clamour of my children that kept me travelling. Now it is something you might call desire. Ghosts, unlike angels, have no duties to perform, no messages to deliver. How can I persuade you of this? Shall I tell you how, when I walk through the gardens in Yalta, I often come across the ghost of our most distinguished dramatist and writer of short stories? Always with a pair of cranes hopping after him, as if begging to have their feathers stroked or snapped, the way Anton Pavlovich fondles or snips the heads of his roses. When I mention my second son, it is only to say how terrified he was by a story Anton Pavlovich once wrote, a story about a doctor who finds himself committed to a hospital for the insane, the very hospital whose inmates he's been tending.

Do you understand? Anton Pavlovich and I discuss my son as if he were a character in a novel someone else has written. This is the great privilege of being a ghost—it's as though someone has taken a sponge and wiped you clean of the sweat and blood and dirt that have dressed your skin from birth. It's not that you cease to feel; rather, all you feel now is freedom so strong it makes a sail of your hair, your skin, and carries you off into the air, forever. You will notice, gentlemen, that whether I stand or sit, there is always a space no thicker than a little finger between me and the earth. As for phantoms that moan and tug a fathom's worth of chains, they are the images of your own fears, your own failings. True ghosts have to do with helium, not hell; you would do well to remember this.

Just by the way you tap your feet against the snow, I can see you've had enough of this. After all, you've come to me with a request made for the good, not of a mere government, but of Russia herself—Russia and all the world outside her, the world, you keep reminding me, my second son altered so unspeakably. You want a yes or no to your request that I open my arms and fold my child back into me. You urge me to forsake my volatility, my complete detachment as a ghost—to open my mouth and swallow all the earth packed over me. To become what you call me: Lenin's mother. Gentlemen, have you heard even one of the words I've given you?

I was twenty-eight when I married Ilya Nikolaevich. I was sick of snow and calico. I had grown up in a household where no stimulants were permitted, not even tea or coffee; you can imagine how heady a temptation marriage seemed to me. And I was acquiring not so much a husband as a high moral purpose. In the course of his short life, my husband was responsible for the building of 450 schools and the begetting of six children, one of whom died so young his name is never mentioned in the history books. We went to live in Simbirsk. Do you know that town, gentlemen? It is built on a steep hill overlooking a river that starts nowhere and goes on forever. Moscow is 560 miles away; Petersbourg, 935. In spring the orchards buzz with blossoms that turn into small, hard, green apples at the end of summer. From July to August there is nothing but dust. It crawls like caterpillars over the leaves and the latticework on the verandahs; it is thicker than the wood and brick from which the town is built.

To create his schools my husband had to travel immense distances; he forsook our bed to sleep in huts with onions strung from the rafters and pigs warming the straw. For seventeen years he spent himself thin as the skin of his hands, and then dropped dead of a stroke at forty-five. When I walk across the fields outside Simbirsk, I often see my husband and our small son, the one whose name nobody wishes to uncover, riding on his shoulders, learning to whistle the songs of all the birds that nest along the Volga. I did not choose to end my days in Simbirsk, gentlemen, although I recommend it for the body of my second son. You may bury him under the apple trees in our orchard, apple trees cut down to make way for a factory. It turns out galoshes that do not fasten properly and let in pailfuls of freezing slush.

Our house was on Moscow Street—make of that what you will. We always had a piano, no matter how difficult it was to put bread on the table or eggs in the salad. To get through the evenings I would play arias from Italian operas; my children played chess, or pored over maps, or read *Tom Sawyer* and *Les Misérables.* It has been said of me that I never raised my voice or my hand to my children, that I never kissed their hair or bundled them in my arms. It is said of my children that they always showed me respect and loyalty. The words love, joy, pleasure—*fun*—never entered the lexicon of our four walls, and yet we were a united and devoted family. Never more so than when our house was falling down around us, the floorboards slipping out from under our feet, even the windows collapsing in upon themselves, like dying stars.

But that is poetry, you say, and you want facts. Here then: Vladimir Ilyich was born with a full head of flaming-red hair. The labour was protracted; I kept falling in and out of dreams. In one I was a sparrow laying an ostrich egg, in another, a small dog who'd swallowed an enormous bone she'd been ordered to bury. Vladimir Ilyich grew up with a butterfly net forever in his hand, or else test tubes slender as ice-coated twigs; he was drawn to delicate and fragile things. As a young child he was always breaking pottery and earthenware, but anything truly precious, anything that could be dangerous if reduced to long, fine slivers, these he handled with a care so extreme I can only call it erotic. He was a brilliant student, but all his schoolmasters complained of his coldness and extreme unsociability.

I can tell you that he had no stomach for suffering. When his brother, and later his sister, died so young and in such dire conditions, he refused to weep for them; his face was like a piece of ice on which a skater has just cut a perfect figure. His eyes were small, the colour and hardness of hazelnuts, and his glance was like sun through a magnifying glass: it consumed whatever it was turned upon, and wherever he passed, the air would hold the smell of burning. Yet his nerves were so bad you could watch them jump and twist inside his skin. In exile he was pursued by failed revolutionaries, people who hanged or drowned themselves, or who were going crazy from starvation. He lived in a shoemaker's house and never opened the windows because of the stench of the sausage factory nearby. He and his wife dined solely off scorched oatmeal; his tubercular stomach furled itself like a spent hibiscus flower under that regime.

Why don't you go to that wife of his with your request? But perhaps you tried and couldn't find her; perhaps she's returned to her native element—not earth but water. She reminded everyone who knew her of a fish, a great blubbery bottom-feeder. Nadezhda Konstantinovna Krupskaya. The only thing I ever liked about her was her father, a military governor who got himself arrested in Poland for dancing the mazurka. He was a liberal, like my husband: the kind of man whose weak and inconsistent sympathies my son grew to despise. Krupskaya was the product of poverty and grimness and political fervour; she had a mouth so sullen-looking that anyone who kissed her must have felt lead on his lips. I have never been fair to Krupskaya, and I do not intend to start now. She developed a goiter on her neck and it caused her eyes to pop out from her face as if they grew on stalks. She was as useful and peripheral to my son as his overcoat or the cloth cap he used to shelter the nakedness of his scalp.

No, Krupskaya won't do. Nor his sister Olga, for there is, after all, that case of typhoid fever still between them. Anna? She never strays from her grandfather's estate at Kokuchkino, where she was banished by the tsar. It is the one place I never go: I can't bear to see my daughter's ghost wasting her eyes with crochet work or scratching badly coded messages onto the windowpanes. Anna would have him gladly, but he'd slip away from her, the way he always did. And a sister, you say, has none of the authority, the staying power of a mother. But can't you see that I've already had enough, enough of running after all of them?

The day Vladimir Ilyich left us, left behind his name and his home, like a pair of ruined shoes, was the day I should have embarked on my future as a ghost. He was the fourth of my six children to be lost to me. When he wrote from Siberia, telling how he pursued a rigorous program in calisthenics in a cell five by ten feet with a ceiling six feet high, I wrote back that he'd done the same in my womb, twenty-four years earlier. His letters were like school exercises, dull, abstract, completely instrumental. For example, he would tell us he'd acquired a dog, but never mention the animal's name. Later he sent us instructions, in cipher. Once more we took up travelling, his remaining sister and brother and I. Until the authorities arrested us in Kiev, in 1904.

And that's the last you hear of me in the books about the man who was my son. A man who permitted himself no deflections into curiosity, who conceived no desires, only convictions, and was as much a stranger to imagination as he would have been to a seraglio. In short, he would make a poor ghost, gentlemen, an impossible ghost, in fact, just as he has been an impossible corpse, all these years. You needn't be afraid of him going about, putting in awkward appearances at podiums and parades: he is the kind that, once buried, stays underground, weighted down by all the bronze and marble, the ink and oil paint lavished on his image.

But you are not convinced. Now you're rising to your feet, drawing out your highest card, the one I've been expecting from the moment I saw you come-a-courting. You say it's all very well for me to drift wherever I desire in my clean white dress. You remind me of other places I could be haunting: interrogation cells set up by the secret police my son inherited and did not disband, or all those places where my son's successors practise their designs—the courts where show trials still take place, the chambers where executions are performed, the famine-stricken peasants' huts where, instead of cabbage boiling in the pot, there's a mess of children's bones. You want me to say that all this is my doing; it's this you want me to take off your hands, to close into my body, in the shape of my dead, grown son.

Look at me, gentlemen. If you look close enough you will find that my skin is as airy as steamed milk; the woman you see in a white dress on a park bench has no body at all. How can you expect her to possess a conscience any more than a womb, especially a conscience you've designed to your own specifications, after consulting this month's history book? I have told you once already: ghosts are not angels, they have no messages to deliver or duties to perform. I am not telling you what is just or right, but what I know. It is something of which I caught only a glimpse during my lifetime—only once in all those strictly measured years. I was on one of my endless journeys, gentlemen, on behalf of my children. News had reached us that my oldest son and daughter had been arrested by the police; they were accused of planning to assassinate the tsar. Vladimir Ilyich stood before me, a telegram

from The Banff Centre for the Arts

in his hand, his mouth open but no sound coming out. I snatched the telegram from him, read it, and went directly to my room. I did not lie down; I did not call for priest or smelling salts. I changed my clothes and packed whatever money I had into my corsets. And then I took the lantern and slipped out the back door to the house of the one neighbour in all of Simbirsk whom I could trust, a man whose eyes were green and sharp as Volga apples.

Do not imagine that I am waxing romantic, gentlemen: I had as clear a sense of my situation, my possibilities, then as now. A middle-aged woman, thin with the brittleness of constant worry, my hair pulled back from my face as tightly as my stays were laced. I went to my good neighbour, one of my dead husband's colleagues, who would later swear to the police as to my son's good character and my own ability to keep him out of trouble. From this neighbour I borrowed a horse. Before I set out, he gave me a bowl of soup, to strengthen me for the journey. It was sour cherry soup, thick and deep, deep red. I drank it straight from the bowl, to warm my hands, and left the blood of cherries on his cheek, bidding him farewell.

And then I rode, lungeing into the seventy miles between Simbirsk and the nearest railway station, as if they were of less account than the little yard between our house front and the street. It was near the end of winter, but cold enough that the stars squeaked as they turned in the sky. The cold was a blessing; it kept the ground like iron under my horse's hooves, so that I'd easily make the morning train to Petersbourg. Behind me lay the wooden house with the oil lamp burning in the window and my neighbour's face reflected in the glass. Behind me lay my own house, with those of my children yet to be sentenced, whether by disease or politics. Ahead of me lay everything I had to fear, for my children, for myself. Yet all I felt, galloping so hard the horse's hooves struck fire all around me, was the sudden openness inside my heart. And all I wanted was to ride across the frozen earth, ride and ride into the night, the addictive emptiness of air. Until there was no beyond or before, no outside or in, but only a horizon, new and limitless as the line on which to write, at last, your name, your true and only name, tart and certain in your mouth as the taste of sour cherry soup or small green Volga apples.

Elizabeth Smart, 70

JANICE KULYK KEEFER

I have travelled so far
from the country of my birth
that my body's become a lunar Sahara.
In the craters of my eyes, light burns out
with the superb slowness of stars.
Remembering that girl, her hair soft as butter,
you say it hurts to look at me.

Look at the garden, then—I made it
out of a gravel dump, quarrying roses
like Carrara marble. If you want skin
without stitches, fresh-smelling involutions,
pay attention to the tuberoses, not to me.

I don't know why you're so mopey.
Look at my flowers, my children, their children:
look at my book—you carry it like a furled
umbrella, as if reluctant to remind me

that the Muses have whispered their milk
into my lips. Does this embarrass you,
the casual terms I am on with greatness?

I will remind you only once:
I want to be respected by those who are dead.
I want to sing and make my soul occur.

The first time I lit a cigarette, I was so nervous
I held it like a pen. For a while I wrote fire.
Now my eyes are blood and ashes:
no water can bring back their white skies.

He is dead, and I am nearly there.
What is there to talk about?
Come sit for a while in this garden;
the bees will astound you with their whisky hum,
and the snapdragons, that never stop
shutting up.

Burial

CARMINE SARRACINO

My mother's tumour is much worse now and is cutting off circulation to her legs, especially the right leg. And our poor cat Sita, in the middle of all this she is so ill, and won't make it much longer.

—Journal, July 2, 1992

I don't know how I did it
Whether by steeling or by going slack
My elbows straightened, my fingers uncurled
And the vet turned his back with our cat in his arms.

For weeks we'd said goodbye.
Mincing steaks, liver, and shrimp
As if cost could nourish, or the gods
Be moved by expenses not spared
By love and protein lavished.

We met each other with "She ate
All the shrimp!" sure it was a sign
Though she thinned, drifted sideways
When she stood, her pink ears pale
As flowers you have to throw away.

Protests! Prayers! The heart
Is that newsreel woman in the red kerchief
Tugging the cuffs of the firing squad Captain
And falling silent all at once
Pressing knuckles into her mouth.

I wrapped Sita in her blanket
And laid her small body on pine cones
At the bottom of a deep hole.

Filling the hole, heaping the earth over,
Dropping flowers—It all seemed like a metaphor:

Imagine if we could do this. Heart,
    If we could do this.

Berlin Suite

MYRA DAVIES

IN PARTICLES PHYSICS, an event is said to occur when two particles meet in time and space. Events cause change. Nothing remains as it was, and yet it does, in Berlin.

TAXI — *Real-time documentation of a seven-minute taxi ride through Schöneburg*

Around midnight two people got into a cab. It was raining heavily or maybe it wasn't but the streets were shining black and wet. As the car picked up speed, a woman tried to see out the window, to get some idea of where they were. But at night in a foreign city, in a blur of stone facades, broken by flashes of white light, fractured by rivulets of water, running up and down the windows, nothing clear. Except that the big bad city wasn't as bad as the fashion magazines would like it to be. Maybe it used to be. Or maybe it never was.

It was a velour-lined English taxi, one of those dove grey wombs. No it wasn't. It couldn't have been. It had to be a four-door Mercedes sedan. Cold, hard, plastic covers on the seats. Moving fast through wet black streets assaulted from all directions by glare. Searing cold flashes in the unknown darkness. She retreated into the seat, shrink-wrapped in artificial intelligence, to observe the sensation of leaden fatalism as it spread itself like a drug through her body.

On the other side of the car a man stared morosely into the water on the window. He mumbled something about his girlfriend never having treated him that way before. Sometimes the worm turns. Is that fortunate for the worm? Maybe. He wondered aloud why he felt nothing in his heart. Whether to play the tormented Master or the suffering Slave. Burning questions in the drama of Love. Martyrs, fervently pursuing a place on the rack, won't settle for less until they've had their fill of it, until they have satisfied the appetite for Damage. It is ridiculous.

The laws of probability posit that there is likely to be a molecule from Caesar's last gasp in any breath we take, so I guess it's safe to assume there was the odd photon or two of moonlight banging about in the back seat of that cab. But for the most part the light was incandescent, fluorescent, and neon. An eerie grey light, punctured by land-mine flashes illuminating a thin profile, shivering. His eyelids were too heavy for him. The head, unsteady on its neck. The spine, deserted by the muscles, having a hard time holding up the skull. Able to do so only by balancing it at the top of the vertebra column like a Chinese acrobat balances a stack of plates on a stick. It occurred to her that if the neck lost its balance his head would fall off. This she thought would be interesting. She waited for it.

The taxi stopped. Take a jar of syrup out of the fridge. Turn it upside down. Slowly the syrup moves down the bottle toward the lip, where it builds behind the ring of crystals encrusted there. The lump swells until it reaches the weight required to push it over the edge. In quantities far greater than desired, it dumps fast and heavy onto what it was intended to sweeten, turning the whole to a sticky mess. Time was like that. Or maybe it wasn't. But it slowed to a crawl and yet continued to move on. The taxi was stopped.

Robotics. She lifted the right hand and directed it to travel out into the void between them. The hand hesitated, daring to accuse her of manipulative cunning. Then reluctantly it did as ordered. She watched it move through space. A lunar vehicle, it came to rest on the left side of his head. Then, faithful little servant that it was (how could she have considered cutting it off?), it sent back the following sense data: "the hair is extremely fine, making overall a soft surface—dry, cool, pleasant." The touch was not effective. Far from conveying warmth, it was as remote, as pale, as lifeless, as its object. He leaned across the chasm, his head moving toward her until his lips landed gently on the bone-line of her cheek. Attic marble in the Pergamon Museum. A kiss inarticulate, and a lie in its chastity.

The man opened the door and got out of the car. In an instant he vanished in the rain, the reflections, the light, and the night. The taxi drove on. What's the matter? Probably nothing.

TATTOO — *Recorded conversation in a Kreutzberg bar*

"You should have a tattoo. It is beautiful and the experience is ... what should I say ... therapeutic. I have a tattoo. I could show you if you want." I gave him the Go signal "Yes" and noticed how carefully he moved his chair back before he stood up to pull his T-shirt out of his leather pants. He lifted it. Lifted it a lot higher than Christ would have done to show the wound. So high that his lean, white, hairless torso was exposed all the way from his belt to his throat.

I saw a fantastic beast. Its left arm slung over his shoulder. The claws of its right hand sunk in the flesh of his breast. The body of the thing, neither lizard nor snake, rolled down his rib cage, decreasing in diameter until it came to an end in a delicate tail that hung from his bottom rib like a silk stocking on a towel rail. Aha, I thought, the Animal Style, as my head exploded with images of the ancestors of this pop cliché, from the Lindisfarne Gospels, the prows of Viking ships. Strong fighting beasts bred of a mix of Celtic and Germanic influences, nostrils flaring, gums bared, rows of teeth curved like scimitars and bodies. Bodies covered with lines in geometric patterns betraying the contempt or was it fear, of their makers for empty spaces.

"I'm going to have another one done." He put his clothes and chair carefully back into order and sat down. Time for another Go line. "Doesn't it hurt?" (Sometimes you just give them what they want.) "Of course it hurts." (The snarl of contempt, *leitmotif* for the men of Berlin.) "Of course it hurts. That is why one does it. Don't you understand? One must have the experience of pain that is the design going into the flesh. This experience is total. You and your body and the pain are one. All separation is erased. One must embrace this to come away clean." While he was talking I was noticing his mouth resembled a sphincter. He was tall even sitting down, a mind at work on top of a pole.

"Perhaps what I am saying is difficult for you to understand. This ability to see beauty in pain is something very German. We Germans have always seen the beauty and the truth that is in pain and only in pain. You North Americans give greater value to comfort. You see pain as something to be avoided by taking a tablet. We in Germany value the experience of feeling. Whether it is pleasure or pain is not so important as the feeling something. And there is more in the feeling of pain. I mean to say more in the sense of intensity, more substance, more, I think one could say, spiritual value, in pain, than in other kinds of feelings. But this, I think, is difficult for you to understand."

FINGERS — *Berlin Mitte in American film noir*

Four fingers lying on a white linen cloth. They looked out of place. I stared at them wondering what they were doing there. They were fat, sort of stubby and quite pink. I didn't recognize them so they couldn't be his. I wouldn't have forgotten fingers like that, so out of agreement with the rest of him. But there they were.

The fingers lay in plain view on the white linen. I couldn't see the rest of the hand. One would have to assume it was there concealed below the table edge. One would also have to assume the unseen hand was connected to an arm presumably occupying the sleeve of his suit jacket. Well, there was something occupying the sleeve. I assumed it was an arm.

But even with all these assumptions, I was still having trouble with the fingers, a matched set of four lying slightly splayed on the linen. I panned from the fingers to the sleeve, from the sleeve to the shoulder, from the shoulder over to the collar. Nothing strange about the neck. The neck supported a head that looked for all intents and purposes like his head. It was wearing his face. I knew that face too well.

I had to dismiss the argument that the fingers belonged to somebody else. But one thing kept nagging at me. If they're his, then those fingers have been all over me and I don't even know them. That didn't feel right. I didn't like it. And I still didn't recognize them. The big question was why. And the facts pointed to one conclusion. I'd never noticed them. You see I thought I knew so much. But I guess I just assumed. I guess I assumed a lot in those days. Funny how that happens.

I looked back at the fingers. They hadn't moved. They lay on the starched white linen like four fresh fish on ice, pink, plump, and slightly splayed. And I thought to myself, My God, those are *his* fingers. And seeing them now as his, I found them touching, beautiful even. But it was a little late for that.

DINNER — *Ending on Potsdammerstrasse by night*

What they ate isn't important and there was no point in lingering over cognac. There was no point in cognac at all. So they skipped it and went out into the street and got a taxi. And they stuffed themselves into opposite corners of the back seat. There wasn't far to go.

The cab pulled up to the curb on a street lit with yellow light, like a stage. With donair sellers and junkies and rats and swarthy men in long leather coats and cheap women walking back and forth and forth and back, eating greasy food out of white greasy paper and kibitzing. *Potsdammerstrasse bei Nacht.*

As the cab pulled up to the curb with the two dark things in opposite corners of the back seat, the two dark things looked away from each other out the side windows. And their looks went out the windows and all the way around the planet and back in the opposite side windows. So though they looked away, they still managed to lick at each other with looks by going the long way around.

Her white hand lay forgotten on the back seat. Easily within reach of his fleshy fingers. Maybe the fleshy fingers reached out and brushed the white hand slightly. Yes, I believe they did reach out and brush the white hand slightly. But the fleshy fingers didn't pick it up. They couldn't pick it up. They didn't dare. For the sad truth was the fleshy fingers were cowards.

She got out of the cab and, passing through the crowd of swarthy men in long coats and cheap women and donair sellers, junkies, and rats, she disappeared into the wall. Only the cab driver saw her disappear because only he was watching. She disappeared like positive into negative. She disappeared into the wall as though she'd never been there at all.

Schaferscapes

KAREN MULHALLEN

(an excerpt)

Bewitched by musicians and bothered by the vagaries of the Goddess of Fame, writer and editor Karen Mulhallen takes herself to The Banff Centre, to investigate the world of R. Murray Schafer, Canada's composer, music educator, environmentalist, literary scholar, visual artist, man of the theatre, and occasional provocateur. Bewildered that the distinguished, innovative, and prolific Schafer is celebrated worldwide but unknown at home, Mulhallen reviews his astonishing career, revisits the Alberta site of a memorable performance of The Princess of the Stars, *an environmental music theatre work performed outdoors on a lake in the Rocky Mountains, and checks out what Schafer, a national treasure, is up to now. She figures it's high time we all did a little Schafer-style ear cleaning.*

IT'S A LONG WAY BACK from this window, in my studio at The Banff Centre, on a warm summer day, looking down a rift populous with deer and elk, framed by a highway running up to Tunnel Mountain—to 1972, when I first remember noticing who composer R. Murray Schafer was. There is something about Schafer in August that always gets to me, and so although it is now June, it feels again like August in my mind. But every August is a different August, even if it has the same name, or is it?

The first August was a kind of psychedelic August. I'd gotten a divorce, I was going blind, and my lover had drowned in the Tiber River in Rome. The Tiber, said somebody, how could anyone drown in the Tiber River? He was just celebrating, I said, offering something that was almost a non sequitur. And that, as they say, was that.

I was teaching a night course, up there at the college in the wilds of Scarborough. I needed the money, and my best friend had an overflow from her course in fiction. Her idea was that we'd go together into a big lecture hall, tell the students our stories, and let them choose which of us they wanted. All sounded democratic enough. It was a free-form era and there were plenty of visions around—from the goosestepping moral rearmament of the Company of Canadians, to the "if you haven't tasted your own menstrual blood and slept with another woman" kind of feminism, and people were switching partners, and lifestyles, and homes, with astonishing abandon. So there we were, my best friend and I, in the cold hall that Australian architect John Andrews had designed to be community-friendly, and she says "I'll go first." I remember not having any objections. I'd just gotten this job three hours ago and hadn't a clue what to say anyhow. She was wearing a little brown crepe dress, with a very short pleated skirt, and long sleeves decorated with knee-length fringes. Sort of like an elongated cowboy shirt. But she didn't look like Annie Oakley. Her shirt was undone to her waist, and her straight red hair was waist-length as well, and hung like a shimmering shawl framing her beautiful pale face. She swung right in, and in a squeaky nervous voice introduced herself. "Hi, I'm Susie, and I'm interested in sex. If that's what you're interested in, you can come along to my classroom, number 106." That's a hard act to follow.

"I'm Karen," I said, "I don't care at all about sex. I'm interested in the texts as texts, and if you want to learn how to read, just follow me to room 108." I left the hall assuming that was the end of that gig, but surprisingly about half the group did show up in my room and we sailed like eunuchs through Wilkie Collins's *The Woman in White,* and John Fowles's *The French Lieutenant's Woman,* and Djuna Barnes's *Nightwood,* and Norman Mailer's *Armies of the Night,* and Herman Melville's *Billy Budd,* and Michael Ondaatje's *The Collected Works of Billy the Kid.* The canon was masculine; we pushed it a bit and had closed down the shop by midsummer. I frittered away July, working on my Ph.D. dissertation on William Faulkner, trying desperately to learn a whole new field, linguistics, and new tools, computer analysis. Come August, I began my annual summer migration to southwestern Ontario to see my parents and go to the Stratford Festival, as I had every summer since I'd been on the edge of adolescence. Schafer's *Requiems for the Party Girl (Patria 2)* opened the week I stepped down from the train and made my way over the long grasses grown up through the train-track ties to the pay phone to call for a ride home. Home. Homeland. *Patria.*

You could say I come from a theatre family. We all had a gift for the dramatic. My father ran two vaudeville shows in the local movie theatre, which had once been an opera house, and my mother was the star of the little local theatre. I'd spent many a boring evening before I escaped to university hearing her lines. *Blithe Spirit, The Glass Menagerie, Our Town, View from the*

Bridge, Death of a Salesman, Harvey, Dial M for Murder, they were all etched on my brainpan, and no amount of psychedelics, or valium, was erasing the welter of words pressing against my forehead in a perpetual headache that was making me blind. I was in no shape to see Murray Schafer's *Requiems for the Party Girl.*

The Festival had opened up a "controversial" new playing space in an old rink by the Avon River, sited next to the green where the local citizens bowl in warm weather and just across from those pesky long-necked swans ever hopeful that Zeus would come down and make princesses out of them. On the outside it still looked like the old arena.

The audience was seated on bleachers facing each other on a diagonal, looking at each other right through the players, who were acting out their lives in an insane asylum; us folks here in the bleachers were out on a day pass. This was a technique I was already acquainted with through Peter Brooke's production of Peter Weiss's *Marat-Sade.* Only the heroine spoke English, and everybody was sounding off at cross-purposes. It was like an Orson Wells movie. The text was Schafer's own, with borrowings from Kafka and Camus. In the opening aria, sung by mezzo-soprano Phyllis Mailing, the Party Girl announced that she was about to commit suicide. "Voices gossiping in other rooms, but no one listens. Outstretched hands are rare." "Everywhere I go I leave parts of myself. Wherever I go, I leave a paper on my desk for visitors to sign and no one signs." You get the picture. She's called the Party Girl because that's what she does, and beneath that persona are the hints of terror and alienation. It was a role cast in the stripe of the times, had to be from Vancouver, I thought, and I did my best to forget it.

It was cold comfort on that muggy August evening that I'd already heard the superb cycle of connected arias, documenting the collapse and suicide of the Party Girl, written for Mailing, Schafer's first wife, on CBC radio, which had commissioned them way back in '66. Scarcely home from Europe, installed as artist-in-residence at Memorial University in Newfoundland, and already beginning to make his mark as a composer and musical bad boy, Schafer was teaching himself the techniques of avant-garde music, experimenting with tonality, using long extended series of rhythms, and playing with intervals. In *Requiems for the Party Girl,* you can hear that when she kills herself. At the moment she dies, the strings begin a long sustained chord very softly, like a funeral organ tone. The work ends with throngs of bells as—angrily, unevenly, pulsatingly—the Party Girl repeats the word "Requiem." Schafer was also creating passionate, openly political, works, like *Canzoni for Prisoners,* based on texts by jailed East European poets. He was in his thirties.

In 1970, Suzanne Ball had written in *The Music Scene:* "Murray Schafer is like religion and politics ... you don't argue about him in polite company. You're either very much for him, or very much against him, and if you belong in the latter category chances are you won't see 50 again." Five years or so later,

Ian Bradley, in *Twentieth Century Canadian Composers,* was recording Schafer's "meteoric rise to fame ... relatively unknown even a decade ago, but today he is without question one of Canada's most successful composers. His fame and reputation are world-wide ..." I'd been following all this music stuff myself at the grassroots level, but probably didn't notice Schafer collect a couple from Fromm Foundation awards. The *Washington Star*'s Irving Lowens pegged Schafer as a composer to watch. At the summer 1967 Tanglewood Festival of American Music, Schafer "ran away from the field with his *Gita,* a brilliantly expressive setting for chorus, brass and electronic instruments of a poem in Sanskrit."

Folk music and non-Western music were part of the pulse of the times, and so were the music experiments and theories of American composer John Cage. Cage extended the range of what we could call music, all the way from silence to random noise, and I'd had a hand with a bunch of other teachers at Ryerson Polytechnic University in bringing John Cage to Toronto to play a chess game with Marcel Duchamp on the Ryerson Theatre stage. Their electronically wired moves made music, of course, and Columbia Records recorded it for posterity, which brings me back to the Party Girl, and those pesky Stratford swans hanging about waiting to be transformed.

By the time the next August rolled around, I'd begun to emerge from the darkness. Avoiding the preparation for my fall lectures, I idly picked up a *Globe and Mail* at the corner box, and wandered up Brunswick Avenue to my rambling second-storey apartment. I made a pot of coffee and took it and the paper into my sunroom from which I conducted my surveillance of my neighbours and my eldest brother, who was living downstairs that summer. What caught my eye was the sort of filing the *Globe* treats as filler, a cultural event out in the provinces, which in this case was Vancouver. It was reported as provocative, meaning not serious—some nutty composer who'd put a snowmobile up on the stage with the National Youth Orchestra. One hundred kids with instruments, and a snowmobile in the percussion section. It wasn't snowing in Toronto, and I'd be willing to eat my bathing suit if anybody could show me it was snowing in Vancouver. The whole symphony lasted for only ten or twelve minutes and ended when the percussionist got to rev the snowmobile for a couple minutes at the climax and drown out the orchestra.

After that I got sick with an annual disease I'd contracted in Mexico from conversing with a parrot in a lending library, high on a hill overlooking the Pacific, while showing a book by Simone Weil to a sailor from Berkeley, who'd been a telephone linesman before building a trimaran and sailing south, down the Baja coast, where the spirits are strong, and around to Zihuatenejo. But through that busy fall, as I reconstructed my life, I kept thinking about that snowmobile, back there in August, and a little bit as well about the telephone linesman, who had a blond ponytail and wasn't crazy about motors and had bought me my first Paul Horn album, Paul Horn playing alto flute in the Taj

Mahal, the wonderful riffs echoing about in that marble monument to love.

I'd once seen Schafer, at a distance, lying on the floor of the Town Hall stage, holding a mallet in the air. He looked ridiculous, but no more so than the other two composer-percussionists who lay next to him howling with laughter. It was December 1965; I was a student, of course, which I guess is my doom, and had got in the habit of following the new music scene in Toronto. I was fresh from a country town, wondering a little when I would start having the eight children I had promised myself. I was taking instruction in Roman Catholicism and was madly in love with a fallen priest whose name I now realize not coincidentally was August. So August and I, in December, watched flautist Bob Aitken playing a new piece by Jack Behrens with his head stuck inside an enormous metal sculpture by Gerald Gladstone while composers John Beckwith, Bruce Mather, and Murray Schafer scratched, scrubbed, and belted away at Gladstone's huge steel tub, until they couldn't keep themselves from breaking up with laughter. There were happenings everywhere. I was involved in a few myself, having managed for example an event where a Swiss-Canadian firebreather from Vancouver, known as El Diablo the Human Volcano, blew six-foot flames at the audience, while an English teacher and electronics musician named Rick Kitaeff played on a synthesizer, and Pierre Coupey recited poetry. But Toronto was still a conservative town, and Schafer wasn't even allowed to use the electronic music studio at the university's Faculty of Music, from which he'd been physically ejected in '55.

After the Town Hall concert, Schafer headed west, and August and I got on with our separate lives, which brings me back to the weird way the Augusts of my life have become Murray Schafer's Augusts. I don't think in the seventies it was possible to come of age without being ripped apart by politics, and it wasn't politics over there but politics right here, because Canada was full of Vietnam dodgers, the airwaves were crowded with the images, the U.S. was eating its own children. We all openly raised our fists against the patriarchy and American imperialism and took to the streets to make sure no one missed us this time round. We were foolhardy optimists, my best friend got fired for not wearing a bra, and I was given a warning. Shortly after, on a heady August afternoon, I joined the *Canadian Forum* editorial collective, which agreed on only three issues—economic nationalism, cultural nationalism, Québécois sovereignty.

I'd grown up with the *Forum,* my mother had been the editor of the *Quinte Sun* in the thirties, when it was the cheapest place in the province to print, so all those great old pipe-smoking professorial English-Canadian socialists, like Underhill and Grube, had gotten into those heavy rumble-seated cars, heavily decorated with chrome, and carted those radical sheets off to the press in Belleville, where my mother would run them through after the printing of the daily paper. My parents had met in the newsroom at the *Quinte Sun,* where my father came with his ads for the Trenton movie theatre. So I was conceived, so to speak, under the *Forum,* and as a child went dutifully with my parents to visit many of the old *Forum* editors. When I came on the *Forum* as poetry editor, there were no regular arts features, although the *Forum* from its earliest days had had a close relationship with artists like the Group of Seven and with cultural analysis, Northrop Frye having once been its editor. At university I'd shopped about a fair bit, which added up to knowing not too much about an awful lot. And what I did know I'd mainly cobbled together. My comrades at the *Forum* promptly created the arts features editor position for me; it opened up my world immediately, and so, you've guessed it, one August came a phone call inviting me to attend and write about a musical event, near Bancroft, Ontario, at O'Grady Lake, *Music for Wilderness Lake,* by R. Murray Schafer. The score called for twelve trombones and a small lake. The trombones, of the trombone ensemble Sonaré, were distributed in the underbrush around the shoreline of the lake. And the composer, that's Schafer, cued the musicians with flags from a raft in the middle of the lake. The landscape was part of the composition, and my caller, a documentary filmmaker, read to me enthusiastically from Schafer's notes on his score, about returning "to an era when music took its bearings from the natural environment, a time when musicians played to the water and to the trees and then listened for them to play back." Schafer divided the piece in two, to be performed, at dusk and at dawn, when the wind was slightest and the echoes greatest. He had hoped for a late spring performance, "because then the birds are at their singing peak." But it looked like he'd settled for summer this time.

I remember as a student going to folk festivals out in the country and sleeping very little, and wherever I could get a space to lie down. But I was way past folk festivals at this point, and the idea of a night in the country under the stars by a lake wasn't much of a draw. Nonetheless, Music, Environment, Film, National Landscape, Canadian Composer—there were all those uppercase topics, and I assigned a writer to go in my stead. The writer was a musicologist, a trained botanist, and a visual artist, and I patted myself on the back for the aptness of my choice, scheduled the article for the next issue of the *Forum,* and promptly put the matter out of my head. But a month or so later, I still hadn't seen the piece, so I began to ask, gently at first, then more insistently. At the turn of the year, the essay did show up under my office-closet door at Ryerson in the English Department, where I was teaching. Yikes. A thirty-page attack on modern music, celebrating in ponderous detail the compositional structure of music before Schoenberg and calling for a return at least to Beethoven, maybe even to Mozart and Haydn. As I write these words, I can hear Schafer in my ear: "Mozart, that pop musician. Phfuhhh. Mozart wore lace panties."

⊥⊥

By 1979, Schafer's c.v. was pretty impressive—articles, translations, pamphlets, and books, including British Composers in Interview, *music education studies like* The Composer in the Classroom *and* Ear Cleaning, *critical commentaries on the German Romantic composer E. T. A. Hoffmann, and on the music of poet Ezra Pound, as well as an analysis of our sonic environment,* The Tuning of the World, *based on his pioneering work in soundscape at Simon Fraser University. The list of his compositions was several pages long, and he'd picked up commissions and awards all over the world, as well as in Canada. It also began to look as though he was in the midst of shaping a cycle,* Patria, *of opera-theatre pieces—he calls them co-operas—with a repeating case of characters and the general storyline of the search for identity through the eventual marriage of the two principals, Wolf and Ariadne.*

I might have put Schafer completely out of my mind, and in a way I did for years. I'd seen him only once, and never met him, and knew he was important, but not much else. I was overloaded myself, teaching five courses, running *Descant,* a literary magazine that had grown up when we were all students at the university, and, combined with the *Forum* editing, I felt like a juggler waiting for the balls to come all a-tumbling down. I stayed with the *Canadian Forum* under several editors, being in some way comfortable with the perilous publishing of the alternative press. I could publish anything I wanted, write anything I wanted, and growing up smart and exotic-looking in a small town meant I already was familiar with the anxiety of margins. Schafer created excitement in May of 1983 with his production of *Ra, (Patria 6),* based partly on *The Egyptian Book of the Dead,* at the Science Centre in Toronto. A couple of the editors went to the performance, reporting on it as a kind of happening where they stayed up all night, feasted with strangers, had their bodies massaged with oil, napped on mats in a room drenched in sandalwood incense, and heard music with a Middle Eastern flavour coming from hidden recesses, but no one thought to write about it that I remember. By now I was living in a comfortable first-floor apartment in the university area and beginning to do more writing in the charged borderzones where politics and art meet. I probably would have gone to *Ra,* if it had come to my attention, since I began my life as an Arabist, but in 1983 I was worrying about Isaac Newton and the impact of Newtonian scientific models on perception in the eighteenth and nineteenth centuries, and that's a fair piece away from Schafer in August. That's what I thought then, but technology is technology, and I can hear that snowmobile revving up over the bird calls, drowning out the woodpecker, as I write up here in the mountains.

In August—yep, there it is again, kismet, destiny—of 1985, I made my way westward to The Banff Centre, where my friend John McEwen was erecting a life-sized, steel sculpture, *Stelco's Cabin,* on the section of the campus that overhangs the Banff townsite. Inside the skeletal steel frame of a house on a platform, a steel flame-cut wolf-dog in outline leans over, looking down to town. Behind him—I happen to know the actors in this drama are masculine—seated on the lawn gazing at Stelco is another wolf-dog. McEwen's art celebrates the rich parallel world of animals, and when I found out that a Schafer piece of musical theatre, *The Princess of the Stars,* in which the hero is a Wolf, or a Wolf-man, was being staged right then at Two Jack Lake, one of a series of small lakes in the mountain basin in which the townsite sits, I just had to shrug my shoulders at the Hardyesque coincidence. I was beginning to feel a little bit mystified at the way Schaferscapes were coming to inhabit my August moods.

The Banff Centre campus was into Schafer overdrive; they'd been building since April and, the week I got there, were just going into actual performance. I got a good look at the principals in the drama before they took to the water: the hero, a ten-foot-high Wolf with a movable head, and his antagonist, the Three-Horned Enemy, with a superstructure of twenty-one feet, including movable tentacles. They're a formidable pair grounded and I had no idea how they were going to fare, borne on canoes in a lake at dawn. Since my Wolf-man was totally preoccupied with his own wolves, I thought I'd better get out there to hear someone else's take on a scenario featuring a princess. The middle of the night isn't my time, I'm really only active about three hours of the day, somewhere between 11 A.M. and 2 P.M., but I pulled myself out of bed at 3 A.M. The weather gods were putting on an inauspicious display; it was pouring rain and mighty cold. This is mountain country, after all. Two Jack is about three miles outside the townsite, and I assumed I'd be nearly alone to watch the spectacle. I headed out of town and came up toward the lake. There was a ribbon of headlights as far as the eye could see coming along Highway Number 1 from Calgary. I parked the truck and began to stumble through the pitch black down the wooded hill. I could feel other people in the darkness, stumbling, rustling. Silent, black hooded figures carrying torches came through the trees to guide us to a lightly treed spot. We sat quietly on the ground for a long time in the darkness as the rain stopped and our eyes adjusted. We could hear the lapping of water, the dripping from the trees, the rustling of many other bodies near to ours. Slowly we began to see the trees, the lake only a few feet before us, the far shore, the treeline, and the mountains.

The grass beneath me is soft and slippery. I can smell the pine and spruce damp from the rain. Into the silence comes a female voice, echoing over the water. It urges the dawn birds to sing and the sun to rise. From above the trees at the far shore of the lake, there is a flash of light as the sun responds to her call. Then a male voice cries out and the female begins again, as instruments begin to tinkle. The chanting comes closer, overlaid and underlaid with texture, the sound of paddles dipping, an occasional cough. Suddenly, close by me, at the shoreline, in a canoe on the water, an ancient figure in rags looms from the darkness, greets us, and begins recounting a simple story of the fall of the Princess of the Stars. Hearing Wolf's call, she leaned too far from heaven and is even now being dragged to the bottom of this lake, says the ancient one, and the mist on the lake is a sign of her struggle. As a horn sounds across the lake, the ancient figure bestows invisibility on us, so that we can witness the struggle between the Three-Horned Enemy and Wolf over the Princess. I begin to lose my sense of where I am. A wolf howls. I begin to shiver. I cannot understand the words. The clapping is behind me and in front of me. I am surrounded by clanging. I cannot move. Stronger and stronger comes the beating of drums. Angry giant forms appear on the water's surface, jousting as ponderously as triremes, and then a Sun Disc surrounded by birds, flapping their enormous coloured wings. The ripples on the lake turn deep pink, while the sun begins to rise, touching the snow-capped tip of Mount Rundle. Cymbals clang, gongs and horns sound, and I hear the birds of dawn singing, louder and louder. Before me are the giant forms, floating on the lake. Everything is doubled, upside down, mountains, trees, sky, giant forms. The woman begins to cry, calling me, as the mist rises on the lake. The conductor on the wharf to my right flaps his coloured flags. Around me, people stand, stretch, and begin to climb slowly up the hill toward their cars strung along the edge of the road. I point John's truck in the direction of the Centre and head back to my own domesticated wolves.

I bought my first house in five minutes in the summer of 1986, partly as a way of changing the cast of characters in my life, and around then I began to hang out with a writer who was one of Schafer's former students. Also by this time, *Descant* had grown from its original mimeograph form to a quarterly bound journal, and one of Schafer's colleagues—the singer, writer, and performance artist Paul Dutton—had joined the editorial collective of which I was the chief. Paul had been performing for Schafer for more than a decade and had played the Wolf in *The Princess of the Stars.* Once he came to *Descant,* there was the sound of Schafer in the air. By then I knew about Schafer's World Soundscape Project, and I knew something of Schafer's groundbreaking work as a music educator. From Paul, I heard about Schafer's novels, about his study of mythology, about his explorations of language, and his experiments with space and sound and audience, some of which I had already had a taste of in *The Party Girl* and *The Princess.* And Paul showed me samples of Schafer's elaborately drawn scores, which resembled nothing so much as my favourite manuscripts in the British Museum, the hieroglyphics of *The Egyptian Book of the Dead* in *The Hunefer Papyrus* and the windblown expressive sketchy drawings in the *Utrecht Psalter.* Manuscripts I've peered at in glass cases, as I've made my way through the high wooden-floored halls toward the Manuscript Department's guarded glass door, separating the world out here, from the scholar in there.

By now I could feel that destiny was hell-bent on bringing the Composer (that's Schafer) and the Editor (that's me) face to face, though I expected the event to be forestalled until August. But destiny has its own agenda and it was May 1987, when English Canadian writers from all over Canada donned their plumage, left their solitary nests, formed a V, and flew to Ontario for an event known as the AGM, the annual general meeting of the Writers' Union of Canada. It's their version of a bacchanal and natch it's May, *Walpurgisnacht.* Witches and wizards frolic together, and all the talk is of Canco, PLR, canon, race, gender, and voice appropriation.

My writer-houseguest, in town for the AGM, wanted to have dinner with Schafer, his former teacher, and wanted to take him out to dinner, rather than share with him a domestic intimacy. In the month of May, it's hard to get in to a popular restaurant in the city of Toronto. There is much kicking up of heels and pushing away of the winter blahs, even if it's only sixty degrees Fahrenheit, as it was on this particular evening. Still, I picked up the telephone and called the hottest restaurant in town that week, a little bistro on Queen Street West that I hadn't ever before been able to get into. Le voila, that old kismet again. We were on for 8 P.M. You're not going to be surprised when I tell you that the restaurant, a tiny hole in the wall, was called Stella, Star, because everything in my relationship with Schafer, as I was coming to believe, is written in the stars. Not that he's astrologically inclined, any more than I am.

This is the serious or moving part of this story. I've had to change my persona for the evening, but I figure you'll recognize me anyway.

The Chauffeur sits with her back to the door, shivering. Across the table her friend is looking raptly at the other man, hanging on his every word. She's never seen him look at anyone this way. She's curious about the other man, whom she's picked up in Lower Forest Hill Village an hour or so ago. She is sitting in the driver's seat of her black Subaru while her friend—let's call him the Writer—goes to fetch the Composer from the coachhouse where he is staying. Two tall men approach her car, the younger one, the Writer, three inches or so taller than the other. Both have grey hair, the younger is clean-shaven, the elder has a salt-and-pepper beard. The younger is dressed all in black, the other is wearing a green felt vest, alpine fashion, and is smoking a pipe. It's a good ten years since she's seen a man smoke a pipe. Driving down the hill, the two men amuse themselves talking about constellations and how to sight Orion in the Toronto night sky. Now in the restaurant, she's getting a good look at the Composer's amiable, friendly face. He's focussed on the Writer, giving her a chance to make a thorough inventory. There is something arresting about the face. It may be the heavy laugh wrinkles about the pale blue eyes or the way he looks right at you. But those are clichés, aren't they? And so is the fact that he laughs a lot. She'd like to say it was the soul of the man shining through his form, but she can't manage on such short acquaintance such a weighty pronouncement. He certainly stands out in his country attire in this restaurant of black-garbed waiters and clients. The three of them begin to talk about myth as the structure of civilization, and about memory. She says something about the memory theatres of the Renaissance imagination, and she asks the Composer if that is what he's trying to accomplish with his latest music-theatre work, *The Greatest Show (Patria 3).* She's heard that he's setting up an entire midway out there in the country, near Peterborough, with a hundred acts, and that the audience buys tickets and moves about inside the piece, but no one could possibly see all the acts in a single night. Early on, in a sideshow act, his heroine Ariadne is dismembered, and throughout the event parts of her body turn up in different acts. The Chauffeur has begun to wonder if he's gone too far. There's a big imagination here, and it's pretty self-confident, because the Composer is deconstructing his own works and spoofing his texts and his critics. Within the network of playing areas, there's a University Theatre where various professors wrangle about the significance of the *Patria* works before a single bench holding at the most four people. Schafer himself gives a lecture in this tiny theatre dressed as Wagner. There's an illustrated slide-lecture on Schafer's novel *Dicamus et Labyrinthos,* a psychiatrist's analysis of *Requiems for the Party Girl,* a description of *Wolfman (Patria 1),* and a skit called anti-opera in which music-director Hermann Geiger Torell vilifies Schafer, claiming his work is stolen from Wagner, Claudel, Brecht, and Disney. At the end, the three-Horned Enemy from *The Princess of the Stars* appears and destroys the fairgrounds of *The Greatest Show.* Then the Chauffeur wonders aloud if the acts are the externalizing of Schafer's own memory cells. For the first time he seems to notice her, dressed in black like her car and the restaurant clientele. He acknowledges her by telling her she understands myth and memory in a way most people don't. Then the Chauffeur and the Composer begin to talk about construction, and deconstruction, and reconstruction.

She tells him about Ronnie, the slender peroxide-blonde lady from Rochester, with the boyish haircut. The child is sitting alone in the darkened old opera house in Woodstock, Ontario. It stinks of the afternoon bodies, and the floor is sticky with spilled Coke and chewing gum, festooned with unpopped popcorn. Ghostly handkerchiefs whiz about her, approaching and receding up into the darkness. Ronnie is in a large white box on a wheeled platform on the bright stage. The saw is raised and lowered, the box is pulled apart. Now there are two boxes. Ronnie's head sticks out of one box. She waves and speaks. Her legs, capped by red-patent high heels, wiggle out of the end of the other box. Then the Chauffeur is seated at home in the dining room at the large table. On her right is her father, across from her is the magician, who before he leaves town will steal her father's cufflinks, beside her is

Ronnie, in one piece. A happy ending. The Composer is intrigued by their mutual interest in magic. Always recruiting, he invites the Chauffeur to take part in his *Greatest Show*. She says no; no matter what she looks like, she knows she's got the soul of a librarian, and she wants to keep all her brain cells carefully catalogued in a climate-controlled environment.

But the three of them now go for a long walk in the cool summer night along Queen Street, past San Francesco's, where even at this hour people are lined up for a veal meatball sandwich, past the shop windows—many like Das Nerve long ago closed—filled with black clothing, black boots, and metal accessories. They continue talking about myth and the stars. The Composer lights his pipe, his green felt vest bright in the light falling from the street lights and against the black uniforms of the teenagers lined up outside the BoomBoom Room.

WHEN I think of Murray Schafer, I do not think of him as some innocent abroad in the darkness of the city. That is how he was that night, but that was one night, and that was seven years ago. I've settled in, to my house in that neighbourhood, to my garden, to my neighbours, to the Kensington Market to the east, and the watering holes to the west. The Writer has gone on with his life, and the Composer and I have become friends. When I contemplate Schafer now, I think of his urbanity, of his accomplishments as a citizen in and of the world. There are the countries he's lived in, all over the globe, studying folk music in Bulgaria, ex-Yugoslavia, Hungary, Greece, and the Middle East. There are the languages, Italian, German, Greek, French, Arabic. There are the texts, medieval German, Coptic Egyptian, Tibetan sacred, western contemporary. There are the cities, Vienna, London, Paris, Athens. There are the people, the great Ezra Pound, Marshall McLuhan, John Cage, Yehudi Menuhin, and the folk of the villages, wherever he is, and the students in his classrooms, and the wide circle of friends, and his family.

Ask me how I picture him at this very moment, as I sit writing in my studio window while two female elk, newly calved, lie in the grass below my balcony, whisking their ears, chewing their cuds, guarding me as I journey; ask me now, and he springs to mind standing on the concrete pathway between two townhouses leading into the alley where I walk my little dog Lou. He's still a tall man, slim with an erect carriage. He's dressed for winter, booted, and wearing some sort of microfibre sea-green down-filled jacket. He's on his way west to Brandon, Manitoba, where he has spent the season in the Stanley Knowles Chair at the university. There's that open, welcoming smile and those bright pale blue eyes above that salt-and-pepper beard. And he's wearing a magnificent and luxurious fur hat, like a Renaissance Flemish portrait, like the groom in Jan Van Eyck's *The Arnolfini Wedding*, and he's laughing . . . *(Originally written 1987)*

Esmeralda

KAREN CONNELLY

SHE HAD AN OUTLANDISH NAME, and her appearance was outlandish, too. Esmé, she was called, although on the inside of her exercise books "Esmeralda" was printed in small green letters. Had her face not been so striking, people might have thought she was ugly because her body was heavy, almost ungainly. If she walked quickly, her limp was very pronounced; one knee seemed to have a permanent kink. She'd broken her leg as a child and the village doctor botched the delicate setting of the bones. Her eyes were the same amber and honey colour as her hair. In contrast to her round body, her face was narrow, sometimes painfully sharp. A long aquiline nose. If you were sitting close to her, you could see the complex latticework of veins in her ears. When she played, her nostrils flared and her face flushed. Even those who didn't care for her thought she was beautiful then.

She leaned very close to the piano and did not coax it to life but demanded that it rise up and make itself heard. Her way of speaking and dealing with people was gentle, although most people never knew it because she spent so much time alone. She loved to sing, and once, after we had become close, I managed to persuade her to sing for us. This surprised the people who thought her aloof, even unkind; her voice was deep and warm as flesh. During the final great snowstorm of the year, when we all gathered to say goodbye and feel the heat burst out of the fireplace for the last time, Esmé told the story of her song, then sang it in a language none of us could understand. It was the kind of time we all have occasionally, fleetingly, when we feel close to the human beings around us and are filled with hope for them and for ourselves, when we pray quickly and silently, even if we don't believe in a god, that something will keep us safe and help us to become ourselves. The painters, musicians, sculptors, piano tuners, kitchen staff: gathered in a ragged circle of firelight, faces warm under the red shadows, we listened to Esmé sing as though we were hearing a hymn we had loved since we were children.

BEFORE I went to the colony in the mountains, I visited the piranhas at the bank, paid off my loan, and put a thousand down on my Visa card. I flicked paint out from under my fingernails while a woman in pointed shoes thanked me for being such a good customer. As I left, she urged me to continue doing business with the bank. Ha! I thought, and whistled myself through the shiny doors. That very afternoon, free at last, I boarded a bus with a duffle bag stuffed full of paints, pastels, brushes, and a bag of powdered graphite, used to simulate illumination. I was interested, at that time in my life, in making light come out of the canvas.

As soon as I arrived at the colony, I lugged my bag to my high-ceilinged studio in the woods; I wasn't interested in seeing my room in residence because I was only going to sleep there. It was the first time in my life I hadn't had a money-grubbing job to do while I painted, and I was determined to take advantage of every moment of my liberation. That same afternoon, after twelve hours on a bus, I set up my rows of paints and the photographs I wanted to work from. I walked for an hour through the trees collecting pine cones and rocks and small, inspiring twigs—I'd always liked to have things to touch—then returned to my studio and sketched for two hours to loosen up my fingers. I gobbled down the stale muffin I had bought the day before in Vancouver because I thought going to supper in the cafeteria would be a waste of time. I was twenty-four, and my favourite phrase was Heinrich Boll's declaration: It's a crime to sleep!

For two weeks I worked constantly, stopping only for a few hours at a time to sleep or rush off to grab something to eat. I didn't bathe; I ate nothing before noon. I ran back and forth through the snow from my studio to the cafeteria, startling hungry deer. I'd met almost no one in the colony, although I knew the place was full of other artists. Sometimes I heard wild piano music pounding through the cold air. There was a lounge and a beautiful swimming pool and a famous library, but I hadn't gone anywhere except into my studio and into the trees where the shadows of the spruce dropped sharp and dark against the snow. I ignored other people because I didn't have money to spend on drinking, and I didn't want to get roped into boring conversations or have any melodramatic love affairs.

Esmeralda changed my mind about listening to other people. I met her just as my first flush of painter's mania was subsiding and I was returning, a little, to the world of bathtubs and breakfast.

⊹⊹

SHE had a strange, almost magical way of perceiving the world; people felt nervous around her, intimidated. During a master class, the principal oboist from the Boston Symphony asked, "In your opinion, what does music mean to most musicians?" He was a chubby, laughing man; the atmosphere of the class was conversational. The other musicians and composers were being witty, sharp-tongued, a little stupid, saying that music was a harmonious way to make a buck or to meet rich women in evening gowns. In response to his question, Esmé answered, "Like anything we love, music is salvation." She did not notice the lack of seriousness around her, the giggles, the restless feet.

She acquired the reputation of being too serious, high-minded, possibly miserable, but that was not true. When she was with someone she trusted, she laughed often. She had grown up in a certain darkness, in a country of secrets, and only by great external seriousness was she able to get as far as she had. When I knew her, she was twenty-six, already one of the most talented pianists in the Soviet Union. She came from a village in Moldavia and was without connections of any kind.

At fourteen, playing in a school concert, she interpreted a piece by Prokofiev almost faultlessly, with an unrushed power rarely observed in amateur musicians. One of the people in the audience was a visitor from Moscow, himself a pianist, an instructor at the conservatory. He spoke briefly with Esmé's parents. He said he would do everything in his power... Esmé's father, a pharmacist, and her mother, a worker in a zipper factory, received a call from Moscow. A month later, Esmé was living in a dormitory. She could see the Kremlin walls from her window. She studied music history and theory five hours a day and received lessons from one of the most famous piano teachers in Europe.

"It was like a huge wind tore through my life, blew everything apart. For longer than a year, I was stunned, well-stunned, like a cow before slaughter. I could not believe what had happened to me. When I had time to wander around Moscow, I had to consciously keep my mouth closed, or else I would have looked like an idiot. After three months, I was allowed to go home for a week of vacation, and though I loved my little town and my people, I suddenly realized, I understood for the first time: I had escaped. I would not grow up to work in the zipper factory. I would not study chemistry. I would play the piano. I would live in music. Do you see what that is? What that means? When I returned to Moldavia, I went back to the little school where I had learned to play. The upright piano with all its chips and forever out-of-tune strings made me weep. In Moscow, I had already been assigned a huge grand piano in a room with a mirror and a window. The piano in my school looked like a broken toy. I was only fourteen years old, but I knew a miracle had befallen me. For the last twelve years, I have tried to understand why. The gifts in our lives are the greatest mysteries we ever know."

WHEN Esmé was twenty-three, she attended a music competition in Poland, where she heard from a playwright about a renowned "centre for artists" in Canada. He had spent four months there and told her of the musicians he'd known, how they were given freedom and space and time to work. He gave her the address.

Esmé already had a considerable reputation. She had played abroad, recorded in England, won several major competitions. She was known in Russia as "the dark angel," even though she was pale and almost blonde. Her style was marked by a severity of interpretation rare in someone so young, and her playing, though grave, was surprisingly open and deep. She had a vulnerability, an honesty that most musicians never attain: she gave.

Every few months since her twenty-third year, when she'd heard about the artist centre, she had applied for permission to leave her position at the conservatory and study in Canada. Her teachers and advisers claimed that an extended sabbatical would be the end of her career. In an unstructured program, her discipline would evaporate, people would question her dedication. She would lose a great deal of what she had worked so hard to gain. The director of the conservatory met with her several times to warn her, dissuade her from leaving, remind her of the dangers, the temptations.

But four months later, at the beginning of September, Esmé made her first unaccompanied journey out of eastern Europe. She was twenty-six years old. While flying through darkness over the North Pole, she thought how wonderful it would be if the plane crashed. "Death," she explained, "can be the most potent revenge." She knew that she was to experience freedom for the first time in her life. She could not sleep for fear of nightmares. "The idea of doing whatever I wanted for more than an hour made me very anxious. I began to suspect that they were right, that I would become lazy, lose technique, fail to play well without the pressure of a schedule."

That did not happen. If people went to the colony with a desire to work, they worked. I discovered later that my flurry of creativity was not unique. The heat of creation made that mountainside warmer than others; the snow melted faster there, wildflowers opened sooner. Some of the sculptors began to work in epic proportions. At night they dreamt of bronze mountains high enough to scrape Orion's feet. Painters rushed around with paint on their elbows and foreheads. After they played and played, the musicians saw the faces of Elektra and Stravinsky in the clouds. In the evenings, we went swimming or drank beer or recited filthy limericks. Some of us stayed in our rooms and studios and thought about how far we were from creating anything that would live beyond us. We moaned, cried, laughed. We joked about becoming secretaries or zookeepers or engineers. I learned there that my life, and Esmé's life, all our lives, were nearly invisible fibres in a long, ancient thread. I tried to be unafraid of being so small. At the tail end of those nights, when I had been thinking too hard, I often ventured up the mountain paths until I was compelled to stop and stare at the sky with an open mouth. At first I was afraid to believe it, but I heard the stars singing.

I once asked Esmé if she had ever heard such a thing. She looked at me curiously, as if I was joking. "Jacqueline, stars don't sing. They never sing. They weep. Sometimes in sorrow, sometimes in joy. That is why they seem to tremble. They are crying."

AFTER my first few weeks of mad painting, when my inhuman pace had slowed down, I began spending the late afternoon in the library, studying beautiful art books and sketching notes to myself. When I paused at my work, I watched the musicians who came in to listen to music. Often they were so concentrated on the storms and reveries coming out of their earphones that I could sketch their motionless faces and bodies for more than half an hour at a time. Others grew restless, though, listening to the world's great composers. They rubbed their foreheads and hands violently, trying to press comparable music out of their own skin.

I noticed Esmé because she went to the library as often as I did. I did not know she was a musician because she rarely listened to music. She read the newspapers, then flipped through the new photography magazines and literary journals. She had bought a great deal of the turquoise jewellery so popular in those mountains; as she turned pages, her bracelets jangled and rang. Enjoying the silvery disturbance in that quiet place, I often tried to sit close behind her or off to her side, just out of her line of vision. I loved sketching her arms and hands because they were very fine, long, lightly veined and muscled. I came to expect her in the library. If she was not there I felt vaguely disappointed. One afternoon I watched her writing furiously on loose sheets of paper, copying something from one of the books on her table. When she rose and disappeared between the bookshelves, I stood and walked slowly past the books—all writings by Solzhenitsyn. As she was still hidden among the bookshelves, I leaned over and looked at what she was writing in her notebook. It was in Russian.

Uneven footsteps thumped behind me. I was caught in the act. I swung around with an apology in my mouth, but she spoke first. "A reprint of his Nobel lecture. I am memorizing it," she said. "Incredible, isn't it? Though he wrote it in Russian, I am memorizing a translation of it in English." Solzhenitsyn had won the prize five years before, in 1970. "But I have never seen a copy of this lecture in Russian. And I have read only part of *One Day in the Life of Ivan Denisovich*. It is very difficult to find that novel. I don't think he has been able to publish anything else in the Soviet Union."

"I didn't mean to ... I'm sorry I—"

"No, do not apologize. It is nice to meet you finally. My name is Esmé." She put out her hand. "And you?"

"Jacqueline."

"We seem to work here always at the same time. You are a painter, aren't you?" I nodded, groped for a book, put my other hand in my pocket. Her eyes held mine. "May I ask you a question, Jacqueline?" I nodded again and returned the book to its place. "Why do you always draw just my hands?"

Even as I looked away, I felt the bright flush rising in my cheeks, my jaw. I laughed.

She leaned over and shook my hand again. "Let's go and have a cup of coffee. I'll tell you."

Several days after I'd noticed her, I had left my sketch pads on the table and gone to the bathroom. Esmé, having felt me watching her, did exactly what I had done: she had gone over to look at my work, flipped through my sketchbook, where she recognized her own hands, the blue-studded bracelets. "But you did not catch me," she said, sipping her coffee. "Russians are quick like that. I was on the other side of the library by the time you came back." We spent the rest of the afternoon together and ate supper at the same table. Suddenly I was talking more than I had in weeks.

What is more extraordinary than the unexpected discovery of another human being? We talked so much that first night, of our work, our lives, our beliefs. She had an easy sense of humour, even though we often discussed Vietnam, governments, their abuses of freedom. She talked often of the Soviet Union, but she did not rage or wallow. She asked, "Who understands these things? There is nothing evil in the world except for human beings. I was eleven years old when I realized that; I wanted to stop being a girl and change into a horse. Then I began to love music, and I was happy. Music, my own hands, taught me that human beings also know what is beautiful and good."

Our greatest similarity was our love of water, the freedom of motion it creates. "It's flying," Esmé said. "It's the closest we'll ever come to being free of our bodies." We began to meet in the change room before swimming, then we would leap into the pool and do lengths until we felt our arms turning to rubber. We usually swam for about forty-five minutes, then we would play for another ten, walk on our hands, turn over and over in the deep end like seals, try to swim the length of the pool underwater. We would also race. Unless she was being kind, Esmé always won. After hopping out and rinsing off, we usually sat in the sauna for ten minutes, laughing about the swimmers who slapped about like wounded fish, or the ones who did two lengths for every one of ours. These fast, technically flawless swimmers she jokingly called "the Soviet Athletes." We came to recognize them on dry land, too; as they walked by, Esmé or I would whisper to the other, "Ahh, one of the Soviets!"

In the change room and the sauna alike, Esmé was almost careless about her body. She was not ashamed of it. She never told me exactly how she had achieved that particular freedom, having grown up in a restrictive country. She only said, "Beneath every tough comrade lives a Russian with warm blood." Even "liberated" women who had various lovers still needed to wrap a towel around themselves in the presence of their own sex. Esmé, naked and built like a well-fed Italian duchess, would have none of it.

Sweating in the wet heat, Esmé said, "The atmosphere of the Earth was just like this when amoebas decided to become gazelles." She loved the sauna. We usually spent too much time in there and came out feeling light-headed. Once, when we were alone, Esmé began doing a series of elaborate stretches that embarrassed me. She was always embarrassing me in the sauna, either by stretching or examining her own body with her hands or spreading oil over herself with the careless strength of a groom rubbing down a horse. I had to turn away from watching this or close my eyes and cross my legs. Esmé never crossed her legs; she said that it was bad for the circulation and didn't fool anybody. "Everyone knows what you have down there, Jacqueline," she once said in a thick, sexy voice, and I laughed, uncrossed my legs, then crossed them again the other way. I was thankful for the heat and half-darkness of the sauna because Esmé could never catch me blushing.

At that time, I was working steadily on studies for my paintings, two of which were commissions by a wealthy doctor who had worked years before in India. He had given me a couple of black-and-white photographs of laughing children wearing raggedy saris, and he wanted two paintings of these same photographs in colour. "I've never seen it before," he said, "the colour I saw there. It made me think I had wasted most of my life by wearing navy blue and grey and hospital green. I still dream about India sometimes. It was a hell of a place to work, but it was beautiful."

I had spent weeks doing studies from the photographs and mixing oils and flipping through various books in search of Asian colours. I was saturated; I wanted to begin. One evening in the sauna, I told Esmé I was somehow reluctant to go ahead on canvas. I had a perfect vision in my mind and was afraid I might not be able to release it without doing damage. "Hmmm, yes," she said, and began to braid her wet hair. "This happens also to composers. They hear the creature singing in their minds, but sometimes they believe writing the notes will silence it, kill it. Strange. When this happens to me, I just begin another work, a playful work, something that does not matter to me, what I call a little mouse piece. Then, when the little mouse comes out, I fool the lion into following it, and suddenly the mouse is devoured and my other work is roaring around the room." She poured more water onto the coals and stood naked over the hiss of new steam. Her back was broad and smooth. "Why don't you paint me first?" she asked, turning around, smiling. "I will be your mouse."

The idea of Esmé being a mouse was preposterous. She knew it, and I knew it, but I agreed to do some work with her as a model. She came to my studio the next day. She walked around, touching things lightly, smelling the paint, looking in closets. It was strange to watch her do this, like a cat in a new house. She made the place her own. It was only natural that she should take off her clothes and stand naked for me. I sketched her in charcoal first, then painted in watercolours, then did indeed get some canvas and work over her skin with pale oils. I went very quickly, messily, without much concentration. A thousand times I asked her if her feet were cold, if she was tired, if she wanted to change positions or rest. She always said no and kept her body perfectly still, one arm raised, hand behind her neck, the other hand on her upper abdomen, her thumb between her breasts. A couple of times we stopped and drank tea. Esmé sat cross-legged on her feet with a blanket draped loosely around her shoulders. She wore a small enigmatic grin on her face. "What are you smiling about?" I asked her.

She raised her eyebrows. "I'm just happy," she said, standing up. The blanket around her fell to the floor. Because I was sitting on a low stool, I was suddenly looking directly at her thighs. I stood up, too.

"Can I see what you've done?" She walked over to the easel and flipped through the charcoal sketches, making little sounds of approval when she came to something she liked.

It worked. That night, after spending three hours with Esmé during the day, I began the Indian paintings and stayed in my studio until two in the morning. Before leaving, I flipped through some of the studies on Esmé, looking carefully at what had been in front of me all day. She had a wonderful body, all hills and basins, roundnesses, long lines. I put the sketches on a shelf and pulled on my boots for the short walk through the trees. That night, in a dream, she came to my studio while I was working on a portrait of her. She ran her hand through the charcoal and smeared the image of her face. "That is not my skin," she said, and reached for my hand the same way she had when we first met, not to shake it again, but to lift it and press the charcoal in my fingers against her cheek. "This is my skin." And the charcoal did not appear black on her face but turquoise blue, like her bracelets, like the water in the pool. "It's flying," she whispered. I heard the sound of her deep, easy laughter and woke, thinking she had come into my room.

A week later, we sat in the sauna together, alone, inhaling the smell of wood and wet heat. Although I was naked from the waist up and quelling a powerful desire to cross my arms, I still wore a towel around my hips. After lolling for a few minutes, Esmé stood in all her pink glory and poured more water over the coals. She glanced at me and put her hands on the backs of her hips, squeezing two handfuls of flesh. "If you can't stand your own naked body, with all its flaws and beauties, then you will never be able to enjoy sex honestly." I was so embarrassed by this that I did cross my arms. Esmé laughed, unpinned her hair, and let it fall over her breasts. "There," she said, looking down at herself, "you can't see mine either."

She laughed at me again and stepped from the first bench to the second, where the air was hotter. After a few seconds of stillness—my eyes were closed—I felt her manoeuvre herself behind me. She began to massage my shoulders with one hand, then the other, then both. This surprised me at first, but I relaxed under the strength of her fingers. I swivelled my neck around, feeling oiled, pliant as an otter. I thought I felt her breath on my neck. Then she kissed me, very lightly, just under the ear. Before I could say anything, or even absorb the sensation, we were both caught off guard as two other women entered the sauna, laughing and chattering.

Esmé left almost immediately, saying goodbye to all three of us, and I stayed in the heat for ten more minutes, my mind turning somersaults. It was only the heat making me feel so dazed. I left the sauna when I felt sure that Esmé had already dressed and gone. Glowing and glazed with sweat, I immediately stumbled to the washroom taps and drank water like a draught horse, swallowing great slow mouthfuls. Through the routine of showering, drying myself, dressing, I kept thinking about having been kissed (but had I really? was I imagining it?) by a woman, on the neck. I tried to remember that sensation, that rising pressure through the centre of my body, that buoy floating up, pulling the thick net of desire through my skin. Impossible, that flush radiating from just under my belly. I was imagining it. Or I had been thinking of a man. I looked at my flushed face in the mirror, my black hair, still wet, my mouth, my eyes. I looked fine, perfectly normal.

AFTER that, tension shifted and clicked in between us. We still went swimming together, we still sat in the sauna, but it seemed that everyone sat in the sauna, trying to escape the suddenly brutal cold outside. We were never alone for more than two minutes. We never spoke of what had happened (or not happened) that evening, but I thought about it. Esmé and I still talked for hours together over coffee and hot chocolate, growing closer, weaving ourselves through each other's lives. Another layer existed, too, a deep, untouchable place that was also the most touchable, because it lived in our very skin, our eyes. But I did not quite believe it existed, and I was afraid to go there.

Sometimes, after talking late into the night, warming our bodies with tea and memory, we walked together down the road toward the little town at the base of the mountain. "We are in Switzerland," she said once, opening her blue-gloved hands to catch the snow. A moment later, we heard someone whistle high and long for a loose dog, then heard him call, his voice lower and less powerful, barely touching us. He whistled again, spearing both wood and stone with one long note. Esmé and I stood breathless in the dark, listening, feeling the nerves pluck and quiver in the backs of our legs. Why does a high whistle through a cold night stir sadness? Without any awkward words we turned and hugged each other.

During the next weeks, she talked so much about Russia that I went back to the paintings of Chagall, hoping to know the colours in Esmé's mind. I returned to graphite, hard charcoal, and bright oils; flowers, mythical monsters, and Indian children's faces inhabited my fingers, came rushing out whenever I worked. I did not sketch Esmé again because I was working easily from the photographs and my own vision; a model would distract me. She did not mention anything about it. I went to her lunchtime and evening concerts. After every one of these recitals, I went backstage and gave her a hug and a kiss and never once did I experience the sensation I had felt in the sauna.

THEN, in the middle of December, we had a Christmas party.

Over one hundred people gathered in the common room, laughing, drinking, dancing, saying goodbye. Some artists in the photography and music studios were leaving, returning to their Canadian cities or different countries; others were only going home for two or three weeks and would return for the second term. Esmé and I went together. When we arrived, we found people crowded around the fireplace at the back of the lounge. A British ceramicist was singing "Winter Wonderland" at the top of her lungs, with dirty words substituted for the regular lyrics. She accompanied her song with gyrating hips and shimmying shoulders, making everyone think of a nightclub act in Las Vegas because she wore a red sequined dress.

It was a very good party. Several conversations in the works were neither trivial nor depressing. Esmé did not have her usual mineral water but instead drank screwdrivers with plenty of orange juice, "to drown out the taste of this sad vodka," she said. We danced. I taught her the lyrics to a few Christmas carols. We even stayed after the midnight toast and had a cup of coffee laced with whisky, chocolate, and cinnamon, topped with whipped cream. A great pot of this stuff brewed in the kitchen, and the entire lounge smelled like a chocolate factory full of scotch drinkers. The scent of cinnamon lingered in our mouths. Esmé laughed as we drank, saying, "This is dessert, dessert! I want one of these for breakfast! I will become alcoholic!" When we finally left, we were still quite drunk and very happy, leaning on each other, laughing.

Outside, between the lounge and Jackson Hall, we tried to have a snowball fight. Defeated by our poor and drunken aim, we dropped the snowballs and tried to push each other into the snowbanks on either side of the pathway. When our jaws numbed from laughing in such cold air, we declared a truce and began walking together up the path. Passing a snow-laden pine tree, Esmé could not resist reaching up and shaking it over my head. I was blind with snow for a few seconds and stunned by the icy whips down my neck. I lunged for her with a scream, pushing her right over the snowbank under the great boughs of the pine tree. She disappeared completely in the hole made by the wall of snow and tree. I was breathless and laughing, still scooping snow out of the collar of my coat. "Esmé?" I leaned over the snowbank to peer into the trees. Darkness. I could see the icy soles of her boots. She had fallen upside down.

I heard a moan.

"Esmé? Are you all right?" Then I was afraid that she'd banked her head at the base of the tree or hurt her back. "Esmé! What's wrong?"

She coughed. "I'm so cold," she said, and her feet wriggled beneath my chin. "I think I'm drunk enough to fall asleep like this, but I am freezing." A few warm words of Russian came, a sputtered laugh. "I have snow in my mouth!" She struggled like a turtle knocked backwards on its shell. Kicking away snow, I reached in to pull her out. She was quite heavy; each time I pulled, her coat slid up her back, exposing bare skin. "I'm freezing!" she said a few times. "I have snow everywhere." Rising at last, encrusted in snow and ice, she jogged stiffly toward the hall. I ran along beside her. "I'm sorry, Esmé, I didn't know you were going to drown in there! I'm so sorry!"

When she opened her coat, kerchiefs of snow fell to the floor. I went with her to her room, opened the door for her, ran the bath. She was shivering. "Take off your clothes," I said. Her chattering teeth filled the room with the sound of tiny castanets. "Hop in the bath." She pulled off her damp sweater and pushed her skirt to her ankles, giggling and whispering in Russian as she fell backwards onto the bed in a heroic struggle with her tights. As soon as I drew them off her calves, she jumped up, her naked body blotched red with cold, and ran to the bathroom.

"Aye! Aye! It's too hot! You're trying to kill me." I heard the splash and dance of water as it rose up the sides of the tub. When I entered, she was doing a jog, lifting up one foot and then the other. I put my hand in. "It's not too hot. It's your skin. Your skin's still cold." She rolled her eyes and, grabbing on to the enamel sides of the tub, lowered herself. She moaned and smiled. "Will you give me the oil?" she asked, pointing to the counter. She did not pour it into the water. She poured a small pool into her hand and began to rub it on her chest. Closing the door, I left the bathroom. Beside her bed, I slowly hung up her clothes. I felt the texture of the red sweater, the black skirt, the black tights, Esmé's clothes. Esmé, in the bathtub, the sound of the water still running there, hot over her feet.

I opened the bathroom door and said, "I think I'll go to bed now." She smiled and said, "Come here first." I closed the door behind me to keep the steam in and squatted beside the tub. She lifted out of the water a little. (The faint perfume of bath oil, the scent of wet heat, wet skin, her breath, her breasts and belly and wide shoulders rising up, an ocean opening, sliding down her hips.) Then she laid her hand on my face—it was wet and very warm—and she kissed me, my mouth. I felt the moist warmth of her lips with my own. Her hands slipped down my neck, eased away the collar of my blouse. The hair on my arms rose. For a moment, I thought I might cry, these touches were so gentle.

⊹

WE did not sleep until much later, almost dawn. Many times, surfacing from a deep kiss or suddenly feeling the contours of her body against mine, I said, "What's happening?" but, as in a dream, there was no answer, only her face appearing before my own, beautiful and opened as I had never seen it before. She did not stop smiling. I kissed her the way I had kissed the older boys of my adolescence, hopefully, recklessly, in a heady state of joy. But I felt guiltless and sure of myself now, despite my external awkwardness. There was passion, and want, and the anxious way of muscles under skin flexing and tensing, but I was hardly able to name the act a sexual one. It was innocent lovemaking, not sex. I felt very young, younger than any teenager ever feels in her storm of flesh and emotion.

So soft, so open, so different, to feel breasts where you have always felt a hard chest. We buried ourselves under the covers of her narrow bed and hugged each other. Her hair was still wet. She smelled like flowers. The wall beyond us was speckled and darkened by the shadows of the pines. For a moment, we stopped moving and held our breath to listen to the wind rocking and teasing the trees. Esmé whispered, "The ocean. It sounds like the ocean."

I touched her neck, the white slope of her chest. "Esmé, I don't really know what to do, you know." She laughed. Her neck stretched back; the hollows of her collarbones became blue pools of shadow. I saw the brightness of her teeth as she lowered her head and traced kisses over my belly.

The sound of my own breath surprised me, as her tongue touched me, as her mouth, like wet satin folding, unfolding, rubbing, braided itself into my own flesh, Esmé's mouth, and the curve of her back rising beyond me in shadow, darkness, my own body falling into the darkness of many colours, the deepest darkness of the body, the blood, where everything disappears but living feeling, pleasure in the skin, and I cried her name.

She glided up to me again, leaned over to wipe her mouth on the covers. She was smiling. Her arms looped over me; her leg rested on my stomach. After a while, I said, "What about you?"

"We have time," she whispered. "We have time. I have been wanting to be with you for so long." We fell asleep on that single bed, holding each other, breathing the perfume of women's sex.

When I woke in the morning, she was not beside me. I sat up and looked around, thinking perhaps I was in my own room; I had dreamt the whole thing. "Esmé?" I whispered. She had made love to me the night before.

Just as I was about to get out of bed, she came in with muffins and coffee. She kissed me. "Hello. How are you? No, no, don't get up. We'll eat in bed." And we did. Then we showered together, washed each other slick and fragrant, leaned together again and again, trying to fit our bodies together. We made love with the hot spray of water pounding our backs and legs and bellies. I could not believe how happy I was, how free I felt with her.

Later we lay in bed, touching each other's backs with our fingertips. Esmé talked about what it was like for her to live in Russia. "Sometimes you can see the faint signs, a certain way of talking that no one would recognize but another lesbian. Homosexuals are considered deviant, abnormal, sick, but lesbians! Lesbians are unthinkable! Lesbians aren't even mentioned in the criminal code because it's assumed they don't exist, unless they are just two women getting together for the pleasure of a man. It is difficult in the world of culture, of restricted culture, to be what I am. And it is such an evil for the privileged, not like beating your wife or children. Much worse than that. So unspeakable. So undisciplined—the greatest of sins. By the time I was about fourteen, I knew that I was different. I struggled with it, cried, made endless promises to myself. I thought about killing myself: there seemed to be no other answer. I was convinced I was the only woman on Earth who loved other women. I was so lonely with my self-knowledge that I thought I might as well die. A good friend saved me, an older boy who played the cello. Drawn together because we were both loners, we became close enough to talk about sex. That was when I found out that homosexuals existed, and we convinced each other that there had to be other people like us. finally I accepted it, accepted my desire, accepted myself. I found out what an orgasm was and nearly went crazy with joy. I watched the ballet classes in the conservatory with such lust that I had to run upstairs sometimes and masturbate under my piano.

"When I was eighteen, a new teacher came from Kiev, a well-known pianist originally from East Germany. She was very beautiful. Tall, blonde, quite thin. Too thin. fine, fine bones. I dreamt about her, wrote love poems to her, longed for her, wanted her. This went on for about a year and a half. When I was nineteen, she and my classmates made a trip to Warsaw for a music festival. Our hotel had somehow halved our reservations, so we ended up sleeping four or five to a room. Lena and I were assigned a double bed; there were two other students in the room, sleeping on cots. All through the evening of the first series of concerts, I was terrified that when we went back to the hotel, Lena would ask one of the other girls to sleep with her. But when we prepared ourselves for bed that evening, she just talked and joked in her usual way. We all said good night, lay down. One of the other girls turned out the light. The room was so small that if I stretched my arm out of the bed, I could touch the next cot.

"Of course I could not go to sleep. I breathed in deeply, slowly, smelling the scent of her face cream, her hair. She lay with her back to me but I was close enough to feel the warmth of her body. I could see the shape of her neck in the pillow. I lay absolutely still, trying to hear the pulse of her heart, thinking of the times she had leaned over me when I was playing to see that my posture was correct. I remembered the time I had seen the lace of her bra, the curve of her breast. I was a virgin, but I felt that I would die if I did not touch her.

"I rested my hand close to her back, felt the material of her nightdress, but not the skin beneath. I did not move for over an hour. I heard three bodies breathing regularly. finally, slowly—it seemed so loud—I shifted so that the whole side of my hand was pressing against her back. She did not stir at all. I thought she was asleep. I opened my hand, touched her very, very lightly, travelled up toward her neck, her hair. Tears were in my eyes, I was so happy to touch human flesh.

"When she rolled over, I felt my stomach turn in fear. I pulled my hand away and closed my eyes. Then I felt her face come close to my own, her breath on my chin, my neck. She whispered into my ear so quietly that I did not hear every word. I had to piece her sentences together from rhythm and syllable. "Not here. Wait until we are alone. Yes. I want you." And she kissed me very lightly. I opened my eyes to see her face but she was already turning over again.

"I did not sleep all night. My mind was full of noise and moving like a train. I imagined everything for us. I lay in bed and hugged myself so hard that I bruised my arms with my own fingers.

"We became lovers. I was dazed with glory. I ran up stairs, I sang in elevators, I stared down the ugliest streets with a foolish smile on my face.

She changed my life by allowing me to love her. And she loved me back, I think, although perhaps not in the way I wanted, not as absolutely as I loved her. For a long time, I wondered if she loved her brother more than she loved me, but now I know that something like that cannot be measured or judged.

"It was the happiest time of my life. We became even better friends. My playing grew very strong, energetic, lively. I grew confident; I was placed in several important concerts. Lena's brother was a well-known violinist. I remember him telling me how wonderful it was that I was finding a style. He really liked me. Once, the three of us went to my town in Moldavia to visit my parents.

"It was because of her brother that she left. We had been together for two years when she disappeared. I was twenty-one. Lena was thirty-four. Her brother defected while on a tour of Austria. He went out to buy cigarettes and ended up at the American embassy.

"I don't know what happened to Lena. I don't think she went with him—though she did go with him on tour, because she had friends in Austria and wanted to see them. If she had defected as well, she would have been publicly denounced. And she would have gotten some message to me, somehow. She would have told someone. I still don't know what happened to her. It has been over five years. I've never been able to find out if she aided him somehow, or if she was simply punished—is being punished—for what he did. Or perhaps she is teaching piano in New York. Perhaps she is afraid to communicate with me for my sake. I don't know. I do not like to think that she is wasting her life in some Siberian desert. But I don't know.

"I was sick after her disappearance. I could not play. And then, when I was better, I refused to play. I was so angry, so alone, and no one would tell me what had happened in Austria. All the musicians who had been on the tour had seen nothing, heard nothing. I went to the director. He claimed it was a mystery; no one knew what had happened, where she was. I wrote letters to committees, heads of state, the newspaper. I risked a great deal by being so vocal, so full of questions, so furious. I contacted someone who worked for Amnesty International. I went mad with grief because I could tell no one how much I really needed her.

"The autumn recitals were coming up in Moscow. Much earlier in the year, before Lena's disappearance, I had been chosen to represent the conservatory. I told them my hands were dead. I had stopped playing. I lost over ten kilograms. I smoked. I contemplated suicide but did not have the courage for that. I knew that if I was sent back to Moldavia, my career as a pianist would be over. I would become a chemist, or perhaps I would work in the factory. This thought filled me with sadistic pleasure. I would waste my gift. Like a perverted alchemist, I would turn gold to shit. There is a certain kind of despair that fools you into believing your pain will weaken if you poison others with it. I was going to transmit my suffering to everyone who had worked with me, encouraged me, moulded me.

"A psychiatrist was brought in. For some reason, perhaps because he was so ugly, I was terrified. I knew what could happen. After a long interview, he asked me to play, surveying me with an eye that showed how pathetic he thought I was, how pale and weak and thin. I said to myself, Fuck him, I will play so well that he will fall down on his knees and worship me. And that is how I played. A miserable but vengeful goddess.

"That went on for a long time. My furious interpretations were thought to be a little strange, much too extreme, but I was working again. I was practising for ten hours a day sometimes, straining the muscles in my forearms. I used to crack my nails by playing so hard and bleed on the ivory keys. If the director and my advisers were horrified, they were also impressed by my new power. I played all the music as if it were a battle, or as if it were dying right there on the page. I interpreted nothing light or glorious. I despised waltzes and gentle pieces—they were sentimental, unworthy. My Mozart sounded diseased. My *allegro vivace* movements were criminal, like a war of butterflies. I loved Rachmaninoff and the lonely music of Bartok and Beethoven's darker works. Everything I played I transformed into the music of sorrow . . ."

Esmé told me a lifetime, several lifetimes, in the months we were together. Her great-great-grandfather, Philippe Lassaigne Maritam, had been a French professor of European history and literature who taught in Moscow. As a young man in Paris he had met Victor Hugo many times. Each of his seven children was named after characters from Hugo's books. Sometimes the names were adapted to Russian, sometimes they remained as they had been in French. Esmé's mother, grandmother, and great-grandmother were called Esmeralda, Esmerina, and Esmerazia.

My Esmeralda knew nothing of her namesake's story until she came here. One evening, I went to her practice studio with an English copy of *The Hunchback of Notre Dame.* In candlelight, sitting among five down pillows, a blanket, and a bottle of cheap, sweet Hungarian wine, I read everything there was about Esmeralda, the gypsy woman with her trickster goat. She laughed every time I came to a passage that described the downtrodden Esmeralda. "Aye! What a name, what a gift!" We fell in love with Quasimodo. We spilled wine on the pillows. She reached over to me with both arms, kissed my throat, and whispered, "Have you ever made love under a piano?" Her mouth tasted of fruit. I looked over at the Blüthner grand, polished to a high black gleam. We blew out the candles and rolled under the piano, our mouths already open to each other's skin.

A certain sadness shadowed us now, because it was already the end of February. Esmé would leave Canada in April. We did not talk about it very much. We did not make promises as other lovers do, knowing we had no right to think of promises or pacts.

A few people knew we were in love simply by the way we spoke to each other. In 1976, there were no other lesbians that we knew of at the colony, but there was a pair of very enthusiastic homosexuals from Chicago who looked like twins. They were photographers who took the most amazing pictures of each other. I became friends with them, but Esmé tended to draw away. Her fear of being discovered or penalized never disappeared, although it diminished while she lived here. She was still afraid of what could happen outside herself, what could be done to her, but she was not afraid of her heart. "I sometimes experience moments of such bitterness," she once told me, "and such anger, anger at the way my world has been, because I have not been free. And I do not even mean in a political sense, though I suppose everything becomes political eventually. It is the same for deviants here, I think. There are so many risks, so many lies, so great a denial of the self." She often called herself a deviant: "When I was learning English, I always remembered it by associating it with the word 'devil.'"

In late March, Esmé announced one morning that she planned to play *Carnaval* by Schumann for her last concert. She lay beside me in bed stretching one leg, then the other toward the ceiling. Light poured through the curtains; our window was open. It would still snow in the mountains, but the heat and movement of spring already roiled in the sky and under the ground. The clouds were high, round sometimes, summer clouds. It was warm; new birds returned from the south. We could smell pine sap whenever the wind was blowing.

Esmé said, "*Carnaval* is romantic, full of light, soft. I haven't played a piece like it since I was with Lena. It's the last time you'll hear me play for . . . a long time. So I want to play something happy for us. We have been happy together, haven't we?" After reaching down to kiss my foot, she jumped out of bed. For a few moments, she turned around and around the room, her body naked and dazzled with sunlight, her hair lit with gold. She had the dignity of a dancer who did not know she was wounded, or simply did not care.

The concert was in April, four days before she was scheduled to go home. It was held at the old hotel on the river, a great stone chateau originally built for the elite travellers who came to the mountains in the early 1900s. Members of the orchestra from the city were going to play, and reviewers came, and most of the rich people staying at the hotel. As I walked through the plush foyer, past the velvet and leather chairs, I heard the sound of a harp, a woman singing in French. I became disoriented, took several wrong turns, circled back, and came to the foyer again. The ceiling was very high, domed in places, like a cathedral. I felt as if I'd lost myself in a castle. Someone had told me that the concert hall was on the third floor, close to a gallery of old paintings, but when I went up there, I met an acre of round oak tables, where old ladies clinked their wineglasses and laughed beneath enormous chandeliers. I turned and ran all the way down the stairs again, tripping on my high heels, out of breath. I began to whisper Esmé's name. I was afraid she would begin to play without me. I asked one of the busboys where the concert was. He said, "I think it's already started, on the second floor, east wing." I was in the opposite end of the hotel, going up and down the wrong flights of stairs. I ran through the gilded hallways, shoes in my hand, catching glimpses of myself in the grand mirrors. I was afraid I would miss her or they wouldn't let me in. People turned around to look at me, point. I heard someone say, "Miss, Miss ..." Then I was pulling my skirt up over my knees to take the stairs two at a time. I begged the doormen to let me sneak into the hall. They asked me to put on my shoes, which I did, then they slivered open the door and I slipped in. I stood at the back for her whole performance, but I could see her face. She had been playing for perhaps two minutes.

Now, years later, I listen to *Carnaval* whenever I want to remember her. I see Esmé playing gently, expansively, as though the hope hidden in the notes had stretched her fingers. No one has ever played for me as she did that night, with such faith and longing. Her hands were like doves.

I remember her beyond me, beyond this world where I live now, my life so various, so busy, so changed. I haven't become a great painter, though I am quite good. I am good enough. These days, when I swim in a river of paint, my small daughter often swims beside me, leaving her smudged fingerprints on big sheets of yellow construction paper taped to the lower half of my studio walls. I have been very lucky. I know what is beautiful and good. Esmé and I wrote for almost five years. Then I married. And I had Katrin. Then I left my husband ... Everything, my life, happened. Is happening now. Time and distance. Esmé and I lost each other in the translation.

But I remember her voice as she spoke of music the day before she left, when we sat in her studio and the reality of her departure fell on us like part of a mountain. The piano faced the window and both of us sat on the bench. "If only we could be the music," she said, "instead of being the vessel for its power. Because it only touches us lightly. It never stays. It isn't the world. It raises us up, doesn't it? But then it finishes. It stops. We fall again, and the silence is even deeper than before.

"Doesn't every musician want to become her music? Can you imagine the freedom of a bird? That is music, Jacqueline, that is flying. But how much of it belongs to us? The notes rise up and turn to light. We can't keep them. Yet if we don't let them go, they stay in our hands and grow silent before us. *That* is why I have to play. To let something *live*."

She closed her eyes, bent herself over the piano, and laid her hands on its black surface. After a while, she raised her head, but her eyes remained closed. Putting my hand beneath her chin, I turned her face to mine. Then I leaned forward and kissed her eyelids. They were very white. Her eyelashes were the colour of doeskin. I felt them against my lips. We sat for a long time, barely touching, our faces turned toward the trees outside. It was a windless day, and the pines were threaded with the flight of birds. Both of us heard the music dance and slip from their small, warm throats.

Shanghai

LAYLE SILBERT

CHINA! Every morning she woke to China with joy. This morning, while blissfully looking forward to seeing the onion-shaped dome of the Russian church in the bathroom window, Ellen remembered. Money. She was running out. How much longer would Ben, with a look of long suffering, hand her thick packets of the inflated currency every few days? She had to ask because she hadn't been able to find a job.

She watched the chickens in the lane and put off thinking where she could look today. She knew very well that she'd run out of places to try. Just then the woman across the way opened the door of her room giving out onto the lane, which thus became her living room. Her name was Luba. So far everything was Russian, nevertheless still China.

Leaning her elbows on the windowsill, she decided that later she'd go and have lunch, no, tiffin, with Ben. Then she'd have to tell him she hadn't looked anywhere this morning. Let him face it; there were no jobs for her. What would he say? Sometimes he was more disappointed than she was when she came back without a job from one of her excursions. Who in Shanghai wanted to hire an American researcher? Right after she'd written a sample radio script about Grey's Cigarettes for the English-language radio station on the Bund, the station ran out of money.

Still watching the lane, she saw a stranger come in like a medieval stroller, a squat, bare-headed Russian in a leather jacket with a balalaika. He stopped, set his legs apart, threw his head back, and began to sing and play. Somebody from a floor above in the apartment house threw down a small object wrapped in newspaper. Barely stopping, the man stooped to pick it up and thrust it in his pocket. A beggar. Somebody else without a job. Look what happened to him.

Later, on rue Paul Henri, she was in Frenchtown, a part of the city that had been the French concession before the war, which had ended two years earlier. "You should have been here then," their new friend, Fritz, a German refugee who'd been here through it all, said again and again. "It was so much better." But she was satisfied with what had survived. The apartment buildings were modelled after chateaux, with balconies and windows that opened outward to catch the night air during tropical summers. Not a Frenchman in sight anymore, with one exception at the office of the United Nations Relief and Rehabilitation Administration, known everywhere as UNRRA, where Ben worked. All she saw now were Chinese and bored-looking Russians. Even the beggar on their street who could be a forgotten Romanov looked bored and superior.

On Nanking Road she waited for transport while watching the river of Jeeps, trucks, automobiles, carts, rickshaws, pedicabs, although so far no sedan chairs. Just as she noticed an open Jeep driven by a uniformed chauffeur and a Chinese man and woman in splendour on brocade-covered seats, the cheesebox came.

A cheesebox, she learned when she'd arrived at the beginning of the month in the heart of winter, was a kind of U.S. Army truck with an open back and benches inside. She scrambled in and stayed at the end of a bench, where the view of the passing street was best. The odours of burning charcoal and tung oil joined the sights to make for beguilement with Shanghai on the way to the Bund, across the bridge over Soochow Creek and to the Embankment Building. Late in the morning, but some people were just going to work. If she ever did get a job, she might be late, too. That would never happen to Ben. Dear Ben, soon she'd have to tell him one more time that she still had no work.

In the anteroom to Ben's office she encountered his secretary, a white-haired Australian lady named Miss Prendergast. She'd lived in Shanghai since she was twenty, through battles, wars, occupation, and sieges, had never learned Shanghai dialect or any other and looked after Ben like a mother. Ellen approved, since she didn't know how to remind Ben to take his rubbers and umbrella. She often forgot them herself.

"There's someone there with him," the secretary said.

"No matter," said Ellen as though for a moment she'd turned Australian, too. She'd expected to find Ben as usual at his desk, his back to the window and the view, so engrossed that at first he wouldn't know her. Then he'd smile as usual and say, "Oh, hello. Let me finish this sentence."

After that she'd settle back with an army service novel bought at a stall, to wait or simply watch him working. The day before, he'd been pondering a document on rice paper, the top covered with columns of Chinese characters, the lower part with English primly crossing the page. He said, "A Harvard graduate. Such English," as he clapped his forehead in dismay. He turned to her as if to make sure she was there and went back to the document.

Now in his anteroom, Ellen hesitated, wondering if she should say right away she'd given up the useless search.

Just then Newton came out of Ben's office.

"Hello," she said.

"Oh hello, Ellen," said Newton and rushed off. Maybe his wife was in his office waiting to take tiffin with him.

She took a deep breath and went in. Ben was leaning back in his chair twiddling his thumbs. She hadn't known he knew how or would ever do anything so literary.

"What's wrong?" she asked, seeing his expression.

"Bad news," said Ben. "Two UNRRA officers froze to death last week. They were in a freight car stuck in Sian, escorting a shipment of powdered milk, grain, and shoes. The news just came through."

"Chinese don't drink milk."

"Well, that's what it was," said Ben. "They were waiting nobody knows how long for the track to be cleared. Wouldn't leave the stuff."

"Did you know them?" Neither said what they both knew, that the reason the shipment couldn't be abandoned was to keep it from local officials who would sell it.

"Don't even know their names. Newton heard it in the dispatcher's office. They were Yugoslavs who went through the war. One was a doctor. Everybody feels bad." Ben shoved his papers away and said, "I don't feel like doing anything. Let's eat."

They sailed past Miss Prendergast into the corridor.

"What are you looking at?" he said.

"I'm looking out other people's windows," Ellen said. Through open office doors, she was catching glimpses of the junks in Soochow Creek, children sitting perilously at the edges, laundry like bunting on bamboo poles.

He raised his eyebrows to show what he thought of people who did such things. "If you had a job, you wouldn't be looking out windows. Did you turn up anything today?"

The moment was here. By now he should know anyway. If she'd found work she would have announced it as soon as she came in. She said, "I don't know where to go anymore."

Ellen wished he didn't shake his head. He sighed. How could he be angry? It wasn't her fault. Was he having trouble seeing her not being the working woman he'd known from the day they'd met? How shocked he'd been to see that not only was she getting used to being without work; she even liked it. As for herself, she did want to work all right, but lately she was admitting to herself that she could really have been born to idleness. Would it take all of China to uncover her true nature?

The hard part, of course, in not making money was asking for it and then taking it. Ben didn't know how to give her money and she didn't know how to ask. She was going to have to ask him right now at lunch.

"OK," he said as though reading her mind, "that means you need money."

She looked at him in gratitude as they came to a stop outside the dining room.

He pulled his billfold, swollen with inflated Chinese national currency, from his pocket. This currency, printed by the American Banknote Company, was unsuited to delicate commerce between men and their wives, especially as it lost value by the day, even by the hour. Their friend Fritz, who visited Ben in his office without an invitation, another sign of how China was not America, carried his money in a briefcase.

"What's the rate today?" Ellen asked, as did everyone. Ben always knew. Watching him, she saw that for all that he wanted her to work, he took pleasure in giving her money.

After he told her the rate, she said, "The faster it goes up the more often I have to ask for money. Put it back. Wait until we sit down." As much as she hated taking money, she couldn't but think how easily she came by these thick packets.

He put his billfold back.

"It's like stage money," she went on. "A rickshaw ride to the Central Bank is a thousand CNC. When I hand over a pile of bills, I laugh. The puller laughs, too."

In the dining room, where white tablecloths hung to the floor because there was enough help to keep them changed, nearly everybody spoke English. With a jolt, Ellen realized she understood what people said. They were talking about the two dead Yugoslavs. To her, the Chinese spoken on the streets was an ongoing music always available. It pleased her not to know what people were saying, content with the cadences and intonations of Chinese, hearing everything but the meaning.

Were she to get a job after all, she'd be penned up in some office where English was spoken, away from the wonderful Chinese noises. She didn't say this to Ben.

"Well," he said as they seated themselves, "jobs are still frozen here."

"What do I do? I told you they treated me like Miss America at the USIS until I said I didn't know stenography. That hurt. Where can I look now?"

"There's always Mr. Kuo." Mr. Kuo was Ben's Chinese assistant, native to Shanghai, forever bounding with goodwill and happy to be their private information centre. At the Chinese opera, he never stopped explaining and translating.

"Besides that, it's hard for me to get around. I don't know where anything is. I don't know how to tell the pedicab man where I want to go."

"What about people who go to work on streetcars?"

Were they going to quarrel? Yes, they were quarrelling. Their voices were rising. They were as riven by her not working as the country was by the civil war tearing it apart since the end of the big world war two years before. They hadn't met anybody who doubted the outcome of the civil war in China, that the corrupt nationalist government would crumple. How would their private civil war come out?

As he saw her smothering herself in China, maybe Ben secretly wanted to be free too to wander and look at everything. Ellen remembered the lyrical descriptions in his letters before she could come to be with him, of long peering walks through the city on weekends. Looking at him as he studied the menu, she thought, He's worried for me. He himself could never bear to be without work, but he'd never have to be. Can't he see I'm different? For him, to be alive is to work. I'm alive without it. But for her too, the road to happiness was through work as long as she was wife to Ben. Without outside work, the wife usually cleaved. With work she cleaved but less. That was what Ben was risking.

"How I envy you." Another voice. There would be no quarrel. Newton had come to join them at tiffin, without his wife after all. By chance she had arrived sooner than Ellen, before the job freeze. What did Newton and his working wife quarrel about?

"Who? Me?" said Ellen. What would Ben make of this? There was more than one way to think of an idle wife. "Sit down."

"If I had your free time, I'd be looking in curio shops for export porcelain. It's wonderful stuff. Some day I'll show you what I've bought so far."

She looked at Ben, saw no new understanding. What he said was, "Let's have dinner some time."

"OK," said Newton. "We should try a new place I heard about. It's called the Kingkong."

Ellen growled to sound like a movie character. Ben and Newton laughed.

Newton said, "It's Szechuan. The only one in Shanghai."

News of restaurants was traded in the dining room like baseball cards. The week before, she and Ben had found the Kavkaz, an old Russian restaurant, in Frenchtown.

"What about this evening? I could call Georgina and have her meet us after work."

"Good," said Ellen, ready for a treat.

"No, no, wait a minute," said Ben. "I think tonight we're invited somewhere."

"Where?" said Ellen.

"Professor Ma Yin chu. For Chinese New Year's."

"Excuse me," said Newton in mock respect. "You consort with the great and famous."

"Only an economist."

"Like you," said Ellen to Ben. "Like you," she said to Newton.

"Watch what I do," Ben said in the Jeep that evening as they drove over. Since he'd come to Shanghai two months before she had, he was her authority on proper conduct, including the use of chopsticks. For Ellen this visit to real Chinese people in their home was what she wanted of China, to engage with it directly.

They fell quiet as the Jeep made its way to an outlying section of the city. Then Ben spoke. "Maybe you'd better go back home to the States, get your old job back."

"No, oh no," said Ellen, pressing her fingers into his arm. "I want to be with you. You don't mean it, do you?"

"Well," he said, looking at her. "I guess I don't. No, I don't."

"Why?" asked Ellen. "I don't understand. All over the world men feed and house and love their wives. Let me see what it feels like, too."

"Chattel," said Ben. Then, with a wry smile and a glint she caught in the light of a passing street lamp, he seemed suddenly to make a discovery. "That's it. I don't know what to do with a chattel. I don't want it. Doesn't it mean I can tell you what to do? Make you take my shoes to the shoemaker, my suits to the dry cleaner because I pay you to do it?"

"Not just for going to the shoemaker either." She put her arm around his woolly shoulders, then nuzzled the prickly stuff for a moment.

He sighed. Was it his sigh for giving in?

"Not for nothing an economist," she went on. "Those ladies who play cards in the afternoon. I always wondered what kind of life that was."

"Cards?" said Ben, shocked. "You want to play cards? I have to support you so you can play cards?"

"Don't worry," said Ellen. "Not me. All I'll do is read and go roaming. I'll really take your shoes to the shoemaker if you want me to. Where is the shoemaker?"

"On Sitzang Loo. I'll show you."

"See. You know how. It's begun. Take advantage. It won't last forever. I won't let it."

"Not a joking matter. It's your life." In the uneven darkness was he looking to see if she understood?

"I'll find something to do. You wait," she said. Would these discussions come to an end at last? Still shaken by the very notion she might go back to the States any sooner than the last possible moment, when they would go together, but at the same time beginning to feel comforted, she followed Ben to the apartment-house entrance.

Wong, their driver, who wore a lumber jacket with a map of Burma embroidered on the back, would wait. "He'll buy something to eat from a street vendor," Ben explained.

As they crossed the threshold, she felt herself setting aside Ben's imperatives. Here, at last, they'd reached the interior of the country. Professor Ma's flat, unheated as was their room in Frenchtown, lit by small naked bulbs suspended from the ceiling, looked dismal. It's home for them, she thought as she smiled to his welcome. Right off, they were led into the dining room without being asked to take off their coats. The warmth of the bodies of the seven elderly Chinese economists already there did little against the chill.

As honoured American guests, Ellen and Ben were seated at the head of the long table occupied by these Chinese gentlemen in their gowns padded with silk waste. Nobody seemed to consider whether she was working or indeed had gone so far in their thinking as to consider the question. Here she was, the American wife of an American economist, and nothing she did could change that.

Professor Ma put himself at Ben's right like a mentor, maybe to make sure they did use their chopsticks properly and that they ate of each dish as it was offered. In the poor light his glossy bald head shone and his face was ruddy. He was known for saying to everybody when he met them, "I take a cold bath every day." Again, as they were bustled into the room, Ellen had the jolt of understanding what was being said. Here everybody spoke in English, surely for their benefit.

Now she remembered that Professor Ma was a leading member of the Democratic League, that during the war Chiang Kai shek had put him in prison for his politics. In wonder Ben had said that even with his dangerous politics he followed the conservative economics of Irving Fisher, then laughed at the disparity.

The Chinese economists were acknowledging the introductions with surprising deference to Ben, easily half the age of any of them. Each spoke his particular kind of English. "Professor Chen, Yale, 1911." Professor Chen rose. "Professor Li, Princeton, 1912."

"Ph.D.," Ben whispered.

Then the others. Here Ellen had a new name consisting of Ben's last name heroically mispronounced, followed by the honorific.

A comfortable middle-aged woman, her hair pulled back into a knot, entered the room without a word. Dressed in a plain blue Chinese gown, she bore an astonishing resemblance to Professor Ma. She carried a large covered platter that gave off a remarkable odour of unknown food. It changed everything for another woman to be in the room.

"This is my wife," said Professor Ma. "She does not speak English." In Chinese he directed her in serving the guests. First Ellen, then Ben, the seven other economists and finally Professor Ma himself.

China! thought Ellen as she watched his wife go around the table. Where would she sit? All the places were taken.

"You," said Professor Ma, meaning all Europeans including Americans, "call these thousand-year eggs." Leaning across Ben, he assisted Ellen in lifting a slippery fermented egg with her chopsticks. Just then she saw his wife, having finished her round, leave the room and her master, surely for the kitchen. Don't go, Ellen called but kept it to herself. Come back. She glanced at Ben. What would he do if she said the words out loud? It was only because she was a foreigner and Ben's wife that she'd even been allowed into this company.

"China!" she said aloud.

"I beg your pardon," said Professor Ma.

Indeed, she thought, go get your wife and seat her with us. Again she laughed the clarifying laugh she's learned to use when there was no clear basis for understanding.

The egg plopped back into her rice bowl. She lifted it again. "Very good," she said, tasting a strange beguiling texture. Not the time to make decisions now, but just then she knew what she would do. She would talk to Mr. Kuo, ask him if he knew anybody who wanted to learn English, could fairly see his crinkly pleased smile as she asked. She would say that she would be the perfect teacher because she could never cheat by slipping into Shanghai dialect, standard Mandarin, or anything else.

She tried to catch Ben's eye as though somehow she could convey her decision to him right now. He was deftly lifting his thousand-year egg; he let it slip whole into his mouth, which silenced him for quite a while. No matter, there was time. Watching Professor Ma masterfully plying his chopsticks, she thought of his wife, who'd given in long ago because that must have been all there was. For her, Ellen, it wasn't the same at all. She exulted, then, ashamed of herself, sorrowed and after that let the whole thing go. The extraordinary polite banter of the seven elderly economists filled the room, and China surrounded them like a great and various sea.

Brief Visitation

JUDY MICHAELS

He says he births people into death,
but he seems gentle, this hospital chaplain,
and he doesn't move in close or insist
on praying with me, instead he notices:
the writing pad on my knees, too many books
for one weekend's infusion. I'm still
on the drips that are meant to defuse,
confuse, generally fuck up, the chemo's side effects,
and I like how he listens, we talk words,
how we love them, especially in the early morning.

I hold up Rita Dove, he writes her down
and says he looks for words to touch
people into love, says he cries easily, sings, too,
but I don't want him midwifing me
away from pain into new life with
God. I *will* him to stay right where he is, halfway
into the room, strong, centred, telling me
how the Bible is a well whose Word
(I prefer words, like dirt, milk, greed) finds

and fills him every day. And I am comforted,
touched from my hospital distance, touched to my
wired, drugged, space-invaded core. My breathing
slows to match his and I remember how my
mother's desperate, rasping breaths and my kiss,
the last warm breath she knew, made some kind
of horrible sense. "But not me," my pain is saying,
loud and rude, "not yet, I'm on the rise,
I've got more to say, I'm touched into love."

Shed No Tears

DOROTHY SPEAK

(an excerpt)

December 18

Dear girls,

. . . Your father wept when I left him at the hospital that first night, the day of the fingers accident, the day the Wife Tree was mutilated. I'm sorry, Hortense, he said. Hush, William, I told him. I'm sorry. I'm sorry, he said over and over. What was he sorry for? I didn't want to know. Maybe he thought he was less a person, less a man, without the three and a half fingers and that therefore I'd love him less. Little did he know that it would take a lot more than three and a half fingers to make me love him, that he could acquire fifty more, he could have a hundred of them growing on his hand, and it could not make me love him again. But I suspect that he was sorry for something else, something we'd lost together a long time before, something neither of us could name.

At the moment when the tears began to pour down your father's face, I'd been about to disappear into the hallway, take the elevator to the ground floor, walk home in blessed solitude through the soft night. I stood there at the door of his hospital room watching him cry and I found I couldn't take the steps toward his bed. It would not have been a difficult thing to cross the room to him. Just three steps and I could have been there to offer comfort. I did not say—as I might have liked to—I did not say, Is there not a time, William, when sorrow is too late? Nor did I tell him that all I could think of was his unwelcome fingers feeling all those years in the night for the hem of my nightgown and that perhaps now I'd be spared that ordeal. All I wanted was to run home to our double bed, which for fifteen years I'd never enjoyed all to myself, and where there was now room enough for me to dream of the Indian doctor.

Earlier that day, I'd met him in the hallway, the Indian doctor, a tall, elegant man who seemed to float toward me like a prophet in white vestments. He spoke to me so softly about your father's hand, his voice full of wonder at the human body.

The bone chips were sharp, he told me. I had to file them down, then stretch the skin over them. There wasn't much to work with. But skin is cooperative. It's quite elastic. It fuses miraculously. It was the three middle fingers your husband lost. The tip of the baby finger went, too. But he's still got the thumb. The thumb came away undamaged. We can thank God for that. That will be his saving. With the thumb and most of the baby finger, he'll be able to manage. He'll adapt fairly easily. Poor William, I said. And how about you? the Indian doctor asked, touching my elbow kindly. How are you doing with all of this? I'm equally concerned about how *you're* adapting, because when limbs are lost, all family members go through a period of grief, especially the spouse. It's all right, you know, he said, to cry. But I'd no tears to weep. Not for your father. Not for myself. If you need anyone to talk to, I'm here, he told me. Just ask for me at the desk. And your son? How is he? I've been thinking about him all day long.

His sympathetic words flowed over my soul like honey. Hearing his calm foreign voice, I smelled the curries of India, saw the saffron dusts blowing, the dry heat rising in waves from the poor Indian earth. I yearned to step forward, to press my body along the length of his golden skin, to walk into his country and never return. I looked at his beautiful fingers and wished it was me he'd touched. I pictured him sewing with patient stitches, drawing the heavy thread through the frayed epidermis, the soft brown pads of his thumb and fingers pinching, forcing the raw flesh together over the fresh bone like clay.

That night I dreamt of the doctor, white India cotton loosely wrapped round and round his body. In this dream I was unwinding these robes and discovering beneath them his smooth Asian skin, his brown limbs, his bare feet, their toes perfect and intact and polished as riverstones. I welcomed the nights alone in bed without your father, while I dreamt of the Indian doctor dipping his fingers again and again into a vessel of honey, drawing them out, and bringing the sweet dripping fingers to my lips.

A week later, when your father came home, he went straight out to the backyard, squatted down like an Indian scout, ran the fingers of his good hand over the blades of grass. Morris stood behind him, shifting nervously on his feet. I don't understand, your father said. They should be here. I saw them land. They're not here, Dad, Morris answered patiently. I told you. Merilee looked. She didn't find anything. Maybe the squirrels got 'em. Maybe the crows. Why didn't you come home and look yourself? your father asked Morris. I thought I should stay at the hospital. I thought you needed me there, Morris told him. If you'd kept the grass cut like you were supposed to, your father rebuked Morris. If the grass hadn't been so long, he said angrily. How could I do that, with the mower broken? Morris answered quietly. It's been broken for over a month, Dad. Remember? Your father held up his injured hand, which, bandaged, was big as a football. I owe this to you, he told Morris. If you'd held on to that ladder. If you could keep a simple instruction in that empty head of yours. Now you listen to me. I don't want you cutting this grass yet. I don't want those fingers chewed up for fertilizer. I tell you, they were whole.

Do you remember how hard it was those first few days to watch your father pace the backyard, out of his mind with pain, waiting for the moment when he was permitted to swallow more morphine? He awoke in the night, in a fever of agony, gripping my arm so hard that I too cried out in pain. The fingers are still there on my hand, Hortense, he hissed in the dark. I know it. I can feel them. They must be. They're hot as pokers.

That Indian son of a bitch, he said soon after he came home. He hasn't given me enough painkiller. These pills aren't strong enough. I'm going crazy. That Indian bastard is putting me through hell, he said. When we rushed him down to the hospital, the Indian obliged him and brought out a syringe, pushing the needle into your father's arm. If they hadn't given me a goddamned wog for a doctor, said your father to the Indian's face, and all I could do was look down at the floor in shame.

A week later, the bandages came off, the Indian doctor unwinding them slowly, revealing the hand at last, which now resembled a large blunt-headed insect with two antennas, formed by the thumb and baby finger, sticking up. I sat in the small white treatment room, where there was an examination table and a hard vinyl chair for me and a stool for the doctor. I watched the Indian pull the thick, dark, tough threads out of the tender blue wound, snipping away with his surgical scissors, gently tugging with tweezers. And the longer I looked at him—the longer I watched the action of his fine, skilful hands—the more my body trembled, and it seemed to me that he too was trembling a little, and afterwards, when the nurse was swabbing the wound, the Indian doctor caught me for a moment alone in the hallway and said under his breath, There's a park near here. The old park with the iron benches. Do you know it? I go there for lunch sometimes. I'm going there tomorrow, Wednesday. I'll arrive at twelve o'clock sharp.

William joked about his hand on the way home. It reminds me of the accidents we used to have on the farms out west, he said cheerfully. That's a real prairie hand, Hortense, he said with forced pride, holding it up. But later, when I looked out the bedroom window, I saw him sitting in the backyard, cradling the bad hand in the good one and weeping, his head bent, his shoulders shaking, grieving not only for the fingers but probably for all the stupid careless wasteful unnecessary losses of his life. Another wife might have put down her dust rag and gone outdoors, swiftly crossed the lawn, wrapped her arms protectively around his head. Not I. I could not go out and console him. I went about my vacuuming and my baking because I didn't care about his losses. I cared not that his mother had died when he was six years old or that, once, his father beat his bare buttocks with a rod until they were blue with bruises. All I cared about was the Indian doctor. I was counting the hours until I could go to him.

It was about this time that we began to see the Canada geese. They flew over the house every day around lunchtime, flock after flock, forming their arrows pointing north. Your father had always loved the sight of them, admiring the genius of their formation, moved by their brave, plaintive cry. When he heard them coming, he used to run out of the house to see them, leaping, lithe and excited as a boy, down the porch steps. But now, drunk with morphine, stretched out in a canvas chair in the backyard, he pressed his eyes closed as the geese passed, thinking perhaps of the hummingbirds that flew away.

And so, while the hummingbirds skimmed across your father's eyelids, and while the geese winged their way overhead, their long necks stretched northward, their cries calling to me of both longing and ecstasy, I too made my passage north, past the elementary school, past the Legion Hall, past the hospital, and on to the park, my bra strap freshly repaired, vanilla extract dabbed behind my ears and on my wrists, the slip I'd worn under my wedding dress, preserved all these years in the bottom of a drawer, clinging now to my perspiring body.

On the park bench, which was intricately wrought with iron roses and larks, the Indian doctor placed his hand on my thigh. At first I thought, This is all he means to do—to heal me with the laying on of his medical hands—for his fingers remained still, unmoving on my leg, though beneath them my flesh was quaking. But then he began to explore; he squeezed, lightly at first. From across the park came the voices of children splashing through the shallow waters of a wading pool, their screams of rapture as a jet shot streams at them. The Indian doctor turned and pressed his mouth to mine, his kisses soft, respectful, and I thought, Is this the way of India, this gentleness? This reverence?

I wonder, my daughters, if you have ever found, in the heat of Nepal, the kind of splendour I experienced when the Indian doctor kissed me in the sun on the park bench behind a clump of dogwood while, out of the corner of my eye, I saw the slender candle-white limbs of the children glimmering as they ran through the silver fan of water, heard their cries of murderous joy. And of course, though we were screened by the dogwood branches, it was very foolish for us to be touching each other in broad daylight, for this park was not far from the hospital, and any of the doctor's colleagues, flashing down the boulevard in their expensive Oldsmobiles, might have spotted us. Later, much later, I was to wonder if perhaps the Indian doctor in fact *wanted* to be seen, to be discovered in the act of adultery, because it might have made his wife of twenty years notice him and love him again.

But if he'd wanted only to inflame the passions of a jealous wife, would he have taken the fingers that had miraculously pressed the flesh of your father's hand together and closed up his wound—would he have used those same fingers to open me up like a flower, to reach between my legs and part my lips like petals, exploring with the knowledge of a surgeon's hands—hands that brimmed every day with human flesh, overflowed with it, forcing it, shaping it into something new, repairing the accidents of life, the ruptures, the violations to the body? Would he?

Soon there were gardeners in the park, pulling up the spent tulip bulbs, replacing them with tuberous begonias, dusty miller, coleus in shades of lime and magenta, their seedlings laid in the black soil in star and diamond patterns. With their shovels, they turned the fragrant earth, bending to their task, their chests, their bare backs glistening in the sun. Over the following weeks, the magnolia trees bloomed, their waxy flowers like white doves perched among the leaves, milkweed blew like snow across the park, great cloudy pink blossoms exploded in the smoke bushes, crabapples grew large and red in the trees. We watched the low flight of white birds wheeling and banking and skimming the lawns and the children splashing in the wading pool waters and the mothers pushing their expensive prams along the winding cinder paths, the carriages riding high on silver wheels, and baseball players running and sliding through the dust on a distant diamond. It was a summer of warm dry winds and cloudless skies. Crossing the park to meet the Indian doctor, I heard the burnt lawn crackle like broken glass beneath my feet. Seeing him waiting there for me on the lovers' bench, I wanted to rush forth across the grass, pull my dress open, shamelessly offer my breasts to his restorative hands. By the end of July, the sun's position had shifted and our bench was thrown into deep shade, making us feel like we were invisible.

At this point your father had stopped pacing the backyard, his bad hand clutched in his good one, mumbling, That son of a bitch. That goddamned Indian ... And instead, he sat around reading war novels, thick volumes he'd found at the public library, his wounded hand resting in his lap, like a soldier home from the front. Hortense, what are all these walks you're taking, just when you should be eating lunch with me? he asked. But I didn't answer and gave not a thought to him sitting alone with his sandwich and his bitter tea and his crippled hand, which could still make him weep spontaneously—I thought not about these while the Indian doctor pushed his long brown surgeon's fingers, sometimes smelling faintly of sweet curry, up inside of me. Your father, in turn, noticed no change in my appearance, though I myself could see that my skin glowed and I felt all of my body swollen with anticipation and pleasure, like a ripened fruit. The transformation did not go undetected by your grandmother. One day when I tried to bathe her, she said angrily, Get away from me. Get out of my house. I see what you're up to, you hussy. You're after my husband, aren't you? I see lust written all over your face. I'll have no slut like you touching me.

One afternoon in September, as the Indian doctor and I sat on our bench, the first falling leaf of autumn dropped into my lap. I was wearing, that day, a sundress from my youth. It had a small pale green check and unusual straps cut like broad oak leaves, embroidered with heavy black floss. I had on my white shoes with the open toe. The leaf spun down and landed so unexpectedly on my knee that, startled, I turned to the Indian doctor and asked, Why will you not love me? All summer I'd been telling him, I love you. I love you. Over and over, as early as May. I'd said it a hundred times, to which his only reply was a gentle smile. Why will you not take me somewhere? I asked him the day the leaf fell. Please take me somewhere private and enter me. But to that he only answered with a calm scorn, Do you want to have a brown baby? What would your husband have to say about that?

This occurred on the day when you, my children, were sitting down in school for the autumn term. You were receiving your new scribblers, their pages fresh and virgin and harmoniously organized with thousands of fine aqua lines. You were given your soft pink erasers velvety as flesh, your thick pencils with their black buttery lead, while the shining fields of goldenrod beside the school swayed in the wind and the nuns bent like tall black crows over your desks, their fat wooden rosary beads clattering hollowly. There was a first-day-of-school lineup at the pencil sharpener and the autumn jackets hung so neatly in the closets at the back of the classrooms and the unmarked chalkboards were black and deep and mysterious as night and you had fallen in love with your new teachers and at that moment it was still possible that you might love them beyond the first day and possibly forever.

It had been every Wednesday that the Indian doctor and I met. The following week, he wasn't on the bench when I arrived. I sat down and waited, but he didn't come. I waited all afternoon, while the dying leaves rained down across the silent park. There were no more children. The wading pool had been closed for the season, the jets turned off and all the children imprisoned in the schools. The sumacs, their red, fist-sized blossoms hanging in the branches like dozens of human hearts, had begun to turn crimson. Overhead, the great maples moved restlessly, dark and foreboding in the heavy autumn winds. I waited until the sun sank below the treetops and the sky began to turn lavender and I knew that you, my children, had left school, carrying your empty tin lunch boxes, your new square lunch boxes decorated in patterns of tartan or checks or flowers. You were walking home, first along the high white winding fairgrounds fence, then through deep pools of shade in the leafy twisting streets. finally I got up and headed south. Passing the hospital, I couldn't resist going in. My heart heavy as a brick in my chest, I climbed the stairs to the Indian doctor's office.

Dr. Seth—the receptionist said—Dr. Seth is in the operating room. But it's Wednesday, I told her. He doesn't operate on Wednesdays. Well, he's operating today, she said. He's filling in for another doctor. Are you sure? I asked, because I could see from her face that she was lying. She grew impatient. Dr. Seth has asked that you not come here, that you leave him alone. What do you mean? I said numbly. He's very busy, she said. He doesn't have time to see you. Could I at least call him? I asked. Could he call me? Mrs. Hazzard, the woman leaned toward me severely. It's very simple. He doesn't want you to bother him again, do you understand?

That evening, knowing that the Indian doctor would never again press his lips to my collarbones, never draw his fingers out from between my legs and put them in his mouth, in my mouth, and seeing William idle in the backyard, nursing a beer, I said bitterly, I expect you're happy about losing those fingers. Now you have an excuse not to find a job. I saw his jaw harden as he bit down on this new wound I'd dealt him. The next day he began to search for employment. Soon he'd found a position as a motor vehicle inspector, which required that he wear a uniform. The first day of work, I helped him on with his jacket. It was still difficult for him to dress himself. Don't touch the scar, he told me. I can't stand anything touching the scar. The feeling makes me climb the walls. I fastened the brass buttons down his chest. I never thought I'd see the day when I'd be working for the goddamned government, he told me. We've been married for fifteen years, William, I told him, and this is your first steady job, the first paycheque I could ever count on, the first guarantee the children will be fed. You look just like a soldier, I said, meaning to encourage him. I survived the military uniform, Hortense, he said grimly, but this one will kill me . . .

Mora de Ebro

DARLENE BARRY QUAIFE

(an excerpt)

HE SHOULD BE PACKING, but there he sat staring at the map wondering why after all these years he had opened this Pandora's box? He was sixty-six, married to the same woman for forty-five years and he had never told her, never once been inclined to reveal what he had found in Spain. And now they were going, leaving tomorrow for Barcelona. There, in the Spanish countryside, he would show her his father's grave, but what would he tell her?

The letters were in another box, a safety deposit box under his name only. The letters from Luz and his father's Communist Party card. It wasn't guilt that kept him silent all these years. He had met and married Nancy more than a year after he had returned home to Calgary from Spain. He saw no reason to stop writing to a friend simply because he had married. Yes, the friend was a woman, an ex-lover, but her life was elsewhere, as was his. In all, he had 342 letters from Luz, the first in November of 1951 and the most recent, yesterday, May 19, 1998, his birthday.

In his hand was the Suunto Global Compass Nancy had given him tucked inside the folds of a map of the world. Her birthday present, with a card that read, "For a man who never asks directions!" Love, Nan. With the straight edge of the compass case he drew a line from the village of Mora de Ebro in northeastern Spain, a Colombian line across the Atlantic to Havana, Cuba, then another dark, thin score from Havana to Calgary, Alberta, Canada. What remained unfinished was the opposite side of a strange triangle. He couldn't bring himself to draw the closing line.

Under the map was a letter from Cuba inside a handmade card. The card, a piece of heavy artist's drawing paper folded in four. When opened it was a single drawing, a sketch really, of the porter's lodge in Barcelona's Parque Güell. It was signed and dated, "Luz Fernández, September 1951."

SHE had gone up on top of the platform overlooking the Parque Güell's plaza to capture the detail on the rooftop pavilion of the porter's lodge across the way. The young man she sat beside watched her work for some time before he spoke, in English.

This caused her to look up and take him in more fully. Young, yes, at the most twenty, perhaps less, hair that brownish red called auburn, blue eyes, lean and tall. Ordinary except for the set of his mouth—determined, angry, sad—only his words, if he had any beyond the niceties of the classroom Spanish he had switched to, would tell her which of these traits belonged to him.

His name was Stephen, Stephen La Croix from Canada. He'd come to find his father's grave.

They talked as she worked.

"I've followed him through Spain," Stephen said in English. They had discovered that Luz's English was far superior to his Spanish.

"How?" Luz gazed at the lodge roof, trying to separate the patterns made by the *trencadís,* the broken ceramic tiling.

"From his letters mostly ... my mother kept them. And some newspaper clippings." Stephen seemed as absorbed in the Hansel and Gretel fancy as she was.

"What about your government?" Luz sketched the undulating profile of the roof where it met the brown flagstone walls.

"They were no help to him and even less help to me." Stephen looked away from the sketch, away from the gingerbread house to the pure sky.

"But how can that be?"

"The Canadian government didn't want him to come here, but he came anyway."

"Oh, the International Brigades."

"Yes, he joined in 1937."

"You remember?"

"Vaguely. I was only five. I remember there were lots of arguments."

"Your mother and father?"

"No, my uncles mostly and my father's friends. It was like there were two camps and my mother and I were in no man's land."

There was silence.

Luz's sketches were always painstaking. Unlike many artists, she could not work in rapid strokes. From the outset she had to get it right, and this required concentration. The roof had many peaks that looked like those formed in stiffly beaten egg whites. A kind of white foam with bits of coloured candy sticking to it.

After a time, Stephen said to the sky, "I have his letters. My mother let me take them. It's all she's got and she still let me take them. But they're not much, really. All he wrote about was ideas. Not even the war so much, or the people here. No, everything was popular fronts, solidarity, *la causa,* fascism. The only person he referred to more than once was someone called La Pasionaria, a woman . . ."

"Dolores Ibarrui, the Spanish Communist Party leader?" Luz had heard something in Stephen's voice.

"Yeah, her. He would write things she said. How she called the international soldiers 'crusaders for freedom,' 'heroes of progressive mankind' . . . stuff like that."

"It must have been a difficult time for your mother."

"You said it. No money, no work. We went to the weekly Communist Party meetings. Mom took Dad's place. But for all that, I think she went because it meant we got a cup of tea and a sandwich."

At last Luz was completing the crown of the roof with its blue cupola. She squinted, blocking out the glare of the sun off the tiles while trying to separate shape from detail. What was this thing surging up at the very apex of this unimaginable house? Her mind's eye imposed an answer on the blur. This tower, pavilion, cupola, call it what you will, resembled an erect penis, the circumcised glans surrounded by frothy semen.

Luz made a note in a corner of the sketch and then remembered Stephen. She looked up to find him watching her. Did he read Spanish? Would the word "pene" register in his English-speaking brain? She was too much the modern woman to be coy. Her university classes in anatomy and life drawing had given her access to the human body and its language. Nevertheless, Stephen was a stranger despite what she knew of him. Intimacy requires much more. A journey.

They had talked, gone for dinner, walked through Barcelona into the night. They argued causes and she had sided with Stephen's father. But the son could not concede he was less important than idealism. His father's letters had been full of ideology not love. At least his father could have loved him and his mother more for the sacrifice they made. But the crusader for freedom took their pain for granted. If this was progressive—the squandering of love—then he wanted nothing to do with ideologues and causes.

Their world views were opposed. Luz was bred to revolution. *La causa* was Cuba. Luz was Cuba. But Stephen was intelligent and obviously had thought hard about his father's path and his own. Stephen's arguments were emotionally sound.

Gilbert La Croix had been part of the Retreats, the Republican army's withdrawal down the valley of the Ebro River to the Mediterranean Sea. By Batea, the Mac-Paps, Mackenzie-Papineau Battalion, was decimated and scattered. After Batea, Stephen's father disappeared from sight and ultimately the memory of those Canadian comrades who survived.

Stephen had searched the Republican line from Batea to Gandesa. While he was in Maella, a man had tried to tell him about a place called Mora de Ebro. A small town on the banks of the Ebro where the Republicans had established a new defensive line during the Retreats. There they had blown up the bridge and those comrades caught on the other side had to swim the river, if they could. Many died and were washed up on the banks.

But Stephen could not understand from the man what was to be found at Mora de Ebro. At this point, Stephen had come back to Barcelona in need of money, from home, if possible.

The money came, and he and Luz boarded a southbound train. Once they were settled in the car, a shyness seemed to come over Stephen. It was as if he was unsure of what Luz expected in return for her help. At first he had just been happy to have an interpreter, not to mention that this need had been met in the form of a worldly young woman. Was she expecting romance?

For her part, Luz read his shyness as introspection—after all, his search for his father might be coming to an end. Would he find what he needed?

"What will you do after?" Luz finally asked.

"After?"

"After Mora de Ebro, after Spain?"

Stephen noted she didn't say, 'After me.' "Pick fruit," he said. "For my uncle."

"This will be your job?"

What did she mean? His life's work? "Why not?" he asked.

"I didn't ask 'why.' It's a family business, that's where you belong. When I go home to Cuba, I will work in my father's cigar shop." Luz noticed that the other passengers in the cramped train car had lost interest in them. Their English, no longer a novelty, was probably more of an irritating buzz, like the flies in the window.

"But you're educated?" Stephen was still leaning toward her, trying to keep their conversation private. He had seen the man next to Luz slide a look over her when she mentioned Cuba.

"Ah, yes, but it will take time and hard work to make a place for myself. There are no women practising architecture in Cuba. I will first have to convince someone to take me on as an apprentice. That will not be easy."

"Because you're a woman?"

"Yes, Cuba is very macho, ah ... like España." Luz was aware of her neighbour's renewed interest and gave the word "macho" a dismissive inflection.

"Macho? Male? My Spanish…" Stephen eyed the man across from him.

"Male pride, machismo, women are inferior, all that rubbish. But I also have a reputation…"

"Oh?"

The man was now watching Stephen with undisguised curiosity.

"As a political activist. Like your father, I'm prepared to fight for justice."

"You? fight?"

"Machismo must be a germ *any* man can catch."

Stephen was young enough to blush, especially under Luz's censorious gaze. "My father fought in trenches full of lice and unburied dead." He straightened in his seat and gave the man a dark look.

"It may come to that for Cubans. It has happened in the past. And women fought with rifles, just as they did here against Franco."

"Could you?" Stephen leaned across to Luz. "I've tried to imagine what my father went through. The killing, seeing friends die. I don't know…" Stephen had the demonstrative hands of his father's Gallic ancestors, and in speaking his heart he had grazed Luz's knee, disturbing her skirt.

The man took this as a sign of ownership. He opened his newspaper.

Luz moved to close the space between her and Stephen. "He fought to stay alive." Her voice was low, her face close to his.

"But he didn't have to be here. He wasn't protecting his family, he gave us up. This wasn't his home. What was the stupid bastard doing here? That's all I want to know."

Luz looked out the window. Could she? Could she kill another human being? In the name of justice, freedom, in the name of God?

To Stephen she said, "Some people do not value life. Some value it too much. Somewhere in between are those who must act so that life is worth living."

"Whose life?" Stephen's angry hiss drew quick looks from the other passengers in the compartment.

"Human life. Your life. Your father like many others knew that the fascists would not be content with Spain or Italy or Germany. Tyrants care for power, not people."

"And what of Cuba? There are no fascists there."

"Tyrants come in many guises."

MORA de Ebro caught them both deep in thought. The landscape of dry hills and *barrancas* passing outside the train window had been a plain screen on which they projected their turmoil. The olive grove before the station washed them in a green and silver relief, like shade to eyes that have stared too long into the sun.

From the station they made their way to the central plaza where they would find food and talk. Conversation with the locals was most often veiled, this was part of the problem Stephen had encountered in his earlier search. No matter who they talked to—survivors of the civil war, Republicans, Nationalists—now, they all lived under Franco's thumb. Spain had been subject to the rule of an authoritarian regime since 1939.

The woman who sold them some strong homemade beer suggested they sit on the steps of a stone monument prominent in one corner of the plaza's garden.

She directed them to a squat marble tablet not unlike those standing stones used to mark graves in Canadian cemeteries. Twice as large as most headstones, this marker was engraved with row upon row of names. Chiselled in the top of the stone was "1936–1939." Luz read off the names: all Spanish surnames, many of which repeated themselves to encompass whole families. These were the town's dead. To break the burden of name after name, the carver had periodically inserted a line of fancy work. Interested in the motif, her artist's eye followed the scroll pattern of the first line. The next line was an ogee, a double-S curve. It was among the stylized olive leaves of the third line that Luz realized there was something more at work. What she thought to be the individual, rather eccentric, touch of the carver was in fact letters worked into the design. She pointed this out to Stephen. Together they examined every line of decoration. Each contained different letters, two, sometimes three, like initials.

Stephen discovered a line of "G. L."

They asked directions to the stonecutter's yard.

The man did not seem surprised to see them. He believed the dead also had needs that they found ways to fulfill. After speaking with Luz, he handed Stephen a fat pencil and had him print his father's name on the smooth surface of a piece of cut stone.

Luz and Stephen waited as the stonecutter lost himself among the great slabs of rock in his yard. He returned with a yellowed card for Stephen: his father's Communist Party card with the stamps that acknowledged he had paid the party's monthly five cents right up until he left Canada for Spain. All his dues paid as he left them waving goodbye from the platform in the Calgary train station.

He had drowned in the Ebro. Weighted down by poverty and ideals like so many stones in his pockets. He had floated onto the bank, a wretched corpse in a tattered uniform, rotten boots, and ammunition belt with no bullets. There were no pictures in his wallet, nothing other than the card. It is possible that he had been robbed, his body looted as it lay in the sun. Anything was possible.

All this flowed through Luz from the stonecutter to Stephen. The old man directed them to a mass grave in the cemetery, marked with a single white cross dedicated to the year these nameless men ceased to struggle.

Stephen sat on the grass at the foot of the cross, staring at his father's faded Communist Party card. "You know, in Canada this card got you black-balled from relief camps, from non-union jobs. It was some cop's or union buster's ticket to beat the crap out of you. My mom wanted him to leave it at home when he went out, but he carried it in defiance of her, of the bulls and big shots. He wasn't going to be pushed around just because he was out of work and poor. My uncle told me before I left that my dad saw what so many didn't at the time. Saw through the Great Depression to the real problem. His favourite expression was 'It's not the Depression that's killing the working man, it's the repression.'"

Luz stood silently behind the cross, behind Stephen.

"You see, I understand that. I know things were bad at home, but to come here? The fight was in Canada. It was all such a waste."

"Would you say so if the Republicans had won?"

From outside Stephen's grief, Luz could see the larger struggle, the threat that ultimately pulled Canada into world conflict.

"It would have made no difference. If it hadn't been Franco, it would have been Mussolini or Hitler overrunning Spain. *La causa* was hopeless. He was here because they'd let him play soldier."

"That's pretty hard." Luz came from behind the cross.

"The truth is neither pretty nor easy to swallow."

She sat resting her head against his shoulder. "Your truth, Stephen. What did you expect to find in Spain?"

"A grave. Just a grave. He couldn't be lost in action for the rest of my life. No one can ever be lost in action."

Lost, Luz thought. Action is better than being lost. The human impulse to take control, even—or perhaps *especially*—in the face of lost causes. What else is there? Surrender?

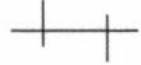

THERE were photos among the letters from Cuba. Luz in uniform with a rifle, Luz with Che Guevara, Luz with Fidel Castro and his other ministers, Luz with her children. Did her husband know about the letters? Stephen has never asked. He addressed his letters to her ministry office, she to his business.

From under the world map, Stephen pulled Luz's sketch. He looked at her notes in the corner, pencilled letters smudged into what could be a grey cloud above the cupola of the porter's lodge. What had she written all those years ago? His Spanish was excellent now. He had been writing to Luz in her mother tongue for decades.

Stephen reached for the magnifying glass on his desk. A few words came out of the cloud: "verde," "azul," some word beginning "pen—" the rest gone. Then several phrases Luz had pressed harder with her pencil to record: "Truth cannot be erased. Neither can lies. Nothing is lost."

Stephen gathered up the compass, the map, and Luz's letter and sketch. He packed it all in his travel wallet with his passport.

The Yellow Canoe

RACHEL WYATT

"YELLOW," Peter said.

Myra let him get away with his "yellow" because it was the first positive thing he'd said in weeks and she was downright tired of snipping the ends off string beans. Anything to get him out of his garden. He'd been working out there with a sullen kind of energy ever since he'd let slip he was afraid of dying.

"Isn't everybody," she'd said, hurrying out of the door with her stop sign and her orange vest. She regretted later not paying attention to him, not saying to him that when she thought about it, it gave her the creeping heebie-jeebies, too. Death.

"Yellow," he said again.

The nearby lake had a coliform count well over the reasonable limit and no one was advised to trail a hand in the water let alone fall into it. It wasn't only a matter of the internal organs; the skin could turn a peculiar shade, if not actually break into a mottled rash. Peter, not caring about all that, thinking most likely of cleaner lakes a bit farther away, murmured something about the bark of the birch tree.

Out for their walk the Sunday before, they'd watched as a family of three piled into a canoe, loaded it with a cooler, and set off. They hadn't spoken, that family, mother, father, daughter, but had begun to paddle intently, each of them knowing exactly what to do, making a clear line across the lake toward the far shore. And Peter had stopped still, in a kind of dream, muttering something about sunbeams on the water.

Myra had felt the magic of that silent moment also. So after breakfast she tidied up, put a touch of rose pink blush on her cheeks, a purple comb in her hair to hold it back, donned her blue jacket that was wearing a bit thin but still looked smart, and followed him out to the car.

"Yellow," he repeated.

When he'd returned to Canada in '48 and she'd followed on, she'd expected adventure and now it was quite overdue. It was a long time since they'd amazed each other, or anyone else for that matter. Perhaps it was time. Peter beside her was humming a tuneless tune, recalled from his two summers at camp. She was remembering the day by the lake when she'd seen him kissing Amber Papadakis, her faithless childhood friend, and Amber had left without a word the next day, lost again to her world of dimly lit theatres.

The Discover Your World store smelled like the inside of a tent on a hot day. There was everything: ropes, stoves, lamps, tents, boats, axes, hiking boots, mountain bikes, water bottles, backpacks, knives for skinning animals, inflatable rafts, hats that were rainproof, and pans that fitted inside other pans. There were coolers, bikes that folded, and boots for climbing. The whole place shrieked of danger.

Peter and Myra stood silent before it all as if they were already started on their journey, hung about with equipment, perched on a Himalayan slope or moonwalking deep below the ocean taking pictures of each other swimming with dolphins.

The salesman, more like salesboy, came up to them and said, "Can I help you?"

"A canoe," Peter replied, continuing decisive. "We want to buy a canoe."

The slim boats were strung up on the wall like ornaments. Beautiful in their shape. Blue, yellow, brown. Not one of them was made of the bark of the birch tree.

The boy in his jeans and T-shirt said, "The fourteen-foot one weighs about fifty-five kilos. Comes in at around nine hundred dollars. We might include the paddles. Even throw in the cover. It's getting kind of late in the season."

A hundred and odd pounds! Myra was finding it difficult these days to lift ten pounds let alone eleven times that. As for Peter, he puffed and wheezed for minutes after he carried the groceries into the kitchen. But he was standing there staring at the yellow canoe on the wall as if he was capable of portaging it on his head round Niagara Falls.

She said, "We have to discuss this. Considering we have to get a roof rack and life jackets and there's tax. We could be looking at more than a thousand dollars."

"Paddles," Peter said.

"I have a lightweight one," the boy said, not releasing them.

"We'll go away and talk it over."

"Costs a little more. Around twenty-three hundred dollars. Could throw in the life jackets."

Peter had his belligerent I'll-take-three look on his face, a look provoked lately by salesmen who patronized him, knowing he was living on a pension, who wanted to save him money. What the salesboy saw was an elderly man with wispy grey hair, blue slacks, a green cotton shirt, and a jacket he'd bought for five dollars at Goodwill. He couldn't see the one-time union official, spare-time soccer coach, erstwhile lover.

"We'll have lunch and come back," Myra said.

Peter trailed out of the store behind her, followed her to the Vital Signs Café for lunch, not catching up, acting like a disappointed boy.

"We'd have to get used to it," he said. "That's all."

"It's more than that."

"My father. Those photos. Of him in a punt on the Thames."

"Your father in that picture was less than thirty and besides no one ever asked him to put the punt on the top of his motorbike or carry it round the locks."

Myra's own memory of boating was on the pond in the park, threepence an hour. An hour of bumping into other boats, trailing your hand in the mucky water, crossly returning when the man shouted your number. *Come in fourteen. Your time's up.* That was all long ago when life was still full of surprises and you could buy an hour of pleasure for the equivalent of half a cent in today's money. But that call, harsh and mean as if it was always only fifty-five minutes and never the full hour, had stayed in her head like an old echo. *Come in number fourteen.*

She watched the people coming into the café. All the different hairdos, pink, spikes, clothes all ragged and baggy. How was it possible to be outrageous anymore? What on earth could a person do to make another person turn and stare these days? Only maybe walk in with his genitals hanging out, and today even that wouldn't make people take a second look.

In their decor, the management had tried for strange, but assorted dinosaurs and antique cookie boxes on a shelf above the juice machine didn't succeed.

The waiter put cornbread on the table in a basket and took their orders for one veggie sandwich and one soup of the day.

"If I could have lived at any time I chose," she said to Peter, "if I could have chosen my century, it would've been the last one. Imagine all the surprise of trains, electricity, telegraph."

"Every age has its surprises," Peter replied, not understanding.

"What lately has amazed you?" she asked.

There were crumbs round his mouth. Given half a chance he would list unfolding leaves, the sudden flight of birds, the rise and fall of tides. But she turned her head to look at the shiny coffee machine that whirred and groaned and churned out coffee not much better than instant.

She passed half the sandwich to him. He began on the soup and would leave half of it for her. He sipped and nodded. It was good soup.

The waiter came and stood by their table. His infinite hairy legs rose up into the shortest shorts, and the little apron made him seem like an exploited waitress of earlier, and perhaps present, times. Myra wanted to reach out and put her hand on his thigh but held back.

"Is everything satisfactory?" he asked.

"No it isn't. There's nothing amazing here."

"We try," he said. "But there's no way we can keep up. We truly strive for surprise. We change the menu daily. We hire and fire staff like it's a revolving door. I took Phenomena as a major at university and look where it got me."

"My wife's been reading," Peter said, trying to explain her away as he had done in the past but had not bothered to do lately. "I'll have your fruit pie with cream. If the cream's fresh."

"I'm always hoping for something new myself," the waiter said, waiting. "You've got to keep your eyes open."

"And I'll have an oatmeal square, please," Myra told him.

Peter said to her, "We'd use it on sunny mornings."

"Mornings!"

"There's a lot of good weather left. It's quiet after the kids go back."

And this year the kids were going back without her. She'd taken the job on as a kind of volunteer thing after the wool and fancy needlework store closed down due to lack of customers and left her free. She hadn't expected there to be an age limit on seeing kids across the road three times a day. She'd loved their cheerful morning faces, the bits of their lives they told her as they waited for her to give them the go-ahead. Her eyes weren't perfect but she could still see cars coming, for cripe's sake. But in June the council had taken her reflector jacket and her stop sign away and said, Thank you very much, goodbye. So she was free for the first time in the fall. Probably forever. Till her number was called.

"We'll go back and look," she said to Peter, to let him down gently.

Getting a canoe had been a moment's silly dream. A mad idea. Kim and her friend Sharon would laugh their heads off and tell their friends that the old folks had finally lost it. Imagine, at their age!

He was thinking about his father in the punt. His mother lying back there with her hair in a long braid over her shoulder. A girl light as a feather who brought the moonlight and the starlight. They weren't married then, his parents. They were a couple ahead of their time, in that postwar madness, the twenties. They lived out a kind of homage paid to the lost ones, living two lives if they could, living on behalf of the dead. And then emigrating to the New World to give their boy a better life.

"We might be able to lift it."

"Our feet would get wet," she said.

"I don't mind that."

She wanted him to mind. She wanted him to wince when he put his feet in that chill water and feel the sharp pain in his calf muscles after. And the rest of the day and lie awake at night twisting and turning. She wanted him to cry out in agony as he had when she'd accidentally unwound his Marlene Dietrich cassette. The new ones, he said when she'd offered to replace it, had nothing like the same quality.

THE salesboy was surprised to see them back. In his experience, customers who said they were going to talk it over didn't return. And these two old folks! Humour them. Maybe they had more money than they showed.

"We've come to try your canoe," Myra said. "If you could just get it down off the wall."

The boy and another young man reached for it with two sticks with hooks on the end and lowered it to the ground. And there it stood, a streamlined shell of curved wood, painted, metal tips, waiting only for two adventurers.

Peter bent down at the bow. She took the stern. They each got a grip and tried to lift it. Only six inches off the ground and she felt the old sharp pain in her stomach and let go. He dropped his end and gasped.

The boy kindly said nothing for a moment.

Peter stood there looking around him at little things, at the floats stacked three deep, the water wings, the Frisbees.

"About all we could do in that is grow geraniums," Myra said. "Even if we could get it home."

"You can rent a canoe by the hour," the boy said. "Place by the lake. They'll put it in the water for you."

Peter was making paddling motions, muttering about birchbark again.

The boy, in his glance, sized them up not only as old but lost to reality and continued, "You know. And get it out again."

Peter began to walk away, leaving her standing there.

"Wait a minute," Myra said, so loudly that other people turned to stare.

And then, because Peter's dreams had been stamped on too often, she said to the salesman, "Let's look at your lightweight one."

They had bits of money here and there. There was nothing worth watching on TV these days anyway, and the old set could last awhile longer. They could save too on heat in winter.

The boy came toward them, easily carrying another perfect canoe. He set it down at their feet.

"Oh," Peter said, stroking the side of the lovely boat, "it's not yellow but it's pretty near the same colour as birch."

The young fellow helped them get the fine brown boat outside and onto the brand-new roof rack and put the life jackets in the trunk. The paddles were the best they had, he said, light and strong. He offered them respect and waved as they drove down the street.

When they got home, Peter got out and limped round and opened the door at Myra's side. As she stepped out of the car, he kissed her.

"Come on, Hiawatha," she said, "let's lift it down."

One afternoon before long, afternoon because neither of them was all that agile in the morning, they would launch their craft, get their feet wet, and paddle off across the water to see what was on the farther shore. Without fear. And even, Myra thought as she found a place for the paddles under the stairs, if the sun was shining and they were feeling good, even with joy.

Vital Signs

NANCY POTTER

I. Marlborough-Blenheim

Four days into the new year, they are neatly blowing up another Atlantic City hotel. They have tucked four hundred pounds of dynamite into the pockets and seams of the Blenheim. They have wired the charges to balconies, filigree, lattice, and each of the three fancy domes. The canary cages are out of the solarium. The string trio has vacated the music room. No one pulls a sheet of faint blue paper from the lacquered writing desk in the library.

It is ten o'clock. For eleven seconds the towers seem to sigh, then rise, shudder, bow inward, and crash. A big cloud of dust and particles drifts over the boardwalk and the rubble stands twenty feet high. "Wow!" the crowd says. "She fell exactly the way we planned," brags the demolition expert. It is too cold to stand here, and there's nothing more to see, anyway.

II. Ice Fishing on Beach Pond

A queer place, you may say, to make a fresh start. The pond's surface has become a shanty town, fragile as a carnival. Under the dense ice floor, under the flagged and baited hooks, twenty feet down, the lukewarm perch and pickerel feel their way around the chilled lily roots, spiny tree stumps, and rusted cans. I've dragged this stiff body into a wooden hut, but not to fish. I'm only subletting. Am here to take instruction. How to drain light from the waiting trees on the shore. How to catch March stealing along the ice faults. How to catch indifference from the trout. It is, after all, presumptuous to claim to be lonelier than the stars.

III. Blizzard

Whoever thought snow was fun? Admiral Byrd? Heidi's grandfather? Sheets of sleet sting the windows. Trees snap like rifles. No winter wonderland. Neither heat nor water nor plumbing. We sit in boots and hats and mittens in the frigid house forgotten by everyone, behind a five-foot drift. Somewhere out there, road crews grind down the roads. On the second day the outlaw plowman arrives, red-eyed, unshaven, sleepless, and dangerous, demanding scandalous tribute. Waiting for the snow to stop has worn us out. In the raw wind we mince across a rutted parking lot but fall anyway under a week's worth of groceries. Three homeless men die in their cardboard boxes.

IV. Failure to Thrive

Ring the plague bell for yet another. Spring rain soils the pavement and floods the new grass. They have converted the old Lying In to a hospice. He fades into the pillow, croaks out a sentence. I bend closer. "When I was a child I thought I was born in the Lions Inn." I have brought the bravest daffodils from my garden, tough and starchy, but the nurse seizes them firmly and carries them elsewhere. This is stern stuff, and she disapproves of jokes. "I knew a guy once who tried to steal a ferris wheel ..." His eyes flutter and the power dims. I walk out. We will give him an exquisite memorial service.

V. Spring Cleanup

We had to be in awe of them. They were such gentle, concerned folk, enough to make us nervous. They wore plastic shoes, mended torn butterfly wings, washed oil-logged seagulls, picketed fur stores. They apologized to the carrots for pulling them. In May rabbits got into their young lettuce and squirrels chewed their crocuses. They sent away for the most commodious Have a Heart traps and bagged three of each immediately. They loaded the cages into the back of their Volvo and started up Route 138 on the way to release them in the state forest. At that nasty curve just past the glassblower's, a doe rushed out of a thicket. Swerving to avoid her, they plowed head-on into Pop Labonte's pickup. All three people died instantly, but in the back seat of the Volvo, the three rabbits and three squirrels waited impatiently. We cannot be sorry enough.

VI. Superstitions

"Someone is always getting married in the garden. I don't know who they are," the senile grandmother says. The groom thinks, "This is my first wedding." The bride asks, "Who are these people?" The ushers are passing around bags of bird seed. No confetti or rice permitted here and no flashbulbs either. The gates close at sundown. The best man realizes he's forgotten the rings. But no one notices. A sudden torrent drenches the smart crowd, sending them under the beech trees. The bridesmaids' gowns leave purple streaks on their legs and hands. At least when the lightning strikes only a distant cousin is carried away. It can't get any worse, we think. But it will. "I warned them not to cut the hawthorn bush," the grandmother says, "it always brings bad luck."

VII. Mid-Summer in Mid-Europe—History Lessons

This summer in Poland it is always morning. One cannot rise before the sun has already slanted over the old ridges of the Tatras. All day in the meadow the women in long skirts are tossing veils of newly mown hay into the sunlight. Before breakfast the students run two miles, dappled in green shadows among the hemlocks. At breakfast they are memorizing Dickinson. "Explain us this line, please, 'Tell all the Truth but tell it slant.' Is not dishonourable to tell slanted truth?" I tell them Truth has hard edges. In Krakow we walk through Warwel Castle, where distant history is neatly arranged in rows of kings. Their favourite is the consort of King Sigismund I —Queen Bona Sforza lately of Milan. It was Bona Sforza who brought green vegetables to Poland. And her Italian paintings. We walk through Jagiellonian University. They remind me that Copernicus was once, like them, only an undergraduate. We stare at a sixteenth-century clock in the shape of a globe that shows a tiny new continent, freshly discovered just off the coast of Africa. They instruct me to go alone to the Remuh Cemetery, near the old synagogue. "That was our saddest time," they say. "Our grandmothers were alive then." And so were the old women tossing the hay in the meadow.

VIII. High Wind in Puglia

Whatever its name—doldrum, mistral, sirocco—the wind blows constantly. Sand invades the lips and shoes and seams. Palm fronds slap. Shutters and hinges groan. The clouds are spectacular. The highest window is full of glory. "I will miss the sky most when I die," the old man said. "More than faces or music or food. But not the wind. I can do without that." Ostuni is a glistening white snail, under the big wind and the huge sky. "I am related to everyone in this town, but I am too tired to explain how," the old man said. He was actually a prince, but he had forgotten that, too. "Watch out for the Albanians," he said finally. "They are not artists like us." It is sour and mouldy in all the great houses. Pigeons live in the attics and mice in the floors below. The prince's son turns reluctantly from his computer screen to show the view from his window—clouds and St. Lawrence on a pillar. St. Lawrence once saved the city from plague. Mice threaten the computer, and St. Lawrence cannot protect them from the Albanians. Clumps of smaller, darker people, heavily draped, unload their trucks at the edge of the city. They live in converted buses that empty moustached men and boys wearing crocheted caps. Amid the straw and weeds and blowing papers they set out their wares—scissors, watches, knives, pulleys, ropes, and whistles. One of the smallest boys stands at a distance amid the poppies and whistles a thin song lost in the wind.

IX. The Wind Blows West

Try as we may, we're only human. Before some triumphant crossing points, we stand on tiptoe, holding our breath—Chartres, Machu Picchu, Angkor Wat, the Parthenon, the Sphinx. Heavy with expectation, we grope to make our summaries. But to other places we come, curious and silent pilgrims. Bare mysterious places before our story. Who made the circles at Stonehenge, the massive heads on Easter Island, the stylish animal shapes at Nazca? The Burren is of the age of stone. Before the torn pages of any manuscript. Even before the memory in any song or name. No one can now speak a sentence in that language. This limestone karst, a muddle of boulders and outcroppings, perilous to the ankles, is good only for the careful sheep and the shy fast flocks of swallows that swirl and twist soundlessly. The constant wind blows over the saffron spotted stone, bends the tiny bright flowers. No one knows who built that dolmen. Deep below, even the ancient rivers are lost. Bones of long-vanished animals wait in the uncharted caves. The wind blows all the way from the Cliffs of Moher across these chalky fragments, over roofless Kilmacduagh toward Coole. The great house is gone, but a few swans float amid the fallen leaves on the pond beside Yeats' tower.

X. Ground Truth

Without finding the pot shards, the flute carved from a femur, the quartz arrowheads, even the fragment of Blue Willow plate or the broken plastic comb or the buffalo nickel, there can be no belief in the culture of the tribe. How can we know that anyone lived or died here? We need to see the scorched boulder that was at the bottom of the cooking pit, the foundations of the ghost house, the porcupine quills discarded after necklace making. That's ground truth for the theories. Last October, in the final stage of a long drought, the city reservoir began to shrink. At the edges, tangled tree roots became brown filigree. Suddenly chimneys and modest doorsteps appeared. Coming in low to the municipal airport we got a view of the outlines of the hat factory and the racetrack, and, of course, Maple Grove Cemetery with its clustered granite obelisks. But before we could find the IGA, Pluto's Service Station, the Dairy Queen, and the Meadow Drive-In, November rains began. By winter, ground truth will lie under twenty feet of fluorinated water.

XI. The Ghosts

A formal man, Uncle Harry stands in coat and vest amid his tied-up cartons in the attic. Cobwebs and dust cover his shoulders. "Things," he whines. "They're killing me. If only I could find the right person." He is trying to arrange matches for everything. Keys to burned-down houses, leashes for dead dogs. A left sandal, genuine lizard. Everything that was too good to use then is now going into storage.

Dry leaves shudder. Don't look back. The past will ambush you. Walk straight on purposefully beyond the flea market, where your errors are on view. Take off that silly costume you selected. What are you, anyway? Regret? Guilt? Open the door and greet the little monsters who have opened their pillowcases wide before they set us on fire. But they are only the five-year-old twins from next door done up as Beauty and the Beast, and they are scared to death.

XII. First Night

Somehow we have survived another year. Chance. Luck. Nothing to do but muddle onward. So many didn't. The New Year's Eve party casts a wider net to fill in with survivors. We have been attending this party for years and have our roles down pat. We are the designated listeners. Soon it will be our turn to offload memories but not just yet. Prepare for charades. Shake out the gauze and fluff up the silk. Write out the most outrageous prophecy for the Year of the Snake on an index card. Kiss the hostess and remember who is deaf and what chairs are safe for sitting. The old apartment on the top of the triple-decker is crowded with abandoned treasures. We escape to the porch at midnight. In the snowy sky the Roman candles pop into blue fuzz, the rockets flare red and white, and the giant fountains fall emerald, ruby, and diamond. We square our shoulders and prepare for the terrorists.

The Organized Woman Story

BIRK SPROXTON

CAROL IS AN ORGANIZED WOMAN. You will understand what I mean by an organized woman when I tell you about her love life, or what I know of her love life, for she has never been in love with me. Not like that, anyway. I have the wrong name.

By organized, I don't mean that she can always find her car keys, though it is true, or that she can remember to phone her third cousin Sally on the third Sunday of every third month, though she does that too. She phones me on the same day, the third Sunday of every third month, and she tells me that Sally has taken to lassooing the children at suppertime, or whatever it is that Sally is up to, and she tells me the latest news about Michael. Michael and I correspond every few days on electronic mail, but no matter. She calls me regularly. On the third Sunday.

I first realized she was an organized woman when she fell in love with my friend. He is her second husband named Michael. The second Michael, my friend, is a different man from the first, but they have the same first name. Then I realized that she always falls in love with men named Michael. Not every Michael, of course, for she can be a very fussy woman, but every man she falls in love with turns out to be named Michael.

You may think that because her brother is named Michael and her father is named Michael that she is simply picking variants of her father, each man a copy of her father with his quiet laugh and confident walk, the way you fall in love with, say, a special kind of doughnut and each time you hanker for a doughnut you go to the same shop, the warm yeasty smells as you open the door always remind you of what you want, and you order the same kind of doughnut you did the last time you were struck by the doughnut urge. Something like that.

Now you may argue husbands are not like doughnuts, but I must tell you I once said that to her, I said, Men are not like doughnuts, you don't have to choose the same kind every time, and she pointed out, in a rather peckish way I thought, that I certainly had not divorced myself from my last round of doughnuts, that in fact I seem to embrace and nurture and hold on to doughnuts and let them root and ripen and grow into huge balloon tires around my waist. I, she said—meaning me, your storyteller—seem to have clutched those chocolate doughnuts to my very loins for life. She has this way of zeroing in on your weak spots. So I dropped the subject.

But she was not looking for variants of her father.

I know this because she was once courted by Wayne, a pharmacist in my neighbourhood. In fact, she was infatuated with Wayne, quite wrapped up in him, you might say, after she chucked out her first husband named Michael, even to the point of trying to persuade her brother to go by the name Wayne.

"After all," she said to her brother, "Wayne is your second name, and this Wayne is very nice. I'd like you to be Wayne, too." She did not approach her father, of course, whose second name is also Wayne, because she knew that he would give in to anything his darling-poo wanted and so it would not be a proper test. Therefore she approached her brother first. But her brother remained adamant. Michael was the name he preferred. Wayne wouldn't do, even if it was his second name and one she was currently infatuated with. So she dropped him. The pharmacist, I mean. If she could not get all her men to go by the name Wayne, if she was stuck with Michael, then Michael it would be. She'd have to find another Michael.

Wayne the pharmacist had to go. She thanked him very much for giving her the cardboard boxes she had used to pack up her first husband's things, and for allowing her a small discount on the several tons of packing paper she had used to wrap every single item that Michael owned, each sock in its own wrapper, before she chucked him out.

That was the Saturday she broke tradition. She phoned me, even though it was Saturday, to say that Michael had departed, his possessions all neatly wrapped in tissue paper and tucked in solid cardboard cartons the nice pharmacist had given her. I thought I would say something to cheer her up, though she gave no sign of being upset, so I said, No, Michael hadn't gone; in fact he was sitting in my living room.

She said, "Oh, you silly man, what's he doing at your place?" And I, thinking she deserved a diversion, though I knew she would find my place a deplorable mess, said, "Well, why don't you come over and find out?"

So she came over and that's how she met Michael, my friend, and that's why Michael and I now use electronic mail to talk. She phoned me the next day, Sunday, the third Sunday of the month, to say that Sally was building a huge jungle gym for the kids to climb on, she was bolting planks onto the third storey Sally was, and then she, Carol, apologized for hauling Michael off like that last night, and wasn't he a nice man?

I said, Of course you think he's a nice man because his name is Michael.

It was the wrong thing to say. I won't tell you exactly what she replied for it may make her look bad, but it had something to do with my feeling sorry for myself about all the poems I can't get anybody to buy, or read, and why didn't I get off my blossoming derrière and lift the telephone receiver and give Sally a call, she of the lasso and the jungle gym and the herd of howling kids.

So I did. I lifted the phone and did that very thing. That very day. The third Sunday of the month. Right after I fortified myself with a little nibble of chocolate doughnut and a somewhat larger nip on a heel of Johnny Walker Red Label and a thorough re-read of the more kindly rejection letters I have in my files.

"Sally," I said, in my most charming poet-voice, "Sally, I'm coming over."

"But," she said, "I don't even know you."

"So what," said I, "I don't know you either. That makes us even. Besides that, you have a lasso."

She said, "What will we do when you get here?"

I said, "I will read you my poems."

She said, with only a small hesitation, "What kind of poems?"

"Apple poems," I said. "Peach and orange and banana poems. Pomegranate and eggplant and rhubarb poems. I have apricots, I have blueberries, I have kiwi and squash, I have scarlet runners and carrots and beets, I have peas and pumpkins and pears and kohlrabi. I have delicate grapes and crunchy celery, I have potato poems, flowering reds and bristling whites, I have turnips and cabbage and broccoli and Brussels sprouts—"

She interrupted me. It's a small failing of hers, not to be a telephone person; long telephone calls don't agree with her.

Then she said, in a quiet voice, she said, "I want a salad, I want you to read me a salad."

A minute ago the phone rang. You can hear it plainly from up here on the third floor of the jungle gym, despite the cries of the children and despite the tiny wet bottom planted on my knee. That will be Carol calling. She will be talking now to Sally. It is the third Sunday of the month. Carol will be asking us to drop over after supper for a visit. Bring the kids, she will say. And Wayne, bring him too, tell him I have some chocolate doughnuts.

She's an organized woman, Carol is. They won't talk long. We will drive over, and sit and visit, and Michael will ask about my latest crop of poems. Have you thought of maybe doing some weeding? he will ask in his gentle way. Then I will say, no, no weeding, I'm a fertilizer man, let them grow.

And Carol will agree with me, "Fertilizer, I'll say," and then give the little laugh that makes Michael's eyes shine.

And Sally, well, Sally will say in her sing-song voice how she likes the fruits and vegetables we grow together and how the kids grow like bad weeds and maybe we should gather them up now if we can disentangle them from the jungle of Michael's computer cords and get on our way, for we have to stop at the pharmacy to buy some radish seeds.

And then Sally will turn to me and say, "Wayne, it's time to lasso those kids and tuck them in the back seat."

And I will lasso those kids and tuck them and strap them tight with belts and hugs and kisses, and Sally will drive us home to make poems and salads together until the next time the phone rings on the third Sunday of the month. Then I will dust the fertilizer from my latest poems. The kids will howl as only kids can do. Sally will twirl her lasso as she picks up the receiver. It will be Carol. She's an organized woman.

Mirror Image

BETTY JANE WYLIE

(an excerpt)

THE NEXT NIGHT IN THE BEDROOM Eve handed Bob her Polaroid camera and told him his assignment: a set of pictures of her posing in the nude.

"I'm going to like this," he said.

"I thought you would."

"But I'd like to know what it's for."

"My next painting," Eve said. "A self-portrait. Most self-portraits are head only. I want to do my whole body, while I still have one. Maybe I'll do one every ten years, to catch the decay, the aging process. That may be depressing, but very interesting. No one to my knowledge has ever done it before."

"Are you sure?" Suddenly Bob was very serious.

"No, but I can check it out in the art library at the university."

"I don't mean the elapsed time idea, I mean, are you sure you want to do this painting?"

"Very sure. Are you shocked?"

"No. No, not about the nude part. It's the self-portrait I'm worried about—and you. You had a hard time dealing with yourself doing the other painting. You got awfully tense . . ."

"I was tired."

"It was more than that. You were . . . you said yourself that narcissism isn't easy, introspection is hard. Maybe it will be too much for you."

"I want to do it, Bob."

"Can it wait?"

"No. Are you going to take my picture?"

"With pleasure. Do you know how you want to pose?"

"Like a Tintoretto Venus, with a hand mirror reflecting my face," she answered promptly. "But this won't be Vanity. It's so crazy, all these lecherous male artists over the years have been painting nude women with mirrors and calling them vain. Their paintings were the *Playboy* centrefolds of their time, catering to the male audience."

"Without staples in the navel," said Bob.

"Right. All the mirror did was turn the woman into an object, make her a surveyor of herself, offering herself to the audience. And they called her vain!"

"So what are you going to do that's different?" asked Bob.

"This will be introspection."

Eve threw a huge embroidered Spanish shawl across the bed, piled up the pillows to support her shoulders, stripped, and lay down. She twisted into different positions and told Bob when to shoot her. She had obviously given it a lot of thought. Full frontal nudity, but with a sideways twist, pulling away from the viewer, not offering herself wholly. She held a hand mirror, a silver-backed one with a long handle from a dressing table set her mother had given her for her twenty-first birthday, when she would have preferred a tour of the art galleries of Europe. (She went anyway.) The mirror had always to be angled so as to reflect her face into the camera.

Bob soon got interested in the assignment, as she had expected he would, from the technical point of view. Fortunately, she had bought a number of cartridges of film. Bob opened a bottle of wine and they sipped and worked together for several hours. They studied each shot as it emerged, criticizing it and analyzing it, then readjusted her poses until they had enough photographs for her to work from.

"It's rare for me to be touching you only with my eyes," Bob said.

"And drinking," she added.

"What?"

"Drinking to me only with thine eyes?"

"Oh—right. That too."

She shivered.

"Are you cold?"

"A little. I've been naked for hours."

"And I've been too busy to keep you warm."

"And I guess it's too late now." She wrapped the Spanish shawl around her shoulders and stood up. The session, it seemed, was over.

"What about a close-up?" said Bob.

"I can work with the hand mirror for that."

"I don't mean that kind of close-up," he said.

"Are you sure you're not too tired?" she asked.

"I'm not. What about you?"

"I'm orgasmic from auto-eroticism."

"That sounds terribly technical for what I had in mind," he said.

"Show me what you had in mind."

He showed her.

"I liked that assignment," he said later, as he turned out the light.

"I knew you would," she murmured, almost asleep.

The full moon woke her an hour or so later, shining across the closet-door mirror, which reflected it into her eyes. She lay awake for a few minutes, thinking, then rose and went to stand naked before the door, gazing at her silver body in the glass. Her skin seemed to glow with an inner light, reflecting the moon—her skin or the glass? Her double's eyes were in shadow; Eve could see only a gleam of light coming from them, no colour. Nevertheless she felt their gaze penetrate her. She swayed toward the mirror and took a half-step toward it. She saw a hand reach out to her.

"No—keep your distance," she whispered. To whom?

They were all late and cranky the next morning. Only three more days of school, and the strain was showing. The kids wanted it to be over NOW.

"Tell you what," said Eve, to cheer them up. "I'll meet you after school and we'll all walk over to the library. You can sign up for your summer reading program and I can gather a heap of stuff about mirrors. Then we'll stagger home and I'll cook a beef stroganoff with the leftover roast."

"Do I have to read this summer?" asked Dood.

"No. And you don't have to watch television, and you don't have to swim, and you don't have to go to summer camp, and you don't have to eat one wiener or one marshmallow all summer."

"Yeah, yeah."

"I'd like to get a cookbook and do some cooking," said Ibbi. "There must be more to cooking than Waldorf salad and corn chowder," she added, naming the food she had learned to cook at school.

"I have cookbooks," said Eve.

"Too fancy," said Ibbi. "I want to learn to cook real food."

"You don't consider beef stroganoff real food?" asked Eve.

"What about me?" asked Bob quickly, before the stroganoff set off an international incident.

"You can help me with the lighting of my new painting tonight. I want to experiment with candles," she said.

"I'll bring some home," said Bob. "It's called bringing home the beacon."

Everyone groaned and went off to work and school while Eve set about to polish the mirrors, finally, in honour of summer light. She had done every mirror in the house, with the exception of the one in the loft and those in her bedroom. She was glowing with the exercise, her arms slightly stiff from so much stretching back and forth, though she had kept changing hands to distribute the stress. She started on her closet mirror, close to lunchtime now, but she had enough time to finish.

"Hello, friend," she said to her vigorous double as she attacked her image with a wad of crumpled newspaper. "I wouldn't let you touch me last night, but now you'll get properly scrubbed down." She was already warmed to her work and she had developed a good sweep with her alternating arms. She hunkered down on her buttocks as she wiped the lower range of the mirror. As she stretched to do the upper areas of the mirror, above her head, her body unavoidably fronted and touched her image, something she hadn't done for several weeks, not since she had pressed her naked breasts against this glass. She remembered that moment now and looked herself in the eye.

"I know what you're thinking," she said. "None of that now. There's no time." But on an impulse, she kissed herself in the glass.

And exploded.

A stabbing pain went through her lips, into her throat, up to her head, and burst into bright fragments of light behind her eyes. She screamed and fell to the floor, unconscious.

Ibbi found her. "Mommy, Mommy!" she was shouting in panic as Eve regained consciousness. "What happened? Are you all right?"

"I'm fine," said Eve. "I must have fainted. Could you get me a glass of water, dear?" She felt something like a monumental hangover in her head. Perhaps water would help, though she doubted it. She sat up and looked at her double while Ibbi was getting her water. "We won't do that again, will we?" she said. She looked suitably subdued, very pale and serious.

"Don't tell Dad about this, will you, Ibbi?" Eve asked her daughter when she brought the water. "He'll just say I've been working too hard, and I don't want to worry him."

"Okay," said Ibbi. "But maybe you shouldn't work so hard."

"I'm allergic to housework, that's all. We'll have fun at the library this afternoon."

It was exertion, that was all. She was low down, polishing the bottom of the mirror, and stood up too fast—just a sudden change of position and lack of oxygen. It could happen to anyone. She was a very healthy woman, and not old. She certainly wasn't going to have a stroke or anything like that, she told herself. Later she told her double that, too, as she got ready to go out. "You look marvellous," she said, combing her hair. She pinned it quickly and expertly into a french roll. "And I'm just as well as you are." She went to meet the kids at school.

The library was a favourite place for all of them. In the children's department there was already a big mural in place—a picture of a castle on a hill, with a moat and a drawbridge. In the foreground, in serried ranks all along the base of the drawing, were little paper cutouts of knights on horseback, each pinned in place with a thumbtack. Some of them already had names written on their shields. Ibbi and Dood were duly registered and each picked out a knight to bear the family's honour. As they read and reported on the books they read that summer, their knights would ride up the hill, cross the drawbridge, and storm the castle. The first thirty riders would be feted with a dinner at the library at the end of the summer. It was the best bribe Eve had found to keep her children happily occupied for at least part of each summer.

She left them choosing their books while she went into the adult section looking for what she wanted: information about mirrors. She took a few notes and checked out some art books as well. When she went to get Ibbi and Dood, she decided that she had to have a copy of *Snow White* for herself.

"Why did you get that book, Mom?" asked Ibbi. "I'm too old for fairy tales like that, and Dood hates them."

"It's for me," said Eve. "Mirror, mirror, on the wall, Who is fairest of them all?"

"I know all about that," said Ibbi.

"Mean old stepmother," said Dood, "giving that poor kid a poison apple. The mirror's neat, though."

"How do you know?" asked Eve.

"It's on Disney."

"Oh—television. And what's the mirror like?"

"It sort of clouds up," said Dood, "and then she sees a picture in it and finds out where Snow White is, sort of like a magic TV screen. I wouldn't mind a mirror like that."

"It's a truth-telling mirror," said Eve, "or maybe it's a projection of the stepmother's envy."

"What does that mean?"

"It means, I think, that the mirror is jealous of her."

"Of who?" asked Ibbi.

"That's what I have to find out," said Eve. "Come on. Knights in armour deserve ice cream to cool off."

A Palimpsest

VEN BEGAMUDRÉ

(an excerpt)

I.

THIS IS A STORY about two houses a thousand miles apart. And so in different time zones. It's about the people who moved into them. The people who moved out in body if not in spirit. About a sudden, inexplicable death.

This is not a nice story, though it has its moments.

The smaller house first, a character home:

- Hardwood floors

- A brick fireplace with a tiled, ceramic hearth

- Windows made of old glass, which bends light filtering through the branches of the neighbourhood's many elms

Kathryn listed these and other features over the phone to her fiancé, Hugh, after her first visit. She made this visit with her mother since he was finishing his residency at a children's hospital, far away. Kathryn told him, "I never dreamt we'd start out in such a nice place. I'm so happy, I could die."

To which he said, "Don't."

"You're such a romantic," she teased. "Did you know marriage is the second greatest adventure? After death, of course."

"Honey," he said, "sometimes I don't know about you."

"Oh good."

"So," he asked, "what about the people?"

"No major illnesses they'll admit to."

"That's not what I meant, and you know it."

She let this pass. Their enforced separation had been a trial. They had broken their engagement twice in the past year without telling anyone, especially not her parents. There were some things parents did not need to know. One more day and he would be back in town. One more week and they could move into the house. A month after this, they would turn from a minister to face their loved ones and friends. He would say, "Please welcome Hugh and Kathryn Blunt." Everyone would applaud—even her mother, though she disapproved of their living arrangements in the meantime.

"The people," Kathryn said. "Well, they are interesting."

"Which means?"

"The husband's an artist. He's Indian."

"Oh."

"Don't worry, it's not that kind of neighbourhood. I meant from India, though I think he was born here. He's, I don't know, dull, for an artist. Doesn't say much. She's the interesting one, what with researching the greenhouse effect on plants. During her sabbatical. The husband and daughter are going along."

"There's a kid in the house?"

"It's okay. The walls aren't marked up or anything. She's twelve. Quiet like her father but a different kind of quiet, like she's always watching the grown-ups to figure out where she stands. Mom didn't like her much. Says kids like that give her the willies."

"Everything gives your mom the willies."

"Now, Hugh," Kathryn said, "don't start." She waited for his "Sorry" before going on. "They're leaving the place completely furnished, dishes and all, but I said maybe they could take some of the artwork down. All of it, in fact."

"The husband's artwork?"

"That's the strange part. Hardly any of the stuff on the walls is his except a couple of photos of mosques."

"Moths?"

"Arab temples. He said they're so old they don't bother him anymore. His wife said he was being modest. He mainly paints now, and the stuff sells before it's dry. No, most of what's up is hers I think, even though it's so, well, Indian, if you know what I mean. It's just not us. I never said so but she guessed."

"Feminine intuition?"

Kathryn let this pass, too. "Once you see the house and we settle on the rent, we'll go room by room and decide how we want them left. Which bookshelves we'd like cleared out, that kind of thing. They're into Ikea. I told her we don't have nearly as much as them. She said they didn't have much either when they started out. Oh, but I did say we'll want to use our own bed."

"This is after I see the house, right? And what if we can't talk them down a hundred a month?"

"My dear distant fiancé," Kathryn said. "My sweet husband-to-be, whom I've known since senior high, and I do mean in the Biblical sense, if you don't like the house, the wedding is off."

Hugh liked the house. Why wouldn't he? Kathryn had impeccable taste. In response to his counter-offer, the owners lowered the rent slightly as a gesture of goodwill. He compromised, though not at once. He didn't care for the couple—not even the interesting wife—but Kathryn had a gift for making friends. If not making friends, then establishing a strange rapport.

They have now moved into what she is already calling their honeymoon house. But life is never simple. Only people—some people—are simple. The wedding is less than a month away and, for the first time since she had chicken pox as a girl, Kathryn has fallen ill.

2.

The larger house now. Not exactly a character home but not without its advantages:

- Wall-to-wall carpeting
- Closets in every room of the four-level split
- In one corner of the huge lot, a workshop that can double as a studio, complete with skylights

Ravi and Margaret rented the house sight unseen, but the owners had faxed more than enough information. Besides, one of Margaret's many friends—soon to be her dean for a year—had inspected the house and pronounced it fine. She'd especially liked the garden, with its wooden bridge curving over a pond.

Ravi arranged his studio first and left Margaret and their daughter, Tara, to the bedrooms and kitchen. He had his priorities, and art came before sleep or food. Still, he caught himself scowling at his easels—a small one for sketches, a large one for work he sold. He scowled because he couldn't decide whether he was battling an artist's equivalent of writer's block or whether he was facing a midlife crisis. At thirty-nine.

"If it is a midlife crisis," Margaret had said, "don't let it interfere with my work." This while he'd helped her assemble their stereo.

Opening a box of CDs, Tara made a face. When he grinned at her, she turned to begin sorting them.

He fought down his helplessness. He would have preferred a wisecrack like, "Yeah, you watch yourself." He didn't know how to cope with Tara's silence, with her constantly turning away.

He asked Margaret, "When have I ever let anything interfere with your work? I moved, too, didn't I?"

"I know, I know." She bussed his cheek while passing. "You deserve to be canonized."

"Bah, humbug." He hooked one arm around her waist, then kissed her on the back of the neck while she tried to get free. But she did laugh. He pretended not to notice when Tara rolled her eyes.

Now, setting out his books—most of them large-format art books—he tossed one into a trashcan. He'd bought this book on impulse at a store catering to self-help. It still annoyed him—the content, not the impulse. The book was called *Help Yourself Through that Midlife Crisis.* It annoyed him because most of the case studies were of successful men—doctors, lawyers, executives—who dropped out for a year to write a novel. Or weld sculptures from used auto parts. What should he do? Stop painting for a year and join IBM?

He sat back on his favourite paint-covered stool and catalogued the equipment moved against the walls. Table saw, band saw, jointer, thickness planer, routing table, belt sander, drill press. Tools hung on pegboards above workbenches, also moved aside. Arnold Bower—not Arnie, Arnold—had said Ravi could help himself to the equipment, even the hand tools. Some of them were so old, their wooden handles were stained with honest sweat.

Arnold had made this offer the day before, just after Ravi, Margaret, and Tara had moved in. Now Arnold and his wife, Dora, were flying east. Like Margaret, Dora would spend her sabbatical doing research. Not on the greenhouse effect. On the emotional stability of gifted children. She'd mentioned this while looking at Tara, and Tara had looked away. She was no genius—certainly not borderline crazy—but she was gifted. She'd also recently overcome a passing hatred for school, though she still claimed most boys her age were, as she put it, intellectually challenged. Alone with Arnold in the workshop, Ravi said woodwork might just do the trick, thanks. He'd even framed in a darkroom before giving up on photography.

"This used to be a darkroom," Arnold said. "Not so long ago either. I ripped out the inside walls. Put in this other skylight to match." He took a dovetail saw from a pegboard and thumbed the blade. "So why'd you give it up?"

Ravi shruggged. Then he decided Arnold deserved better. "I stopped believing in the power of documentary photography to change things." He laughed over sounding like a prof, which he wasn't. "Society. Injustice. You know."

Arnold chuckled. "I was into peace marches, myself."

"And now here I am," Ravi said, "getting tired of painting for profit."

Arnold nodded with understanding.

Trying to think of what else to say—wishing he could have more time with this older, wiser man—Ravi eyed the floor between them. It was concrete. The red paint had bubbled from years of moisture. In one spot the concrete was pitted as though someone had dropped a bottle of acid. What kind of acid would leave such scars? Of course, muriatic. Arnold must have dropped a bottle of muriatic acid after cleaning an especially grimy toilet. Ravi considered buying an area rug, a gift for having survived the move. He'd seen one in the latest Ikea catalogue. It was four feet by six and would easily cover the scars. It would also be impractical in a studio.

"I took a year off once," Arnold said. "Did everything I promised myself I'd do when I retired. Sailed, played tennis. Even took up golf. That's the problem with a midlife crisis." He sighted along the dovetail saw. "It's not that you bore everyone around you. You end up boring yourself. In the end you're glad to get back to the real world, whatever your real world is." He hung the saw in its place on the board. Leaning back against a workbench, he looked about, as though sorry to leave all this. "But, hey," he added, "if you're lucky, all you've got is writer's block. Artist's block? Though if a friend of mine's right, it has less to do with not being able to paint than it does with something a hundred times worse."

"Which is?"

"Loss of faith." This time Arnold laughed, not over sounding like a prof—he taught in a junior college—but over trying to be profound.

Tired of unpacking now, Ravi left the studio. Halfway to the house he stopped to admire the garden. He caught himself imagining a boy running back and forth on the curving, wooden bridge. Four. The boy would have been four next week. Ravi could have bought him his very own paint box. Margaret could have sewn a small blue smock. Tara could have given him her children's easel. More angry than sad, Ravi turned away. He hardly ever thought about the son he'd lost.

He wondered whether Margaret thought about him and decided yes, of course, why wouldn't she? Even if she never spoke about him.

And Tara? She had her books, her clothes, and her stuffed animals. She could trust things more than people. People left, and they couldn't be replaced.

Ravi entered the house through the back. He was heading for the basement family room—Margaret wanted it rearranged to suit Tara—but he stopped to examine the guest room. Even with a sofa bed under the long window, the room had been Dora's study, complete with a computer table. All the equipment was heading east with her. Somehow he knew Arnold avoided this room. Arnold had even said Dora avoided the workshop, then looked annoyed with himself at having said this. Ravi hadn't wanted to pry.

He entered the guest room and stood in front of the sliding closet doors. Margaret had suggested he put the Bowers' artwork in here because she'd brought so much of her own. "I mean," she'd added, "so much of ours." He slid the doors open. The space on the long shelf and under the hanger bar had been cleared out. Yes, the Bowers' artwork would fit in the left half and still leave the right half clear. He was about to turn away—to start on the family room for Tara—when he noticed a pile of frames.

They sat almost out of sight in a far corner of the high shelf. Only someone like him, taller than Arnold, would have noticed.

Ravi was not impressed. The frames had been piled one on top of the other and never been dusted. He simply had to set things right. He returned to his studio for cardboard and re-entered the guest room. He took down the top frame and tried to blow dust off the glass. The dust barely stirred. It had thickened over the years into a pasty soot. He laid the frame face up on the computer table and covered the glass with cardboard. Without bothering with the dust on the second frame, he laid it face down. The third went face up, and on top of this went another piece of cardboard.

He didn't care for the images. He'd liked such work once, before he'd become a serious artist. Or, as Margaret had once said, an artist who took himself seriously. The images were watercolours of a castle, a sunset, and a café, all of which he'd painted as a boy.

He took the last frame and flipped it face down. He cringed and hissed, "God damn it!"

Something sharp had sliced his index finger. The slice was like a paper cut—shallow—and it stung. The glass was broken like ice on a pond, the cracks radiating outward from the hole. He sucked on his finger while glaring at the image.

No castle, no sunset, no café. Not even a watercolour. This last frame held an informal wedding photo taken at a reception twenty years before. The man wore a wide tie. The woman wore a translucent batik top. She was Dora Bower, no mistake: the same curly red hair, the same broad forehead. The same eyes. In person, especially if Arnold was in the room, her eyes were a laughing green Ravi found alluring. Here the eyes were moist with a different kind of happiness, a gushing sentimentality. But the man beside her was not Arnold. This man had a sour, almost brutish face. It was hard to see more since the flash had bounced off his pale skin.

Ravi was tempted to criss-cross masking tape on the broken glass but decided he couldn't be bothered. He put the photo face down again, then replaced the stack of frames on the high shelf. No one else could see them now. Not Margaret. Not Tara. He guessed Arnold had never seen them. And now, though Ravi told himself not to be ridiculous, he felt as if he was conniving with Dora—as if, by hiding the photo again, he'd become an accessory after the fact.

He puzzled over this while searching for a Band-Aid.

3.

Kathryn woke first on Sunday morning, the day after she and Hugh moved into their honeymoon house. The skin on her right thigh burned. Moving quietly so she wouldn't wake him, she hobbled into the bathroom. Here she sat on the toilet, lifted her nightgown past her knees, and started to cry. When she hung her head, tears ran down to collect on her chin.

Three days before, on Thursday, she'd woken with a single blister above the knee. Now blisters covered her entire thigh.

She felt like retching. Squeezing her arms against her stomach, she said, "No, not now." She searched among her toiletries in a box and found a bottle of calamine lotion. The bottle was almost empty. She couldn't bear to touch the blisters, so she used a wad of toilet paper to dab lotion on them. Without thinking, she dropped the empty bottle into the plastic wastebasket.

The noise woke Hugh. "Honey?" he called. "You okay?"

"It's nothing!" She used the toilet, washed up, and returned to the bedroom. Trying to sound casual while pulling on her bathrobe, she finally said, "It's hurting." Then she said, less casually, "Oh God, it hurts."

It had started as a tingle the previous weekend, the weekend of Hugh's return. She hadn't told her parents about the problem. Why would she? At first he had said it might be sunburn, though the skin hadn't looked burned to her. She never lay about in the sun, even at her favourite outdoor pool. She swam her laps in the morning, then showered and dressed for work. The next day he'd suggested it might be prickly heat. She'd refused to let him examine the thigh.

She never let him play doctor with her. She took their love life, on hold for months now, too seriously. The most she allowed him was the question he sometimes asked after they made love. "So, how's my bedside manner?" She would reply, playing Sophia Loren to his Peter Sellers, "Well, goodness gracious me!" The "Doctor, Doctor" song was an old one, but all of Hugh's friends knew the words. It was a crowd pleaser at Hospital Follies. These days a female played Peter Sellers and the most masculine male—Hugh, once—played Sophia Loren.

Kathryn's doctor knew the song, too. Her name was Lil. They had attended school together since grade one. In grade twelve she'd introduced Kathryn to Hugh. In those days Lil had been what people called a seasonal girl. She'd dated Hugh during the football season and dropped him after the finals. As she later put it, Kathryn had picked up the fumble and hung on for the touchdown. As Lil also put it, she wasn't seeing anyone just now. Except patients.

Kathryn had gone to see Lil on Thursday afternoon. After hearing the verdict, Kathryn had moaned, "Shingles? I don't have time for shingles." She pulled her skirt down over her knees.

"Well, they've found time for you." Lil unwrapped a lollipop. She had cartons of them because she'd stopped giving her younger patients lollipops. Now she stamped the backs of their hands. Given a choice between Bugs Bunny and Roger Rabbit, most children chose Roger. "It's a virus we've all got in our nervous system," she said. "Related to chicken pox. In fact, you can't get shingles unless you've had chicken pox. And you have. It's a real shame, Kat. I'm sorry."

"Me too. So now what?"

Lil's tone changed, as it had a habit of changing—one moment serious, the next foolish. She could even sound offhand, though never callous. "Now? Nothing. If you'd come sooner, I could've given you an antiviral to head off the blisters. Could be a lot worse, though. Could hurt like hell. So what is it? The wedding or the move?"

Kathryn rocked on the examining table. "It can't be the wedding. Though God knows Mom's doing her best to turn it into a circus. She's still on about that honeymoon in Puerto Vallarta. Says it'll be her present to us—from Dad too, it's his money—but we put our foot down. Who's got time for mariachi?"

"Is that a collective foot or a royal foot?"

Kathryn managed a laugh. Without thinking, she placed her hands on her thighs. She winced. "It must be the move."

"If you say so." Lil crunched the rest of her lollipop. After pocketing the stick, she pulled Hugh's file out from under Kathryn's. "In the meantime, I wouldn't get too close to Young Doctor Blunt for the next two and a half weeks. The incubation period's three, so—"

"But we'll be living together! finally."

"Doesn't mean you have to sleep with the guy. Or kiss him. No slurpy kisses, anyway. Don't even sneeze on him. They haven't quarantined people for this in ages but there's no point taking a chance." Lil opened Hugh's file, glanced at the contents, and closed it. "Especially with him starting work next week. All those kids. Good thing your shingles can't give him chicken pox, since he's had that already. But his own nerves could act up. Mind you, knowing him, he'll refuse to catch anything."

Kathryn nodded. Even as an intern, Hugh had had his theories. He pretended to scoff at holistic medicine but his favourite theory was *it's all in the mind.* He didn't claim to be original.

"Speaking of which," Lil said, "how long are you planning to wait?"

"What brought that on?"

Lil unwrapped another lollipop. "Just an associative thinker, I guess. Young Doctor Blunt. Pediatrician. Birds and bees. Fucking."

Kathryn flushed.

"Sorry, I meant the natural instinct of *Homo sapiens* to reproduce. Carry on the line. Go forth and multiply."

"I get the point." Kathryn shrugged. "Till he gets settled. Till I'm promoted. Till we get a house. Our own house. Then we'll have time for kids. It's not like I have to look too far for the father."

"Gee, thanks. And it's not like I'm your sister or anything, but do me a favour, Kat. Kitty-Kat—"

"What!"

Lil grew serious. "Don't wait. There's a lineup at the sperm bank."

Now, while Hugh cleared away Sunday morning dishes, Kathryn sat in the kitchen and watched Lil scrawl a prescription. She'd driven over as soon as Hugh had phoned. Kathryn hadn't wanted him to phone, but she also hadn't wanted him to examine her. Even now. She'd tried not to hobble while making pancakes—like everything else in the kitchen, the griddle had come with the house—but she hadn't been able to hide the pain. He'd agreed to eat her pancakes if she would let him phone Lil.

"This is killer stuff," Lil said. She tore the prescription off her pad. "Not in all my five long years of practising the medical arts have I seen a case this revolting. You may be unique in the annals of modern—"

"Enough already," Kathryn said.

"Liquid antibiotic," Lil announced. "To keep the blisters from getting infected and dry them up. Easier to absorb than pills, so your stomach shouldn't get too upset. Four teaspoons, four times a day. We're talking megalitres here." She slapped the prescription onto the kitchen table. "And, in case you need a good buzz, Tylenol with codeine. You don't get points for ignoring pain." Her chair scraped on the flowered linoleum. She stood and brushed a fingertip down Kathryn's cheek. "Do me a favour."

"Don't wait?"

Turning from the dishwasher, Hugh frowned, but Kathryn refused to enlighten him. She hoped Lil would control her urge to think associatively. Kathryn said, "Thanks for dropping by. Really."

Three hours later she woke from a restless sleep. She'd taken the first dose of antibiotic, filled at the nearest pharmacy, and a Tylenol with codeine. She felt disoriented. She'd been dreaming about flying in deep, dark space. The tour guide had been a jolly alien with a genetically engineered microphone for a voice box. He'd been cooing about pulsars and quasars. She lay on her back with her face turned from the window. Narrow bands of light, creeping through the closed blinds, picked out the other pillow. It would soon be Hugh's. One more day and he would be back in town. One more week and they could move into the house. She blinked. He was back. They had moved in the day before. She was resting while he unpacked. So why couldn't she hear him moving about downstairs?

She decided he was taking a break to read—out back in the garden. During his residency he'd rediscovered the novels of A. J. Cronin. Hugh was reading *The Citadel* for the second time in as many years. When she'd asked for a plot summary, he'd said, "A country doctor becomes a city doctor and loses touch with reality." Only when she'd pressed for more had Hugh admitted, "The wife dies."

Kathryn drifted back to sleep. The next time she woke, she felt a hand shaking her left shoulder. It was a small, gentle hand, too small for Hugh's, too gentle for Lil's. Kathryn opened her eyes and squinted. Someone had opened the blinds.

A girl stood beside the bed. At least, whoever this was, she was too small to be a grown-up.

Kathryn tried to focus. She couldn't see the girl's face because light bending out from behind her shadowed her features. She looked like Tara—Margaret and Ravi's girl—but Kathryn decided this couldn't be the Tara she'd met.

"That girl gives me the willies," her mother had said.

Kathryn shivered.

This was a younger Tara, about nine. She didn't wear a loose sweatshirt, as the older Tara had, to hide her small breasts. This girl wore a T-shirt. Nor did she have short hair. Ribbons dangled from her braids. If she wasn't the Tara Kathryn had met, where had this girl come from? Of course, another house in the neighbourhood. But how had she got in?

Kathryn flinched when the small hand tugged at the comforter. And when the girl pressed Kathryn's arm, the hand felt cold.

"He won't play with me," the girl said.

"What?" Kathryn's lips felt dry. She tried to sit up and found she couldn't move. The comforter felt like a lead blanket in an X-ray lab. "Who?"

This time the girl whispered, but she sounded less plaintive. She sounded fierce. "He won't play with me!" She turned and left. Kathryn didn't hear her skip down the stairs. She'd run along the short hallway toward the front rooms.

Kathryn tried moving her legs again. The codeine had worn off. Her right thigh burned once more. She extricated herself from the comforter, eased out of bed, and hobbled into the hallway. Standing erect with difficulty, gripping the jamb, she looked at the smaller of the two front rooms. Its blinds were closed, and the room was dark.

Ravi had used it as his study but she'd guessed he hadn't spent much time here. He rented a studio in the warehouse district, he'd said. The room had looked neater than the larger one to the right—Margaret's off-campus office. Her retreat, she'd called it, from the balls of academe. Kathryn and Margaret had laughed while Ravi, who'd likely heard the joke before, had nodded in appreciation.

Yet Kathryn sensed the girl hadn't entered this larger room. She had entered the small one, directly ahead.

A door creaked shut.

Moving slowly, reluctantly, Kathryn entered. When she switched on the light, it flashed with a fizzing click. She looked at the cupboard door. It was ajar. The cupboard looked even darker than the room.

The only time she'd peeked inside, when Ravi and Margaret had shown her around, Kathryn had found it full of boxes. They'd been marked "Old

Art Mags," "Arches Paper." Ravi had said he wanted to leave the boxes here, and she'd said sure. He hadn't said—nor had Margaret—that before this room had become his study it had been a nursery. Kathryn had guessed this from the yellow walls and goldenrod trim. She had also guessed the room hadn't been a nursery for some time—perhaps not since Tara, whose bedroom was in the basement, had been small. Now there was still no hint of alphabet pictures taped to the walls. No hint of mobiles dangling over a crib. There were simply a desk, a chair, and Ikea shelves.

And there was the cupboard.

Hide and seek, Kathryn decided. The girl was waiting to be found. Kathryn grew impatient. She did not feel like playing games and yet she wanted to know who refused to play with the girl. A boy? Why should he? The girl hadn't looked like someone who played with other children. Especially not boys. Then again, Kathryn hadn't seen her face clearly.

Kathryn wanted to leave. She couldn't. She wanted to find the girl but couldn't do this either. Her thigh ached, and she fought the temptation to stoop. She told herself she should return to bed. What if she still was in bed? After all, she wasn't well. Of course—she was dreaming. She'd been dreaming about an alien tour guide, then dreamt Hugh hadn't returned, then dreamt someone had woken her. Still, how could she dream about a younger version of a girl she hadn't met until only weeks before? A girl who hadn't said a word then and yet, moments ago, had woken her to say, "He won't play with me"?

The answer lay in the cupboard. Why else had the door creaked? Why else had Kathryn felt drawn to this room? Before she could scare herself witless, she opened the door.

This time it didn't creak. She marvelled at the design. Starting at waist height to clear the stairwell, the cupboard rose to a sloped ceiling. How clever. She was about to close the door when she saw the eyes. They glinted in the shadows above a box marked "Old Art Mags." They glinted once more when whoever it was—whatever it was—growled, "No one plays with me."

Inordinate Light

ROSEMARY NIXON

(an excerpt)

ALLEGRA SITS IN Foothills Neonatal Intensive Care Unit and imagines a daughter. Fluorescent lights stare down, a worker vacuums. Ninety machines hum. Her baby. Her girl. The baby next to Cassandra's isolette was born last night without a brain. His eyes stare out. *There's nothing in there.* Allegra has to look away. The mother sits beside his isolette. Unmoving. Iceberg face. Allegra feels choked-up laughter. *You look just like your baby.* Looks down at Cassandra. Her eyes are closed, legs splayed, blue diaper dwarfing. Her daughter. Inside burning. She will be reckless, this daughter, Cassandra. She will play hard, be a tomboy, scrape shins, throw a football, throw herself into her history.

Throw away this picture, Allegra.

A friend of Allegra's sister is sitting on a hard bench in the waiting room. Allegra hardly knows her. The husband left her two, three months ago. Allegra has seen the woman, Judith, on occasion, at the grocery store, at church. Has never talked to her. What would one say? This morning Judith showed up at the hospital. She wears a dark coat, no earrings.

You can't stay, Allegra said. They only allow family. You can't stay. Even my sisters have trouble getting in.

Two hours now. There she sits, on a bench in the waiting room. Offering no words.

Allegra looks over at the arctic mother.

Dr. Norton enters the nursery. The one doctor who never dresses like a doctor, who neglects to take on that identity. Dr. Norton will not last the month. Today she's wearing a floral print dress; it shows beneath her lab coat. She carries a chart, moves to the isolette next to Cassandra's. Her sleeve touches that mother cast in ice.

Good morning, Mrs. Angonata. The woman doesn't answer. The doctor pulls up a stool, sits down beside her. Expels a breath. There's not a lot we can do for your son. This is hard. He's being kept warm and safe.

A twitch. The woman begins shaking. A shimmer. She shimmers in this cold blue-lit neonatal nursery.

We don't know how long. Some hours? Perhaps several days. No, you don't have to hold him. No, some mothers choose not to. I can offer you little more than honesty. We're here for you. Please, call me any time. Wait, no it's not too hard. It's just the cords get caught. I'll help you lift him out. Of course it's good. This baby needs you. She lifts the empty baby, empty dangling legs, stare fixed on nothing. Lifts him from the mess of wires into a frozen mother's arms. Mother. Doctor. Allegra. Judith on a hard bench. Under fluorescent lights, four women without a language stare into the present.

October 8
#524010
Draeger, Girl
Diagnosis
Problem List:

1. Respiratory distress
2. Dysmorphic features
3. Auditory-evoked responses show abnormal
4. Draeger, girl has decreased calcium and magnesium
5. Has feeding difficulties acquiring a gastrostomy tube
6. Was put on digoxin 0.1 mg p.o. bid, and is being followed by Doctor Vanioc
7. Draeger, girl kept on 38% oxygen—goes off-colour during feeds

The news is like staring into an eclipse of the sun. Look at it straight and you'll go blind.

Garnet prepared. He prepared for this child to be born.

He has not prepared for this.

Garnet stands at the window of his physics classroom and looks out past his plants. He can see down to the smoking door. Kids huddled in bunches without their coats. Their breath rising, even cloudy spirals.

Roses. He must bring Allegra roses. For a moment, shifting through papers on his desk, hunting for a missing wire, Garnet forgot. Forgot he has a baby. This baby. But remembrance caught him, scorched his stomach, and he dragged his breath and bent into his chair. His physics students sit quiet in their desks. Some are looking at him, others look away. Garnet says,

When a wave passes from deep water into shallow, the ray refracts toward the normal. Sixteen years you have survived, he wants to say. The students go about their work, filling water tables, generating waves. They haven't noticed they've turned sixteen, have functioning kidneys, breathe. When water rolls from deep to shallow, he says, it can create a tidal wave.

Miraculously, the day ends.

Garnet packs his satchel with student lab reports, drives to a florist. Asks for a dozen roses. The young woman behind the counter winks, says, Oooh, have we got hopes tonight! then gets glum when Garnet doesn't answer.

At the hospital, Garnet steps off on fifth floor. Wonders how he got here.

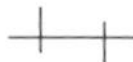

FOOTHILLS Neonatal ICU breathes story. Stories weave the isolettes, suction machines, heart monitors, oxygen tubes, heaving ventilators. They cling to the hems of nursing uniforms and ride the lapels of doctors' lab coats. They smell, these stories, these angry prayers.

Allegra holds Cassandra on her lap. An intravenous needle stuck in the baby's head. Yellow bruises criss-cross the shaved scalp where intravenous needles went interstitial. Even needles fail her baby. When Allegra was a child, farm boys caught frogs, cut off their legs, and let them go. The frenetic gyrate of legs, the bulging eyes. Stop it! I hate you! Allegra crying. The boys laughing.

Just being boys.

Cassandra fights like that when the nurses suction her. Her fists punch out, head wheels from side to side. Allegra conserves strength for those suction episodes—fifteen, twenty times a day. A tube inserted up Cassandra's nose, mouth open in a gag, push farther, farther, Cassandra's frog legs jerking, a nurse hauling tubing like a hose snaked down a drain hole. White-green gunk sucking up the hose, spastic limbs, her baby's face a caricature of anguish. Allegra sobs quietly beside the isolette, hand pressed into her face. The nurses step around her, doing their job.

Dr. Summers enters. One of the boys. The head nurse is also one of the boys. This is an old boys club and Allegra has crashed it. Nobody likes her here. Nobody likes her baby. Allegra asks permission to bathe Cassandra. To lift Cassandra into a warm water basin. The surprise of skin on skin. Baby, you exist. We're really touching. Allegra knows to arrange the gastrostomy tube inserted in Cassandra's stomach, to keep hold of it five inches down the tube so gravity doesn't pressure and pull it free, to arrange the oxygen tube, the heart monitor attachment tubes, her intravenous lines. Allegra's fingers support the baby at the small of her neck. Cassandra finds herself in water; her expression is surprise. Allegra laps water against her belly, the soles of her feet. Cheek against the baby's head until Cassandra's features lose their tenseness, her head moves to touch cheek to her mother, and she kicks. For one strange moment the institution smell lifts, and Allegra is a live whole mom holding a live whole baby.

NO bath. Nurse says no time this morning. Beepers are going off. Babies are trying to die. The nurse has filled a basin with water, then abandons it when the baby next to Cassandra goes into cardiac arrest. The nurse moves fast, her elbow catches Cassandra's foot, which hits the basin, knocks it to the floor, and now the cleaning staff have been called in—more bodies, more equipment.

Allegra hums. It's an act of rebellion. Hums to Cassandra, who ignores her bath water sweeping across the neonatal floor.

Allegra, standing before Cassandra's isolette, sees Cassandra's life here at Foothills Hospital as one big awful song. Ninety-nine bottles of beer on the wall. Ninety-nine bottles of beer. Fragments. Bleak and rhythmic. The sickening repetitive pattern. Pass one down. Hand it around. Same tune, same words. Fewer bottles.

IT'S not a question of lowering her expectations. On the radio, driving to the hospital, Allegra hears a man say, Humans have to have a culture in order to survive. You don't have to be cruel to be a torturer, he says, you just have to be obedient. Survival. Seven P.M. A long bleak night. Cassandra's intravenous went interstitial. She's aspirated again. They've had to turn up her oxygen. Babies go blind from too much oxygen. Mottled green bruises lace her scalp and hands. Six needles plucked from her scalp in a twenty-minute period. The pain on her baby's face is a child's pain, too deep to enter. Let's try this again, the nurse says with hearty falseness.

Sure, why not keep stabbing spears into my baby? Don't worry if you can't hit the vein right away. Babies don't feel pain. They can't. If they did, you'd be deranged instead of merely obedient.

The man on the radio says, We have to believe the things that matter to us are going to survive. Allegra remembers studying the word "believe" for a spelling test. Mixing the *e* and the *i*. There's a lie in believe, Allegra's mother said.

Allegra eyes the needles on the tray, stares at the nurse's precise hands. Wants to grab those hands. Jab! Jab! Oh, sorry. Did that hurt? I thought nurses didn't feel pain.

THE angled doors of Foothills Hospital slide apart, and Garnet enters the smells—floor polish, corned beef, flowers, medication, coffee.

Garnet thinks, We exist because of an explosion of stars. O_2, CO_2, H_2.

Garnet got the mail before he drove here. Allegra's mother sent a baby quilt. A starburst pattern. Tiny triangles of brown and blue and yellow, green, patterned, cotton, linen, gabardine, handstitched patches, leftovers from Allegra's childhood. Garnet thinks of Allegra's mother, her hands stitching glimpses of her daughter's past to this baby's future. Praying someone can stitch the baby a childhood.

This morning Garnet explained Schrödinger's cat to his Physics 30 students. A box, an unfortunate cat shoved in a box, radioactive material, and a potentially lethal device. This device could kill the cat, depending on whether the radioactive pellet emits a particle and triggers the device. There is a 50-50 chance. The scientists outside the closed box have no idea of the fate of the cat, who thus remains in a state of limbo, the cat alive *and* dead, or neither alive *nor* dead, until an observer opens the box and looks inside. Garnet scrubs his hands, dons a yellow gown. He opens the heavy door and steps into the cold sharp neonatal climate. Breathes in its absences. A stroller ride. Tugs on a mother's nipple. A winter toque. His baby has no history. My sweet, you come from stardust. A series of beeps. A nurse calls, Brady. Baby Heisler. Got it.

These babies are bereft of the smell of oranges, autumn quilts, iced tea. A room full of babies who cannot see the stars. Garnet stands by his baby's isolette. She breathes in great gulps, as if air were uncertain, retreating from her. Einstein never accepted Schrodinger's quantum mechanics. Einstein said God doesn't play dice with the universe.

Garnet reaches into the baby's isolette, rubs a thumb, like one would rub Aladdin's lamp, against his baby's forehead. Feels the face of agonizing hope burst across his skin. Pulls up a stool. Straightens the cords, arranges the files flung atop her isolette. Collects two pens, some lint, and a napkin from the floor. Order in the world.

ALLEGRA believes she'll give birth jogging. Well, you could hardly call this jogging, now in her ninth month, but the doctor says exercise is paramount, and despite this weight that sails before her, Allegra can speed-walk at a fast roll. October. Winter pushing up between the cracks. Birds winging south, this cold landscape no longer trusted. Allegra carries *her* space within her. No chilling winds. Her womb a cloud break in the seasons. Look ahead. There's clear blue sky. The baby due on Halloween. This baby, squeezed with love, wet face against the buckle of her womb.

Allegra was born at the stroke of midnight. Her mother got to choose her birthdate. Picked the day before. Allegra feels wonderfully witchy as she moves along the leaf-strewn path. Her energy telescoped within her. Three weeks to D-date. Allegra images her water breaking. A splat on the jogging trail, like seagull droppings, and out pushes the head, a fast and furious birth, baby waving, Hello gravel, hello joggers, hello world!

Her sister would tell and retell the story. Trust Allegra, they'd say. She could never wait for anything. Had her baby on the jogging trail.

Allegra's legs ache. She's not hungry, but she'd kill for fruit. A man on a park bench is eating a nectarine, very yellow, a bit bruised, and Allegra considers moving by him, snaking out her hand, whipping it from his dripping fingers, like the whisky-jacks at Moraine Lake. Feels a thief's exhilaration. The baby kicks, shoves an elbow against groin. This baby's bones are yoked to her bones, this baby's heartbeat, hers.

Let's walk together, baby. Allegra sinks her chin into her monstrous coat, cocoons herself into the baby's cadence, fast walks her toward the future, toward the trajectory of birth. Baby, let's steal a bit of brilliant sunshine. Baby, baby, autumn baby, Allegra calls her with a lover's tongue.

Radio Waves

GEOFFREY URSELL

"It is curious that a hundred years ago radio waves were completely unknown as a physical entity."

DR. J.S. HEY, Radio astronomer, 1985

"Radio waves can never be used for communication."

HEINRICH HERTZ, Physicist, 1895

DR. DARIA LINESKIW was not feeling well, not feeling very well at all. She had left her office at the university early and was now driving north on Avenue Road, heading for home. But with the CBC burbling away some bland classical trivia, and with the windows rolled up and the air conditioning on, she felt at least somewhat insulated from the traffic, from the noise, from the godawful sopping August heat. She turned right, into the shadow of a hovering tower of a building, and the CBC went all fuzzy—"Goddamn useless car antenna!"—and clear again as she escaped the building's presence. She felt she had to get home—had to.

Things were just getting to be too much. Trivial things, massive things, equally oppressive, equally too much. Her apartment highrise and its several giant companions loomed up in the windshield. She squealed the tires on the scorching road, turning around the corner, squealed them into the sloping driveway leading under the building. Gave the radio control button on the dash an impatient push, only to have to bring the car to a sharp, front-end-dipping stop when the garage door didn't budge. "Shit! Not again!"

Mr. Kargin couldn't leave the automatic door alone, couldn't believe that she actually knew how to fix it. He kept fiddling with the range finder, so that sometimes the door would go up and down by itself uselessly and unexpectedly, while other times it would refuse, absolutely refuse to budge until you were practically nudging it with your fender. Several people had put substantial dents in it, assuming that it would open as usual—and it wouldn't. She let the car roll nearer, pushed the control button again, held it down, extracting a one-second pulse of radio waves from the device for every thirty seconds it was pressed. The door began to slide up. With only just enough clearance, Dr. Lineskiw laid rubber, got through, and was instantly almost blind. She slammed on the brakes. The door slid down, totally immersing her in darkness: the lights were off. Kargin was saving electricity again.

She flipped the headlights on, drove to the parking stall, shut the car off, got out; by memory and sliding a hand along the concrete wall, she found her way to the elevator. Groping, found the button, brought the cage down. The blaze of illumination revealed by the opening doors was in its turn blinding. She got in, eyes narrowed against the glare, pushed 38, leaned against the back wall. The door silently slid shut, the machine began to lift. She closed her eyes, bowed her head. And opened her eyes again when the machine came to a stop, to find her entering footprints outlined in black on the orange-carpeted floor. She bent down to look—car oil, car grease. "Serves that stupid son of a bitch right." She took her shoes off and, carefully stepping over the marks, walked along the hall to her apartment. Entered. Shut the door.

"A drink, for God's sake, give me a drink," she told herself. Took ice from the fridge, the whisky from the kitchen counter, poured a good, deep shot. Jameson's Irish—a sentimental favourite of all her colleagues: Guiseppi Marconi had stolen away the youngest daughter of the whisky barons of Dublin back in 1864. Their son was the crazy Marconi, Guglielmo Marconi, where it all began.

Dr. Lineskiw went into her living room, eased herself into a chair, picked up the remote, and turned on the television. The picture leaped onto the screen. It was all fuzzy, it wavered, jumped. The sound was a buzzing blur of words. She flicked through several channels, past scenes from game shows, soap operas, commercials. Paused at the image of a woman in a red-and-blue, skin-tight covering, a red cape fluttering behind, fighting her way through an electronic haze. She was on her stomach, arms extended above her head, resting on nothing—flying. An old *Super Girl* rerun. Dr. Lineskiw flipped on. None of the channels were clear. "Wonderful," she pronounced. "More than fifty goddamn channels pushing signals at us and what can you get? The marvels of satellite dishes. Simply astonishing." More of Mr.

Kargin's work perhaps? She took another long sip of Jameson's. "Oh well... last resort."

She snapped the television off, went to the stereo, set the now chill and dripping glass on the white shag, chose a record, put it on. Turned the power switch, moved the start lever, stretched out on the rug, and waited for the music. The tone arm moved across, lowered itself, the needle made contact with the revolving plastic. She heard a faint ghost of the sound she wanted. Then remembered: the amplifier was buggered—she had meant to take it in this morning—had forgotten. Couldn't even get FM now, not even—"God help me should I want it"—AM. CHUM and all its cohorts. CHUM? Shit! *Hemno!* Shit and nothing but shit!

She moved the lever to Reject, turned the power to Off, got up, and moved to the window. Parted the thick brown curtains with her left hand and took another dose of whisky. Looking out to the fog-shrouded towers of downtown Toronto several miles away, she tried to see the lake. Too much haze. But through the haze, and somehow distinctly visible for almost its entire length although more than two-thirds immersed in murky air, rose the CN Tower. Its Sky Pod was wedged like a doughnut on a pole, glistened pale silver in the weak sunlight, seemed to be floating on the layer of vapour.

She had taken her young niece there once, on a dazzlingly bright winter morning. The girl had stood with her nose pressed against the outside glass of the elevator, Daria beside her with one hand on the child's shoulder, watching the earth, the concrete, whoosh away below them as they were lifted—almost flung—into the air. They had investigated both observation decks—from the highest, Lake Ontario was a frozen blankness edged by thin grey roads swarming with tiny vehicles, by pillars of steam, strings of smoke rising straight up in the stillness, by distance and haze. They had seen the dining room, the lounge, heard about the broadcasting equipment, the microwave facilities. And then, coming down, her body quivering uncontrollably under Daria's comforting hands, the girl had huddled against the wall farthest from the Plexiglas, hands pressed hard over squeezed-shut eyes, as the earth once more fell up into view.

Now, staring out at the tower, Dr. Lineskiw saw its tip, the "business end" of the hypodermic—290 tons of steel carrying nearly two dozen television and radio station antennas—glinting fiercely. She remembered seeing posters someone had put up all around the base of the tower—for blocks around—out to the limits of where the concrete and steel would come thundering down were it ever to topple. The posters warned people. And that wasn't even the half of it, she had decided.

Visible from everywhere in the city, from several cities around, from far out upon the lake, the tower stood, beaming its electromagnetic waves in a circle for hundreds of miles or more, beaming them ceaselessly.

And Dr. Daria Lineskiw turned away from the window, both her trembling hands clutching the nearly empty glass of whisky, suddenly recalling that she was not feeling very well, not very well at all.

November 17, 1901, Poldhu, Cornwall, England

From a slight rise I look toward Marconi's aerials. Is the sea behind me or in front? To the left or to the right? It is always misty, the sky a blank greyish white whichever way I turn.

Sometimes the force of the sea strengthens, the winds gather might, whistle the flowing air through the taut guy wires. No one has ever heard a sound like this on land before. In storms the air shrieks: these new aerials, carrying aloft the copper antenna, slim and erect and unbending. I have stood beside them in such gales, both hands grasping their quivering, humming wood, my head tipped back, searching for the swaying, circling tips (invisible in the wrack of clouds) 150 feet above.

I was in the transmitting building, rechecking the wiring of the oscillators, the night of the cyclone. It built up so stealthily, and I was so lost in the work, that I didn't realize what danger I was in until I heard the first splintering crack—I thought for a moment that a circuit had shorted, was burning out the wiring of one of our precious oscillators, and I leaped toward them.

And then the thundering crashes of the falling aerial supports smashing across the roof had me cringing on the floor, forearms thrown up and over my head. Then, not silence—only the wind pushing against the brick walls that sheltered me. The moaning scream and wail of our circle of towering posts and guy wires and aerial cables gone, vanished in an instant.

I stumbled to the window. In the quick sheets of illumination from the lightning, I saw a jumbled, broken mound of wood and wire, the few remaining supports canted over by the thrust of the storm.

Marconi came from Poole the next morning, was imperturbable. Planned and got us working on this jury-rig within the day. There is a passion in the man I have never seen, never imagined before. This thing must work: *he* must make it work.

From a slight rise I look toward the aerials. The photographer in front of and somewhat below me places the cover on his aperture to end the exposure.

SHE was lying on her bed, all the curtains drawn, all the lights extinguished, attempting to ready herself for the interview. The person from the CBC should be arriving within an hour, wanting at least half an hour of usable tape from Dr. Daria Lineskiw, radio astronomer, upon her election as a Fellow of the Royal Society of Science in Canada—F.R.S.S.C. Dr. Lineskiw began imagining possible questions, imagining possible answers, trying not to aggravate the sharp ache in the middle of the back of her skull, trying not to intensify the sensation of nausea still hovering not far from the pit of her stomach.

"You're awfully young to be elected to the fellowship, aren't you? Only thirty-two?" she asked herself.

Prepared an answer: Perhaps. But radio astronomy is a very young science, not more than ten years older than myself really, and so it's still possible to make what will soon appear to be quite elementary discoveries, to do what will soon appear to be quite elementary research, and I have had the good fortune to be a part of that research and to make some of those discoveries.

"Could you tell me how you got interested in astronomy in the first place? And why *radio* astronomy?"

Walking . . . walking with Father in the woods. He worked on the night shift in the mine, slept the sun away, and in the evenings, after his breakfast, would take me for walks when mother didn't want to go and sometimes when she did, all of us walking, summer and winter. Whenever the stars were out. He knew the stars and we never lost our way, no matter how far we went: he knew how the stars moved across the sky, their patterns, and that it was truly Earth turning that made the sky seem to move, the stars in fact remaining set and still in the dark, in the inexpressibly distant reaches of the universe. "What is beyond the stars, *batko?*" she had asked him. "Where does the universe end?"

The sounds and smells of the northern woods flowing into me through all the spinning circle of Earth around the sun: Jack pine and muskeg, owls and loons, the flowers of spring—trillium, violets, columbine. And in winter the cover of snow reflecting the brightness of starlight and moonlight, wolves howling at the pulsing, shimmering movement of northern lights, sometimes far, far away, sometimes dipping as almost to touch you, surround and caress you, the sound and lights merging mysteriously. The night sky so clear, so close. And the presence of *batko,* so fierce when he had to be, organizing for the union when men who did that were filthy Reds, were—especially if Ukrainian—Foreign Scum, were in danger of being beaten up, of being in an "accident" in the mine. He, drinking in the peace—at least as seen from Earth—of the stars as a balance, a ballast. And yet, once as we watched the flashing descent of a meteor shower race across our vision, he told me, "You know, *dorohenko,* for all the drilling, the blasting, the danger down there where I slave, you know it feels so peaceful really, down there, *myr, myr.*"

And radio . . . radio astronomy? Remembering *vuiko* Ivar, who built the first radio ever to be seen in Timmins, in 1925—taking his instructions from a book, a radio book in Ukrainian that he sent away for and got from the Old Country, God knows why, because there were no stations transmitting a strong enough signal for him to hear anything on it until four years later. Sending away to a supply house in Toledo, Ohio—William B. Duck Co., Radio and Electrical Supplies (William B. Duck!)—for parts. And making the goddamn thing. And not knowing if it worked for four years. Which it did. Old *vuiko,* 53, old to me, giving me a crystal radio set on my tenth birthday, letting me try to put it together myself, bless him. Helping me, only when I asked, to attach it to an aerial, and listening with me as I moved the "cat's whisker" over the crystal until I brought in the local station on the headphones.

The stars and the radio—*batko* and *vuiko* didn't know how tied together those things are. Radio waves, star waves, X-rays—putting your feet, newly shod, into a machine and watching your own bones wriggle, right through the flesh and the sock and the leather! Watching your bones! All different lengths of energy waves, all of us bathed in a flood of energy waves, waves miles long and waves so short that 10 million would fit in the width of a thumbnail—electromagnetic waves. Infrared heat rays and gamma rays and ultraviolet rays and cosmic rays and radio waves. Light rays. All the same. flooding through the universe, the universe awash with radiation. And we only noticing so little for so long: light waves, less than a thousandth part of the whole spectrum. Streaming untouched through our atmosphere, letting us in on a universal secret. And, finally, radio waves, also stealing through our barrier of air, partially absorbed, letting us "see" more and more into space. We, before knowing that, before realizing they are everywhere, fashioning our own.

December 1, 1901, SS Sardinia, *longitude 37°18´, latitude 49°54´, mid-Atlantic*
Unending fog and a chilling drizzle on deck. Choppy waves from the north hitting us nearly broadside. We have lost all communication with the rest of the world. The captain only guesses where we are by dead reckoning. I have felt ill enough not to want to eat, but well enough to keep the food down ever since we cleared Ireland. Only four and a half more days now.

Marconi says that we have gone over the top of Earth's curve, as if the bulging round of the planet were a mountain barrier nearly 200 miles high. That is what our signals have to climb. If they moved in straight lines, they would be 1000 miles above the nearest point of land in Canada.

Marconi says they will climb; he says they will curve.

+++

"YOU worked with Sir Bernard Lovell at Jodrell Bank, didn't you?"

Yes, yes, Jodrell Bank—the mecca I learned about at Carlton. Riding out on a green, single-decker bus into the countryside, away from my tiny "bedsit" with Manchester factory grime—a sludgy past of dust and soot and God knows what kinds of industrial effluents—in a thick layer in all the corners, more thinly spread on the walls, on the ceiling. "When the birds wake up in the morning in Manchester they don't chirp, they cough ... ha, ha." Out through the winter mist and chill swirling over the Cheshire fields to take my turn at sitting on a wooden straight-back chair for hours in front of a bank of machinery, monitoring the graph paper to make sure the telescope was tracking the proper path, following the right coordinates. The telescope a big metal dish that can move, nothing more, that can gather and strengthen signals from outer space—from the stars.

That first interview with Lovell himself—a surprisingly small man—when he asked me what line of research I wanted to pursue. And I said that I really didn't know yet. "There's no hurry," he said. "You'll want some time to settle in, get used to the equipment." Finally, after Cambridge had discovered them and, three months later, announced them, all of us at Jodrell getting caught up in the rush to learn as much as we could as quickly as we could about "pulsars," something in space sending sharp pulses of radio energy at astonishingly regular intervals, some up to thirty times a second, others every two seconds, many in between. Space beacons for intelligent beings: the LGM theory—Little Green *Men* (the bunch of chauvinist twits!)—Little Green Men. And first discovered by a woman, Jocelyn Bell, anyway!

"Do you believe in extraterrestrial life?"

The inevitable question.

Well, in this case we found out differently. Rotating stars ... stars that have run out of fuel, that have exploded—supernovas—and what's left continues to collapse in upon itself. Getting denser and denser—one cubic inch weighing maybe hundreds of billions of tons. Collapsars! Keeping the same spin momentum as they shrink—all this happening in seconds. Spinning faster and faster as they get smaller. Accelerating particles of atoms, like crack-the-whip on a frozen pond. Until some have to let go, get spewed out. The star spewing out radio waves with every spin. Pulsars. Stars that pulse.

But extraterrestrial life, of course, of course. The odds are more than high, they're inevitable. Ten thousand stars like the sun within 100 light-years. In *this* galaxy. And there are billions of galaxies. Of course, other beings. And we could have attracted them without even knowing it, you see. Because we have a "halo" of radio waves around Earth that goes out in all directions, a spreading miasma of radio waves that began—faintly, then stronger and stronger—as soon as we started broadcasting and that goes out into space for as many light-years—because radio waves, like all electromagnetic waves, travel at the speed of light—for as many years as we've been using radio. Maybe for seventy or eighty light-years now.

So somewhere our first radio signals, which just go on forever and ever once they're transmitted, could be being received. And "Aha!" some creature could be saying, "That's what they're up to on that planet." And by our radio waves we shall be known, God help us! Who could blame them if they don't want to get in touch with us, hearing that? Some of them must be smarter than us, must be!

"Well, then, flying saucers—do you believe they exist, too?"

Why not? No one has proved they don't, no one has proved they do. Lots of sightings of something. Sure, flying saucers could easily exist. Visitors. Occupants of some dimension we don't know about—just as we didn't know about radio waves, for God's sake, until 1932. Oh, we knew how to generate them before then—Hertz did that in 1888. But to know they were all around us, everywhere, everywhere. We didn't know! What else don't we know? What else??

December 11, 1901, Signal Hill, Newfoundland

We lost our balloon today. We had filled it with hydrogen gas from the cylinders, attached the aerial and the restraining line, and watched it lift into the white sky. Marconi raced back into the building, leaving Kemp and me to guard the mooring. We hung on to the line, paying it gradually out into the growing wind. It began lifting faster than we wished, the wind buffeting it about almost uncontrollably. I could feel the line thrumming in my hands, chafing against my thick leather gloves. Kemp yelled to bring it down, and we had just begun—the wind gathering force against our efforts—when the rope snapped like a piece of cotton! The balloon flew out to sea, disappearing in a flash behind the blank wall of cloud and mist.

Marconi came running out, and I could barely hear him, huddling together as we were, say that he was almost certain he had detected signals from Poldhu!

I helped to find more pulsars, I wrote up my research on pulse shapes, I passed my oral examination, and I got the hell out of there. Out of Manchester, out of the noise, the filth, away from the masses of people—I once figured out that there were, within a radius of forty kilometres around me, more than 50 million people! I started to get human claustrophobia.

Like being shut in a small room, the walls, the ceiling, the floor of which were made of human bodies—all ages, all kinds, all conditions of human bodies—and the room kept getting smaller and smaller. Away from studying in the sleeping bag I had *batko* ship over, the small gas heater on one wall of my room like a dwarf sun in a frozen universe. Away from the student pub where everybody stood jammed together and shouted at one another to be heard, the air a stinking haze of smoke, the television screaming out soccer goals in the corner. Away from the pseudo-intimate discussion of theories of the creation of the universe: did I prefer the Big Bang or the Steady State? When they didn't give a shit what I said, as long as I got the idea. Yes, the hell out of that, of all of that!

And back to the northern woods, to the National Research Council's Algonquin Radio Observatory. Driving up the valley from Ottawa on Number 17, past Arnprior and Renfrew and Pembroke, and taking the narrow paved highway to the left, into the park, into Traverse Lake and the telescope, the computer building, the cabins—encircled by forest, by Jack pine and spruce. Back to the peace and the familiar sounds and scents of the woods, the familiar motion of time, the seasons progressing as they should. And at night the stars clear as ice crystals in the black, black sky, which didn't matter a damn for the research since radio waves come through whatever the weather—but for my sanity it mattered, yes, it did indeed matter. Watching the swirl of a blizzard, twenty-five or thirty below outside, then stepping into that first sharp gasp of a chill, frozen wind driven into your lungs, watching from a warm, warm room. Alone in the cabin, the nearest town hundreds of miles away, firelight making the ceiling flicker and shift into sleep, into dreams.

"But why was the observatory located in Algonquin Park, so far away from everything?"

The noise. The noise we're churning out. It used to be in B.C., at Penticton. Then, in 1962, they had to shut it down, had to spend months finding a place with as little interference as possible. Interference from commercial radio, from television, from microwaves, from airlines, taxicabs, motors, appliances, citizen band freaks, from the military. There are more than 10,000 radio, more than 3000 television transmitters in the world—large power transmitters. Commercial radio is just the tip of an iceberg. There are about 60 civilian, nearly 300 military communications satellites in orbit around the world. And those are only the ones we know about. In ten years from now there may not be any more radio astronomy. The radio spectrum will simply be overwhelmed. We won't be able to hear anything from outside Earth. We'll be stuck with listening to ourselves, will hear only our own voices.

You know, it has occurred to me that perhaps people who go crazy are simply receiving all these signals more acutely than is normal—their minds are getting overloaded, are short-circuiting. (No. I will *not* say that. Let them draw their own conclusions. The facts are crazy enough.)

"You began some new research for the NRC at the time that led to several discoveries?"

Yes, new research. Beyond pulsars. What happens then? Sometimes the collapse has gone on, the gravitational field becomes so strong that nothing, not even light, can escape. The pulsar has become a black hole. You could shine a searchlight with the power of the sun into it and see nothing. It would swallow the light, capture it, consume it. In effect, the star that has turned into a black hole disappears from the visible universe, becomes a bottomless, wall-less pit. If anything goes near, the black hole sucks it in. It may be, in fact, that black holes have consumed most of the matter that used to be in the universe, that the stars and galaxies now visible are just the remaining grains of luminous dust, the last particles of—to this point—unengulfed, undigested matter.

"But if the black hole is invisible, how do you know it's there?"

That's what I was working on—methods of detection. You see, if there's a visible star near the black hole, the star will appear to oscillate, to shudder, as it circles this incredibly strong centre of gravity. And we can track that. Or, if material from that star, or any other matter in the vicinity, is sucked into the black hole, X-rays are given off, almost as if the matter that is being swallowed is screaming as it vanishes.

I've watched, in the sense of seeing the evidence on X-ray plates, that happening. Great whorls and fantastic whirlpools of screaming light, of screaming matter, being sucked out of the universe into this invisible, colourless maw—the black hole. And no one knows what happens after that. It may be open-ended, moving through time and space, disappearing and reappearing in separate places in the universe. We just don't know. We don't know if we'll ever know.

December 12, 1901, Signal Hill, Newfoundland

The weather was even worse this morning, so Marconi decided to try the kites. The first one broke away, plummeting into the sea. But we soon had a second one raised, more than 400 feet high in the gale, surging up and down and tugging at its aerial wire. Kemp and Marconi retired to the receiving room, while I remained to attend to the kite. An icy rain beat into my face all the while, as I tried, without much success, to keep the kite at a constant level.

Shortly after 12:30, Kemp, scarf tight around his neck, cap pulled securely down to his ears, came dashing out from the building. "We've heard it!" he was shouting at me, the wind carrying away the sense of his words until he came near. "We've heard it! Marconi wants you to go in and listen. Go in!"

I made sure he had some control of the guideline and hurried in. Marconi handed me the earphones as soon as I sat down, asked me, "Can you hear anything, Mr. Paget?" I pushed the earphone against my best ear, straining to hear the three dots—the Morse "S"—that Poldhu was meant to be transmitting. Marconi was looking fiercely into my eyes when I glanced at him. I could hear nothing more than the louder, then softer, then louder again rushing crackle of the atmospherics. "Not the signals," I was forced to admit.

"Listen, Paget, listen!" he commanded. And for several minutes I did so, still not hearing the signal. Finally Marconi took the earphones back and, while I sipped a cup of hot cocoa, continued his watch. Again, at 1:10 he announced, "Here it is, yes, here it is!" and after a few moments returned the earpiece to me. Again, I heard nothing. "Go fetch Kemp!" Marconi told me. And I did. Kemp heard the signals, albeit much later, at 2:20.

I am forced to the conclusion that I was rather more careful with the height of the aerial than he, so that the signals came in stronger when it was I who was outside attending to the guideline.

"WHY did you leave Algonquin if you liked it there so much and your work was going well?"

I needed a rest, an intellectual rest, a time to consider the implications of all the discoveries that were being made. I mean, how long could *you* go on thinking about what is beyond the beyond without wanting to take a mental breath? And then the University of Toronto offered me a very tempting job, a moderate amount of teaching and the chance to continue with whatever research I wanted. Of course, I still have access to the NRC facilities, and last summer I was up there with a new scanning program.

And these are lies. All lies.

And the truth is it's not even because of Bjorn—he went back to Norway a year ago and we hardly ever write anymore—only when one of us has come across something new in the neutrino research that I have now thrown my whole life into. No, not Bjorn himself: he just gave me the opportunity to discover what *batko* was really talking about.

Bjorn—at that Ottawa conference where I first saw him—standing on the Governor General's lawn at the opening, afternoon reception, his bushy blond hair lit up like a corona. Some strange kind of physical attraction that I knew immediately was not whatever people mean when they say "love." But I wanted to be with him, to spend some time in his company. And he was pleasant to me, we had dinner together on the Sunday evening after the conference ended. I drove him to the airport, didn't try to make him stay the night. I let him go, because that's not what I wanted, not a casual night of screwing.

So last August, after I'd finished at Algonquin, I phoned him. Said, "Bjorn, this is Daria Lineskiw. I'd like to take a look at your work." And he said, "Sure, of course, I'd like to see you again, talk with you about it." He was just going to the mine, to check the equipment and ready it for their collecting procedures. So we agreed to meet there.

The plane: out from Ottawa to Regina, the first 1000 miles forest and water drifting by underneath, clouds masking Lake Superior, a cloud cover close above as well. Until just after we stopped for a few minutes at Winnipeg, took off again, the clouds melting away, the prairies opening wide, golden fields floating out to all the horizons, burnished with grain, like flying over the face of the sun, I thought. The light seemed to rise up from the land. From Regina the next morning, south, following the blue-grey twists of the Missouri River to the Black Hills, the sacred mountains of the Sioux.

Bjorn met me at the airport, we dropped my bags at the motel where he had gotten me a room, a single room, his next door. A discreet and charming man, making no assumptions. Then in his car, into the hills, to the mine, where the telescope of their project was. One mile deep in a gold mine, to screen it from cosmic-ray particles, to enable it to capture neutrinos and only neutrinos. And when a neutrino passed through the telescope—a tank, immersed in water, holding 100,000 gallons of tetrachloroethylene—it might, if it hit an atom exactly right, change one of the chlorine atoms into a radioactive argon atom. This seemed to be happening about once every two days, even though more than 80 million billion trillion or so neutrinos were reaching and passing through the earth with every second.

Neutrinos, ghostly particles of pure energy, weighing absolutely nothing, flooding out from the very centre of the sun, surging through the universe at the speed of light, passing through the planets as if they were no more than thinnest mist, at least 100 thousand billion billion moving through the human body during three-score years and ten: perhaps *one* neutrino interacting, merging with body tissue, during all that time. Flowing more easily than light through glass.

We entered the mine, began the series of descents that would take us to the neutrino room. Men were still working some of the middle levels, and some travelled down with us in the first four or five cages. Then we were alone. What if we had a power failure, what if one of the cages got jammed, what if, once we reached the bottom, several kilometres below the surface, the earth shifted, the shafts were squeezed, plugged with thousands of tons of rock? And as we slowly fell, almost silently, deeper and deeper, passing from one cage to another, from one to another, these questions seemed to float away, to drift and be lost on the air that moved in a slow, ever-warmer flow, up and along our bodies, to be left forever behind.

Falling, an hour and more of falling into the depths, dark rock walls sliding by through our light, sliding out of darkness, sliding into darkness again. Imperturbable rock. We had stopped talking about halfway down. Sitting side by side on the wooden bench, we had listened to the whine of the motor at the top of each shaft sounding fainter and fainter, the metal cages—solid floors, thick wire-mesh walls—emitting small creaks and groans.

I never went with *batko* down into the mine. The company would not allow it. I knew that, but I also knew that other children—boys—had gone with their fathers, smuggled in for a few hours. And I had wanted to ride like this, down into the earth, into his place of *myr*. My mother had said, "We could never take the chance of losing you down there. We could not live with that." But now I have lost both of them, and I don't know how I live with that.

The cage stopped. We sat motionless for a moment, our bodies recollecting themselves. Then Bjorn stood, pulled the final folding metal door open from right to left. We got out, looked into each other's face. There was absolutely no other sound than that of our beings pursuing their separate existences. Our soft breathing was loud sighing in my ears. Bjorn pointed the way along the only tunnel.

All down its length a string of naked bulbs hung from the apex of its rounded shape. On the floor a pair of metal tracks emerged from the cage and ran straight for a distant bend. We walked toward the bend. Further on, a thick cream-coloured door appeared on our left, set back from the main passage. Hidden stairs led below water level to the pumps for the tetrachlor.

We moved round the bend, saw the small silver cylinder on wheels for holding the sample, passed the door and window of the control room on our right, entered the chamber that held the neutrino telescope through another thick door with vapour-tight seals all around its rim. Bjorn pulled it closed behind us.

We walked out on a narrow metal platform that had an even narrower extension jutting out to the left at its end. The air was very warm, almost dripping with moisture. We leaned on the metal railing, peered down into the water—a shield for the telescope against neutrons—that lay close beneath the platform, stretched placidly out to the rock walls on every side, sealed itself perfectly against them. Small rings of ripples were slowly sliding across the surface, radiating out from the poles that supported the platform.

I turned my eyes toward Bjorn and he looked into them. "Can we have the lights out?" I asked.

He nodded, said that everyone who came down to the telescope wanted to have that experience, that some couldn't take it for more than a moment. That he himself often slept here on an air mattress, that there was food, tablets to purify the water.

"I'd like to be here for a while without the lights," I told him—and, "Bjorn," I said, "bring the air mattress."

So he did, shining a small pocket flashlight to help him come back, carrying the mattress. We sat down on it. He turned out the flashlight.

It was purely dark. I could find no dimensions with my sight. Bright stars came dancing into my vision—my eyes struggling to create their own illumination. I closed them. I opened them. No difference. I listened to my own breath, quiet and soft, to Bjorn's. My whole being seemed to be floating in a pool of transcendent peacefulness. My mind was coming to rest. I felt it was like one of those glass domes filled with a winter scene: it had been turned upside down, shaken, the snow had clouded it, and now it was settling, becoming still. I could see into it.

In the bright northern light of the sun, I had been searching the sky for swallowing darkness; here, in the dark, I was bathed in pure force from the sun. No other radiation, no electromagnetic wave of any kind was getting through. Only neutrinos, simply neutrinos, just minutes away from their birth in the sun, in the incandescent core of the sun. "*Batko,* dear *batko,* I know what you meant. *Myr . . . myr.*"

We sat motionless for a long time. Then I reached over for Bjorn's hand, held it in mine. Turned to him and tried to reach my arms around him. He held me, I held him. I lifted his T-shirt, caressed his chest. He stroked my breasts, his hands slowly slipping, naked and warm, along my soft skin, fingering my nipples. We helped each other undress, purely by touch, and lay down on the mattress.

I felt so calm, so unafraid. We spoke no words, no names. Our deeper breathing, our moans were the only sounds to surround us in that place. We kissed and had no time for kissing. I rolled on top of Bjorn, straddled him, held his throbbing cock in both my hands, and moved him into me. Wanting him in me, touching me there. Grabbing his arms. His hands on my breasts. As he moved farther and farther in. Easing and pushing and sliding inside.

The first time a man touched me there. With the power of the sun passing through rock like air, pouring over us both. And my body filled with light, the light pulsing through me, through Bjorn, until we throbbed and throbbed and throbbed with light in the deep and splendid dark.

December 15, 1901, Signal Hill, Newfoundland
Marconi gave word to the local press today of our reception of wireless signals from England. The governor, of course, had been informed the evening of the actual event and now most graciously held a reception in our honour. The news had reached England as well. Marconi yesterday sent a message to the company, which I had carried to the offices of the Anglo-American Telegraph for him: "Signals are being received. Weather makes continuous tests very difficult."

After the reception, we went with the government officials and a photographer to the hill again, where, inside the tower, our picture was taken, we all dressed in our coats and hats the very way we were on Thursday last. We sat most quietly for the man, Marconi and I perched upon the wicker basket that held our balloons and kites, Kemp standing behind. I looked straight into the aperture. Marconi and Kemp, I think, were fixing their gaze on more distant objects.

Then another of Marconi by himself, coat doffed, in the room in the other building where he first received the signals. The apparatus was laid out, as it was on that day, before him.

I am slowly, I think, coming to some understanding of what that moment means. We have sent signals across the ocean—2000 miles—riding on nothing but air. Through the gale of winds, through the layers of cloud, over and around the curve of the globe. To one small kite on top of a small pinnacle of rock, into pieces of metal that click when the signal strikes them. Click Click Click. That moment: in England. That moment: here.

Marconi says he will send those clicks around the world. Around the world.

IN her dream there is a blur of red and blue across the sky, a scream of wind, and then the Girl of Steel plunges down into the earth! Down, down she goes, deep into the very depths of the planet, down to the edge of the molten core itself, to where her X-ray vision has revealed a melted pool of the ore she seeks.

In a twinkling she fastens her cape into a container for her fiery burden. Seconds later, she makes her way back to the surface, where, moving at super-speed, she shapes the barely cooling molten metal around her body into an impregnable suit of lead. Squeezing some sand together with a piece of the lead in her hands, she melts them into one to form a thick shield of leaded glass for her eyes. The Daughter of Krypton is ready now to meet those who would destroy her with the awesome power of their deadly ray!

Somehow, they have collected a mighty mound of the strangely glowing chunks of emerald metal. Somehow, they have fashioned a weapon that collects the invisible emanations from that metal and forces them into one fearsome beam. Super Girl knows they are waiting for her. She knows the frightful fate they have in store, the eerie illness that will empty her of energy. But she hopes, by all the moons of Krypton, that this time she will be ready for them.

Ghost Story for December

ALICE FRIMAN

Would it be any comfort to know the dead we love
are looking out from behind thick glass at us . . .

EAMON GRENNAN

In Virginia, snow lasts two days
then melts, leaving doilies on lawns
and lumps of swan on the berm.

A woman shivers in a yellow parka
carrying her gloves. She walks
looking for signs of her father,
last reported not moving
and aloof in his satin cupboard
waiting for seepage. She needs
to know he'll stay there
through spring rain and the root
inching a rope toward his heart.

Already she's heard the first fly
of next year buzzing her pane, notes
in her journal how grass in Virginia
gets a head start, holding its green

through winter. She worries
what a twitch of warmth can budge
deep in the sift of soil. And if here
spring comes early, what does it mean
for the father buried in Florida
where hibiscus and heliotrope
and red passionflower
lush as pain keep coming coming
as if there were no such thing as death?

Cave hic poetae. Beware of poets
who play with the dead. It's no comfort
to know her father watches
from behind glass. Or rises
to the surface of a lake—dead fish—
repeating her old name *rotten daughter*
rotten daughter through his mouth hole.

The father she wanted was given,
five days before the end. And that
in the form of a baby whose last breath
settled the lid on a gift. Don't open it.

White Shoulders

LINDA SVENDSEN

MY OLDEST SISTER'S NAME is Irene de Haan and she has never hurt anybody. She lives with cancer, in remission, and she has stayed married to the same undemonstrative Belgian Canadian, a brake specialist, going on thirty years. In the family's crumbling domestic empire, Irene and Peter's union has been, quietly, and despite tragedy, what our mother calls the lone success.

Back in the late summer of 1984, before Irene was admitted into the hospital for removal of her left breast, I flew home from New York to Vancouver to be with her. We hadn't seen each other for four years, and since I didn't start teaching ESL night classes until mid-September, I was free, at loose ends, unlike the rest of her family. Over the past months, Peter had used up vacation and personal days shuttling her to numerous tests, but he finally had to get back to work. He still had a mortgage. Their only child, Jill, who'd just turned seventeen, was entering her last year of high school. Until junior high, she'd been one of those unnaturally well-rounded kids—taking classes in the high dive, water ballet, drawing, and drama, and boy-hunting in the mall on Saturdays with a posse of dizzy friends. Then, Irene said, overnight she became unathletic, withdrawn, and bookish: an academic drone. At any rate, for Jill and Peter's sake, Irene didn't intend to allow her illness to interfere with their life. She wanted everything to proceed as normally as possible. As who wouldn't.

In a way, and this will sound callous, the timing had worked out. Earlier that summer, my ex-husband had been offered a temporary teaching position across the country, and after a long dinner at our old Szechuan dive, I'd agreed to temporarily revise our custody arrangement. With his newfound bounty, Bill would rent a California townhouse for nine months and royally support the kids. "Dine and Disney," he'd said.

I'd blessed this, but then missed them. I found myself dead asleep in the middle of the day in Jane's lower bunk, or tuning in late afternoons to my six-year-old son's, and Bill's, obsession, *People's Court.* My arms ached when I saw other women holding sticky hands, pulling frenzied children along behind them in the August dog days. So I flew west. To be a mother again, I'd jokingly told Irene over the phone. To serve that very need.

⊹⊹

PETER was late meeting me at the airport. We gave each other a minimal hug, and then he shouldered my bags and walked ahead out into the rain. The Datsun was double-parked, hazards flashing, with a homemade sign taped on the rear window that said "Stud. Driver." "Jill," he said, loading the trunk. "Irene's been teaching her so she can pick up the groceries. Help out for a change." I got in, he turned on easy listening, and we headed north toward the grey mountains.

Irene had been in love with him since I was a child; he'd been orphaned in Belgium during World War II, which moved both Irene and our mother. He'd also reminded us of Emile, the Frenchman in *South Pacific,* because he was greying, autocratic, and seemed misunderstood. But the European charm had gradually worn thin; over the years, I'd been startled by Peter's racism and petty tyranny. I'd often wished that the young Irene had been fondled off her two feet by a breadwinner more tender, more local. Nobody else in the family agreed and Mum had even hinted that I'd become bitter since the demise of my own marriage.

"So how is she?" I finally asked Peter.

"She's got a cold," he said, "worrying herself sick. And other than that, it's hard to say." His tone was markedly guarded. He said prospects were poor; the lump was large and she had the fast-growing, speedy sort of cancer. "But she thinks the Paki quack will get it when he cuts," he said.

I sat with that. "And how's Jill?"

"Grouchy," he said. "Bitchy." This gave me pause, and it seemed to have the same effect on him.

We pulled into the garage of the brick house they'd lived in since Jill's birth, and he waved me on while he handled the luggage. The house seemed smaller now, tucked under tall Douglas firs and fringed with baskets of acutely pink geraniums and baby's breath. The back door was open, so I walked in. The master bedroom door was ajar, but I knocked first. She wasn't there. Jill called, "Aunt Adele?" and I headed back down the hall to the guest room and stuck my head in.

A wan version of my sister rested on a waterbed in the dark. When I plunked down I made a tiny wave. Irene almost smiled. She was thin as a fine chain; in my embrace, her flesh barely did the favour of keeping her bones company. Her blondish hair was quite short, and she looked ordinary, like a middle-aged matron who probably worked at a bank and kept a no-fail punch recipe filed away. I had to hold her, barely, close again. Behind us, the closet was full of her conservative garments—flannel, floral—and I understood that this was her room now. She slept here alone. She didn't frolic with Peter anymore, have sex.

"Don't cling," Irene said slowly, but with her old warmth. "Don't get melodramatic. I'm not dying. It's just a cold."

"Aunt Adele," Jill said.

I turned around. I'd forgotten my niece was even there, and she was sitting right on the bed, wedged against a bolster. We kissed hello with loud smooch effects—our ritual—and while she kept a hand on Irene's shoulder, she stuttered answers to my questions about school and her summer. Irene kept an eye on a mute TV—the U.S. Open—although she didn't have much interest in tennis; I sensed, really, that she didn't have any extra energy available for banter. This was conservation, not rudeness.

Jill looked different. In fact, the change in her appearance and demeanour exceeded the ordinary drama of puberty; she seemed to be another girl—shy, unsure, and unable to look me in the eye. She wore silver-wire glasses, no makeup, jeans with an oversize kelly green sweatshirt, and many extra pounds. Her soft straw-coloured hair was pulled back with a swan barrette, the swan's eye downcast. When she passed Irene a glass of water and a pill, Irene managed a swallow, then passed it back, and Jill drank, too. To me, it seemed she took great care, twisting the glass in her hand, to sip from the very spot her mother's lips had touched.

Peter came in, sat down on Jill's side of the bed, and stretched both arms around to raise the back of his shirt. He bared red, hairless skin and said, "Scratch."

"But I'm watching tennis," Jill said softly.

"But you're my daughter," he said. "And I have an itch."

Peter looked at Irene and she gave Jill a sharp nudge. "Do your poor dad," she said. "You don't even have to get up."

"But aren't I watching something?" Jill said. She glanced around, searching for an ally.

"Vrouw," Peter spoke up. "This girl, she doesn't do anything except mope, eat, mope, eat."

Jill's shoulders sagged slightly, as if all air had suddenly abandoned her body, and then she slowly got up. "I'll see you after, Aunt Adele," she whispered, and I said, "Yes, sure," and then she walked out.

Irene looked dismally at Peter; he made a perverse sort of face—skewing his lips south. Then she reached over and started to scratch his bare back. It was an effort. "Be patient with her, Peter," she said. "She's worried about the surgery."

"She's worried you won't be around to wait on her," Peter said, then instructed, "Go a little higher." Irene's fingers crept obediently up. "Tell Adele what Jill said."

Irene shook her head. "I don't remember."

Peter turned to me. "When Irene told her about the cancer, she said, 'Don't die on me, Mum, or I'll kill you.' And she said this so serious. Can you imagine?" Peter laughed uninhibitedly, and then Irene joined in, too, although her quiet accompaniment was forced. There wasn't any recollected pleasure in her eyes at all; rather, it seemed as if she didn't want Peter to laugh alone, to appear as odd as he did. "Don't die or I'll kill you," he said again.

IRENE had always been private about her marriage. If there were disagreements with Peter, and there had been—I'd once dropped in unannounced and witnessed a string of Christmas lights whip against the fireplace and shatter—they were never rebroadcast to the rest of the family. If she was ever discouraged or lonely, she didn't confide in anyone, unless she kept a journal or spoke to her own god. She had never said a word against the man.

The night before Irene's surgery, after many earnest wishes and ugly flowers had been delivered, she asked me to stay late with her at Lion's Gate Hospital. The room had emptied. Peter had absconded with Jill—and she'd gone reluctantly, asking to stay until I left—and our mother, who'd been so nervous and sad that an intern had fed her Valium from his pocket. "Why is this happening to her?" Mum said to him. "To my only happy child."

Irene, leashed to an IV, raised herself to the edge of the bed and looked out at the parking lot and the kind Pacific twilight. "That Jill," Irene said. She allowed her head to fall, arms crossed in front of her. "She should lift a finger for her father."

"Well," I said, watching my step, aware she needed peace, "Peter's not exactly the most easygoing."

"No," she said weakly.

We sat for a long time, Irene in her white gown, me beside her in my orange-and-avocado track suit, until I began to think I'd been too tough on Peter and had distressed her. Then she spoke. "Sometimes I wish I'd learned more Dutch," she said neutrally. "When I met Peter, we married not speaking the same language, really. And that made a difference."

She didn't expect a comment—she raised her head and stared out the half-open window—but I was too shocked to respond anyway. I'd never heard her remotely suggest that her and Peter's marriage had been less than a living storybook. "You don't like him, do you?" she said. "You don't care for his Belgian manner."

I didn't answer; it didn't need to be said aloud. I turned away. "I'm probably not the woman who can best judge these things," I said.

Out in the hall, a female patient talked on the phone. Irene and I both listened. "I left it in the top drawer," she said wearily. "No. The *bedroom.*" There was a pause. "The desk in the hall, try that." Another pause. "Then ask Susan where she put it, because I'm tired of this and I need it." I turned as she hung up the phone and saw her check to see if money had tumbled back. The hospital was quiet again. Irene did not move, but she was shaking. I found it difficult to watch this and reached out and took her hand.

"What is it?" I said. "Irene."

She told me she was scared. Not for herself, but for Peter. That when she had first explained to him about the cancer, he hadn't spoken to her for three weeks. Or touched her. Or kissed her. He'd slept in the guest room, until she'd offered to move there. And he'd been after Jill to butter his toast, change the sheets, iron his pants. Irene had speculated about this, she said, until she'd realized he was acting this way because of what had happened to him when he was little. In Belgium. Bruges, the war. He had only confided in her once. He'd said all the women he'd ever loved had left him. His mother killed, his sister. "And now me," Irene said. "The big C, which leads to the big D. If I move on, I leave two children. And I've told Jill they have to stick together."

I got off the bed. "But, Irene," I said, "she's not on Earth to please her father. Who can be unreasonable. In my opinion."

By this time, a medical team was touring the room. The junior member paused by Irene and said, "Give me your vein."

"In a minute," she said to him, "please," and he left. There were dark areas, the colour of new bruises, under her eyes. "I want you to promise me something."

"Yes."

"If I die," she said, "and I'm not going to, but if I do, I don't want Jill to live with you in New York. Because that's what she wants to do. I want her to stay with Peter. Even if she runs to you, send her back."

"I can't promise that," I said. "Because you're not going to go anywhere."

She looked at me. Pale, fragile. She was my oldest sister, who'd always been zealous about the silver lining in that cloud; now it seemed she might be dying, in her forties—too soon—and she needed to believe I could relieve her of this burden. So I nodded. *Yes.*

WHEN I got back, by cab, to Irene and Peter's that night, the house was dark. I groped up the back steps, ascending through a hovering scent of honeysuckle, stepped inside, and turned on the kitchen light. The TV was going—some ultra-loud camera commercial—in the living room. Nobody was watching. "Jill?" I said. "Peter?"

I wandered down the long hall, snapping on switches: Irene's sickroom, the upstairs bathroom, the master bedroom, Peter's domain. I did a double take—he was there. Naked, lying on top of the bed, his still hand holding his penis—as if to keep it warm and safe—the head shining. The blades of the ceiling fan cut in slow circles above him. His eyes were vague and didn't turn my way; he was staring up. "Oh, sorry," I whispered, "God, sorry," and flicked the light off again.

I headed back to the living room and sat for a few seconds. When I'd collected myself, I went to find Jill. She wasn't in her downstairs room, which seemed typically adolescent in its decor—Boy George poster, socks multiplying in a corner—until I spotted a quote from Rilke, in careful purple handwriting, taped to her long mirror: "Beauty is only the first touch of terror we can still bear."

I finally spotted the light under the basement bathroom door.

"Jill," I said. "It's me."

"I'm in the bathroom," she said.

"I know," I said. "I want to talk."

She unlocked the door and let me in. She looked tense and peculiar; it looked as if she'd just thrown water on her face. She was still dressed in her clothes from the hospital—and from the day before, the kelly green sweat job—and she'd obviously been sitting on the edge of the tub, writing. There was a pen, a pad of yellow legal paper. The top sheet was covered with verses of tiny backward-slanting words. There was also last night's pot of Kraft Dinner on the sink.

"You're all locked in," I said.

She didn't comment, and when the silence stretched on too long I said, "Homework?" and pointed to the legal pad.

"No," she said. Then she gave me a look and said, "Poem."

"Oh," I said, and I *was* surprised. "Do you ever show them? Or it?"

"No," she said. "They're not very good." She sat back down on the tub. "But maybe I'd show you, Aunt Adele."

"Good," I said. "Not that I'm a judge." I told her Irene was tucked in and that she was in a better, more positive frame of mind. More like herself. This seemed to relax Jill so much, I marched the lie a step further. "Once your mom is out of the woods," I said, "your father may lighten up."

"That day will never come," she said.

"Never say never," I said. I gave her a hug—she was so much bigger than my daughter, but I embraced her the same way I had Jane since she was born: a hand and a held kiss on the top of the head.

She hugged me back. "Maybe I'll come live with you, Auntie A."

"Maybe," I said, mindful of Irene's wishes. "You and everybody," and saw the disappointment on her streaked face. So I added, "Everything will be all right. Wait and see. She'll be all right."

⊥⊥

AND Irene was. They claimed they'd got it, and ten days later she came home, earlier than expected. When Peter, Jill, and I were gathered around her in the sickroom, Irene started cracking jokes about her future prosthetic fitting. "How about the Dolly Parton, hon?" she said to Peter. "Then I'd be a handful."

I was surprised to see Peter envelop her in his arms; I hadn't ever seen him offer an affectionate gesture. He told her he didn't care what size boob she bought, because breasts were for the hungry babies—not so much for the husband. "I have these," he said. "These are mine. These big white shoulders." And he rested his head against her shoulder and looked placidly at Jill; he was heavy, but Irene used her other arm to bolster herself, hold him up, and she closed her eyes in what seemed to be joy. Jill came and sat by me.

⊥⊥

IRENE took it easy the next few days. I stuck by, as did Jill, when she ventured in after school. I was shocked that there weren't more calls, or cards, or visitors except for Mum, and I realized my sister's life was actually very narrow, or extremely focused: family came first. Even Jill didn't seem to have any friends at all; the phone never rang for her.

Then Irene suddenly started to push herself—she prepared a complicated deep-fried Belgian dish; in the afternoon, she sat with Jill, in the Datsun, while Jill practised parallel parking in front of the house and lobbied for a mother-daughter trip to lovely downtown Brooklyn for Christmas. And then, after a long nap and little dinner, Irene insisted on attending the open house at Jill's school.

We were sitting listening to the band rehearse, a *Flashdance* medley, when I became aware of Irene's body heat—she was on my right—and asked if she might not want to head home. She was burning up. "Let me get through this," she said. Then Jill, on my other side, suddenly said in a small tight voice, "Mum." She was staring at her mother's blouse, where a bright stitch of scarlet had shown up. Irene had bled through her dressing. Irene looked down. "Oh," she said. "Peter."

On the tear to the hospital, Peter said he'd sue Irene's stupid "Paki bugger" doctor. He also said he should take his stupid wife to court for loss of sex. He should get a divorce for no-nookie. For supporting a one-tit wonder. And on and on.

Irene wasn't in any shape to respond. I doubt she would have anyway.

Beside me in the back seat, Jill turned to stare out the window; she was white, sitting on her hands.

I found my voice. "I don't think we need to hear this right now, Peter," I said.

"Oh, Adele," Irene said warningly. Disappointed.

He pulled over, smoothly, into a bus zone. Some of the people waiting for the bus weren't pleased. Peter turned and faced me, his finger punctuating. "This is my wife, my daughter, my Datsun." He paused. "I can say what the hell I want. And you're welcome to walk." He reached over and opened my door.

Two women at the bus shelter hurried away, correctly sensing an incident.

"I'm going with Aunt—" Jill was barely audible.

"No," said Irene. "You stay here."

I sat there, paralyzed. I wanted to get out, but didn't want to leave Irene and Jill alone with him; Irene was very ill, Jill seemed defenceless. "Look," I said to Peter, "forget I said anything. Let's just get Irene there, okay?"

He pulled the door shut, then turned front, checked me in the rear-view one last time—cold, intimidating—and headed off again. Jill was crying silently. The insides of her glasses were smeared. I shifted over beside her and she linked her arm through mine tight, tight. Up front, Irene did not move.

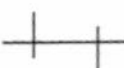

THEY said it was an infection that had spread to the chest wall, requiring antibiotics and hospital admission. They were also going to perform more tests.

Peter took off with Jill, saying they both had to get up in the morning.

Before I left Irene, she spoke to me privately, in a curtain cubicle in Emergency, and asked if I could stay at our mother's for the last few days of my visit. Irene didn't want to hurt me, but she thought it would be better, for all concerned, if I cleared out.

And then she went on. Her fever was high, but she was lucid and fighting hard to stay that way. Could I keep quiet about this to our mother? And stop gushing about the East to Jill, going on about the Statue of Liberty and the view of the water from the window in the crown? And worry a little more about my own lost children and less about her daughter? And try to be more understanding of her husband, who sometimes wasn't able to exercise control over his emotions? Irene said Peter needed more love, more time—more of her, God willing. After that, she couldn't speak. And, frankly, neither could I.

I gave in to everything she asked. Jill and Peter dropped in together during the evening to see her; I visited Irene, with Mum, during the day, when Peter was at work. Our conversations were banal and strained—they didn't seem to do either of us much good. After I left her one afternoon, I didn't know where I was going and ended up at my father's grave. I just sat there, on top of it, on the lap of the stone.

The day before my New York flight, I borrowed my mother's car to pick up a prescription for her at the mall. I was window-shopping my way back to the parking lot when I saw somebody resembling my niece sitting on a bench outside a sporting goods store. At first, the girl seemed too dishevelled, too dirty-looking, actually, to be Jill, but as I approached, it became clear it was her. She wasn't doing anything. She sat there, draped in her mother's London Fog raincoat, her hands resting on her thickish thighs, clicking a barrette open, closed, open, closed. It was ten in the morning; she should have been at school. In English. For a moment, it crossed my mind that she might be on drugs. This was a relief—it would explain everything. But I didn't think she was. I was going to go over and simply say, "Yo, Jill, let's do tea," and then I remembered my sister's frightening talk with me at the hospital and thought, Fuck it. Butt out, Adele, and walked the long way round. I turned my back.

ONE sultry Saturday morning in late September—after I'd been back in Brooklyn for a few weeks—I was on the roof preparing the first lessons for classes when the super brought up a handful of mail. He'd been delivering it personally to tenants since the box had been ripped out of the entrance wall. It was the usual stuff and a thin white envelope from Canada. From Jill. I opened it: "Dearlingest [sic] Aunt Adele, These are my only copies. Love, your only niece, Jill. P.S. I'm going to get a job and come see you at Easter."

There were two. The poems were carefully written, each neat on their single page, with the script leaning left, as if blown by a stiff breeze. "Black Milk" was about three deaths: before her beloved husband leaves for war, a nursing mother shares a bottle of old wine with him, saved from their wedding day, and unknowingly poisons her child and then herself. Dying, she rocks her dying child in her arms, but her last conscious thought is for her husband at the front. Jill had misspelled "wedding"; she'd put "weeding."

from The Banff Centre for the Arts

"Belgium" described a young girl skating across a frozen lake—Jill had been to Belgium with her parents two times—fleeing an unnamed pursuer. During each quick, desperate glide, the ice melts beneath her until, at the end, she is underwater: "In the deep cold / Face to face / Look, he comes now / My Father / My Maker." The girl wakes up; it was a bad dream. And then her earthly father appears in her bed and, "He makes night / Come again / All night," by covering her eyes with his large, heavy hand.

I read these, and read them again, and I wept. I looked out, past the steeples and the tar roofs, where I thought I saw the heat rising, toward the green of Prospect Park, and held the poems on my lap, flat under my two hands. I didn't know what to do; I didn't know what to do right away; I thought I should wait until I knew clearly what to say and whom to say it to.

IN late October, Mum phoned, crying, and said that Irene's cancer had not been caught by the mastectomy. Stray cells had been detected in other areas of her body. Chemotherapy was advised. Irene had switched doctors; she was seeing a naturopath. She was paying big money for an American miracle gum, among other things.

Mum also said that Jill had disappeared for thirty-two hours. Irene claimed that Jill had been upset because of a grade—a C in phys. ed. Mum didn't believe it was really that; she thought Irene's condition was disturbing Jill, but hadn't said that to Irene.

She didn't volunteer any information about the other member of Irene's family and I did not ask.

IN November, Bill came east for a visit and brought the children, as scheduled; he also brought a woman named Cheryl Oak. The day before Thanksgiving, the two of them were invited to a dinner party, and I took Graham and Jane, taller and both painfully shy with me, to Central Park. It was a crisp, windy night. We watched the ginormous balloons being blown up for the Macy's parade and bought roasted chestnuts, not to eat, but to warm the palms of our hands. I walked them back to their hotel and delivered them to the quiet, intelligent person who would probably become their stepmother and be good to them, as she'd obviously been for Bill. Later, back in Brooklyn, I was still awake—wondering how another woman had succeeded with my husband and, now, my own little ones—when Irene phoned at 3 A.M. She told me Jill was dead. "There's been an accident," she said.

A few days later, my mother and stepfather picked me up at the Vancouver airport on a warm, cloudy morning. On the way to the funeral, they tried to tell me, between them—between breakdowns—what had happened. She had died of hypothermia; the impact of hitting the water had most likely rendered her unconscious. She probably hadn't been aware of drowning, but she'd done that, too. She'd driven the Datsun to Stanley Park—she'd told Irene she was going to the library—left the key in the ignition, walked not quite to the middle of the bridge, and hoisted herself over the railing. There was one eyewitness—a guy who worked in a video store. He'd kept saying, "It was like a movie. I saw this little dumpling girl just throw herself off."

The chapel was half empty, and the director mumbled that that was unusual when a teenager passed on. Irene had not known, and neither had Mum, where to reach Joyce, our middle sister, who was missing as usual. Ray, our older brother, gave a short eulogy. He stated that he didn't believe in any god, but Irene did, and he was glad for that this day. He also guessed that when any child takes her own life, the whole family must wonder why, and probably does that forever. The face of my sister was not to be borne. Then we all sang "The Water Is Wide," which Jill had once performed in an elementary-school talent show. She'd won Honourable Mention.

After the congregation dispersed, Peter remained on his knees, his head in his hands, while Irene approached the casket. Jill wore a pale pink dress and her other glasses, and her hair was pinned back, as usual, with a barrette—this time, a dove. Irene bent and kissed her on the mouth, on the forehead, then tugged at Jill's lace collar, adjusting it just so. It was the eternal mother's gesture, that finishing touch, before your daughter sails out the door on her big date.

I drank to excess at the reception—we all did, and needed to. Irene and I did not exchange a word; we just held each other for a long minute. From a distance, and that distance was necessary, I heard Peter talking about Belgium and memories of his childhood. On his fifth birthday, his sister, Kristin, had sent him a pencil from Paris, a new one, unsharpened, and he had used it until the lead was gone and it was so short he could barely hold it between his fingers. On the morning his mother was shot, in cold blood, he'd been dressing in the dark. The last thing she had said, to the Germans, was, "Don't hurt my little boy." This was when Mum and I saw Irene go to him and take his hand. She led him down the hall to his bedroom and closed the door behind them. "Thank God," Mum said. "Thank God, they have each other. Thank God, she has him."

And for that moment, I forgot about the despair that had prompted Jill to do what she did, and my own responsibility and silence, because I was alive and full of needs, sickness, and dreams myself. I thought, No, I will never tell my sister what I suspect, because life is short and very hard, and I thought, Yes, a bad marriage is better than none, and I thought, Adele, let the sun go down on your anger, because it will not bring her back, and I turned to my mother. "Yes," I said. "Thank God."

Five Songs for Relinquishing the Earth

JAN ZWICKY

The rock weeps into whiteness.
Sunny meadow slopes, the gentians,
far above.
The sun, too, tumbles down. A symphony
of spruce boughs in the fiery moss.

Jewel-music, the amber roar of the falls.
No one thinks of home.
Waiting in the cool shadows,
we are dappled with hope.

+ +

Remember how the track swung out
around the cutbank in the full light of noon?
In my dream,

I took off my rings then, my bracelets,
the gold locket.
To stand bare-headed among the pines!

+ +

The fascination of water
is the laughter of geometry.
Wind plunges down the hillside:
        a longing to embrace.

The mountain drifts in twilight.
When we draw the blinds at dusk
is the moment we most want to open
        them again.

+ +

Delicacy of mule deer, the sharp
        dry scent of spruce—
we have been grateful for the smallest kindnesses:
a shelf that holds up books, dry socks.

Rain streaks the windows of the cabin.
Of course, the earth once moved
        on fragile stilts like theirs.
Thought rolls down a crack, is lost.

A sky with holes, a desert
        in the Amazon,
you, black stump, rigid in slash: —
Mist writhes from the surface of the lake.

We are tired.
The wooden bowl is empty.
All night, arguments with strangers, dim
        corridors, panic.

+ +

It is spring. The gullies are dry.
One makes camp in a rocky meadow
        under a plain of stars.

The hands fold themselves in sleep then;
and the ears, the eyes; the tongue
          in its dark cavern.
The mind walks alone to the horizon.

When it returns, its face will be white,
the compass will lie broken
          in its broken hand.

And when the tent flap flutters
in the windy dawn, where the heart lay
          will be nothing.

The Geology of Norway

JAN ZWICKY

But when his last night in Norway came, on 10 December, he greeted it with some relief, writing that it was perfectly possible that he would never return.

—RAY MONK, LUDWIG WITTGENSTEIN

I have wanted there to be
no story. I have wanted
only facts. At any given point in time
there cannot be a story: time,
except as now, does not exist.
A given point in space
is the compression of desire. The difference
between this point and some place else
is a matter of degree.
This is what compression is: a geologic epoch
rendered to a slice of rock you hold between
your finger and your thumb.
That is a fact.
Stories are merely theories. Theories
are dreams.
A dream
is a carving knife

and the scar it opens in the world
is history.
The process of compression gives off thought.
I have wanted
the geology of light.

They tell me despair is a sin.
I believe them.
The hand moving is the hand thinking,
and despair says the body does not exist.
Something to do with bellies and fingers
pressing gut to ebony,
thumbs on keys. Even the hand
writing is the hand thinking. I wanted
speech like diamond because I knew
that music meant too much.

And the fact is, the earth is not a perfect sphere.
And the fact is, it is half-liquid.
And the fact is there are gravitational anomalies. The continents
congeal, and crack, and float like scum on cooling custard.
And the fact is,
the fact is,
and you might think the fact is
we will never get to the bottom of it,
but you would be wrong.
There is a solid inner core.
fifteen hundred miles across, iron alloy,
the pressure on each square inch of its heart
is nearly thirty thousand tons.
That's what I wanted:
words made of that: language
that could bend light.

Evil is not darkness,
it is noise. It crowds out possibility,
which is to say
it crowds out silence.
History is full of it, it says
that no one listens.
The sound of wind in leaves,
that was what puzzled me, it took me years
to understand that it was music.

Into silence, a gesture.
A sentence: that it speaks.
This is the mystery: meaning.
Not that these folds of rock exist
but that their beauty, here,
now, nails us to the sky.

The afternoon blue light in the fjord.
Did I tell you
I can understand the villagers?
Being, I have come to think,
is music; or perhaps
it's silence. I cannot say.
Love, I'm pretty sure,
is light.
            You know, it isn't
what I came for, this bewilderment
by beauty. I came
to find a word, the perfect
syllable, to make it reach up,
grab meaning by the throat
and squeeze it till it spoke to me.
I wanted language
to hold me still, to be a rock,
I wanted to become a rock myself. I thought
if I could find, and say,
the perfect word, I'd nail
mind to the world, and find
release.
The hand moving is the hand thinking:
what I didn't know: even the continents
have no place but earth.

These mountains: once higher
than the Himalayas. Formed in the pucker
of a supercontinental kiss, when Europe
floated south of the equator
and you could hike from Norway
down through Greenland to the peaks
of Appalachia. Before Iceland existed.
Before the Mediterranean
evaporated. Before it filled again.
Before the Rockies were dreamt of.

And before these mountains,
the rock raised in them
chewed by ice that snowed from water
in which no fish had swum. And before that ice,
the almost speechless stretch of the Precambrian:
two billion years, the planet
swathed in air that had no oxygen, the Baltic Shield
older, they think, than life.

So I was wrong.
This doesn't mean
that meaning is a bluff.
History, that's what
confuses us. Time
is not linear, but it's real.
The rock beneath us drifts,
and will, until the slow cacophony of magma
cools and locks the continents in place.
Then weather, light,
and gravity
will be the only things that move.

And will they understand?
Will they have a name for us? — Those
perfect changeless plains,
those deserts,
the beach that was this mountain,
and the tide that rolls for miles across
its vacant slope.

Author Biographies

CAROLINE ADDERSON resided in the Leighton Studio's boat for three snowy weeks in 1993, during which time she polished the manuscript for her first book, *Bad Imaginings* (Porcupine's Quill 1993), which was nominated for a 1993 Governor General's Literary Award and the 1994 Commonwealth Book Prize and won the 1994 Ethel Wilson Fiction Prize. Stories from this book have been widely anthologized and translated. Adderson has also written for film and for CBC Radio. Her first novel, *A History of Forgetting* (Key Porter/Patrick Crean Editions 1999), was nominated for the Writer's Trust Fiction Prize. Adderson lives in Vancouver.

VEN BEGAMUDRÉ worked at the Leighton Studios on a story collection, *Laterna Magika* (Oolichan Books 1997), and on two novels, including *Van de Graaff Days* (Oolichan Books 1993). *Laterna Magika* was a best book finalist in the Canada-Caribbean region for the 1998 Commonwealth Writers Prize. Begamudré has been writer-in-residence in the University of Calgary's Markin-Flanagan Distinguished Writers Programme, the University of Alberta's Department of English, and the Canada-Scotland Exchange.

MAUREEN BRADY's recent stories have been published in *Cabbage and Bones* (Henry Holt and Company 1997), *Mom* (Alyson 1998), and *Pillow Talk* (Alyson 1998). She has received grants and awards from the New York State Council on the Arts, the Barbara Deming Fund, the Ludwig Vogelstein Foundation, MacDowell, the Virginia Center for the Creative Arts, Villa Montalvo, the Tyrone Guthrie Centre, and The Banff

Centre for the Arts. Brady teaches writing at NYU and the Writer's Voice and divides her time between New York City and the Catskills.

KAREN CONNELLY is the author of several books of poetry and non-fiction. She is the recipient of the Pat Lowther Memorial Award for poetry and the Governor General's Literary Award for non-fiction. She is currently working on a novel and a collection of essays about Burma. Connelly's most recent book of poetry is *The Border Surrounds Us* (McClelland & Stewart 2000). Connelly's other books include *Touch the Dragon: A Thai Journal* (Turnstone Press 1992), which won the Governor General's Literary Award for non-fiction and was a national bestseller, as well as *The Small Words in My Body* (Gutter Press 1995), *This Brighter Prison* (Brick Books 1993), *One Room in a Castle—Letters from Spain, France, and Greece* (Turnstone Press 1995) and *The Disorder of Love* (Gutter Press 1997). Connelly's books are published in the U.K., Australia, Germany, and Asia.

MARLENE COOKSHAW is the author of three collections of poems, most recently *Double Somersaults* (Brick Books 1999). Her chapbook of short prose, *Coupling*, was published by Outlaw Editions and reprinted in 1998. She was born in southern Alberta but has lived on the west coast of B.C. since 1979, currently on Pender Island. Cookshaw is the editor of the *Malahat Review* in Victoria.

JULIA DARLING is a playwright, poet, and short story writer who lives in the north of England. Her stories have been published in many anthologies and collections and have won several awards. Her first novel is entitled *Crocodile Soup* (McArthur & Co. 1999), and she is currently working on a second novel, the first draft of which was written in the Leighton Studios.

MYRA DAVIES is a western Canadian writer and recording and performance artist. Since 1991, Davies has been working with Berlin electronica sound artist Gudrun Gut on a collaborative spoken word, recording, and performance project, *MIASMA*. Gut and Davies have released two *MIASMA* CDs and additional individual tracks. They have toured in Europe several times and maintain linked Web sites in Canada and Germany. Davies is writing a book about the Berlin underground music scene.

EMIL A. DRAITSER'S stories have appeared (or are forthcoming) in the *Partisan Review*, *The Kenyon Review*, *The Literary Review*, *International Quarterly*, *Confrontation*, as well as on the Op-Ed pages of the *Los Angeles Times* and *San Francisco Chronicle*. He's a recipient of the New Jersey Council of the Arts Fellowship in Fiction and the City University of New York Grant for Creative Writing. Currently, Draitser teaches Russian at Hunter College in New York.

ALICE FRIMAN, born in New York City, is professor emerita of English and creative writing at the University of Indianapolis. Published in ten countries and anthologized widely, she has produced eight collections of poetry, including *Inverted Fire* (BkMk 1997) and *Zoo* (Arkansas 1999), winner of the Ezra Pound Poetry Award. Among Friman's other awards are three prizes from Poetry Society of America and fellowships from the Arts Council of Indianapolis and the Indiana Arts Commission. Friman was at the Leighton Studios in February 1991.

TERRY JORDAN's short story collection, *It's a Hard Cow* (Thistledown Press 1994), won a Saskatchewan Book Award and was shortlisted for the Commonwealth Writers Prize. He was the first Margaret Laurence Fellow at Trent University in 1996. His latest book, *Beneath that Starry Place* (HarperCollins 1999), was nominated for the 1999 Chapters/Books in Canada First Novel Award. His award-winning plays, *Reunion, Movie Dust,* and *Close Your Eyes* have been produced across the country. Jordan is currently working on a novel and teaches in the English department at Concordia University, Montreal.

JANICE KULYK KEEFER has twice been nominated for a Governor General's Literary Award, is a two-time winner of the CBC Radio Literary Competition, and was awarded the 1999 Marian Engel Award. Kulyk Keefer is the author of numerous works of fiction, poetry, and literary criticism. *Anna's Goat* (Orca 2000) is her first book for children. Kulyk Keefer teaches at the University of Guelph and lives in Toronto.

ROBERT KROETSCH is a novelist, poet, and essayist who was born in Alberta in 1927 and first attended the Banff Summer School for the Arts in 1947. His nine novels include *The Words of My Roaring* (Macmillan of Canada 1966; University of Alberta Press 2000), *The Studhorse Man* (Simon & Schuster 1969; Random House 1988), *Badlands* (General Publishing 1975; Stoddart 2000), and *What the Crow Said* (General Publishing 1978; University of Alberta Press 1998). His longer poems are collected in *Completed Field Notes* (McClelland & Stewart 1989; University of Alberta Press 2000). Kroetsch is currently at work on something but has so far been unable to determine what it might be.

DON MCKAY has published eight books of poetry, including *Birding, or desire* (McClelland & Stewart 1983); *Night Field* (McClelland & Stewart 1991), which received the Governor General's Literary Award; *Apparatus* (McClelland & Stewart 1997); and *Another Gravity* (McClelland & Stewart 2000). His work has also received the National Magazine Award and the Canadian Authors Association Award. Since 1975, McKay has served as editor and publisher with Brick Books. He taught creative writing and English literature at the University of Western Ontario and the University of New Brunswick for twenty-seven years before resigning to write and edit poetry full-time. From 1991 to 1996, McKay edited *The Fiddlehead,* and he has also served as a faculty resource person at the Sage Hill Writing Experience and The Banff Centre for the Arts.

JUDY MICHAELS is a poet in the schools for the Geraldine R. Dodge Foundation and artist-in-residence at Princeton Day School in Princeton, New Jersey. Her book *Risking Intensity* (The National Council of Teachers of English 1999) is about reading and writing poetry with high school students. Her next book, *Dancing with Words,* is to be published in spring 2001. Michaels' poems have appeared or are forthcoming in *Poetry*, *Woman's Review of Books,* and other journals, and she has published book reviews in *America Book Review*.

KAREN MULHALLEN is editor-in-chief of *Descant,* which she has edited for most of its three decades. She has published seven volumes of poetry—*Sheba and Solomon* (Eleftheria 1984), *Modern Love* (Black Moss Press 1990), *War Surgery* (Black Moss Press 1996), *A Sentimental Dialogue* (Pasdeloup 1996), *The Caverns of Ely* (Pasdeloup 1997), *Herm on Tour* (Pasdeloup 1998), and *The Grace of Private Passage* (Black Moss Press 2000). She co-edited *Tasks of Passion: Dennis Lee at Mid-Career* (Descant Editions 1982) and edited *Views from the North: A Travel Anthology* (Porcupine's Quill 1984), as well as *Paper Guitar: Twenty-Seven Writers Celebrate 25 Years of Descant Magazine* (HarperCollins 1995). She is also the author of the prose travel-fiction-memoir *In the Era of Acid Rain* (Black Moss Press 1993). Mulhallen is the author of numerous articles and reviews on the arts, and her essays on literature and culture have appeared both in Canada and abroad. She is the former arts features editor of the *Canadian Forum,* on which she worked for fourteen years, and her column on Canada, "Canadian Diary," appeared in the *Literary Review* (London and Edinburgh). Mulhallen teaches English in Toronto at Ryerson Polytechnic University. She is working on a new book of poetry set on or near water.

ROSEMARY NIXON has published two works of fiction, *Mostly Country* (NeWest Press 1993) and *The Cock's Egg* (NeWest Press 1994), the latter of which won the Howard O'Hagan Award for Short Fiction in 1994. Nixon has published in literary magazines and anthologies across Canada. In the fall of 1996, she was awarded a grant to write for five weeks at the Leighton Studios. Nixon was the 1996–97 Canadian writer-in-residence in the Markin-Flanagan Distinguished Writers Programme.

HELEN FOGWILL PORTER was born and grew up in St. John's, Newfoundland, where she still lives. She has been writing professionally for thirty-five years and has published across Canada and overseas. She writes fiction, non-fiction, poetry, humour, drama, and criticism. Most of Porter's work is set in St. John's; she is keenly interested in regional speech. Porter is completing her second novel, *Finishing School.* Her first poetry collection, *Blood and Water,* is now with her publisher, Breakwater Books. Porter's published books include *Below the Bridge* (Breakwater Books 1980), *January, February, June or July* (Breakwater Books 1988) and *A Long and Lonely Ride* (Breakwater Books 1991). *January, February, June or July* was shortlisted for the W. H. Smith/Books in Canada First Novel Award in 1989 and won the Young Adult Canadian Book Award, presented by the Canadian Library Association.

NANCY POTTER has taught for many years at the University of Rhode Island in Kingston, Rhode Island, where she lives. Her two collections of short stories are *We Have Seen the Best of Our Times* (Alfred A. Knopf 1970) and *Legacies* (University of Illinois 1987). Potter has been a Fulbright teacher of American Studies in Argentina, Chile, and New Zealand, and has been a volunteer worker in Greece, Poland, and Mexico.

TOM POW held the 1992–93 Scottish/Canadian Fellowship based at the University of Alberta. During that time, he travelled from Vancouver to the Yukon, from Cape Breton to Baffin Island. He wrote some of the poems in *Red Letter Day* (Bloodaxe Books 1996) in the Leighton Studios and began work on two radio plays set in Canada for the BBC: *Wilderness Dreams* and *Aglooka: John Rae and the Lost Navigators*. Pow teaches Creative and Cultural Studies at the Crichton Campus of the University of Glasgow in Dumfries.

DARLENE BARRY QUAIFE'S novel *Bone Bird* (Turnstone Press 1989) won a Commonwealth Writers Prize. Her novel *Days & Nights on the Amazon* (Turnstone Press 1995) was voted a "Book for Everybody" by the Canadian Booksellers Association. In fall 2000, Quaife's third novel, *Polar Circus* (Turnstone Press), was published. Also to her credit is a book of popular culture on a ubiquitous theme, *Death Writes: A Curious Notebook* (Arsenal Pulp Press 1997). As a freelance writer, Quaife has contributed to newspapers, magazines, and journals. She has also had some success as a playwright for radio and stage. In addition, Quaife is a founding director of PanCanadian WordFest: The Banff—Calgary International Writers Festival and a past president of the Writers Guild of Alberta.

JAY RUZESKY'S poems and stories have appeared in Canadian and American journals such as *Caliban, Prism international, Canadian Literature, Event, Saturday Night, Descant, Border Crossings,* and *Poetry Northwest*. His books include *Writing on the Wall* (Outlaw Editions 1996), *Painting the Yellow House Blue* (House of Anansi Press 1994), and *Am I Glad to See You* (Thistledown Press 1992). He is on the editorial board of the *Malahat Review* and teaches at Malaspina University-College.

BARBARA SAPERGIA writes fiction—including *South Hill Girls* (Fifth House Publishers 1992) and the recent novel, *Secrets in Water* (Coteau Books 1999)—and drama. Her seven stage productions include *Matty & Rose, Lokkinen* (Playwrights Canada Press 1984) and *Roundup* (Coteau Books 1992). Her radio dramas have been broadcast on *Morningside, Stereodrama,* and the Australian Broadcasting Commission. Sapergia has written several episodes of the *Prairie Berry Pie* children's television series and is currently writing a feature film script for Minds Eye Pictures and Dovzhenko Studios based on her novel *Foreigners* (Coteau Books 1984).

CARMINE SARRACINO grew up in the immigrant neighbourhood of Federal Hill in Providence, Rhode Island, as a second-generation Italian-American. He attended Rhode Island College and the University of Michigan, where he earned a Ph.D. He has published widely on Walt Whitman and is currently putting together a collection of his own poems for a first book, entitled *This Day*. Residing in Pennsylvania, Sarracino is the R. W. Schlosser Professor of English at Elizabethtown College.

GLORIA SAWAI lives in Edmonton. Her first collection of short fiction, *Song for Nettie Johnson,* will be published in spring 2001 by Coteau Books.

LAYLE SILBERT has published more than one hundred stories in literary magazines, as well as poetry and several personal essays. Some of her work is represented in a handful of anthologies. Of the five books she has published, one is a book of poems, three are short stories; the most recent, *The Free Thinkers* (Seven Stories Press 2000), consists of two novellas. Silbert is also known as a photographer of writers.

DOROTHY SPEAK grew up in southern Ontario. She has written two story collections, *The Counsel of the Moon* (Random House 1990) and *Object of Your Love* (Somerville House 1996). Her recently completed novel, of which this excerpt is from an early draft, will be published by Random House in spring 2001. Speak lives in Ottawa.

Born in Flin Flon, Manitoba, BIRK SPROXTON now writes and edits in Red Deer, Alberta. His novel *The Red-Headed Woman with the Black Black Heart* (Turnstone Press 1997) won an award for historical fiction. He is the author of *Headframe:* (Turnstone Press 1985), a long poem, and editor of *Trace: Prairie Writers on Writing* (Turnstone Press 1997) and *Great Stories from the Prairies* (Red Deer Press 2000). Sproxton is the founding editor of an online magazine called "Taking Place: Canadian Prairie Writing."

LINDA SVENDSEN is a fiction writer and screenwriter. *Marine Life* (HarperCollins 1992), her collection of linked stories, was recently made into a film. "White Shoulders" has been anthologized in the *Penguin Anthology of Stories by Canadian Women* (Viking Penguin 1997) and *The Oxford Book of Stories by Canadian Women in English* (Oxford University Press 2000). Her stories have been published in the *Atlantic, Saturday Night,* and *Prairie Schooner,* and she has appeared three times in the O. Henry Awards' *Prize Stories* (Doubleday & Company) and *Best Canadian Stories* (Oberon Press), and has won NEA and Canada Council grants. Svendsen also adapted *The Diviners* and *The Sue Rodriguez Story* for television. She lives with her family in Vancouver and teaches in the Creative Writing Program at the University of British Columbia.

ROYSTON TESTER was born in England's industrial "Black Country" and grew up in Birmingham. Before coming to

Canada in 1979, he lived in Barcelona and Australia. His work has appeared in *Rip-rap* (Banff Centre Press 1999), *Malahat Review, Quickies 2, Prism international, Quarry, The Globe and Mail, B&A New Writing, Church-Wellesley Review,* and *Queen Street Quarterly*. *hands over the body* is his first story collection; "First Steps First" is an excerpt from *Enoch Jones,* a first novel-in-progress. Tester lives in Toronto.

GEOFFREY URSELL is an award-winning writer, composer, publisher, and television producer. His first novel, *Perdue* (Gage Educational Publishing Company 1984), won the Books in Canada Award for First Novels. He has written extensively for stage, radio, and television, most recently creating a children's series, *Prairie Berry Pie*. He has also composed songs for stage and radio. Ursell is a founder and current president of the literary press, Coteau Books, where he has edited many anthologies and single-author titles.

FRED WAH has published poetry, prose-poems, biofiction, and criticism and teaches creative writing and poetics at the University of Calgary. His book of prose-poems, *Waiting for Saskatchewan* (Turnstone Press 1985), received the Governor General's Literary Award in 1986, and *So Far* (Talonbooks 1991) was awarded the Stephanson Award for Poetry in 1992. *Diamond Grill* (NeWest Press 1996), a biofiction about hybridity and growing up in a small-town Chinese-Canadian café, won the Howard O'Hagan Award for Short Fiction.

CHRISTOPHER WISEMAN joined the University of Calgary in 1969 and founded the Creative Writing Program there in 1973. His award-winning work has appeared in many journals and anthologies, and he has published eight books of poetry, the most recent being *Crossing the Salt Flats* (Porcupine's Quill 1999). He has taught writing in many places, including Banff, and has spent time every year since 1986 working in the Leighton Studios. Wiseman lives in Calgary.

RACHEL WYATT was for many years Program Director (Writing) at The Banff Centre for the Arts. Her most recent novel is *Mona Lisa Smiled a Little* (Oolichan Books 1999). Her stage plays include *Crackpot* (Playwrights Canada Press 1995), which was first produced at Alberta Theatre Projects (ATP), Calgary, in 1996. It has also been performed in Winnipeg, Victoria, Philadelphia, and London, England. *Knock Knock* (Playwrights Union of Canada Play Service 2000), her latest play, also premiered at ATP, in January 2000. Wyatt has also written extensively for radio.

BETTY JANE WYLIE was a published poet before anything else, published in the early '60s in such publications as *Fiddlehead* and *Canadian Forum;* then a playwright of puppet plays, produced first in Winnipeg, then in North America by the Puppeteers of America; then a playwright for both children and adults with productions in Canada at the Manitoba Theatre Centre, St. Lawrence Centre, National Arts Centre, Stratford Third Stage, and Stratford New Play Workshop.

When her husband died in 1973, Wylie turned to journalism and non-fiction for income to finish rearing her four children. She has published thirty-five books, including biography, self-help, financial planning, inspiration, cookbooks, children's plays and puppet plays, belles lettres and poetry (two volumes), and some three dozen plays that have been produced in theatres in Canada, the U.S., Britain, and New Zealand—but no fiction.

JAN ZWICKY's books include *Wittgenstein Elegies* (Brick Books 1986), *The New Room* (Coach House Books 1989), *Lyric Philosophy* (University of Toronto Press 1992), and *Songs for Relinquishing the Earth* (Cashion 1996; Brick Books 1998). She has also published widely as an essayist on issues in music, poetry, and philosophy. Zwicky has taught creative writing at the University of New Brunswick, led a number of workshops, and taught in the Writing Program at The Banff Centre for the Arts. Since 1986, she has edited poetry for Brick Books. A native of Alberta, Zwicky is currently living on Vancouver Island, where she teaches in the Philosophy Department at the University of Victoria.

About the Editors

Recipient of the Marian Engel Award and co-winner of the Gerald Lampert Award, EDNA ALFORD has published two collections of short fiction, *A Sleep Full of Dreams* (Oolichan Books 1981) and *The Garden of Eloise Loon* (Oolichan Books 1986). Her work has appeared in numerous journals and anthologies, including most recently *The Oxford Book of Stories by Canadian Women in English* (Oxford University Press 2000). Alford was co-founder and co-editor (with Joan Clark) of *Dandelion Magazine* for five years and fiction editor of *Grain Magazine* for five years. She has served on the editorial board of Coteau Books since 1988 and has edited many short fiction collections, as well as co-editing *Kitchen Talk* (Red Deer College Press 1992), *Meltwater* (Banff Centre Press 1999), *Rip-rap* (Banff Centre Press 1999), and *2000% Cracked Wheat* (Coteau Books 2000). Alford is Associate Director of the Writing Studio at The Banff Centre for the Arts.

RHEA TREGEBOV was born in Saskatoon, raised in Winnipeg, and now lives in Toronto. She has four collections of poetry: *Remembering History* (Guernica Press 1982), which won the 1983 League of Canadian Poets' Pat Lowther Award; *No One We Know* (Aya/Mercury Press 1986); *The Proving Grounds* (Véhicule Press 1991); and *Mapping the Chaos* (Véhicule Press 1995). She has also published five children's picture books and edited the anthologies *Meltwater* (Banff Centre Press 1999), *Rip-rap* (Banff Centre Press 1999), and *Sudden Miracles* (Second Story Press 1991). Tregebov was co-winner of *The Malahat Review* Long Poem Competition in 1994 and also received the 1993 Readers' Choice Award for Poetry from *Prairie Schooner* (Nebraska). She teaches creative writing for Ryerson Polytechnic University's Continuing Education program and works as a freelance editor of adult and young adult fiction and poetry.

Permissions

"Bread and Stone" by Caroline Adderson was previously published in *Bad Imaginings* (Porcupine's Quill 1993). Reprinted by permission of the publisher.

"A Palimpsest" by Ven Begamudré is an excerpt from his novel *Laterna Magik* (Oolichan Books 1997). Reprinted by permission of the publisher.

"Achill Ancestors and a Stranger" by Maureen Brady was previously published in *Cabbage and Bones: An Anthology of Irish American Women's Fiction* (Henry Holt and Co. 1997). Reprinted by permission of the publisher.

"Esmeralda" by Karen Connelly was previously published in *One Room in a Castle* (Turnstone Press 1995). Reprinted by permission of the publisher.

"Bruise" by Marlene Cookshaw was previously published in *Event* (Vol. 28, No. 1, Spring 1999).

"Nesting" by Julia Darling was previously published in *Bloodlines* (Panurge Press 1995). Reprinted by permission of the publisher.

"Taxi" and "Tattoo," from "Berlin Suite" by Myra Davies, were released on the CD *Miasma* (Arabella Musikverlag & Maobeat Musikverlag 1993). "Fingers" and "Dinner" were released on the CD *Miasma 2* (Arabella Musikverlag & Maobeat Musikverlag 1997). Reprinted by permission of BMG Music Publishing Canada.

"Ghost Story for December" by Alice Friman was previously published in the *Malahat Review* (No. 124, Fall 1998).

"Lenin's Mother" by Janice Kulyk Keefer was previously published in the *Malahat Review* (Vol. 109, Winter 1994).

"Elizabeth Smart, 70" by Janice Kulyk Keefer was previously published in *Marrying the Sea* (Brick Books 1998). Reprinted by permission of the publisher.

"Icarus" by Don McKay was previously published in *Another Gravity* (McClelland & Stewart 2000). Reprinted by permission of the publisher.

"Brief Visitation" by Judy Michaels was previously published in *Nimrod: International Journal of Prose and Poetry* (Vol. 42, No. 2, Spring/Summer 1999).

"Schaferscapes" by Karen Mulhallen is an excerpt from a piece previously published in *BorderCrossings* (Vol. 15, No. 1, Winter 1996).

"Inordinate Light" by Rosemary Nixon is an excerpt from a piece previously published in the *New Quarterly* (Vol. XVIII, No. 1, Spring 1998).

"Going Places" by Helen Fogwill Porter was previously published in *Grain* (Vol. 21, No. 1, Spring 1993).

"Vital Signs" by Nancy Potter was previously published in *Pleiades* (Vol. 18:1, Fall 1997). Reprinted by permission of the publisher.

"Buffalo" and "Hazards" by Tom Pow were previously published in *Red Letter Day* (Bloodaxe Books 1996).

"Mora de Ebro" by Darlene Barry Quaife was previously published in *AlbertaViews* (Vol. 2, No. 3, Summer 1999).

"The Garden of Edith Ashdown" by Barbara Sapergia was previously published in *South Hill Girls* (Fifth House Publishers 1992).

"Burial" by Carmine Sarracino was previously published in *Prairie Schooner* (Vol. 71, No. 3, Fall 1997).

"Shanghai" by Layle Silbert was previously published in *Burkah & Other Stories* (Host Publications 1992). Reprinted by permission of the publisher.

"The Organized Woman Story" by Birk Sproxton was previously published in *Dandelion* (Vol. 22, No. 1, 1995) and reprinted in *Due West* (Coteau Books/NeWest Press/Turnstone Press 1996).

"White Shoulders" by Linda Svendsen was previously published in *Marine Life* (HarperCollins 1992). Reprinted by permission of the author and her agent, Robin Straus Agency, Inc.

"First Steps First" by Royston Tester was previously published in *Church-Wellesley Review* (Fall 1999).

"Radio Waves" by Geoffrey Ursell was previously published in *Way Out West* (Fifth House Publishers 1989).

"Diamond Grill" by Fred Wah consists of excerpts from *Diamond Grill* (NeWest Press 1996). Reprinted by permission of the publisher.

"Remembering Mr. Fox" by Christopher Wiseman was previously published in *Remembering Mr. Fox* (Sono Nis Press 1995). It was first published in the journal *Working Title.*

"The Yellow Canoe" by Rachel Wyatt was previously published in *The Day Marlene Dietrich Died* (Oolichan Books 1996). Reprinted by permission of the publisher.

"Five Songs for Relinquishing the Earth" and "The Geology of Norway" by Jan Zwicky were previously published in *Songs for Relinquishing the Earth* (Brick Books 1998). Reprinted by permission of the publisher.

Meltwater

"The *Meltwater* collection illuminates small aspects of the human—whether in stories such as Curtis Gillespie's *The Coffin* or in poems such as Michelle Desbarats Fels's *The Park*—and even at times rises to luminosity.

—THE GLOBE AND MAIL

CONTRIBUTORS

Kristin Andrychuk
Janis Barlow
Brian Bartlett
Ven Begamudré
Astrid Blodgett
Ronna Bloom
Stephanie Bolster
Mary Borsky
Mary Cameron
Warren Cariou
Marlene Cookshaw
Lynn Davies
Jamie Diamond
Marilyn Dumont
Deirdre Dwyer
Michelle Desbarats Fels
Anne Fleming
Cynthia Flood
Rebecca Fredrickson
Bill Gaston
Joanne Leah Gerber
Curtis Gillespie
Susan Goyette
GP Greenwood
Gail Helgason
Greg Hollingshead
Sally Ito
Dayv James-French
Janice Kulyk Keefer
Catherine Kidd
Billie Livingston
Yann Martel
Julie Mason
Ally McKay
Barbara Nickel
Armand Garnet Ruffo
Jay Ruzesky
Jean Rysstad
Diane Schoemperlen
Joan Skogan
Michael Winter

$17.95 CDN / $14.95 US
ISBN 0-920159-55-9
6 x 9 / 284 pages / paper

Rip-rap

"[*Rip-rap* and *Meltwater*] bear witness to a program that continually achieves its goal: to inspire great writing."

—PRAIRIE BOOKS NOW

CONTRIBUTORS

Caroline Adderson
Kelley Aitken
Paul Anderson
Ken Babstock
Rosemary Blake
Lesley-Anne Bourne
Marc André Brouillette
Chris Collins
Méira Cook
John Donlan
Irene Guilford
Naomi Guttman
Stephen Heighton
Bruce Hunter
Maureen Hynes
Michael C. Kenyon
Richard Lemm
John Lent
Elise Levine
Laura Lush
Sue MacLeod
Randall Maggs
Rachna Mara
Joseph Maviglia
Lorie Miseck
Lisa Moore
Sheldon Oberman
Joanne Page
Helen Pereira
Sina Queyras
Chetan Rajani
J. Jill Robinson
Barbara Scott
Anne Simpson
Struan Sinclair
Dorothy Speak
John Steffler
Royston Tester
Barbara Turner-Vesselago
Liz Ukrainetz
Sue Wheeler

$17.95 CDN / $14.95 US
ISBN 0–920159–65–6
6 x 9 / 272 pages / paper